THE
WORLD
ON
BLOOD

THE
WORLD
ON
BLOOD

Jonathan
Nasaw

A DUTTON BOOK

DUTTON
Published by the Penguin Group
Penguin Books USA Inc., 375 Hudson Street,
New York, New York 10014, U.S.A.
Penguin Books Ltd, 27 Wrights Lane,
London W8 5TZ, England
Penguin Books Australia Ltd, Ringwood,
Victoria, Australia
Penguin Books Canada Ltd, 10 Alcorn Avenue,
Toronto, Ontario, Canada M4V 3B2
Penguin Books (N.Z.) Ltd, 182–190 Wairau Road,
Auckland 10, New Zealand

Penguin Books Ltd, Registered Offices:
Harmondsworth, Middlesex, England

First published by Dutton, an imprint of Dutton Signet,
a division of Penguin Books USA Inc.
Distributed in Canada by McClelland & Stewart Inc.

First Printing, April, 1996
10   9   8   7   6   5   4   3   2   1

 REGISTERED TRADEMARK—MARCA REGISTRADA

LIBRARY OF CONGRESS CATALOGING IN PUBLICATION DATA
Nasaw, Jonathan Lewis
    The world on blood / Jonathan Nasaw.
        p.   cm.
    ISBN 0-525-94066-9
    1. Vampires—California, Northern—Fiction.   I. Title.
PS3564.A74W67   1996
813'.54—dc20   95-38195
                                               CIP

Printed in the United States of America
Set in Bernhard Modern and Minion
Designed by Julian Hamer

PUBLISHER'S NOTE
This is a work of fiction. Names, characters, places, and incidents either are the products of the author's imagination or are used fictitiously, and any resemblance to actual persons, living or dead, events, or locales is entirely coincidental.

For Patricia

BOOK ONE

My Life on Blood

ONE

It is possible to steal a baby from a hospital at night. Whistler awoke at sunset with that simple thought shining like a beacon through the murk of his hangover.

It wouldn't be easy, he knew. Daytime would have been easy, but daytime, alas, had not been an option for over twenty-five years.

He opened his eyes, groaned aloud, and sat up gingerly. The wineglass on the bedside table was nearly half full, but a quick sniff told him that the stuff had gone bad overnight—or rather, since morning. With a roll of his eyes, as if it were all too much to bear, he emptied the contents into the potted plant on the bedside table, then dropped to his knees, flipped back the comforter, and from the small refrigerated compartment built into the platform of the king-size bed, he withdrew a 32-oz Clamato Juice jar.

The liquid he poured from the jar into the glass bore only a passing resemblance to Clamato Juice. But then, that was the point. "If there's one thing certain in this sorry world," Nick Santos, who'd invented the trick, used to say, "it's that no thief, housecleaner, overnight guest or midnight muncher is ever going to cop a slash from a jar of off-ish looking Clamato Juice."

At the thought of Nick, Whistler's long jaw tightened for a moment. Then he raised the glass—a toast to absent friends—and tossed the contents back with an understated flourish. Whistler did everything with an understated flourish—or hoped to.

After a shower, and another splash from the jar, Whistler went strolling naked through his walk-in closet, pushing aside rack after rack of custom-made shirts, silk suits from his tailor in Hong King, elaborate dressing gowns and pajamas and leather and vinyl S&M wear, and enough kimonos to stock a geisha house, until finally he reached his rack of hospital costumes: orderly's whites, surgical greens, a lab coat with a stethoscope tucked into the pocket, and two custodian's uniforms, both green—one with *Tony* stitched over the left breast pocket, the other with *Art.*

He selected the latter, quoting his namesake aloud—"Tonight, Ladies and Gentlemen, Art is upon the Town"—and permitting himself a frugal smile.

The baby would have to be a Doe of course, he decided as he stepped into the one-piece coverall. So much cleaner with the Does—no parents to overreact. It was also a happy coincidence that they were almost always brought to the understaffed county hospitals, where the security precautions were . . . not oppressive, to put it kindly. The last one he'd borrowed from a county hospital hadn't even been missed, so far as he'd been able to tell. In any event, there had been nothing in the news about the disappearance—or the return, for that matter.

But the timing would be critical. He checked the hour as he slipped on his wristwatch, a Patek Philippe that had once belonged to his father. (It was no heirloom, though—Whistler had swiped it from the old man in London back in 1966.) Not quite 6:00, he noted. El Sobrante was only fifteen or twenty minutes from the county hospital in Martinez—if they hadn't changed the visiting hours, that gave him a good two or three hours to kill.

He wandered downstairs to the kitchen of the restored white clapboard farmhouse to see about dinner and found a note from Selene on the antique kitchen table. The entire house was furnished in genuine 1930s Depression-era farmhouse kitsch, right down to the Bakelite deco radio on the counter and the Laurel and Hardy salt and pepper shakers on the rubberized checked tablecloth.

Jamey dear—Okay, I'm off to Tahoe to mix up a few brews with the gals. Thanks in advance for the use of the Manor—we'll leave it as we found it. And thanks for dinner last night—the leftovers are in the fridge. I also left you a $1/2$ pint just in case—the way you were drinking last night, I wanted to make sure you had a waker-upper. By the way, I caught one of your little helpers snooping around the house while you were busy with the other one. I'd have turned her into a frog, but it was the one with the boobs, and I know how you feel about boobs. I would have come up to say goodbye in person, but the Creature was rampant, and I still have six months of celibacy left on my vow. Hugs and (chaste) kisses—Selene.

As he rummaged among the take-out cartons in the Frigidaire, Whistler tried to remember the name of the young woman from the night before, so he could ask the service not to send her again. Ah, but what an erotic *tableau vivant* she and the boyish Vietnamese hooker had made against the backdrop of his pearl gray sheets. *Thanks all the same, Selene, but I think I'll take my chances.*

In what Whistler hoped was a stab at humor, Selene had left his half-pint in a creamer shaped like a cow. Before leaving for the hospital, he poured half the contents into a silver hip flask, then held the pitcher above his face like a *bota* and let the remaining liquid cascade from the cow's mouth into his, and trickle down his throat. Being fairly fresh, it started coming on within minutes, and by the time he reached the hospital he was so high that the kidnapping itself was something of an anticlimax.

Shamefully easy for a man of Whistler's ability, in fact. As if for his convenience, they'd shifted the Does all the way to the back of the nursery—no need to have them up by the glass for parental viewing, was apparently the thinking. Art the janitor had only to sweep his way past the nursing station and on through the nursery, snatch up one of the two sleeping Does, and slide out through the back door and down the service stairs.

The hardest part was deciding which one to take, the John or the Jane. After an instant's hesitation, during which he reflected that the last Doe he'd snatched had been a Jane, he selected the John. Not that gender had anything to do with it. He wasn't a child molester, for godsakes.

TWO

El Cerrito is a city in transition. Richmond encroaches from the north, Berkeley from the south. To the east rise wooded hills studded with overpriced homes; to the west, at the edge of the San Francisco Bay, stretches a bleak industrial littoral. Even the little hill for which the town was named lies across the border in Albany.

All in all, it had never been considered a promising location for any new enterprise, let alone a nondenominational twelve-step church with a female pastor. Or so the Reverend Betty Ruth Shoemaker had been advised two years before, by her friends, by her banker, and by conventional wisdom, which, until recently, she'd always thought of as ninety-nine percent convention and one percent wisdom. On a good day.

But on the Friday night after the Thanksgiving of 1991, with the ashes of the great firestorm still blackening the East Bay hills, and the ashes of old Elizabeth Corey resting among them (or stirring, depending on the wind), Betty Ruth found herself staring at the screen of her elderly computer and wondering whether conventional wisdom hadn't been right for once.

For when the firestorm finally enveloped Libby Corey's graceful old Maybeck house that October, it had deprived the Church of the Higher Power of its major benefactress, who at age eighty-two had been up on the roof with a garden hose trying to wet down the shake shingles.

"Eighty-two years old and up on the roof with a hose," said Betty out loud—talking to oneself was a ministerial perquisite: she could always pretend she was praying. "Not a bad way to go at that age. They say the smoke gets you first, you never even feel the flames."

But it occurred to her that *that* was conventional wisdom too. She frowned at her reflection on the screen, superimposed over the church's utterly dismal spreadsheet, then glanced around an office furnished largely with garage-sale spoils: faux-Tiffany desk lamp with a nymph etched in green and gold on the glass shade; Serenity Prayer clock: God grant us the wisdom, etc.; scarred olive-green metal desk; pre-ergonomic desk chair with duct-taped arms. Two filing cabinets, no window. Enough room to swing a cat if you held your elbows close to your sides.

She turned back to the desk to make a few ineffectual stabs at cleaning up—mostly throwing papers and bills into her bulging *To Be Filed* file—but when she looked at the computer screen again, the spreadsheet was still there, still reproachful.

"What we really need is a miracle," she declared. "A three-hundred-and-seventy-five-dollar-a-month miracle." That being the current projected shortfall for the Church of the Higher Power, assuming she forwent her salary. A fair assumption—she hadn't drawn it since the founding of the CHP, managing to survive instead on income from her counseling. "Is that asking too much?" she inquired of the computer, which was apparently sitting in for the deity tonight. "One more twelve-step group to rent the smaller meeting room three nights a week?"

No reply—none expected. She reached around to turn off the old Mac, ignoring once again the yellow *Trust In God But Back Up Your*

Hard Disk Post-it slapped on the side of the monitor, then stepped out into the church, shutting the door behind her.

"Ah, well," she announced to the darkness and the faint smell of cedar. " *'May the wicked cease from troubling, and the weary be at rest.'* "

"Amen to that." A man's voice from somewhere in the shadows of the pews.

Betty gasped, clapping her hand to her chest. She could just make out a face at the back of the church, white and waxen as a camellia in the dark. "Who's there?" Her fingers felt behind her for the row of light switches on the wall, flipped a few at random: two banks of overhead lights clanked on in the rafters, illuminating the chancel and the mourners' bench.

"Sorry, didn't mean to startle you." The man rose from the back pew and stepped out sideways into the aisle. "I'm Nick? Nick Santos?"

His boots tapped the hardwood as he strode up the aisle, and she recognized him when he reached the light—a slender man in his mid-forties, in faded but pressed stonewashed jeans and a soft blue chambray shirt; only a comma of his thick walnut-brown hair had been allowed to fall in studied casualness over one eyebrow. *Let's review,* she thought as he approached. *The perfect man. My age group, well mannered, impeccably dressed, exquisitely groomed, devastatingly handsome. In other words, he's gay.* "Oh, of course. Nick. The A.A. meeting?"

He nodded. "A.A., N.A., M.A., CODA, A.C.A.—you name it, I'm addicted to it."

Alcoholics Anonymous, Narcotics, Marijuana, Codependents, Adult Children of Alcoholics. "What, no S.L.A.?" she joked.

"Sex and Love?" He grinned ruefully. "That gave me up when I gave up all my other addictions."

"I know what you mean," she said, laughing. But his reply had cut a little too close to the bone, and she hurriedly changed the subject. "So what was it you needed to talk to me about?"

"One of my groups renting the smaller meeting room three nights a week."

In her mind's ear, Betty heard old Libby Corey's distinctive cackle, and she caught herself wondering, without a trace of embarrassment, whether she shouldn't have sought a rather larger miracle. Enough to get the damp-rotted bathroom walls repaired, say. Or maybe World Peace. But undermining the elation was a faint dread. She told herself it was only the shock of coincidence, that hearing her own prayer coming back

to her nearly word for word had unsettled her, but the rest of the conversation had an eerie ring nonetheless. "We should be able to fit you in.
Which group did you say it was?"

"I didn't. It's V.A."

"Don't think I've heard of that one. What's the *V* stand for?"

"Very."

"Very Anonymous?"

"Very."

THREE

Nick Santos carried his cordless phone out to the padded chaise on the
redwood deck of his home in the East Bay hills. Below him the lights of
Berkeley tumbled steeply from Grizzly Peak Road down to the flats, and
rolled on to the edge of the black bay. He tugged off his boots and
straightened the hems of his stonewashed jeans, then leaned back to dial
the first number on the V.A. phone list.

"James, it's Nick," he informed an answering machine. "I have a
room for us. The Church of the Higher Power, El Cerrito, corner of
Jackson and Darling. Nine o'clock Saturday night. Meeting room downstairs, on the right. We also have Monday and Wednesday nights, same
time, same place. It's perfect—basement room, no windows, thick door
that locks. See you tomorrow—stay clean in between."

He made nine more calls, and reached three people, five machines,
and a busy signal, then punched auto redial and waited, watching the letters G O O D Y E A R floating mysteriously towards the Bay Bridge—
they were just passing Alcatraz when his phone buzzed to let him know
the call was going through.

"West County Blood Bank, this is Beverly."

"Bev, it's Nick. We've got us a room at the Church of the Higher
Power in El Cerrito." They had been meeting at a branch of the Berkeley
library, now closed for asbestos abatement.

"You know how I feel about churches."

"It's nondenominational—hell, it's a twelve-step church, and we're a
twelve-step program—what do you want, egg in your beer?"

"Any crosses?" Beverly asked.

"There's one on the wall of the meeting room, but it can probably come down."

"I suppose it'll have to do—the situation here can't go on much longer. When's the first meeting?"

"Nine o'clock tomorrow night. When did she last cop?"

"I've been keeping an eye on her since yesterday, so Wednesday at the latest—she's probably getting desperate."

"Might she have any other sources?" Nick wanted to know.

"I don't think so—she's a pure virgin Orphan if there ever was one. If she hadn't gotten the job here, I don't know how she'd be getting it. But what I've done, I've set it up so that she'll have the keys tomorrow night—we always have one person on standby on Saturday nights, in case of a run on the bank. I'm sure the temptation will be too much: all I have to do is tell her I'll be in the office myself after nine, and she'll have to make her move before then. Cheese Louise and I will hide somewhere, then confront her and bring her to the meeting with us."

"How the hell are you going to hide Cheese Louise?"

"Don't be size-ist."

"Sorry. Do you want us to hold off the meeting until you guys get there with . . . what was her name?"

"Lourdes. Lourdes Perez."

"*Loor*-diss?"

"But spelled like the shrine. She's Filipino. Filipin*a*, I guess. Sure, hold the opening prayer for us—if we can't get her to come along, we'll be there ourselves by nine-thirty at the latest."

"Sounds like a plan. Call me if you need me."

"Okay. Take it easy, Nick."

"Easy, and one day at a time."

FOUR

Not until little John Doe had been changed, fed a bottle of warm milk wrist-tested for temperature and fortified with Luzan rum, then rocked to sleep in the wooden trundle bed on the floor of the farmhouse kitchen, did Whistler allow himself to draw its blood. That was all foreplay—the boredom that drove him to baby-blood usually disappeared as soon as he began the hunt, and once he had the baby in hand, no sense of urgency remained.

Still, he took a craftsmanlike pride in his work, finding the thready blue vein in the instep with its hardy but bird-quick pulse, drawing the blood so cleanly through the syringe that the child never stirred, deftly replacing one ampule with another and then a third before sliding the needle out while pressing a cotton ball against the wound with his thumb. When he withdrew the cotton, only a tiny blue pinhole remained.

There weren't a dozen blood techs west of the Rockies who could have done half as well, he noted proudly as he reversed the plunger, sending the contents of the last ampule hissing into a silver-rimmed wineglass. This he held to the light, that he might approve the color, a dark eggplant purple, before taking his first genteel sip.

It took a few minutes for the baby-blood to come on. While he was waiting he checked out his voice mail from the kitchen phone, a two-piece wood and brass wall model, a perfect replica of the phone in Lassie's farmhouse kitchen save for the touch-tone buttons adorning the inside of the handpiece. Nick's was the last message. Whistler listened impassively, replaying it once to jot down the address of the church on the chalkboard next to the phone before erasing the message.

Then as the crystalline clarity of the baby-blood buzz began to build—it wasn't like other drugs, not even like other blood highs— he looked down at the lad in the little crib at his feet, and an idea— rather, a revelation—sprang up full blown and shiny bright. On baby-blood, all ideas sprang up full blown and shiny bright, with the force of revelation.

"I do believe an opportunity has arisen," he remarked confidentially to the infant. "Instead of going right back to that nasty old hospital, how would you like to visit El Cerrito instead?"

Still reserved, but playful now—another effect of the baby-blood—he cocked his head for the reply, then glanced over at the chalkboard. "Yes, darling, that's what I said: the godforsaken flatlands of El Cerrito."

FIVE

Betty Ruth eased herself down into the hot juniper-scented bubble bath she'd been promising herself all day, in lieu of the celebratory drink she wanted so badly. Inch-high votive candles were balanced around the sink and on top of the toilet tank and the wicker hamper; inside each of the tiny bath bubbles flickered an even tinier juniper-green flame.

"A three-hundred-and-seventy-five-dollar-a-month miracle," she sighed, and her sigh echoed through the tiny bathroom of the two-story parsonage that took up the front third of the Church of the Higher Power—only a narrow back staircase connected it with the church proper. Upstairs were a small bedroom, the bath, and an unoccupied nursery, all with low slanted ceilings; she used the ground-floor living room for her clients, though often as not the counseling sessions ended up at the kitchen table.

Being something of a unrecovered workaholic, Betty had brought a notebook into the bath with her—she facilitated a small group of battered lesbians that met on Saturday mornings, and she wanted to review her notes from the last meeting—but she couldn't get her mind off her answered prayer.

" 'Three nights a week.' That's pretty much it, word for word. For word, for word." Betty knew that answered prayers usually meant trouble: "Be careful what you wish for—you just might get it," was a common theme not only in Sufi tales and New Age texts, but even in old horror stories like "The Monkey's Paw." She recalled with a shudder how the bereaved mother's prayer for her dead son's return was answered when his mangled corpse dragged itself to her front door.

But Betty's uneasiness, she suspected, was not entirely based on superstition—she'd been around recovery programs for quite a few years now, and had never heard of one that kept *itself* anonymous, as well as its members. She'd even gone so far as to thumb through her twelve-step source books—no V.A. of any description.

"Anonymous Anonymous," she said, pushing back her bangs and patting her oft-neglected forehead (her gray-brown hair had been cut in the same weatherproof dutch boy for the past twenty years) with a steaming wet washcloth. "Oh well, I suppose it was bound to happen sooner or later."

Then, as she let herself sink down into the welcoming heat until her chin brushed the steaming surface of the water: "I guess an addict is an addict is an addict." With a puff of breath she blew the bubbles away from her mouth, in order to finish her thought. "As long as the check clears, that is." And with a final tight-lipped but satisfied grin, as if to say *Oh what a naughty girl am I,* she disappeared beneath the billowing juniper-scented waves of foam.

It couldn't have been more than twenty minutes later—the water was still warm—when Betty was awakened from a delicious half-doze by the sound of the double doors slamming in the church below. *That's funny,* she thought. *I could have sworn I locked them.* She climbed out of the bath and toweled off hastily, then threw on her shabby corduroy bathrobe and hurried down the musty back staircase, which was so steep and sharply angled that light from the bare bulb at the top barely reached the door at the bottom.

She paused before that door. *A smart person would not turn that knob,* she thought, remembering poor Carol Knox, the Walnut Creek minister who'd been murdered by a pregnant schizophrenic Satan-worshipper in the mid-eighties. *A smart person would go back upstairs and call 911.* Then she heard what sounded like a kitten mewling.

"Another abandoned kitten." She was both annoyed and relieved. "What am I, the SPCA?" But when Betty opened the door she felt a cold breeze blowing through the church, and saw the double doors at the far end smashed inward. Then she heard the mewling again, coming from a back pew; this time she recognized the sound and went racing barefoot down the aisle, ratty bathrobe flying out behind her.

ONE

Lourdes Perez opened her refrigerator door, then knelt to retrieve a clear plastic drip bag of blood from behind a cabbage in the vegetable crisper. It was nearly empty—squeeze and shake it as she might, less than half a shotglass was all she could wring out of it. More than enough to get her out of bed this Saturday night, barely enough to get her out of the house.

Normally she would have taken a bag home with her on Friday, but that bitch Bev had been watching her like a hawk since Thursday. Still, even knowing that her stash was nearly empty, it had taken all the willpower Lourdes possessed not to polish it off before going to bed this morning—she'd settled for a couple Halcion instead. Lucky thing Bev had offered her the standby shift tonight—she didn't know *what* she'd have done otherwise.

When her hands had steadied, Lourdes spent a quick fifteen minutes at her vanity, pulling her glossy black hair into a tight bun, and applying eye shadow externally and Visine internally to her oval-shaped brown eyes. She got her coloring, her eyes, and her wide-bridged nose from her Filipino father. Her mouth, though, was her Okie mother's, thin lipped, neat and hungry: tonight she smoothed on a rich Persian red lip gloss that contrasted nicely with the cream-white cowl-neck wool sweater she'd laid out on the bed.

She chose her beige skirt last. It had to be a skirt because she had only two clear goals for her Saturday night, the second of which was to get laid. And when Lourdes seduced a man, she liked to take her clothes off standing up, while he watched—it sort of got things started off on the right foot. For that purpose, jeans were unsuited—too ungraceful, no matter how good they made her butt look.

The first of her goals, of course, was to procure a bag of blood. She checked her purse to make sure she had the keys to the bank, and hustled out the door practicing the little twitch at the end of her normally liquid stride that would set her skirt a-sway, thereby compensating for her temporary lack of jeans.

Later Lourdes would tell herself that she'd had a premonition at the door of the West County Blood Bank; more likely the little frisson she experienced as she turned the key was associated with the fact that she was, after all, about to commit a crime, albeit a misdemeanor. And once in, she'd apparently felt confident enough to be whistling the *we will we will rock you* refrain as she let herself into the cold-storage room.

The whistling stopped cold when she let herself out, though: Somehow Beverly had materialized in the middle of the office. Behind her, blocking the exit, was a dyke-looking heavy in a crew cut and a woolen poncho, and both of them were looking serious as a heart attack. *Two* heart attacks.

"Oh, hi Bev," Lourdes managed, but it fell so far short of casual that she might as well have performed a double take and a pratfall.

"Hi, Lourdes," said Bev, with what for her was a degree of pleasantness. "Would you like to show me what you've got in your purse there?"

"Not particularly," was the reply. Lourdes had been popped before, though never for blood, and if all her experience (getting busted by her parents for masturbating or stealing their booze and cigarettes, then by truant officers for ditching, and by teachers for drugs, and later by Modesto cops for D.U.I. or just for hanging out with the wrong crowd) had taught her one thing, it was that they always had their minds made up in advance how they were going to deal with you.

No matter who had caught you, or what they said, they already knew whether they were going to ground you or expel you or send you to counseling or take you to jail or let you off with a warning. This may or may not have been an accurate perception, but it was definitely liberating: all you had to do was see how it played out, and then you could give them the appropriate response: sorry or thank you or fuck you very much.

So she didn't even bother to open her purse for the two women, and if she fought at all, it was for mastery over herself—not to let them see how badly shaken she was. And after they'd asked her to have a seat and told her they knew how she was feeling because they'd been there themselves; after they informed her that she had a problem and that they'd like her to come with them to meet some people who'd had the same problem; even after she realized it was counseling they had in mind and responded appropriately (*thank you* out loud, *fuck you sideways* under her breath), the sense of panic still threatened to overwhelm her.

The only way she could stave it off was to persuade herself that they were talking about some sort of twelve-step or support group for kleptos, and throughout the drive to El Cerrito (they let her follow them in her car, which she suspected was some sort of by-the-book *we-trust-you-so-trust-us* bullshit), whenever the panic threatened to boil over, she clung to that little piece of denial like flotsam after a shipwreck. *That's all it is, the stealing. They think my problem is the stealing.* The alternative—whatever it might be—was too awful to think about.

TWO

The battered lesbians had not gotten their money's worth out of a nearly sleepless Betty Ruth on Saturday morning, as the police hadn't finished with their crime scene—laying out reels of yellow tape, measuring the doors and taking samples of the splintered wood, stomping around the lawn looking at footprints they themselves had made, and dusting the pews for fingerprints—until nearly three. They also drank lots of coffee and squawked on their walkie-talkies (*Who could they be talking to?* Betty wondered. *Every cop in El Cerrito is already here*) and interviewed her over and over.

This last annoyance was at least partly her own fault: having fallen desperately in love with the baby in the fifteen minutes it had taken for the cops and the paramedics to show up, she had surrendered it with a lame wisecrack, and after that things were out of her hands.

Or, as the detective from Martinez who'd been the last to interview her had put it: "Reverend Shoemaker, *I personally* don't believe you're our kidnapper here. *I personally* don't really suspect that you drove out to Martinez and took that baby, then brought him back here, smashed in your own church doors, and called nine-one-one. But when I give my chief a report stating that the abducted infant was returned by a child-less female who was overheard by a responding officer to have stated—" He'd flipped back through his leather-bound notebook. "—and I quote: *'I wanted a baby in the worst way, but this wasn't exactly what I had in mind,'* you can understand that he's going to have a few more questions, and I'd better have the answers for him. So—" He glanced down at the notebook again. "You told the lady from Child Protective Services that you've been trying to have a baby for a year, and were feeling hopeless, and that time was running out for you?"

"No no no." Betty felt her rosy cheeks growing hot—she'd assumed she and the woman from CPS were having a woman-to-woman communication. "I said I've been looking for a suitable *sperm donor* for a year. And I didn't say *I* was hopeless—I said the *men* were hopeless and sperm banks were too expensive. As far as time running out, all I said was that at my age, if I didn't make a decision soon, time would make it for me." *What a conversation to be having with a cop.*

"And that is . . . ?"

"The decision? Whether to have—"

"No, your age."

"I'm forty-one." For another few weeks, anyway. But unless they asked for her date of birth, that would be her own damn business.

Then, after the cops had left, there was still the problem of the doors—they'd helped her get them closed again, but only by propping them in place. But a quick glance around reminded her that there wasn't much in the church proper worth stealing, so she settled for locking the office and meeting-room doors, and bolting both staircase doors behind her on her way back up to the parsonage.

She'd spent the remaining hours before dawn lying awake trying to read, listening for prowlers, and finally drifting off to something like sleep with her palms crossed against her chest as if she were still holding the baby, feeling that warm life in her hands again, and that tiny heart beating against her breast.

But then, too soon, the battered lesbians, and the cajoling of the scrap wood from Dolan Lumber, and the rounding up of the volunteers to fix the doors, and then in the afternoon two new clients for couples counseling. Ho hum. *He* wanted more sex and less nagging; *she* wanted vulnerability, and for him to clean the toilet when it was his turn. Betty could have done it in her sleep—and very nearly did.

After the session, exhausted though she was, she knew she'd never be able to get to sleep without calling the hospital to find out how the baby was doing; within ten minutes of receiving the news that he was a little anemic but otherwise thriving, Betty was dead to the world.

When she awoke again, the sky beyond the live oak branches that shaded her window was black, and she felt momentarily dislocated in time—normally when she awoke in darkness it was to the silence of the early morning hours. Then she glanced at the Dream Machine on her bedside table (it had cost a few dollars more than the other clock radios, but she felt it was worth it for the name alone), saw that it was 8:25, and realized she was supposed to be meeting Nick out in front of the church in twenty minutes.

She hurried out of bed and into the shower, a quick glance at the dresser mirror having confirmed that her hair was a disaster area and that pillow lines scored one cheek. It seemed to her that a gay man would notice that sort of thing. He might not *care*, but he'd notice.

After her shower she opened wide the window to avoid worsening the damp-rot problem. Unable to afford the necessary repairs, the best she could do was keep the bathroom aired out until another miracle happened along. Still, she was determined not to pray to her Higher Power for this one—didn't want to seem greedy.

"But if You felt like doing it on Your own," she remarked casually on her way down the back stairs, "we've got a low bid of ten thousand five. That's without a cushion, though, so You might want to make it twelve even, just to be on the safe side."

She hesitated again at the bottom of the staircase, then, reprimanding herself for her timidity, drew the bolt emphatically, and threw the door open with a crash. She immediately felt silly for her dramatics: the church was as peaceful and calm a sanctuarial presence as it had been before the break-in, with only a hint of sawdust in the air, and a slight crack of light knifing in at the far end, where one of the newly repaired double doors no longer hung quite flush against its jamb.

Nick came strolling up the shady walk at precisely 8:45. It was a tranquil Saturday night in El Cerrito, or as tranquil as it gets in the flat-lands, what with the constant hum of traffic along San Pablo Avenue, and the intermittent roar of the BART train along the elevated tracks. Under the shadow of the live oaks the churchyard behind the twisted black wrought-iron fence seemed only a few gravestones short of Dick-ensian to Nick, but the church building itself was a solid and reassuring presence.

"I fell in love with that building the first time I saw it," he called to Betty Ruth, who was waiting for him at the church doors with her hair still damp from the shower. "There's something so . . . *familiar* about it."

"Everybody says that. It's the proportions. I figured it out one time—it's built to the exact proportions of a Monopoly hotel."

He backed up a few steps and cocked his head. "Exactly! All it needs is a coat of red paint."

"Not for a church, I think."

"No, I suppose not. What happened to the doors? I didn't notice any of this last night."

"Nothing serious. Somebody broke in, but they didn't do any other damage."

"Did anything get stolen?"

"No, nothing taken." *Quite the opposite, in fact,* she thought, but she'd already decided to tell as few people as possible about the baby. She held up a piece of paper and a magic marker, and changed the subject. "So did you want me to put up some signs, with arrows down to the basement?"

He pursed his lips, pretending to think about it. "Nooo. It shouldn't be necessary. It's a closed meeting—all our meetings are closed—and everyone has directions."

"Suit yourself."

The Church of the Higher Power was as plain inside as out—wooden pews, low unadorned altar, three high narrow windows set in each long wall. "What was this building before it was the CHP?" he asked as she closed the doors behind them.

"It was built by Holy Rollers back in the twenties. Nothing fancy—but sturdy. The '89 quake didn't even faze her."

"No, they did a nice job," Nick agreed. "See how these pews are pegged with contrasting wood instead of just nailed?"

There was a smudge of fingerprint powder on the back of the last pew—quickly Betty stepped forward to brush it away, then wiped her hand on the back of her roomy jeans. "Are you a carpenter?" she asked him.

He shook his head. "No, just a dabbler. But I appreciate fine workmanship." He turned around to examine the doors. "That's why it's such a damn shame to see that."

Together they looked over the hasty repair work—a blaze of new wood at the hinge of one door, a sheet of stark knotty plywood nailed over the jagged hole in the other. "I know, but it'll have to do," she said finally, torn between appreciating what might be concern and resenting what might be criticism. "We don't exactly have a lot of cushion built into the facility budget."

He stepped forward and knelt to run his fingers over the scarred wood. "Shouldn't take much—some filler here, another inset in that panel there, then restain both doors a little darker to cover."

Resentment won. "Let me rephrase that: we don't have *any* cushion—in fact, we don't have any facility budget."

For Nick, there was no mistaking her peeved tone, and though years of therapy had made him well aware of his two guiding needs—to be approved by women, to dominate men—he still found himself overcompensating with charm. "Oh, no charge," he said, smiling so disarmingly that she was immediately ashamed.

"You mean you . . . I didn't realize . . . You were offering to fix it yourself?"

"If you wouldn't mind letting an amateur take a whack at it."

"Mind? I'd be forever grateful." Betty tried to figure out whom he reminded her of when he smiled. Something about the mischievous lift at the corners of his dark brush of a mustache. Some old friend or lover still capable of sending a faint, barely remembered flutter rippling somewhere deep down inside her. Then she got it—*Magnum P.I.*—and felt even more foolish. Television actors and gay men. *Definite pattern emerging here, Rev,* she told herself. *No wonder I'm having such a hard time finding a sperm donor.*

"Great. I'll stop by tomorrow, take a look at it in the daylight."

He followed her up the aisle and through the door to the steps that led down to the meeting rooms in the basement. She opened the first door on the right with a key and led him in. "It's not much, but it's all yours for an hour and a half. Set up the chairs any way you like, stack 'em when you're done. Leave it unlocked—I'll lock up when I make the rounds. No smoking, of course."

"Of course. And thank you, it'll be perfect. I can't imagine a nicer home for our meeting. Just one thing, though—" He pointed to a black cross made of halved hollow bark hanging on the cinderblock wall across from the round black schoolroom clock. "Would you mind terribly if we took that cross down from the wall? Just for the meeting—we'll put it back before we leave."

"Suit yourself—by charter, the Church of the Higher Power is strictly nondenominational."

"It's only that some of our members are a little oversensitive about crosses."

"Jews, Muslims, atheists," she remarked on her way up the stairs. "I understand."

Somehow I doubt that, thought Nick, nodding politely to her retreating back.

THREE

Lourdes had spent the first few minutes of the ride to El Cerrito fumbling through her purse for her coke stash, and the last few contriving to put enough distance between herself and the Volvo she was following to manage a toot. Or two. Luckily, it was one of those high-tech little Safe-T-Snort bottles where you could turn it upside down, then flip a lever to measure out a convenient dose without taking your eyes off the road. Legend was that it had been invented by an airline pilot.

At the corner of Jackson and Darling, two wide, quiet, tree-shaded streets, Beverly leaned out the window of the Volvo to point out the church for Lourdes, then waved her manicured hand in a vague circling gesture that Lourdes took to mean *Park where you can.*

Taking advantage of this brief moment of freedom to whip her pink Chevy Caprice into a space around the corner of the church, just out of sight of the Volvo, Lourdes barely had time to slouch down low in her seat for one last toot of coke to ease the blood crash she knew was on the way. Then, to ease the crash from the coke, she broke a yellow Percodan in half and swallowed it dry, brushed her forefinger under her nose to remove any telltale Peruvian marching powder, and stepped out of the car just as Beverly and the other woman came trotting around the corner in search of her.

A dead-white gibbous moon hanging high over the hills to the east threw their foreshortened shadows across the churchyard grass as Lourdes followed the two women through the gate and up the walk; their sneakers squeaked up the hardwood aisle and the slap of her white sandals echoed behind them; in the cool stairwell she could hear voices drifting up from the basement.

At the bottom of the stairs Lourdes paused before the only open door, trying to gather herself. She straightened her skirt, tugged her sweater a little tighter across her breasts, and raised her chin like a dancer. *March in there like it was your own idea, girl,* she told herself, but it was not until she felt the first warm glow from the Percodan rising up to fill the void left by the dying coke rush that Lourdes found the strength to cross the threshold.

And inside? Not much: a bare room with eleven people—nine white, one black, one Asian—sitting around in a circle. Someone closed the door behind her as she edged her way around the circle to the only vacant chair. She heard the click of the lock as she took her seat.

"I guess we can get started," said the man seated across from her, looking directly into her eyes. His mustache reminded her of the Marlboro Man. No, the Marlboro Lite Man. "Hello, everybody. Lourdes, we're especially glad that you could join us tonight for the first meeting of V.A. in our new home."

She could feel the terror coming over her, but it was mixed with a curious sense of relief. The Marlboro Man leaned forward, concern all over his handsome face. "Are you all right?" Their glances had locked across the circle; unable to tear her eyes away from him, she managed a nod.

"Here we go, then."

Here we go, her mind echoed numbly.

"My name is Nick, and I'm a vampire."

"Hi Nick," responded ten voices in cheery unison. Lourdes moaned—there was a roaring in her ears, and she felt the room slipping away from her.

A remarkable face swam into focus when Lourdes next opened her eyes: long solemn upper lip; deep vertical creases in the cheeks; wide-set gray eyes that were cold and amused, the color of solder; and a high forehead crowned with a remarkable head of chrome yellow hair, brushed up into a soft, relaxed butch cut. The color, while clearly not natural, was exquisitely chosen.

Perhaps the most remarkable thing of all about the face, other than its pallor, was that it was upside down—only gradually did Lourdes become aware that her head was resting in a lap, and that other people were applauding. Then it all came back to her—the blood bank, Bev, the meeting, the—*oh my god, the vampires.*

The yellow-haired man ignored the applause (which was for his James-Brown-sliding-kneedrop/Willie-Mays-basket-catch of her head, only inches from the concrete floor) and turned the full force of his attention on Lourdes. "Going to live, are we?"

She tried to stare back, but her eyes insisted on turning him into Upside-Down Man, the noseless, mouthless, bearded monster that appears to children staring too long at an upside-down face. The eyebrows *under* the eyes were particularly awful—she turned her head away and he helped her back up onto her chair.

"How do you feel?" The other man, Nick, smiled at her reassuringly across the circle. His incisors appeared to be normal, which she found even more reassuring.

"I'm okay—just embarrassed—I never fainted before in my life."

"No need to be embarrassed about anything—not in these rooms. Just let me know if you start feeling shaky again." He leaned back and crossed his legs. "Most of our meetings are speaker/discussion: a speaker tells his or her story, sharing his or her strength, hope, and experience, then picks a topic, and whoever wants to can speak to that topic, or just talk about whatever's up for them.

"But tonight we have a newcomer for the first time in—Jan, how long have you been coming to meetings?"

The youngest of the vampires, a gangly narrow-skulled girl of twenty or so, edged forward in her chair. Lavender streaks slashed through black hair cut in an angular punk wedge. A torn black leather bomber jacket. Left ear pierced with a half dozen studs, some jagged stars, others irregular splashes of silver. "Eleven mon—oops. I mean, hi, my name is January and I'm a recovering vampire. Eleven months, three weeks." She raised both hands over her head in a victory clasp, but there was in her eyes something of the look of a cat bristling in an empty room, and Lourdes found herself unwilling to meet them.

Nick turned back to Lourdes. "I'll start by reminding us all that the reason we call ourselves vampires, instead of simply blood addicts, which is what we are, is that it helps us remember just how serious this addiction is.

"So serious, in fact, that up until a few years ago, the idea of a vampire going into recovery was nearly unimaginable. Then a man named Leon S. achieved his sobriety by attending other meetings, and saying 'booze' or 'pot' or 'crack' when he meant 'blood.' One night when I had reached my absolute bottom, he showed up out of nowhere and saved my life, and we then dedicated ourselves to reaching as many of our old blood brothers and sisters as we could. One by one, as they bottomed out, we'd be there for them, if only just to serve as examples, to prove it was possible."

Nick shook his head sadly. "In the end, though, it wasn't enough.

What we learned from going to other meetings was that there is no true recovery without honesty, not even for Leon, who ended up taking that Thirteenth Step: the one that leads over the side of the Golden Gate Bridge.

"That's when we realized we were going to need our own meeting, where we could call blood, blood, and deal with our own issues. V.S. started with six of us in Sherman's living room—" He indicated that worthy with his glance, then paused dramatically before turning back to Lourdes. "And now we are twelve. Lourdes, welcome.

"Now for the reading of the literature—we do this every meeting, Lourdes. So who wants to read the Steps?" His eyes scanned the circle, settling on the stocky woman with the woolen poncho and the Gertrude Stein hair who had accompanied Beverly to the blood bank.

"Hi, my name is Louise," she proclaimed, "and I'm addicted to blood." Pulling an A.A. pamphlet out from under her poncho, she began reciting, adapting the words where appropriate: "Step One: We came to realize we were powerless over blood, and that our lives had become un-manageable. Step Two: We came to believe that a Power greater than ourselves could restore us to sanity. . . ."

When she had finished, another woman read the Twelve Traditions, then Nick took the floor again. "In a way, I envy you, Lourdes—you've got the adventure of your life ahead of you. You're getting off the merry-go-round—"

Most of the others recited the rest along with him: "—and onto the roller coaster." They had a group chuckle; Nick continued. "But we do have a few rules that you'll need to know about. Beverly, I believe you're the secretary this month—go ahead."

"Awright, number one: cross-talk. *No* cross-talk." *Numbeh . . . cvrawss-tawk*—Beverly had once been described by a native as one of those New Yorkers who seemed to have moved to California in order to complain about the food. *You cawl this a bagel? This is not a bagel.* "That means no criticizing or responding directly to somebody's share.

"Number two: attendance. You attend three meetings a week for three months, then a minimum of one meeting a week after that. If you're out of town, arrange to call somebody.

"Number three: service. They need somebody else on the refreshment committee—sign up with Louise over there.

"Number four: dues. We don't have any. What we do have is Tradition Seven, which says V.A. ought to be fully self-supporting, declining outside contributions. What that translates to is a minimum of five bucks a person a meeting. If you can't afford it, see the treasurer—who's the treasurer?"

The yellow-haired man who had caught Lourdes tapped her on the shoulder. "That would be—" he began, but the others nagged him:

"*Hiiii,* James . . ."

"Sorry. My name is James. Vampire. Treasurer." He wore a black soft-collared shirt; Lourdes sniffed perfumed licorice on his breath. What was that stuff? Her father had used it. Of course: Sen-Sen.

Beverly picked it up again. "James, then. See James after the meeting. That's about it for the rules. Any questions?"

"You said three meetings a week for three months, then one meeting a week after that, but you didn't say for how long after that." There was no answer at first. Lourdes glanced around the circle—a few of the vampires were smiling. "What, did I say something funny?"

Nick finally responded. "No, not at all," he said gently. "It's just that we don't look at it as 'how long.' We prefer to think of it as 'one day at a time—forever.' "

Lourdes remembered the bag of blood in her purse; suddenly she wanted to be high so much it almost hurt. She crossed her legs and clenched her thighs tightly. "What if I don't want to . . . *recover?*" She tried not to spit the word out, but did not succeed entirely.

Nick again: "Of course you want to. You just don't know it yet—you can't know it until you're detoxed. Now we're going to let you keep the bag you stole tonight. What we recommend is, tonight when you get home, pour about a shotglassful, and sip it over the course of the night to keep the crash off. Then all you have to do is cut the amount down by a teaspoon every night for a week. Taper off—you don't have to do it cold turkey. And remember you're not alone—we've all been through it. You'll have our phone numbers—call us if you need us, someone'll be right over. Twenty-four hours a day."

"But what if I just can't?" Lourdes asked hopelessly—not hopeless about giving up blood, hopeless about communicating with these people.

"If you *want* to, you will. Ask for Higher Power's help, bring your fanny to the meetings, and take it one day at a time."

The rest of the meeting passed slowly—excruciatingly slowly, as far as Lourdes was concerned. She found it somehow surprising that a vampire twelve-step meeting could be just as deadly and boring as the Alateen meetings her counselor at Modesto High had forced her to attend during her senior year, for spending a few too many three-period lunches in

Gracedia Park smoking dope under the trees, or tripping on hundred-mike mini-doses of violet acid, and watching the river flow purple through the valley.

At one point Lourdes even dozed off from the combination of the crash and the Percodan. When she awakened, January had the floor. ". . . so I wake up this morning and do my affirmations, and then I go off to work." January turned to Lourdes and explained in an aside that she worked at the Copy Shoppe on Telegraph Avenue. "It's like, this is *supposedly* my big reward to myself for giving up blood—finally getting to work days after two years on the night shift." She turned back to the circle at large. "Only, as a big reward, it's a total fucking bust. The main difference, working days is more stress, more assholes yapping at me, hurry up, copy this, collate that, staple these, not that way, this way, no this way . . ." Visibly worked up, she took a breath to calm herself.

"So anyway, on my lunch break I go up to People's Park, and I'm sitting on a bench by the volleyball court, and I see this one wino heading up to the bushes at the far end of the park to pass out."

"That was my primo supply, rolling winos and shit," she confided to Lourdes in another aside. This time, Lourdes had to force herself not to draw back. "And while I'm watching him with my eyes, not moving, forcing myself not to get up from that bench, in my mind I'm following him—I see just how I'm gonna do it—I can picture kneeling next to him, a quick slash, dip my face down—I swear, sitting on the bench I can feel the hot blood, the way it smears across your mouth if you catch it still spurting, drips down your neck, you know how it's funny, you might not have a single drop on your chin, but you always manage to get some on your neck anyway—"

She stopped abruptly. "Anyway, that's about it—it was like the pressure to drink was so incredible it came out like that, just like a using dream, only I was wide awake." January thought about that for a moment with her wolfish face cocked slightly to the side. "And I didn't do anything about it, I didn't follow him. I couldn't even make it one day at a time—I took it one minute at a time—just for this minute I'm not going to drink blood—now just for *this* minute, *this* minute—until all the minutes made up a half hour, and it was time to go back to work."

The group, obviously moved, broke into spontaneous applause, and January sat back down, squirming like a puppy under their approval. Lourdes forced herself to applaud along, but her head was spinning. She'd followed January's gory musings with a rapt fascination, repulsed and titillated in equal measure, and it took every ounce of willpower she could summon not to reach into her purse and at least fondle the cool plump bag of blood waiting for her there.

After the last of the vampires had his or her turn to speak, Nick turned to Lourdes again and asked her if she had anything she wanted to share.

"No, not really."

"But we'll see you on Monday night, same time, same place?" It was not a question, so she didn't bother to answer. "Okay then," he continued, "who's going to lead us in the closing prayer?"

Everybody stood up then, and they all joined hands while a short, round-headed, Howdy Doody–faced vampire named Sandy led them in the closing prayer that many twelve-step groups had adapted to their own circumstances from Overeaters Anonymous.

As we stand in this sacred circle, with my hand in yours I know that we can do together what we could never do alone. No longer must I depend upon my own weak will to resist the call of blood, but together we can reach out our hands and find a power and strength, a love and understanding beyond our wildest dreams.

Seconds later, Lourdes was rushing out the door and up the stairs, purse swinging, sandals flapping, without waiting around for the hugs or the cookies or the phone numbers the other vampires were trying to press upon her.

At the church door she heard her name being called, and turned to see James ambling down the aisle after her, his hands jammed casually into the front pockets of his pleated slacks. How had he caught up so quickly, she wondered, when he didn't seem to be hurrying at all? "Lourdes? A word?" His voice was soft and dry, his accent barely British.

"What—"

He took one hand out of his pocket long enough to bring the forefinger to his lips—shhh.

She waited in the doorway until he was close enough to whisper to. "What do you want?"

"Blood," he whispered back. "Only blood, and a beautiful woman to drink with."

Lourdes heard the roaring in her ears again, but this time it was only a BART train. She opened her purse to show him the bag of blood inside. He nodded slowly; his eyes never left hers, but she knew he had seen it all the same, and for the first time that night, Lourdes smiled.

At any rate, it appeared to be a smile: first her lips parted, just wide enough to show her teeth, then her teeth parted, just about wide enough to hold a small olive. "James, was it?" she asked, turning again, pushing open the double doors.

"Please, James is my V.A. name. I despise it." He stepped out beside her, and offered her his arm.

She took it. "What shall I call you then?"

"Whistler." They started down the steps together, her hand resting lightly in the crook of his elbow. "My friends call me Whistler."

Chapter 3

ONE

The Dessert Inn was an upscale joint for El Cerrito. Black-trimmed brick walls, exposed beams, art posters. More important, espresso drinks until one.

The night manager's practiced eye told him instantly that the striking couple were on a date. He was torn between seating them at table eleven, where he'd be able to watch the dark-haired woman in the white sweater and tight beige skirt from behind the register, or at fourteen, which was his girlfriend's station. Wealthy older man, beautiful younger woman—everything about it shrieked big tip.

He settled on fourteen. "This way, please."

But the yellow-haired man pointed instead toward one of the booths, not with an upraised arm, but with a languid flick of forefinger, and a persuasive arch of an eyebrow. "Over there will do, I think," he said with a faintly British inflection.

Something in his manner sucked the night manager right in. "Very good, sir," he found himself saying, with some astonishment: he'd never said "Very good, sir" before in his entire life, as far as he could recall. *On the other hand, there's a lot to be said for a booth,* he thought a moment later watching Lourdes's skirt ride up her bare thigh as she slid sideways into the booth. And up, and up—

Suddenly he felt a hand on his shoulder—Jesus, the old guy had moved fast. And something about his grip intimated that the thumb and forefinger now squeezing from opposite sides of his shoulder could just as easily be meeting in the center of it—that bones were not an obstacle. But the voice was as toney and untroubled as before. "A gentleman never stares," was the advice it whispered in the night manager's ear. "He may peek, but he never stares."

"Thank you, Whistler," said Lourdes, primly smoothing her skirt as the night manager fled. "A creep like that could flat stomp a girl's buzz." They had stolen a quick sip from her bag in the restaurant parking lot— just enough for a buzz, and to keep off the crash.

Something about the turn of the phrase tickled him. *"Stomp a girl's buzz,"* he repeated, laughing delightedly. He'd already decided she was the most breathtaking creature he'd ever seen, vampire or no vampire, with her sleek round skull slightly large for her body, her oval face and clear olive skin, her dark thick-lashed eyes, and the black hair pulled back ballerina-tight, not to mention the legs that had launched a thousand night managers. "I've never heard that before."

"We say it all the time where I'm from."

"And where's that?"

"Modesto. West Mo, actually. How about you?"

The waitress arrived to take their orders—Whistler waited until she was out of earshot before replying. "Maryland born. Raised there, and in the Virgin Islands. London in my teens."

"So what the hell are you doing in El Cerrito?"

"I have a restored farmhouse in El Sobrante, actually, but I divide my time between there and Whistler Manor, my lodge up at Tahoe, and my villa in Greece, and—"

"Stop, stop." She held up a hand, laughing. "I'm sorry, Whistler. But your villa in fucking Greece? Gimme a break—I'm a Filipino Okie from West Modesto. We don't know men with villas in Greece."

To his credit, he laughed back. "Well, you do now."

When their drinks arrived, she threw back her steaming double espresso like a B-girl. "There, that should keep me awake another five minutes, easy." She tugged the neck of her sweater away from her body and fluttered it for a little breeze, although it was not especially warm in the Inn.

"I'm sorry, are you starting to crash again?" he asked with concern.

"Well, it's not a crash, exactly. Just that feeling—do you know what I mean? Do you get it, too? When everything's so—so—"

" 'Weary, stale, flat, and unprofitable'?"

"That's it. That's exactly it."

"Shakespeare," he advised her. *Shakespee-ah*: his English accent had grown more pronounced. It was not quite an affectation, as he had indeed lived in London for nine of his formative years, but it did tend to meander, respecting neither class nor regional boundaries on its wanderings.

Lourdes's eyes widened. "Was he a vam—was he one of us?" Her own speech was northern Central Valley—not quite Valley Girl, more like a Midwesterner with a mouthful of chewing gum.

Whistler shrugged, stirring his cappuccino with the spoon held loosely between thumb and forefinger. She found herself staring at his hands—his fingers were long, tapered, the moons perfect ivory-blue crescents in the elegant nails. "During my brief university career, I once wrote—well, commissioned: I rarely wrote my own papers (which may well account for the brevity of the career)—a little beauty entitled 'Blood and the Bard,' and I can tell you with absolute assurance that there are over eleven hundred references to blood in Shakespeare." He drank, then with his napkin carefully blotted a spot of foam from his long upper lip. "My personal favorite is from *King John*: 'at feasts, full warm of blood.' "

Finally she couldn't stand it any longer—she reached across the booth and took his left hand in hers, turned it over, ran her fingers lightly along the back of it. "Sounds good," she whispered dreamily. "Feasts full warm of blood."

Whistler began some wisecrack or other, but it caught in his throat as he watched her stroking his hand, this beautiful, untutored, newly-Awakened young Orphan. What a world of blood there was to teach her about, he thought, trying to place this peculiar sensation that seemed to be coming over him, this painful, pleasurable sense of fullness in his chest and throat, and behind his eyes. Then it came to him—it was the way you felt just before you broke down and cried.

No wonder it had been hard to place—Whistler hadn't shed a tear since 1988, when Nick and Leon and the others had tied him to a bed in his own lodge in order to wean him from blood.

Could I be falling in love? he thought wonderingly, and then, like an echo in his mind, he heard the voice of the poor drowned Viscount— Nick's first casualty. *Falling in love? What a demned foolish thing for an aging vampire to do.*

TWO

"I never did this *with* anybody before," Lourdes declared as she unloaded the bag of blood from her purse onto her kitchen counter. "You?"

"Every chance I get."

"What's it like?" Just nervous small talk, but he seemed to take it seriously. "Doing it together, I mean."

"You are an Orphan, aren't you? Well, it's interesting."

"That's all—just interesting?"

"At my age, '*interesting*' is praise indeed."

"How old *are* you?"

"Three hundred and twelve."

She gasped, then saw the long vertical seams of his cheeks deepen—there were dimples hidden in there somewhere. "I don't *think* so," she said, employing a catchphrase of the day. "Homey don't play dat. What year were you born?"

"Let's see, eighteen, seventeen, sixteen . . . ninety-two less twelve . . . 1680!"

"Nice try." She held the bag up for his inspection, turning it around so he could read the West County Blood Bank label. "Good shit. Guaranteed HIV-negative."

He took the bag, turning it over thoughtfully. "Not that it makes a difference."

"But I thought—in her share, Beverly said—"

He waved Beverly away as an annoyance. "Party line."

"What're you saying? That you can't get AIDS from drinking blood?"

He shrugged. "No one ever has—no vampire, that is."

"Maybe the stomach acid kills the virus?"

"I doubt it. My god, we practically used to wallow in the stuff—all it would have taken was a cut or a chapped lip or canker sore. And then there's the sex. Even the rawest Orphan finds out soon enough that the most common side effect of blood—to those of us who have that lucky gene or condition or whatever that makes it a drug for us—is that it is, beyond question, the most powerful aphrodisiac imaginable. So when you take into account all the blood, and all the sex, it means that if we're not immune, my dear, then we are all, all of us, walking dead. And I don't mean Nosferatu."

"Speaking of Nosferatu," she said, somewhat indistinctly, as her tongue was busy exploring the inside of her mouth for cracks and cankers, "how come they took down the cross for the meeting?" He handed the bag back to her; she hooked the top over the brass knob of the white lacquered cabinet above the sink. "Wait here, I have to get the good glasses for this."

She brushed past him; he caught a whiff of jasmine-based perfume. "Sally. Our long-necked Ethiope?" he called after her.

"The black girl?"

"Reddish brown, I'd say—yes, that's the one."

"What about her?" She returned with two bulbous Cost Plus brandy snifters, one of which she handed to him; the other she positioned under the outlet tube.

"Her family back in Addis Ababa tried to have her deprogrammed once—exorcised is more like it—by some self-styled North African Van Helsing. Not only does she still carry a brand in the shape of a cross high on her eminently callipygian left buttock, but the smell of garlic sends her into conniptions."

Whistler watched with breathless attention as Lourdes gave the plastic wheel at the bottom of the tube a delicate quarter turn. *Such a wonderful touch,* he thought. *Fingers like a surgeon. Or a harpist. Or a porn star.*

Lourdes gave the wheel a final turn, then tapped the tube, and the blood began to flow, a few drops, then a dark ruby stream that coated the inside of the glass as it fell. She closed the stopcock and held the goblet to the light. "God, I love that color." She handed it to him; he traded her the empty glass. "You know, I was scared to death when Beverly busted me tonight, but now I feel like thanking her."

Whistler rolled the snifter between his hands to warm the blood like a fine brandy. "How so?"

"Because now I know I'm not alone." Lourdes rinsed out the sink, then opened the refrigerator and stooped down to stow the half-empty bag in the crisper, tucking it carefully out of sight behind the cabbage. She was aware of her skirt riding up her thighs again, of Whistler's eyes on her, and for his benefit dipped a little lower.

He had been right, of course: she *had* discovered about sex on blood all by herself. But she'd never had sex with a man who was also high on blood—an omission, she suspected, that was about to be remedied soon.

They carried their glasses through the living room/dining room of her one-bedroom apartment; she parted the white curtains and opened the sliding glass door that led out to a balcony overlooking the flat pebbled roofs of the neighboring apartment buildings. It was a warm night—it had been warm that whole long weekend.

"Boy, my life sure gets strange sometimes," whispered Lourdes, look-ing down at the glass in her hand—the blood was a dull sparkling car-nelian in the moonlight.

"Do you like it that way?"

"I love it. Know any good toasts?"

Whistler smiled, and lifted his goblet to hers. "Of course. 'Other things are all very well in their way, but give me Blood!' "

"Shakespeare again?"

"Dickens. *David Copperfield.* Chapter Twenty-five: *Good and Bad Angels.*"

They clinked glasses, the crystal rang prettily, and they drank.

THREE

An orchard of gnarled Gravenstein apple trees stretched on for half a mile behind Whistler's farmhouse. Looking out through the screen door, Lourdes couldn't quite see to the end of it, even in the moonlight, even on blood, which always sharpened her senses wonderfully.

She was good and high now. The blood had taken its own sweet time coming on—as cold blood was wont to do—but as they drove north from Berkeley in Whistler's '58 Jaguar saloon, on it had come: colors brightened, objects grew sharp-sided and discrete, thoughts spun away into the night like blips in a video game, and the stars began to align themselves along a three-dimensional grid. The world on blood was an awesome piece of work, but delicate too, sparkling like a spiderweb sprinkled with dew.

"It looks like an enchanted orchard," whispered Lourdes, with her nose mashed against the screen. "Like it's alive."

"Everything looks alive on blood." Whistler was high too, but then Whistler, after twenty-five years, drank not to get high, but to stay high: the hallmark of an addict. He reached over her shoulder to unhook the door. "I'm letting the orchard grow wild," he explained. "Must be the Druid in me."

"*I'm* growing wild," she called over her shoulder, racing down into the orchard, white sandals flapping. "It's the blood in me."

He caught up with her where the orchard was the darkest, and the sweet winey smell of the rotting apples the strongest.

"No neighbors?" she asked.

"Not for half a mile." He slid close behind her, reached around with both hands, and pulled her tight against him.

"Stop or I'll scream," she giggled.

"Scrrrream, den." His long solemn face was expressionless, and his yellow hair washed colorless by the moonlight. "Scrrrream all you vant to, my dearrrr. Dere isss no vun to hearrrr you."

"Ooooh." A deep chesty moan. She turned to face him, but when he bent to kiss her pursed lips she danced back a step, dry leaves and applewood twigs crackling underfoot. "Wait." She pulled her white sweater over her head, and draped it over a low spiny branch. Then she let her skirt fall, stepped out of it, and hung it next to the sweater, where it was soon joined by her bra and panties. When she was naked save for her white sandals, she closed her eyes and took a few slow, deep breaths; her wide-set breasts rose and fell, pale fruit in the orchard in the silvery light. "There, that's better," she reported. "Much better. Now where were we?"

"I believe we were about to scream," said Whistler, reaching for his belt buckle—it was in the shape of an ourobouros, a tail-eating snake.

By the time they reached the bedroom on the second floor of the farmhouse, he was as naked as she was, and the Creature—which was Whistler's name for the erection that customarily visited him during a blood high (it seemed not to belong to him; quite the other way around, in fact)—had attained full Creaturedom. She pushed him down across the bed with a gleeful whoop, glorying in her newly regained vampire strength; he seized her wrist and pulled her down just as roughly.

She gasped appreciatively the first time he entered her. She would have gasped appreciatively in any event—still, it was nice not having to pretend. And as he began moving above her, inside her, she felt herself responding—it was as if her Creature was her dancer's body, her whole body: a blush spread out from the center of her chest, and when it reached her eyes the whites flushed Chinese red.

She understood now that she had been wrong about sex with another vampire: it was even better than she had imagined, like being high on all the drugs in the world at the same time—Quaalude-hypno-trance, early-cocaine-engorgement, Ecstasy-empathy with a dash of porn-fever. At first her orgasms were powerful, and prolonged—she'd think she was finished and then, at a smile from him, or a tender touch or just a thought, she'd feel it rippling in her womb, and the orgasm would build from the inside out until her belly skin rippled in sympathetic vibration. And if he was not inside her, if he was lying beside her with the Creature bobbing, perhaps a bead of clear come at the tip, then together they would watch her fluttering gently, and at that moment she would have sworn he was feeling every ripple right along with her.

But after a few more hours, orgasms, though no less frequent, began to seem irrelevant, and it was after one of these (they had by then each donned one of Whistler's kimonos, hers lilac, his black—more for the color and the contrast and the feel of the silk than for warmth or modesty), upon finding themselves entwined in a position so convoluted and unlikely that only a mind on blood could have conceived it, and two bodies on blood achieved it, that Lourdes turned to Whistler and asked, through swollen lips, with what was left of her voice: "Why would they ever imagine I'd want to give up drinking blood in the first place?"

FOUR

"Are you always hard?" Lourdes murmured, lying on her right side on the damp and rumpled pearl-colored satin sheets of the king-size bed. It was nearly dawn—the kimonos and the black down comforter had hit the floor ages ago.

Whistler rolled onto his side to face her, propping himself up on one elbow. He trailed a finger down her rib cage, along the dip of her waist, and over the swell of her hip. "On blood."

She giggled. "You're hard and I'm easy."

"Match made in heaven." He placed the back of his right hand under a breast, hefting it gently, letting it settle back into its delicate curve.

Between them, the Creature began to stir—when its head brushed her thigh Lourdes sat up abruptly, crawled to the end of the bed, and snatched the comforter off the floor to wrap around herself. "Actually, I'm getting kinda sore."

"Coming down?"

"I don't think so. I could use a boost, though—you have any weed around?"

"Do the royal corgis shit on the palace lawn?"

"I don't know. Do they?"

"Frequently, in elegant little turds." From the drawer of the bedside table he produced a small coffin-shaped wooden pipe and a pine green bud the size of a Ping-Pong ball—Humboldt's finest. He filled the bowl, lit it, passed it to her; she inhaled in tight little sips, managing not to cough.

"Whistler baby? Is it dawn yet?"

"Very nearly." In the bedroom heavy black curtains were drawn over closed blinds behind tight-fastened shutters. On top of a black dresser with delicate, almost feminine, bowed legs and brass ourobouros drawer handles, a small tasseled lamp provided just enough wattage to illuminate the genuine Whistler etching—a staircase in Italy—hanging on the wall over the dresser.

"Let's go outside."

"Can't. Turn to ash, y'know."

"I don't *think* so," she laughed. "Homey don't play dat, either."

"If I gazed upon sunlight, m'dear, my eyeballs would feel as if they'd been poached."

"Only direct sunlight really bothers me. I bought some wraparound blue-blockers last month, though—they help a lot."

"You're young yet—have you even been drinking for a year? I thought not. It's a progressive side effect. Soon you'll find yourself avoiding daylight altogether."

"Why do you think drinking blood screws up your eyes?" They were sitting up in bed, passing the pipe; she was looking him up and down, frankly trying to guess his age. His chest was dead white where the kimono had fallen open, and in the aftermath of the blood blush the skin was dry and pebbly.

He shrugged. "Side effects. Heroin constipates the bowels, marijuana rasps the throat, cocaine paranoids the mind. Thorns and roses, y'know—no such thing as a free lunch."

She studied him for another minute. "All right, I give up—how old *are* you, really, and don't give me that 1680 shit again."

"I was born in 1945, and I've been drinking blood for twenty-five years—all but the last three of them blissfully V.A.-free." He sighed, returned the pipe to the drawer, and lay down on his back.

The top sheet was hopelessly lost—Lourdes nestled in next to him, covering them with the comforter. "That's something else I can't figure out—why are you hanging around with those creeps?"

"Well, for one thing, they can make things extremely uncomfortable for anyone who tries to go out. The last chap to try it was Sandy."

"Which one was that?"

"Short? Freckles, reddish hair? Sat next to Nick at the meeting?"

"Huckleberry Finn?"

"The very. Tried to resign two years ago. They broke into his house for an intervention—and mind you, if you'd been less cooperative tonight, they'd have done the same to you—took him out into the country where no one would hear the howling, kept him prisoner for a week, holding meetings in his room, saving him from himself every four or five hours. Now he's the most enthusiastic twelve-stepper in the bunch, poor bastard."

"Is that how they got you involved?"

"At first, yes—they broke into the Manor and tied me to my own bed." He spread his arms by way of illustration; Lourdes reached out and grabbed his wrists, playing at pinning him. "And within twenty-four hours I was willing to do anything, say anything, join anything, to get them to go away so I could get my blood." He pretended to struggle; she pressed her length against him and he went limp. "I was so convincing they left after two days, and I've been convincing them ever since."

"But why didn't you, like, just move someplace else?"

He smiled for the first time since she'd asked him about V.A. Suddenly he broke her grip on his wrists, grabbed hers in turn, whipped her hands down to her sides, and rolled over on top of her. "When I turned twenty-one," he informed her—there was nothing in his tone of voice to indicate he had her pinned beneath him, "I came into a large enough inheritance that I realized it was within my means to live anyplace on the planet." Pause for emphasis. "I chose this one, and here I'll stay until *I* decide it's time for me to leave, and not some gang of Program Nazis."

Gleefully, vainly, she struggled—strong as blood made her, it made him that much stronger. Still, she wouldn't stop fighting him until he brought her wrists to his lips and kissed them, then let them go. She went limp, with her wrists crossed helplessly on the pillow above her head—then he rolled off her. "I dunno," she said, breathing hard. "I still don't buy it. I mean, Whistler, I've *seen* them, and I've seen you, and it's hard to believe they could keep you going to three meetings a week for years if you didn't want to."

He was lying on his side—he propped himself up on an elbow and looked at her carefully, as if he were seeing her for the first time. "You are a perspicacious little Orphan, aren't you?"

It was the second or third time he'd called her an orphan; she assumed that somehow he knew of her parentless state—her mother had drunk and smoked herself to death by 1988, and her beloved father had died just last year. As for perspicacious, she hadn't a clue, but in the context it seemed to be a compliment. "You bet your ass."

"The *whole* truth, then, is a bit more complicated. As I said, at first I attended the A.A. and N.A. meetings with them out of fear. It was quite a shock to my system, after all, being denied blood after more than twenty years. I imagine that for an ordinary person, the equivalent would have been a week's worth of inventive mental, physical, and emotional torture. So I avoided drinking on meeting nights—one or another of them insisted on accompanying me to at least two meetings a week—and worked out all sorts of elaborate ruses to avoid daylight meetings.

"Eventually, though, my fear began to be replaced by anger, and a thirst for revenge. *For now,* I told myself, *I'll out-program-talk the best of them, I'll attend their meetings, I'll play their silly games.* And then some sweet day . . . *boom.*"

He rested his hot forehead against hers, his wide gray eyes boring so intently into her eyes that she imagined he could see his tiny upside-down image at the back of her retina. "Boom?" she whispered, almost into his open mouth.

"Boom. Somehow, someday, I promised myself, they'll all pay. Especially Nick. But then Leon . . ." He hesitated for a moment, then decided against telling her the truth about Leon's demise—it was too early. He lay back. "Leon died, and V.A. was chartered, or rather chartered itself, and one year turned into another, and the strangest thing started happening."

Lourdes frowned. "What?"

"I'd wake up with that old dead feeling—the 'weary, stale, flat, and unprofitable' blues. Lah-de-dah, another evening of ample supplies of the greatest drug in the world, and all the sex I wanted. Lah-de-*fucking*-dah. But perversely enough, if it happened to be the evening of a meeting, I would feel almost energized: Can I get away with it again tonight—can I fool them again? It was almost enough to get me out of bed.

"And then I'd find myself rather enjoying the meetings—they're not that bad, you know, at least when you're high on blood. I could bait Bev, tease Augie, see if I could get a rise out of Nick, and all the while there'd be this element of danger. I especially enjoyed hearing them describe my wicked little lifestyle as if it were something grand and evil."

Lourdes edged a little higher in the bed, and looked down at him.

"Well it wasn't any goddamn fun for me, Whistler—and I hope I never get so fucking bored that it will be."

He propped himself up on his elbow again. "Nor for me, m'dear, nor for me. It's been old and tired for at least a year. No challenge any-more—fooling them is child's play. That's why I risked it all on that one throw of the dice after the meeting. After all, I had no way of knowing whether you'd march right back downstairs and denounce me to the others."

"But I didn't," she said, so earnestly that her breasts bobbled inches from his nose. "And now there's two of us, and we're together, and to-gether we can finish those fuckers off—together we can tear that fucking meeting to the ground."

"Not as easy as it sounds. As the old Sufi tale has it, it's like trying to dismount the tiger without being eaten."

She slid down in the bed until her mouth was at the level of his ear. "I don't care. I don't . . . fucking . . . care! I just want off. I want off so bad I can taste it."

"Are you sure?" When he turned his head his breath smelled of blood and pot, and of her juices as well.

"Sure?" She felt her skin puckering up into goose bumps. "Baby, I been sure my whole life, way before I even knew what being high was." She rolled onto her back beside him. "See, as far back as I can remember, I always knew somehow there was a different way to feel. I remember how when I was five I used to rub myself to sleep—I guess I was, you know, masturbating, but I didn't come or anything, but it was like when I was doing it at some point—*crrk*—everything would kind of like *shift* around me, and it wasn't like *I* changed, it was like the world changed it-self around to fit me.

"When I was about eight I lost it, lost the feeling. Then when I was ten I started sneaking my dad's gin—to get that feeling back. And from the minute the booze hit my stomach I could feel my body just relax all around it, and for a little while anyway, before I'd get sick, I could be in my world again.

"I started smoking pot when I was twelve. My older brother turned me on to it—then he used to do things to me, but I'd let him do whatever he wanted, because when I was toasted it was still almost my world again, whatever he was doing down there. Then by high school I could get my own pot, and acid and 'ludes and coke, but no matter how high I got, it was getting harder and harder to get back to my world, and after a while I gave up on it—being stoned in *this* world seemed like the best I could do, and even that was getting pretty old."

"And you discovered blood how?"

She smiled—a secret smile, a remembering smile. "Anne Rice," she said finally. Whistler nodded knowingly. "It was last summer—this guy took me down to Carmel for a weekend, and I brought along *Interview with the Vampire.* I started reading it Saturday morning—talk about couldn't put it down—I mean, I read all day, finished it at like three in the morning—the guy I was with was really pissed.

"But those first chapters, when Louis describes what a blood high feels like? It was the first time anybody, anywhere, any way, ever even got *close* to how I used to feel back in my little bed, rubbing my little pussy like it was Aladdin's lamp."

Whistler had to turn away onto his side—Lourdes had the comforter pulled up to her throat, but even so, just the sight of her flushed face and bloodshot eyes, and her black hair, loose now, clinging in sweat-soaked tendrils to her neck, had roused the importunate Creature again.

"So a couple weeks later I apply for the blood bank job, and a couple weeks after that I finally get my nerve up at the end of my shift—I was still working days—and boost a bag of O-pos from the refrigerated room, and smuggle it into the bathroom under my sweater, and drink it cold." She closed her eyes again, recalling that first tentative sip—the blood had been salty, and rang like adrenaline in the back of her throat. "And then—"

"Nothing?" suggested Whistler.

"Right. Nothing. Nothing. Finally I drive off to ballet class. I'm feeling so fucking disappointed—prob'ly a little relieved too, but mostly I feel like a *total* asshole. But then I get there, and I'm pulling on my pink leg warmers in the locker room, and all of a sudden I start feeling like I'm on acid—only without hallucinations—everything is realer than real—like you said, alive—I remember telling myself that I never noticed how . . . *woolly* wool is, the pink is totally fucking *electric,* the black is the blackest—

"Anyway, by the time class started I was just totally *floating.* I never danced like that before in my life—my leaps are like flying, and for the first time ever I could *feel* what the teachers were telling me all those years, about sculpting your lines, about imagining your body is hanging from your head instead of balanced on your feet. Only I don't even *have* to *imagine* it. My teacher even told me that if I'd danced like that when we were auditioning the month before, I'd of gotten the role of Swan-hilda instead of Coppelia."

"Sorry, don't know much about ballet."

"Well, the whole thing is typical of how my ballet career's gone. My whole life I never got a lead role, not even a feature role—even after five years with the East Bay Ballet Theater, which is strictly amateur, I *still* never even got out of the corps. Then I finally get a *title* role, and of course it's Coppelia. Because in *Coppelia*, Swanhilda is the lead role. Coppelia doesn't even dance: she's like this mechanical doll who spends the whole ballet being wheeled around in a chair—the high point is when she gets dumped onto the floor in the second act.

"Anyway, when I finally get back to my apartment that night, the blood is still coming on, but it's not like any other high I ever had—I don't know what to do with myself—it doesn't *matter* what I do with myself, it's all so fantastic. Finally I end up taking a bubble bath—I dump in about a quart, and run the water so hot the steam is practically blistering the paint right off the bathroom wall—and I'm so high while I'm lying there I can practically *feel* it every time a soap bubble pops, and I'm closing my eyes, I'm reaching down, I'm touching myself—"

Her voice grew dreamy again as her eyes closed; Whistler felt the comforter shifting rhythmically, whispering a silky song. "And all of a sudden I *knew*—I was three years old again, touching myself in bed—when I was on blood it was my own world again, the world I fit in, the world that fit me."

She stopped, stroking herself oh-so-lightly with her thumb, then pressing against her sex with a cupped palm, feeling the warmth and comfort. The room, the farmhouse, the world on blood, was quiet except for the beating of her heart. She let go of herself, and with that same damp hand seized Whistler's shoulder and tugged him onto his back, whispering urgently. "It took me so many years to find my world again—I haven't even had it back for a year, and they're already trying to take it away."

Lourdes shoved aside the comforter, spat into her palm and slathered the Creature up and down, then climbed on top of Whistler, squatting with her feet planted flat on either side of his hips. She had ballerina's feet, gnarled and strong. "Well I'll tell you what . . ." Eyes open, weight on her heels, head and shoulders thrown back, hands cupped lightly over her flushed breasts, she lowered herself. When she spoke again her voice was choked, husky, triumphant. "Nobody's taking my world away from me again."

She closed her eyes deliberately and began to ride him with graceful determination, using her strong calves and thighs to balance herself. He watched her, delighted, comfortably distant. Her arms floated up over her head. "You're dancing," he remarked.

"Always," she replied, without opening her eyes.

"Not hurting you, is it?"

"A little. But the best come of the night is always the one right after you're totally sure you can't possibly come again."

Whistler's delight knew no bounds. "Take it, baby."

"Oh, I will. Don't worry about that, I will."

Chapter 4

ONE

In the early months of his recovery from blood addiction Nick Santos had liked nothing better on a Sunday morning than spending a few hours out on his redwood deck with the bloated Sunday paper, a pitcher of screwdrivers, a few joints, and a pack of Kools. But over the years his recovery had progressed substance by substance until by now all that was left to him was the paper, the balcony, and the orange juice—a regular Virgin Screw.

Still, he wouldn't trade his sobriety for all the drugs and blood and booze in the world, he told himself. And told himself and told himself, and attended at least one meeting a day to tell somebody else—or have somebody else tell him.

But even clean and sober—*especially* clean and sober (he told himself, etc., etc.)—Nick found himself basking in the *Sunday*-ness of the morning; the deep greens of the hillside, the sun-dazzle on the bay, the mountains of Marin glowing on the far horizon were all denied to the blood addicts, poor bastards.

Poor bastards indeed: he made himself a mental note to bring up the idea of an outreach program again at the next V.A. meeting. Perhaps he and one of the others (probably Sherman—Whistler's program had seemed a little weak lately) could fly out to one of the cities with a large vampire population, New Orleans, say, or New York or Las Vegas, to try to make contact with the locals, maybe isolate one for an intervention.

The very idea energized him—he thought about going inside to do some research on the Internet, then recalled his promise to help Betty Ruth fix her church doors. He loaded his tools into the trunk of his '56 Corvette convertible, and followed the Milky Way—Martin

Luther King Jr. Way—to El Cerrito. He had to park the 'Vette half a block away so as not to leave it under a tree—couldn't subject the hand-rubbed Arctic blue finish to a possible birdshit bombardment.

To his chagrin, when he set down his toolbox on the top step of the church and pulled open the doors to take a closer look at the damage, there was a service in progress inside. Betty, at the slightly raised pulpit, interrupted herself to acknowledge his presence with a smile and a wave; as Nick, his olive complexion darkening in embarrassment, slipped into the empty back pew with his clanking toolbox, several of the twenty or so congregants twisted around in their pews, presumably to get a better look at the idiot who hadn't figured out that there might be a service taking place in a church on a Sunday morning.

But then she introduced him as the man she'd mentioned earlier in her sermon, and now the entire congregation turned to applaud him. Apparently she had turned their encounter of the previous night into some sort of parable, in which Nick had played the part of the man who, upon seeing a problem (i.e. the doors), had turned his immediate attention, not to complaining about it, or to delegating it, but to fixing it.

It was all flattering enough, but good as it felt to be acknowledged, Nick couldn't help noticing how quickly he had jumped to his first conclusion. *It ain't easy, being an egomaniac with an inferiority complex,* he thought, not for the first time.

Betty thanked him again personally after the service. He thanked her back, then complimented her on her outfit: a simple, but undeniably purple, wool dress and a black-and-violet silk scarf. She looked down at herself. "This? I call this my Moby Grape dress."

He grinned. "I remember grape jokes."

"Right—what's purple and big as a house and spouts off every couple of hours?"

"Naah, I have a better one—you should call it your Alexander the Grape dress. You know, what's purple and conquered the world?"

"Well aren't you sweet!" She colored a little herself, though she already had high spots burning on each cheek from delivering her sermon: public speaking was not Betty's favorite part of the job. "Look, let me just say goodbye to a few people and run upstairs to change, then I'll be right back down to give you a hand with the door."

A few minutes later, up in the parsonage, Betty Ruth found herself dithering over what to wear as if Nick were a prospective beau. Then it occurred to her that he was now, in a way.

For Betty had awakened at two-thirty that same morning with her arms folded at her breast again, and a deep sense of loss, having felt the sense-memory of that tiny child in her arms, that tiny heart beating against hers, slipping away from her with the same inevitability as her chance of bearing a child.

So she'd forced herself to run through what they called a "process" in New Age counseling, one of her own devising. She called it telescoping, and it involved starting with the immediate problem (her sense of loss) and telescoping that out into the next larger problem (her inability to find a suitable sperm donor), which in turn extended out into the larger problem of her own ambivalence about becoming a mother.

She could have gone even further—into her fear of the pain of childbirth, her feelings about her own mother and her own mother's feelings about *her* mother, and so on—but suddenly, with what she could only describe as the reverse of an epiphany, some sort of glorious absence, she realized that the issues underlying her ambivalence were moot now: the ambivalence itself had been resolved.

Once again, another New Age axiom had revealed itself as ancient wisdom: the solution to the problem lay in the nature of the problem itself. Of course she wanted to bear a child of her own—that's what this whole damn telescope was about in the first place. The rest was just fear, and fear, of course, was always, and in the end only, about itself.

At that point, the deeper mystery having been solved, the rest of the telescope collapsed in clacking segments that resolved themselves one after the other until she reached the problem of the sperm donor. That's when Nick Santos' face had appeared to her mind's eye with all the discrete, sharp-edged clarity of an hallucination.

Hence the dithering back in the parsonage after Sunday service over which T-shirt to wear: Betty Ruth might soon be asking Nick to father her child, and for that there was no chapter in *Dress for Success.*

After all, she reasoned, she wasn't trying to seduce him, what with him being gay and her being at least situationally celibate. All things considered, she'd be just as happy with the turkey baster the lesbians preferred, or perhaps the direct-to-diaphragm approach currently in vogue among her straight, or not-quite-as-lesbian, friends.

On the other hand, she didn't want to gross him out, either, so she finally settled on an old teal Henley shirt that had seen a painting job or two in its day and that, she hoped, would project just the right note of womanly self-reliance.

When she got downstairs, he was already deeply engrossed in his work. Arrayed about him as he knelt before the open doors were an assortment of stains and putties and plastic wood and liquid wood in cans and tubes, and a collection of paintbrushes and putty knives that ranged in size and shape from housepainter to mascara, from trowel to dentist's pick, as well as a miniature blowtorch and a pink professional-model ConAir blowdrying gun.

"Nick, I'm impressed!"

He looked up, grinning. "I lived in the Castro during the seventies—antiquing was sort of a survival skill. As for the hairdryer, you'll want to stand back when I turn it on—it's got a wash like a Huey chopper."

It was painstaking work, but they found themselves enjoying each other's company, and over the course of the afternoon they managed, with the practiced ease of experienced twelve-steppers, to exchange large slabs of their respective life stories: Betty's Dutch Reform upbringing in Williamsport, Pennsylvania; Nick's coming of age in Detroit, in Greektown down by the river; Betty in divinity school, her conversion to Methodism, her missionary work, her first church and her last, the one she'd lost through drink; Nick at the Air Force Academy, intelligence work, hard duty (eating rats with the Montagnards) and easy duty (language school in Hawaii, monitoring Chinese radio transmissions from a base in Japan), his honorable, if heavily negotiated, discharge.

She talked about the men in her life—the former men in her life—with more humor than bitterness. "The last was about two years ago. We met at—now don't you dare laugh out loud—at a Sex and Love Addicts meeting. I know, I know: how doomed can you get!"

He discussed the only woman in his. "Marie and I were married for about ten minutes back in '69. I knew I wasn't straight, but I guess it seemed like a good career move at the time. Besides, since graduation I'd already raised my saber at the weddings of half the men I'd slept with at the Academy."

There! It wasn't much of an opening, but Betty was through it in the blink of an eye. "So I don't suppose you had any children, you and Marie?" she called over the roar of the blowdryer—he was up on the ladder working on the top of the right-hand door.

"WHAT?"

"I DON'T SUPPOSE YOU HAVE ANY CHILDREN?"

"NO!"

"DID YOU EVER WANT TO?"

"WHAT?"

"HAVE CHILDREN?"

"SURE, I—" He turned off the blowdryer and looked down thought-fully at Betty. "I don't care whether you're a man or a woman, or straight or gay, or a housewife or a priest, when you hit forty without any chil-dren of your own, or even any prospects, you're bound to do a little soul-searching every now and then, come three in the morning."

Now or never/I'm not ready, she thought—they say it's impossible to have two thoughts at the exact same instant, but Betty proved them wrong. "Two-thirty," she said to the door, only inches in front of her face.

"Beg pardon?" No longer shouting.

She looked up at him again. "I did my soul-searching at two-thirty this morning."

Something in her voice brought him down from the ladder—he did not let go of it, though, even when he'd reached the ground. "And what did you decide, if anything?" Trying to keep it light.

"That I wanted to have a child." She hoped he would keep asking ques-tions—that would have been easier—but he just stood there holding on to that stupid ladder, waiting. *Nothing to it but to do it.* "That I was thinking about asking you to be ... the sperm donor." She'd hoped that would sound a little less off-putting than "the father"—instead it rang stiffly in her ears. "I mean, if you could. If there weren't any ... medical problems or anything." Going downhill fast—what a clumsy way to bring up the Big Question: his HIV status. *I knew I wasn't ready.* "There wouldn't be any re-sponsibility involved, if you didn't want." By now there was a flat, trailing quality to her voice. Time to bail. "I guess it was a stupid idea, huh?"

But to her surprise, the corners of his mustache had lifted slightly again. "Not entirely," he said thoughtfully. "Were you thinking of John Henry or the steam drill?"

"Huh? Oh—turkey baster, most likely. Or direct-to-diaphragm."

"But why me? Why someone you've just met?"

"Because I've already rejected all my friends, but I don't want it to be a complete stranger."

"Have you looked into sperm banks?"

"Two hundred dollars for the initial screening, then two-fifty a pop."

"So to speak." Nick couldn't resist.

She laughed nervously. "So to speak." Then, after a moment, "Is this what they call a pregnant pause?"

His turn to laugh. "Not yet."

"Look, there's no hurry about all this. Why don't we take our time, think about all the questions we'll want to ask each other, maybe get to know each other a little better."

Suddenly it occurred to him that *that* might be the real problem here. *How the hell can I tell her about my being a vampire?* Even if he wanted to, he'd need the permission of the entire fellowship—it was written into their charter. *On the other hand, how can I not tell her?* But her eyes were studying his expression intently—to cover his confusion he turned his face away, took her hand, and led her down the walk. "C'mon, let's get a little perspective here."

He let go of her hand at the gate, and they turned to face the church; side by side, they regarded their handiwork. "Not bad," he said after a moment.

"Not bad? Good lord, Nick, those doors look like they should be hanging on a small cathedral from the Middle Ages." She noticed that they had somehow joined hands again.

"A small but *tasteful* cathedral. We do good work, you and me."

She understood that he was not just talking about the doors; without letting go of his hand, she turned to face him. "So you'll think about it?"

He nodded solemnly. "Obsessively, if I know me."

"Fair enough." She stood up on her tiptoes and gave him a quick peck on the cheek. All things considered, it had been a good afternoon's work.

T W O

At the eastern end of the Richmond–San Rafael bridge the Chevron refinery burns like a pit of hell; on the other side looms San Quentin. But if you roll down your windows when you reach the Marin County line, midway across, the bay smells clean, like the ocean, and you can all but hear the abandoned foghorns warning ghostly ships away from Red Rock.

Lourdes couldn't resist firing up a joint as she and Whistler rolled along in the silver Jag an hour or so after sunset on Sunday night. It was another measure of Whistler's apparent wealth that he didn't mind her rolling fat joints out of fine green bud that was going for sixty bucks an eighth on the street, when you could find it. "You still haven't told me where we're going," she reminded him, handing him the joint.

He checked the Jaguar's rearview mirror, then took a hit. "Back to the sixties, m'dear," he hissed between clenched teeth, holding in the smoke. "Over the mountain and back to the sixties."

Only one road leads to the town of Bolinas, in western Marin. Three or four days a year a new road sign marks the turnoff from Route 1; the rest of the year it is unmarked, the townspeople being of the opinion that if you're meant to find the place, you'll find it, and if you need a sign, you weren't meant to.

The Jaguar glided through Stinson Beach, then along the edge of the lagoon; they slowed, and Whistler pointed to a bare signpost on the left. "There. That's the turnoff. Getting sloppy nowadays—in my day we used to break the post off at the ground."

As the woods closed around them, Lourdes edged over and stuck her head out the window. "I miss this in the city," she said.

"Which?"

"You know, the woods—driving through the woods at night."

"Best pull your head in now—this wood is about to get considerably closer." He swung the Jag wide left to line up a right turn onto a narrow dirt driveway; branches scraped the roof.

"Your beautiful shiny car," moaned Lourdes.

Whistler didn't seem concerned. "In the sixties it was part of our security system—cops hated getting their cars scratched as much as they hated walking."

The driveway ran for another quarter mile; at the end of it the headlights picked out a tiny woman in a billowing nightgown standing in the doorway of a weathered A-frame. "Who's that?" Lourdes asked.

"That's Selene."

"Is she a vampire?"

"Of course not. She's a witch."

"Oh."

They parked next to an Eisenhower-era jeep, and Lourdes followed Whistler up a trail of flagstones lined with whitewashed rocks, and flowers and herbs in pots, that climbed the slope to become a railed set of wooden steps. She waited in the doorway while Whistler and the little woman hugged—and hugged, and hugged. She would have been jealous, but her own hug, when it came, was equally prolonged and enveloping: Lourdes found herself humming blissfully into the woman's long dark gray-streaked hair.

Whistler introduced them afterward, which seemed somewhat irrelevant. "I'm so *glad* to meet you," chimed Selene. "It's been years since Jamey's brought anyone with him."

"You call him Jamey?" Lourdes sidled up against Whistler and rubbed her shoulder against his arm like a cat. "Can I call you Jamey, too?" she purred.

"If you'd like," replied Whistler amiably.

The A-frame was one big room with a sleeping loft at the apex. Selene picked up a hurricane lamp and led them straight through and out the back door to a redwood deck with a sunken round redwood hot tub burbling in the middle. "Whoops—forgot the towels," she announced, setting the lantern down. "I'll be right back."

Lourdes took off her leather jacket—actually it was *his* jacket, a glove-soft bottle green Italian number she'd found in his hall closet. He'd quite forgotten about it, as he didn't wear green anymore: green did not suit his pallor. "Is it her blood we're gonna drink?" she whispered.

"Yes." Whistler began unbuttoning his shirt.

"Do you pay her?"

He looked up, annoyed. "I *pay* hookers. Selene, I cherish."

She unzipped her jeans and stepped out of them, balancing first on one foot, then the other. "What's the street price on cherish?" she asked, a trifle meanly—she hadn't liked his tone of voice.

"Well, I *do* own this house, this land. If she ever needs anything, she calls me." Whistler hung his shirt over the deck railing, then turned back to Lourdes. "But it's not the way it sounds."

"It *sounds* like a combination of a mistress and the goose that lays the golden eggs."

An owl hooted somewhere up the hill, and a lizard or a squirrel or something skittered under the deck. When Whistler finally spoke again there was only a trace of his customary archness. "I've never given much thought to how things sound. My relationship with Selene is perhaps the least mercenary I've ever been involved in."

"And if Selene decided to stop laying golden eggs?"

"You don't understand—it's not by *my* choice. I *like* mercenary relationships. But with Selene, everything she does for me, everything I do for her is completely voluntary—on both sides. If she thought for a moment there was any quid pro quo involved, *she's* the one who'd be gone, pfffft, puff of smoke. We were lovers for twenty years before she took her vow of celibacy four years ago, and that hasn't made a bit of difference."

Lourdes hooked her thumbs into the waistband of her peach-colored panties, and as she slid them down she thought of a line from *The Wizard of Oz.* "Is she a good witch or a bad witch?"

"A very good witch indeed," said a voice behind her—Lourdes wheeled around to see Selene coming through the back door with an armload of towels.

"Sorry. Didn't know you were there."

"Not a problem—it's not a dark secret, dearie, it's a religion. Wicca. It means wisdom." Selene dumped the towels next to the lantern, pulled her nightgown over her head, and slipped into the tub. She was even tinier than she'd seemed clothed, round-shouldered and slightly pouch-bellied, with stick-thin arms and legs, more than a sprinkling of moles, and a nasty raggedy scar along the left side of her neck, just above where the collarbone joins the shoulder. Not your classic siren, yet Lourdes, who was strictly heterosexual up to a certain point, that point being the right amount and combination of drugs—or blood, always blood—was briefly stirred. *Maybe she is a real witch after all,* she thought.

Whistler followed Selene into the tub; steam drifted up into the dark fir trees surrounding the deck. "Delightful," he said, lowering himself to the redwood bench that rimmed the tub, eighteen inches below the waterline.

Lourdes was last. She sank down to her neck and let her head float back into the water; looking up, she saw a circle of black autumn sky dusted with crisp stars, and heard herself humming again. Suddenly something struck her. "Jamey?" Trying out the sound of it.

"Yes?"

"I know this is probably a dumb question, but how come we just can't drink each other's blood, and leave out the middleman?"

"Would that we could. Why, if we could get off from drinking each *other's* blood, m'dear, V.A. would be a dating service. But we can't—in fact, that's the surest test for one of us. If you drink someone's blood and nothing happens, then you've found another vampire."

"Speaking of drawing blood . . ." Selene stood up and waded into the center of the tub. She held out her hands; they formed a circle and closed their eyes.

"To the Mystery," intoned Selene.

"To the Mystery," repeated Whistler and Lourdes. Selene turned to her. "I'll need a few minutes to get into my trance, dearie—try not to say anything, or move around too much."

"Then what?"

"Jamey knows. He ought to—we've been doing this for a quarter of a century."

Neither of them had a watch, and if Selene had signaled, Lourdes missed it, but somehow Whistler knew when the time came. He crossed the tub to the shadowy end where Selene sat upright with her eyes closed. He rested his palm over her heart—she crossed her hands over the back of his, then slid forward, slowly, into the water.

Whistler motioned to Lourdes, who put her arms under Selene; they cradled the floating witch between them, her long hair fanning out in the water like a middle-aged Ophelia. Selene was barely breathing, and her pulse had slowed; suddenly she opened one eye and peeked up at Whistler. "The scalpel—it's somewhere over by my nightgown," she said, then slipped smoothly back into her trance.

Lourdes supported Selene by herself while Whistler reached a hand out of the tub and felt around on the deck—it took him a few seconds to come up with the velvet fountain-pen box. He snapped it open and pulled out a scalpel, holding it up to the flickering lantern light for a moment to approve the edge: it glinted handsomely. *God, I love my life,* thought Lourdes.

He beckoned to her—she gently floated Selene across the tub to him, closer to the light, with one hand spread wide under the witch's back and the other under her thighs.

The rest happened quickly. Whistler stepped forward with the scalpel in his right hand; the only sounds were the wind in the firs and the burbling water. With his left hand he reached across Selene's body and rotated her left leg a few degrees outward, locating a small blue vein where thigh met groin—a familiar vein, hatched with tiny white hair's-breadth scars. The scalpel flashed, swiftly he nicked the vein—Lourdes saw only a thin red ribbon of blood before his mouth covered the wound. Soft sucking movements sent the water rippling.

When it came her turn, Lourdes stepped between Selene's legs and squatted down to suck; she could feel the soft damp nest of the witch's pubic hair against her cheek. She drank greedily, and felt her high coming on even as she drank. Whistler had warned her about this. "Live blood, fresh from the vein," he'd cautioned her, without a trace of English accent. "Shit'll kick your ass."

But she hadn't paid much attention, and now, sucking at the pulsing vein, she couldn't have cared less anyway: she would not have been able to stop if Whistler had not been there to gently tug her away with one hand while applying pressure to the cut with the thumb and forefinger of his other hand.

Then it was over, not a drop of blood in the water, Selene floating peacefully, back arched and hips raised. Lourdes, stoned beyond belief— she might as well have been in a trance herself—bent her head to Selene's breast and began nursing rhythmically. The older woman opened her eyes. "That feels very nice, Lourdes," she said sweetly. "But I ought to tell you I'm celibate."

Lourdes turned her head to the side. Her eyes were already beginning to glitter red in the lantern light. "I know," she said. "Does that mean I have to stop?"

"Not right away, dearie."

THREE

Nick Santos's third career (after the military, which he'd told Betty about that afternoon, and the literary, which he had pointedly failed to discuss, having published three vampire novels under the name Nicolas San Georgiou) was as a freelance programmer/analyst specializing in computer security.

This made him an old man in a young man's game, but he knew a few tricks the kids hadn't learned yet, such as if the NSA said encryptions were secure up to eighteen bits, that meant they'd already learned how to crack eighteen-bit cryps. Something else he knew—this was a lesson they'd learned the hard way in Nam—you can only truly protect something if you're willing to destroy it.

So he not only recommended thirty-six-bit cryps for his most sensitive clients, but kept his own private files on unlabeled floppies that were never stored to hard disk; each of the floppies was in turn infected with a doomsday virus which would, if not disabled by a password, cause it to erase itself while at the same time reducing the host computer's operating system to the functional level of—well, to the level of the sitting vice-president: he had dubbed it the Quayle. It was nothing fancy—you just had to be willing to take the risk.

Or minimize the loss: this Sunday night, out of the tens of thousands of dollars of high-tech equipment resting on desk-high shelving braced against three walls—Macs, clones, printers, plotters, modems, faxes, red-lighted surge protectors, thickets of power cords tangled and dense enough to hide Br'er Rabbit—only one monitor, a worthless CGA-board antique, was aglow in the darkened office down the hall from Nick's bedroom, and that in turn was wired up to the oldest computer in the room, an equally worthless first-edition IBM-XT. That way, even if he screwed up while accessing one of his protected files, he wouldn't lose any equipment of value.

Not that he had any security work planned for tonight. He supposed he could have started working after midnight, but the fact was that he'd been keeping his promise to Betty a little too well: he'd obsessed over this sperm-donor idea all through his regular Sunday night A.A. meeting, and afterwards, over coffee and pie at Nation's, his A.A. sponsor had expressed some concern. "You seem awfully distracted, Nick."

"No, no problem," Nick had assured him. "Just trying to get a few things straight in my mind. Nothing I can talk about yet." *Just whether I should tell this woman who wants me to father a kid for her that I'm a recovering vampire.*

"Well if you can't talk it out yet, why don't you write it out?" was his sponsor's suggestion.

To which Nick had replied, in his mind: *Writing? That's what got me into this mess in the first place.*

But he couldn't dismiss the idea as easily as that, he realized a few hours later, settling into his work chair, a state-of-the-art leather and tubed-steel masterpiece that was worth considerably more than the CGA monitor and the XT put together. It might be easier to get a few thoughts down on paper—pros and cons, that sort of thing.

It wasn't until he'd popped in one of his protected disks that it occurred to him that he hadn't written a line of anything but programming or tech specs in nearly twenty years, and that the reason for that had been a writer's block the size of the Transamerica Pyramid.

So he sat there staring at the blank screen for a few minutes, tapping a few keys and then erasing the letters with the back-arrow, until all at once it came to him: *Fuck it. Who'm I kidding? Nobody's ever gonna read this anyway.* And he found himself typing the following sentence: *I thought I was the King of the Castro.* Then he went downstairs to make himself a cup of instant coffee.

By the time he returned, his primitive screensaver program had kicked in, and the room was dark. He settled back down into his chair and tapped the space key. When his sentence reappeared, he nodded. "Yeah," he said to himself. "Fuck it."

Then, on a whim, he backspaced to the top of the screen, inserted the centering code, and typed four words—My Life on Blood—in the largest available font.

His mouth had grown fearfully dry. He took a sip of the hot coffee, set it down on the counter, levered his chair back into a nearly reclining position, took the keyboard onto his lap, reminded himself one more time that no one was ever going to read the damn thing, cursored down to delete the period after Castro, and began to type in earnest.

MY LIFE ON BLOOD

I thought I was the King of the Castro, back in the mid-seventies when the Castro was the only kingdom worth having. Never mind the exact years—numbers don't signify here. It was the Golden Age. It was the time of Before.

The month was October. They say there are no seasons in San Francisco, but there were in the Castro. Autumn meant bunting blooming in the windows of Harvey Milk's camera shop and size ten fuck-me pumps and ruby slippers sprouting up in the shoestore windows weeks before Halloween.

The Bar of the Month that October was Oscar's Place, which we all referred to as the Pistachio Palace, after the rather saprophytic shade of chartreuse with which the owners had seen fit to decorate the walls.

But no one came to the Pistachio Palace for the decor, especially not on Sunday morning. No, you came to brunch for Leon's pepper-shot Bloody Marys, hair of the dog, good fer what ails ya, and a mushroom omelet to die for, if you'd gotten past the praying-to-the-porcelain-god-Ralph stage, and for the deep dish about last night, Saddie Night, Amurrica's Date Night, and who done what to whom and how often?

The drinks were on me again that morning. I was still celebrating a rather obscene advance my publishers had given me for a fourth vampire novel, as yet uncompleted, and I hadn't even managed to spend the money I'd gotten for the mass paper edition of the trilogy. My friends and I were doing our best to remedy *that* little oversight, however, and I'm afraid we were keeping poor Leon rather busy at his shaker.

We were at our regular table, a long narrow Da Vinci Last Supper job in the raised alcove at the back of the dark room (when Leon was working brunch the black drapes were always kept tightly closed), and I remember that for some reason we had rechristened our waiter Benedict, as in *I'll have the eggs, Benedict!*—oh, what cards we were!—and kept calling loutishly across the room for *Drinks, barkeep. More of that voodoo that you do so well.* And it is altogether fitting that at this defining moment of my life, for so it proved to be, I was getting cheap laughs with a story I blush to repeat here, about having been recognized in the Bulldog Baths the night before by a boy newly arrived from Iowa who was performing a rather personal act upon me at the time:

"... so he looked up, and his eyes bugged out to here, and he said—and these are his exact words—he said, *Hahrn't hoo Hick Han-horr-heeho, huh hriter?* and I looked down at him, and replied—and these are *my* exact words—*Dear boy, didn't your mother teach you not to talk with your mouth full?*"

Well, I hardly need tell you that the hilarity was general, and everytime it started to die down, somebody'd start sputtering and repeating fragments of either punchline—*Hahrn't hoo Hick,* or *Dear boy*—and set us all off again, and in the middle of it Leon appeared at our table with another round of Bloody Marys and Tequila Sunrises and Mimosas and god knows what other noxious concoctions we were drinking in those days, and something in his face dried up the last of the giggles.

Which was unusual, for Leon had one of the world's top ten funny faces: a droopy-nosed, long-lobed basset-hound face, like a cross between Yoda of Star Wars and one of the lesser Seven Dwarves. But then, it was unusual for Leon to come out from behind the bar in the first place. "You the one who writes about vam-pies?"

That's *pies,* as in apple or rhubarb: Leon was from some little southern town—I never got the real name—he always referred to it as Deepshit, Jawjah.

I allowed as how I was indeed the one who wrote about vampires.

"Well siss on you, pister, 'cause you don't know so mucking futch." And he turned his back and—what *is* the word for Leon's walk? somewhere between a flounce and a stalk—flalked back to the bar.

Again, the hilarity was general, but although I managed a chortle or two my own bad Pagliacci self, I was not only hurt, but I couldn't imagine for the life of me what had prompted the little man's outburst. I'm sure I never dished him behind his back: I had a friend who had a friend who'd heard a story about him that "could *not* be repeated, my dear," but all I knew about him for certain was that he made the best damn Bloody Mary this side of Market Street.

Benedict didn't know what was going on with Leon either, so I took the check down to the bar myself, and dealt with his effrontery the way real men do: I apologized. Said I didn't remember ever doing anything to offend him, but if I had I was sorry. And he apologized back, and said he didn't know what had gotten into him, and of course we both snickered at that, and then he told me that if I really wanted to learn something about vampires, dot dot dot.

Actually, his voice only trailed off, but he had a very expressive way of speaking, and the ellipsis was definitely implied. And although it was true he was far from my type (anything short of drop-dead gorgeous was far from my type in those callow days, I must confess), it was also true that the above-mentioned obscenely-advanced-upon novel was not only uncompleted, but uncommenced, and unlikely to be commenced if I didn't stop celebrating soon and get to work.

So I humored the little guy. And you know, he was right: I didn't know so mucking futch after all.

Dating—such as it was—was different in the time of Before. Not so much pressure—nobody was auditioning for a life's partner. You could meet, have drinks at the Elephant Walk or the Pistachio Palace, maybe dinner at the Chinese place at the corner of 18th Street with the bamboo-screened booths, and if it wasn't working out you could go to the baths and lose each other at the door, and if you happened upon each other in one of the cubicles or the tubs or the orgy pit in the course of the night, a grin and a courtesy wave would suffice, no hard feelings, heh heh.

That's by and large the way I figured it would go with Leon. Chinese, then lose him in the baths. I mean, I was the King of the Castro, wasn't I? You bet. But by the time the potstickers had arrived there wasn't anyplace on earth I'd rather have been than sitting across from that little goblin of a man, listening to him talk about vam-pies in a voice so full of honeyed southern charm it made Slim Pickens sound like Bugs Bunny.

What we did at first was play a what-if game. What if there really were such things as vampires? What if they weren't superhuman monsters, but only human beings for whom human blood was the greatest drug of all? What if they didn't need to kill their victims, but only take a cup here and a pint there—no more than the blood banks?

I don't know at what point I began to understand that he was not just pitching a plot to me. (That's something that happens not infrequently to novelists—as if plots were in short supply.) I know it was sometime after the arrival, and dispatch, of the velvet prawns, but before the litchi nut ice cream, because once I understood what he was driving at I couldn't eat a bite. Stirred my dessert into white silken mud in the red-rimmed china bowl. And I dearly love litchi nut ice cream.

I hadn't lost my appetite from revulsion, mind you. I was simply nervous as a schoolgirl with a crush, wondering whether he was going to ask me to the prom or not. I already knew what my answer would be, and when he asked me whether I wanted to go back to his room with him I was cool on the outside, I was the King of the Castro, but on the inside I was Molly Bloom and yes I said yes I will Yes.

Somehow when I think back on Leon's apartment above the Pistachio Palace, I think of Blanche DuBois, of paper fans, and weeping willows dripping with Spanish moss. Silly, I know: it was only two rooms overlooking Castro, but Leon could do that—cast a spell like that around him. And there *was* a four-poster bed—that was real. And every carpet and shade and curtain and doily had tassels and deedly-balls, and a beaded curtain separated the bedroom from the living room.

He took my blood at the kitchen table. It was a cafe table. It even had a hole in the center for an umbrella. The chairs were wrought iron cafe chairs. The needle was a larger gauge than you use for injecting drugs—didn't hurt a bit, though, and as I watched him decant the vial into a hollow-stemmed champagne glass and drink it down, slowly, his peach-pit Adam's apple bobbing, I thought to myself: *I must remember this!*

Only nothing much happened. He smacked his lips thoughtfully, and looked up. "Nicolas San Georgiou. Nicolas God-dayam San Georgiou. Who'd a thunk it, who'd a thunk it, who'd a thunkety-thunk thunk it."

"What?"

"Le's give it just a little more time, bud."

"Give what time, bud?"

"Well, you can't tell only from the taste, but with blood this fresh, if I don't get a buzz within the next few minutes then we'll know for sure."

I knew my next line: *Know what for sure?* but I have always resisted the role of straight man, so to speak, so we sat there making small talk, and at the end of the allotted waiting period he reached across the little round table rather formally, and we shook hands, and then he burst into laughter, which did alarming things to his floppy jowls. Didn't bring up his color—he was still white as newspaper stock—but even his Easter Island earlobes were shaking merrily as I sat there with my bare face hanging out, wondering whether it had all been an elaborate prank.

I picked up the empty champagne glass. Red dregs in the stem, tapering to a thin red thread, like a thermometer tube at the very bottom, and a pinkish gleam around the rim, were all that remained of my blood. I ran my finger around the edge of the rim, trying to make the crystal sing, but couldn't get it going. I put the glass back down. "So Leon, ol' buddy, ol' baby-heart, I think it's time for you to tell me what the fuck is going down here."

He got up and walked over to the window, pushed the curtains aside and peeked out. It was a move right out of some classic thirties gangster flick—Bogart or Cagney could have pulled it off, but then, they weren't usually dealing with flounced curtains. "Sorry I laughed. Wadn' at your expense—I was only laughin' from pure delight." The blinking neon light over the bar below cast pale periwinkle stripes across the right side of his face when he turned back to me. "See, the fact is, you' a vam-pie, son."

"Oh, I see."

"No. No you don't. But you will, baby-heart. Very soon, you will."

A discreet bronze plaque marks the entrance to the Parthenon Baths—a discreet bronze plaque and a day-glo lavender door. That good old YMCA-pool smell of chlorine hits you first—it's not until you've negotiated the long black-lighted corridor to the inner door, flashed your membership card, paid your five bucks, and been buzzed through to the locker-room/check-room that you catch your first whiff of the distinctive *ambience* of the bathhouse. For unique as each bathhouse may be (the Bulldog, for instance, has a trucker theme: miniature license plates mark the cubicles, and one can commune with like-minded men in a full-scale mock-up of a Peterbilt eighteen-wheeler cab; while the Parthenon has a classical theme: sunken Roman Baths, and Greek everything else), the smell is always the same: a melange of pool and poppers, sweat and cologne, KY and the latest designer Crisco.

Next comes the ritual of the towel: as delicate and circumscribed as the Japanese Tea Ceremony. First the waist wrap: high if you're fat and low if you're flat. Then the tuck & I-grow-old-I-grow-old-Do-I-dare-to-wear-my-towel-rolled? Depends on whether you want to show your thighs. Some do that shouldn't.

Next order of business: the Stroll. Leon seems to know where he's going: I follow him through the warren of the Parthenon, which is a honeycombed maze of aisles and stairways. We pass up the tubs, the orgy pit, the black-out room, the cubicles. Take your time—no hurry in the baths—here's an open door: a boy beckons. I catch Leon's eye; he shakes his head; I feel the pulse of the Euro-trash synth-rock disco beat that quakes the very walls; regretfully, I pass. Never passed up such a pretty open door before.

On the other hand, I've never cruised for blood before, either, and it isn't until we've passed the vinyl room (the Parthenon is not slavish in its adherence to the classical theme) and headed up a narrow iron stairway that twists first to the left and then to the right, that I realize where he's taking me: to the roof.

Now, there's nothing wrong with the roof of the Parthenon: I'd spent many a lazy morning there, stripped and oiled and toasting in the sun. But the only reason for going up there at night is to get a breath of fresh air if you've overdone the 'ludes, or something. I mention this to Leon, and he taps his temple with his forefinger. "Attaboy. Now you' thinkin' like a vam-pie, bud."

"You bet, bud," I reply, totally mystified until we reach the top of the stairs and open the door to the roof—brrr—and see the boy. Now you're supposed to be twenty-one to get in the baths, but I'm damned if this cutie, sprawled naked on his side, half-on and half-off the thin mattress, an odalisque for the Castro, is a day over seventeen. Leon puts his forefinger to his lips, and circles around to approach the boy from behind. He taps the naked shoulder—no response. "Some nights you get lucky, baby-heart," he whispers to me, across the unconscious lad.

I remember: Gravel underfoot. A cold goddam wind and an overcast so thick and black it is invisible, it is the night itself. Leon turning the boy onto his stomach, pulling a sheathed scalpel from the towel roll at his waist. *Cunning* sheath: hand-worked calfskin. Choosing a small vein at the back of the knee. Lecturing in a whisper: "Choose a different vessel every time. Don't need a major vein, don't want a major artery." Not a slash with the scalpel, but a push and a slide, then a downward swoop of the head; the stringy muscles at the back of his neck strain; his fingers knead the firm thigh-flesh like a baby at the breast.

When he pulls back his eyes are dream-smudged. His lips are black: he licks them pale again. "Your turn, baby-heart." I look down: black blood wells in the hollow of the boy's knee. In the space of a pulse I understand that nothing will ever be the same for me again.

I dip my head to the soft bowl brimming black: the taste is salt and rust. It's like having an out-of-body experience while I'm still in my body. I gather my feet under me and stand, vaguely surprised: it feels as if I could just keep rising, floating into that glorious black fog like an untethered float in the Hudson's Parade.

When I come back to myself, only a few seconds have passed. Leon has wedged the boy's discarded towel against the back of the knee, then bent the leg back to stanch the flow of blood. "Vam-pies are not necessarily sentimental," he explains. "Or unnecessarily. We jus' ab-*hor* to waste blood."

When the bleeding has stopped we clean the boy up with his own towel, toss it over the edge of the roof, carry him back inside and down the stairs as easily as if he were a sack of dog chow, and deposit him in a cubicle. We leave the door open: he'll be safe: no place on earth is safer than the tubs. I love the tubs. I will weep when they are, at long last, closed.

Nick sighed, felt around under his seat and hit the lever to tilt his magical chair forward, then replaced the keyboard on the counter in front of the overheated XT and reached for another sip of coffee. To his surprise, it was cold in the Wedgwood cup, and the cup was cold in the saucer.

He looked down at his watch: 3:00 A.M. He thought of Betty, wondering whether she was awake, and whether she'd changed her mind.

ONE

Sherman Bailey was the featured speaker at the next Sunday night meeting of Vampires Anonymous. In honor of the occasion, he had worn his favorite vintage 1930s Pineapple Joe Hawaiian shirt—a chocolate brown beauty with green coconut palms.

"Hi, my name is Sherman—"

Eleven voices: "Hi Sherman!"

"—and I'm a very nervous recovering vampire." Chuckles from the circle. "I can't believe I still get nervous when it's my turn to tell my story. By the way, happy December seventh, which as everybody knows lives in infamy as the day the Japanese attacked Pearl Bailey. I guess everybody here has heard my story at least once except for Lourdes, so stop me if you get bored."

"Oh, that you meant that," murmured Whistler.

"No cross-talk, James." Beverly called him back to order in a hurry.

"I don't mind," said Sherman.

"Well I do." Beverly folded her arms. "Just the *possibility* of cross-talk makes this less of a safe space for some—"

Whistler interrupted her with a languidly upraised palm. "I apologize—to you, m'dear, as well to our speaker. Sherman, please continue."

Sherman inclined his head after Whistler's own gracious manner, then opened his hands wide, palms up, as if presenting himself as an exhibit. He was a teddy-bearish man, balding, with an assertive reddish brown mustache. "Well here I am, Lourdes. What you see is what you get: in twenty years—my wife Catherine says ten—I'll be Wilford Brim-

ley selling oatmeal. I don't know at what point it gets decided that an innocent little fetus is going to grow up looking like me, but I do know
there are a lot of tubby little guys walking around looking *exactly* like
this, mustache, bald spot, round glasses and all.

"And I'm no different than any of the others. Oh, I've done enough
therapy—since I was eleven, in fact—to know that I should be saying I'm
unique and glorious. But then, by the same reasoning so are all the tubby
little guys, so where does that leave us?

"And probably lots of them are addicts too. The only real difference is that I can get high on blood." He looked up at the corner of the
ceiling as though a thought had just occurred to him—in fact it had
not, it had occurred years ago: he'd liked it and filed it away for his
twelve-step autobiography: "Come to think of it, we don't even know
how many of *them* can *also* get high on blood—most people never
find out.

"As for me, *I* found out—the hard way. I was an Orphan, which
means I discovered my addiction on my own, as opposed to being Awakened by another vampire. I'd been fascinated by vampires when I was a
kid—obsessed by the time I was an adolescent—if I hadn't had the good
sense to keep *those* fantasies from my shrinks, I'm sure I'd have been
locked up years before I ever tasted my first drop.

"And even then, it took an accident. I was in college—psychology, of
course—I thought it might help me figure out whether I was insane—
when one night—one momentous night, as they say—my girlfriend
happened to cut her wrist pretty badly—" The vampires in recovery
leaned forward hungrily: this was everyone's favorite part of everyone
else's story. "—playing with the coke razor."

Sherman raised his forefinger professorially. "Now at a moment like
that, someone *else* might have tried to stop the bleeding first. Someone
else might have called for help. Not me: *I* dumped the crumbs out of an
empty bowl of pretzels and held it under her wrist, and *then* we stopped
the bleeding."

He looked around the circle, smiling slyly. "I told myself at the time I
was trying to save the rug—it was white—but I'm sure it was really my
addict taking over even then—somehow *it* knew before I did. Because, if
it *was* the rug, why did I bother—"

He took a breath for the big finish. Whistler caught Lourdes's eye
again—it was such an oft-told tale he could lip-synch the next words
along with Sherman:

"—dumping the pretzel crumbs out of the bowl first!"

*   *   *

The rest of Sherman's share was somewhat less detailed. He was more interested in talking about his current situation with his wife Catherine—how she was far more interested lately in her Wicca practice than in him, and appeared to be harboring some unspoken discontent. He *seemed* to be saying that he was afraid she was going to leave him, but his declarations were sandwiched, twelve-step style, between qualifications and negations.

"What's coming up for me, if I let myself really feel my feelings, is that I'm afraid it's me she's so unhappy with. Of course, I know I'm probably projecting that. Because, not to take her inventory for her, but I know it's really herself she's unhappy with. So what's probably really happening is that my inner child is afraid that I'm inadequate, and it projects that out on her, that of course it's me she's unhappy with. Or rather, my inner child."

A turgid silence followed. Sherman broke it with a pleased laugh. "I feel better already. Just getting to talk about it—sometimes that helps more than anything." Beverly got up to get herself a cup of coffee from the stainless steel cart at the back of the room. "I guess I'm done," Sherman concluded, to polite applause. "For a topic, I suggest your life on blood—what you miss most, what you have instead. Or whatever's up for you, as usual." He looked around the circle—the heavy woman in the wool poncho caught his eye. "Ch—I mean, Louise?"

"You nearly said Cheese Louise, didn't you?" She chuckled. "Hi, my name is Cheese Louise, and I'm a deli." The circle of vampires broke up laughing. "Actually, my name is Louise, and I'm a recovering vampire. Thanks for the topic, Sherm. The thing I miss most is that feeling of being invulnerable that you get on blood. Speaking as a woman, particularly—sometimes walking to the deli to open up, in the winter particularly—it can be pretty scary, walking down College in the dark. I remember, when I was working nights as a vampire, not only wasn't I ever afraid when I was high on blood, I used to enjoy it if somebody gave me trouble. So I guess I miss that, too—kicking ass."

She chuckled again. "As for what I have instead—I guess mostly it's where I'm walking to—to my own shop. Getting clean and sober, and finding my Higher Power, is what enabled me to have my own store in the first place. If I was still using—especially if I was still using blood—there's no way I'd have that."

Louise rubbed her palms together briskly. "That's all I have to say—

except that I'm grateful for this fellowship, and for all of you." She sat back as several hands shot into the air. "Henderson?"

This proved to be an impossibly tall musician with thin lank hair pulled back into a ponytail, who introduced himself in a lazy Texas drawl, and allowed as how he'd lost 'bout half his chops on the git-tar. "Useta play faster'n Stevie Ray, and sweeter'n Johnny. 'Course, I'm still faster'n Stevie Ray, but that's only 'cause he splashed hissef all over that mountain. Now how 'bout you, Augie?"

A stout, imposing man with a fleshy nose and dark hair brushed back at the sides adjusted the crease of his wool slacks, and identified himself without looking up. "Hello again everyone. My name is August, and I'm a recovering vampire, and what I miss most about drinking blood is . . ." When he lifted his head and scanned the circle of friends there was a beaten look in his eyes, despite his evident prosperity. "Everything! From the waking up at sunset with a desperate thirst, to the scoring itself. The clean way the blood floods the chamber of the hypodermic; the first dark welling of a clean vein cut; the floppy rolling squoosh of a full bag from the blood bank—"

Several of the vampires were nodding: *Tell it, brother.* "And of course the sex. Don't let me get started on that—I haven't had sex with a minor in so long I've nearly forgotten what it's like. But most of all I miss . . . Can you miss an absence? If so, I miss the absence of the . . . Sherman, what's the psychiatric term for the part of your mind that's always judging yourself?"

"The superego. It restrains and censors the ego. An internalization of the moral standards of your parents and society."

"That's the fellow. I miss his absence." He puffed out his already convex cheeks, and blew out a sigh. "Who wants to go next, I'm tired of the sound of my own voice. Toshi?"

The Asian, of course. A Japanese who flushed brick red under a delicate ivory complexion. "My name is Toshiro, and I am a recovering addict to a great many substances, including blood . . . Yes, hi back to all of you. I cannot allow myself to miss any of my drugs. You see, just the other day I received word that I have been given the opportunity of a lifetime—a position of chef has opened up at Chez Panisse—only a fill-in shift on Tuesdays and Wednesdays, and only for the cafe upstairs, but still . . ." There was a smattering of applause. "Thank you. So as you can see, even to think about blood would be a disaster for me at this time." He looked around the circle. "What about yourself, James?"

Whistler, who hadn't had any blood for hours, had nearly nodded off—his chin was halfway to his chest—but he came out of it brightly. "Don't miss a thing about it," he said, looking earnestly around the circle. "Not a single thing, and *that's* the Higher Power's honest truth."

Beverly was waiting avidly, watching not his face but his body language, listening not to his words but to their pitch and cadence. Like many practiced twelve-steppers, she had learned to sense when a share was ending. That way she could have her hand shooting up into the air just as the sharer started looking around for someone to call on.

But Whistler's abruptness caught her warming both hands around the styrofoam cup in her lap—when she looked up to catch his eye, she saw he was already nodding in her direction. She wondered if he had read her thoughts. He used to do that all the time, back when they had been lovers, on baby-blood.

On baby-blood. The thought—and the memory evoked by it—came to her so suddenly that it might well have been his thought first. Another trick of his. Not that it mattered: she knew now what she wanted—needed—to talk about that night. "Hi, I'm still Beverly, and I'm still an addict. This isn't exactly on the topic, but it's what's up for me. I was doing my Fourth Step in N.A. last week, making a Searching and Fearless Moral Inventory of myself, but it's my second time through, and I was having trouble getting any energy into it. So my sponsor suggested I think of the single most immoral thing I had ever done in my life, and when I thought back I remembered a time that my friend and I—I'll protect his anonymity—befriended this newlywed couple we'd met. She was a secretary—mousy little thing—and I was the office manager. From the day she announced she was pregnant we cultivated her and her husband. Had 'em over for dinner, bought 'em expensive presents—I think we even bought the crib."

"Carriage," Whistler interrupted.

"So much for my friend's anonymity," Beverly said dryly. "But you're right—I remember now, it was one of those expensive yuppie baby carriages. Anyway, we kept it up for five months. Every time we saw them, we'd drive home just howling about how stupid and boring and dull they were. Then after she gave birth we visited her in the hospital, and after she'd had the baby home for a few weeks we bought the new parents a night out on the town—dinner, tickets to a show. And ourselves, of course, their dear trusted friends, to baby-sit."

Beverly paused for a sip of wretched coffee—even in a styrofoam cup, it managed to taste of cardboard. "Ten minutes after they were out the door we had the baby on the dining-room table with a needle in its foot."

She put the cup down on the floor, careful to slide it way underneath the folding chair so she wouldn't knock it over. When she looked up, Lourdes had a hand raised tentatively. "Lourdes, you had a question?"

"Yeah—if you were done. I don't want to cross-talk."

"I'm done—what'd you want to know?"

"Just, I keep hearing people mention baby-blood. I mean, what's the story there, why would you go to all that trouble for like, six months, just for a few drops of baby-blood?"

"Bev, if I may?" She nodded, and Whistler took the floor. "We went to all that trouble, Lourdes, because that's how much trouble it took to get it—if it had taken more, we'd have done more. But as for the head, it's as impossible to describe as sex to a virgin. Baby-blood provides an extreme clarity of thought. Very little difference between that and madness, mind you—ask Nicolas sometime."

Whistler smiled blandly across the circle, and observed the tightening of Nick's lips with some satisfaction. He wasn't sure why he was needling his old compatriot at this moment—probably just sheer perversity. But then, sheer perversity had always been good enough for Whistler. "Although oddly enough, the nearest thing I've ever experienced was tripping on acid while drinking blood, which is in a way exactly the opposite head. But again, Nicolas can tell you more about that than I can."

This time Nick's reaction was immediate and unthinking: he started to flip Whistler the bird. It wouldn't have been the first finger to have been raised in anger at a V.A. meeting, but out of the corner of his eye he caught a glimpse of Beverly about to go ballistic, so instead he used the offending digit to brush the carefully disarrayed comma of hair back from his forehead. *Thank* you *James.*" The sarcastic Lawrence Welk cadence had not disguised the angry quaver in his voice. "I'm sure you could tell the story about acid and blood as well as I could. But it is getting late—perhaps Lourdes would rather hear the story after the meeting. I've noticed you two have been spending a lot of time together lately, anyway."

Whistler only grinned, but in a flash Lourdes was halfway out of her chair. "He's my goddamn sponsor, Nick—you got a problem with that?" Nick rose to confront Lourdes, Whistler jumped up to defend her, Beverly leapt to her feet beside Nick shrieking about cross-talk, and Sherman hurried into the center of the circle to interpose himself between the two factions, crying, "Everybody sit down! What is this—Geraldo?"

Suddenly a folding chair flew entirely across the circle, narrowly missing Sherman, clearing Ethiopian Sally's head by a few feet, and smashing into the black schoolroom clock on the opposite wall before crashing to the floor, followed by the clock.

The room lapsed into shocked silence, broken only by the death rattle of the clock, which had landed on edge and rolled halfway across the room before spinning onto its face with a steadily slowing, rhythmic clatter. All eyes turned to January, standing in a gap of the circle of chairs with her fists clenched, bent forward slightly from the waist as if the muscles of her tight belly were clenched as well.

"You selfish selfish fuckers," she screamed. The silver studs in her ear reflected the purple of her hair; an overlarge black U.C. sweatshirt revealed the straps of a sleeveless undershirt; black leggings and square-toed knockoff Doc Martens boots completed the ensemble.

"What?" Sherman was the first to speak—the other four had all sat back down, mouths agape.

"You guys are going on and on about some fucking history, some shit that was over years ago, and not one of you even remembered that tonight was my one-year anniversary. Not one single person in the meeting." She glared around the circle—not an eye met hers. When she reached Whistler, he turned all the way around in his chair—when he turned back, his slim magician's fingers had extracted a small, plush box from the pocket of his leather jacket.

"We usually wait until the end of the meeting to give out chips, January," he said, crossing the circle with the box held out in front of him. "But this seems to be the time for an exception."

January accepted the box numbly, having shifted from overwhelming rage to overwhelming gratitude so swiftly that she seemed to have stripped some emotional gear. Whistler had to open the box for her—inside lay a silver poker chip with ONE DAY AT A TIME inscribed on one side. He lifted it from the box by the gold chain to show her the 365 inscribed on the other side. His duties as treasurer were the only V.A. responsibilities he took seriously—and his jewelry broker took them even more seriously, at a 60-percent markup.

"Shall I?"

She managed a dazed nod. As he stepped closer to reach around her neck, he could feel himself responding to the pure animal heat coming off her, and to her scent, a bitter but not unpleasant coffee-bean sort of smell. Or it might have been the sense of danger—in any event he took care not to brush against her as his fingers expertly fastened the delicate catch.

Meanwhile Sherman had retrieved her chair, while Lourdes hung the poor cracked corpse of a clock back on the wall. As January and Whistler returned to their seats, Nick began the applause—alone at first, one slow clap at a time like Citizen Kane at the opera, and then faster as the others joined in, until finally a weeping January rose from her chair again, this time not to throw it, but to take a bow.

"And now the floor is yours, Miss January," said Whistler, terribly pleased with himself. The cost and quality of the chip alone had represented a more than grand enough gesture—the timing had elevated it to the level of a major coup. "We'd be honored to hear anything you have to tell us."

January sat back down, sniffled once or twice, and the tears disappeared as completely as the rage they had replaced. "Well okay, I been trying to think what I was gonna say tonight. You guys except Lourdes know I always get a little emotional when I start telling my story, but lately, not just at this meeting but at my Violence Addicts Anonymous meeting before it broke up, I hear people all the time starting off their shares talking about dysfunctional families this and dysfunctional families that, until it makes me want to either laugh or scream, one. On account of—and this is the only meeting I can tell the whole truth at, which is why I love it so much and need it so bad—at least most of the people talking at least *had* families. I had Glory.

"Glory—that was my mom's name. She would be qualified for every meeting you can think of. Southern Comfort, pot, speed, smack, coke, uppers, downers.

"I was only allowed to smoke pot, but of course I snuck everything. But not blood—Glory didn't know about blood. Neither did I, until her last boyfriend. He was a Chinese guy named Wayne. One of those tall bony Chinese—if you squinted your eyes you could kind of picture him in a silk beanie and a long droopy mustache.

"We were living in a tiny little two-room house in Stinson Beach. I slept in the living room, but even with their bedroom door closed you just couldn't miss how they were screwing all the time, her and Wayne. I used to go for long walks on the beach at night, but I could of walked all the way to Bolinas and they'd of still been at it when I got back.

"This went on for a year—I was like, twelve—finally I learned to sleep through it, and then in the summer it was kind of cool, 'cause they'd sleep all day with the bedroom blacked out, and screw all night, and I could basically kick with my friends, you know, come and go whenever.

"How I found out I was a vampire too, was I guess Wayne was hitting on Glory a little too hard—you couldn't even miss how she was getting paler and paler every day and had these little cuts—always another band-aid here or there—and I was never exactly clear whether she was in on it or not, but one night he put some chloral hydrate in my Dr Pepper and took a little drinkie outta *me*, and guess what?

"Right. He didn't get high. But he didn't tell her, either. He just waited, and the next night he came to me real late. I was sleeping on the porch out back, facing the beach. I remember the full moon was over the ocean and the clouds were all silver and he woke me up out of a deep sleep and said here drink this and I wasn't even sure I wasn't dreaming but I wasn't scared.

"It was Glory's blood, it was my mother's blood. We shared the cup, and when I was good and high we went into the bedroom and told Glory I was a vampire, and drank some more and fucked each other in every combination there was—the three of us. I wasn't a virgin or anything, but it hadn't ever been anything like that night.

"But then at sunrise, after me and Wayne took our chloral hydrate and fell asleep, she stabbed him through the back with a pair of scissors, and took off her clothes and walked out into the ocean—a couple guys saw her, but they were so busy scoping her bod that they didn't figure it out until she didn't come back.

"She never did come back, either, unless you count when her body floated in the next day. I saw it. It was pretty awful, but by that time I'd already been through waking up next to Wayne's dead body with the scissors sticking out, so it wasn't like, unbearable.

"Only, like I said, don't talk to *me* about dysfunctional families."

TWO

"And what insights did you carry away from the meeting tonight?" asked Whistler archly as the waitress at the Dessert Inn left with their order.

"Two things. One, I want some baby-blood. Two, January scares the shit outta me."

"I knew that Chinese fellow she spoke of, that Wayne," replied Whistler. "The mother, too. He used to bring her to our parties in Bolinas before Selene eighty-sixed him. A sleazebag of the first order—no one was particularly sorry when he was found dead. But we'd always assumed another vampire had done it—it's not as easy as it sounds, driving a scissors that deep."

"You think January—"

"No, I believe her—she's not difficult to read. And wasn't that a sweet scenario—mother, daughter, Chinaman, all abed together?"

"I have to admit, it did get me a little turned on—up to the scissors part, any— Oh, thanks." Her espresso had arrived—she took a scalding sip. "Jamey?"

"M'dear?"

"That week that Beverly gave me off for detox is over. She's switching me back to days so I can make the meetings. I mean, she's expecting me to show up at work on Monday morning."

"Well we'll just have to disappoint her, won't we?"

"But I could get fired. Or she could call an intervention on me."

Whistler spread his hands out flat on the table, palms down, fingers splayed, thumbs touching, as if he were participating in a seance. "Those are two separate problems. And of the two, the first is not a problem— I'll have a year's salary transferred into your bank account in the morning. As for the second, I think it's time to get serious about Operation Dismount-the-Tiger—did you bring your disguise?"

Lourdes was still trying to digest the part about the year's salary— clearly even her wildest imaginings had underestimated Whistler's wealth. Why, if he could toss off $19,850 just like that, he must be a millionaire or something. "I'm sorry, a what?"

"Disguise—remember I asked—"

"Oh, right. Yeah, a hat with a brim, and some big sunglasses. But you still didn't tell me what for."

"For step two of Operation Dismount-the-Tiger, of course."

"I never even heard about step one."

"Ah, but that's the reason we can't go after any baby-blood just yet." He explained about having borrowed the Doe only a week before. "If I'd known I was about to meet you, I'd have waited. As it is, I think we should let a little more time pass before going after another infant. But I promise you, what I have in store for you tonight will be nearly as much fun."

"That's easy for you to say, you just had some last—"

He reached across the table to take her hand. "I promise you, my darling. When the time is right, you shall have all the baby-blood your thirst desires. In the meantime, let's cruise the Ave tonight, pick ourselves up a donor and a playmate all in one."

"You know a hooker who gives blood?"

"Oh, they can all give blood, m'dear. You just have to poke them in the right places."

San Pablo Avenue runs from downtown Oakland all the way to Hercules. Darlene, who worked the Oakland end (but closer to the Berkeley border, as was fitting for a white girl), thought she had seen everything in her year and a half on the Ave, but when the Chevy Caprice pulled up to her corner with a lone white woman behind the wheel, she thought again. *Never seen a dyke cruisin' the Ave before. Trip.*

She sauntered to the curb and tapped on the glass—"You lost, sweet cakes?"—but when the driver leaned over to roll down the passenger-side front window, Darlene stooped down so her assets were practically hanging over the sill, same as if it had been a man.

"No, not lost," said the woman, showing her teeth in a smile; she was wearing a floppy hat and oversized dark glasses—those teeth were about all Darlene could see of her face. "In fact, I think I found what I was looking for. My boyfriend keeps talking about a threesome—tonight's his birthday, and I thought I'd surprise him."

"Surprises are cool," said Darlene. "Might take some deep bank, though."

"Beg pardon?"

"Deep bank. *Might* could be expensive."

"Well, we *might* could be rich."

Driving a Chevy? Darlene thought, but when the woman unlocked the door, she opened it and eased herself into the passenger seat, tugging her long-sleeved low-necked black stretch minisheath down to the top of her thighs. It was nice to be out of the wind that came whipping down the Avenue every night, but the car had a funny smell, like somebody'd been cooking crack with ether. "So where is this boyfriend?" she asked teasingly, as the car pulled away from the curb.

"Closer than you think," said a man's voice behind her—she started to turn—the last thing she remembered was the cotton pad over her face, and that sick sweet sleepy smell.

Darlene opens her eyes: everything's still black. A blindfold. The urge to remove it is barely a thought before she understands that her wrists are tied, her ankles too; she's on a bed, still dressed. Then she remembers the smell of the ether and knows she's going to die.

Though it's a shock to her body—for a second she thinks she's going to vomit (that'll kill you too, she knows, spewing on your back: her friend died that way, choked on chunks in a China-white sleep)—somewhere deep inside she feels almost peaceful. Ever since she ran away from home at twelve, people have been warning her she'd end up this way if she didn't get straight and get out. And now here it is.

Then she thinks about the possibility of pain, and the peaceful feeling dissolves. "Is any—" She has to clear her throat. "Is anybody here?"

"Oh yes," says a man's voice—rich or old or English, something like that—sounds like he's standing at the side of the bed. "It's very like a party, in fact."

"Are you gonna kill me?"

"Oh no. That would *spoil* the party—we're not even going to hurt you."

"Then could you take off the blindfold? I'm getting kinda scared."

"Ah, but then we *would* have to kill you, I'm afraid—if you saw us."

Jesus-fuck, she thinks weakly. "Look, mister, I'm a ho on the Ave— you think the five-oh's gonna give two shits whether you fuck me *tied* down or *upside* down or—"

"Now just relax." That's the woman who picked her up. Sounds like she's standing on the other side of the bed; Darlene feels the mattress shift as she sits down. It's quiet here—no city noises; she wonders how far they've taken her. "I promise, we're not going to hurt you."

"Then why am I all tied up?"

"So you won't dislodge the I.V. Your veins are in terrible condition, y'know." The man's voice reeks of concern. "If my friend here hadn't needed the lesson, we'd have simply opened a vein. As it was, it took me three tries to find a decent one for the I.V., and then I had to run a catheter in to keep it from collapsing. We're taking a little blood from you, you see. So if you *would* keep still for just a *little* while longer, we'll finish up here. Then we can have a drinkie and send you on your way."

The tone is calm and soothing; it makes her feel like a little girl—tender and tired and sad. "I'm cold," she says; her own voice seems farther away than his.

"Here, I'll fix the spread for you."

The woman's voice again; her weight comes off the bed. Darlene smells perfume—jasmine—hears a soft rustle in the air above her, feels the puff of breeze and then the blanket being tucked in around her; for the first time she senses the needle in her left arm. "Did you tell me why?" asks Darlene.

"Why what?" She can feel the woman sitting on the side of the bed again, feel the warmth against her hip, and a soothing hand on her shoulder.

"Taking . . . blood." Sleepy now.

"We drink it. We're vampires."

The thought occurs to Darlene again—this time she says it aloud, a confidence, as if she were among friends: "I'm dead."

"Oh no no no," says the man. "Tch tch tch tch." Clucking as his voice comes nearer. "You're just a bit out of sorts from the chloroform. You'd be surprised how little blood a person really needs." His thumb presses cotton against her vein—the pain wakes her a little—he slides the needle out—that doesn't hurt, but then the catheter slithers out after it, and that stings.

When they loosen the ropes she feels pins and needles as the blood flows back into her hands and feet; with it comes a flow of possibility. "I won't tell anybody, you know. I promise, I swear I won't tell anybody." Desperately: "Even if anybody cared, nobody'd believe me."

"Ah, but I *want* you to tell someone, Darlene. I have in mind one particular person for you to tell, and no one else. I want you to tell that person that vampires took your blood. Nothing else, though—just that vampires took your blood. Then I want you to take the money I'm going to leave in your purse, and never mention what happened here—never even *think* about it—again. If you do, then I *will* kill you, and that would be a loss and a shame."

Darlene cannot trust her voice. She nods; her eyes are open wide behind her blindfold. "Who—" She tries again. "Who—who do you want me to tell?"

"A very nice woman—you'll like her. A minister, in fact." Then Darlene smells that sick sweet sleepy smell again—her chest heaves as she tries to hold her breath, tries to fight the thundering grayness stealing over her.

THREE

Midnight found Nick in his office again, seated before the old XT. All those unbearable memories and feelings that Whistler and the meeting had stirred up made sleep pretty much out of the question anyway—it hadn't taken him five minutes of lying there in the dark for *that* particular revelation to dawn. But all other avenues of escape from his feelings—blood, booze, weed, sleeping pills—being closed off to him by one program or another, he'd found himself thinking about how much like a drug the act of starting *My Life on Blood* last week had affected him.

He'd forgotten that about writing: how it had always taken him out of himself; how for a few hours at a time, anyway, he could leave the regrets and anxieties of his life behind on another continent, while he drifted off into that timeless sea.

Then he remembered Beverly's share at the meeting, and it occurred to him that perhaps *My Life on Blood* was really *his* true Fourth Step, his Searching and Fearless Moral Inventory; that instead of trying to escape from those unbearable memories and feelings, he could use them for his recovery, as yeast for the process.

And what yeast he would have to work with tonight: his friendship with Whistler—and his rivalry; that terrible night on blood and acid; the nightmare of baby-blood. No, not baby-blood. He couldn't face that yet. But that night on acid, that night after which it was no longer possible to pretend that blood was only a recreational drug, that being a vampire was a relatively harmless pursuit—maybe he was ready now, at long last, to drag that out into the light.

Or maybe not—he decided to start with something easier. Whistler, perhaps. That first Halloween. Now there was a nice high jumping-off place. Suddenly he thought of Selene, and a song fragment sprang to mind before he could suppress it. Those were the days, my friend. Those were the fucking days. Not exactly the most appropriate sentiment for a Fourth Step, but sometimes, he knew, you have to be like the Fool in the tarot: you just have to trust in the process, and step off the cliff.

*   *   *

I'm afraid that Leon rather spoiled me—we drank live blood at least twice a week, and fresh blood, not live but recently drawn, the rest of the time. We had donors, whom we paid, and stoners, like our friend on the Parthenon roof; druggees, whom Leon mickeyed at the Pistachio Palace, and thuggees, low-riders from the Mission or white boys from Concord descending on the Castro for a night of fag-bashing.

Meanwhile my education continued. I learned about the vampire red eye, and never went out without my Visine. I learned sunlight burned my eyes like a sonofabitch the day after the night before; soon, when every day was the day after the night before, I learned how to protect my eyes, how to rearrange my life, where to find an all-night this or a twenty-four-hour that. I learned anatomy—the vascular system, anyway—and how to use a hypodermic needle; I learned when to stalk, and when to lie in wait. I learned that one out of a hundred people's blood would not get me high; I learned that that person was a vampire; I learned to let Leon decide whether he or she should be Awakened.

I remember I'd only been a vampire for about three weeks when I started bugging Leon about the other vampires I now knew existed: where were they, how many, when could I meet them? To which he answered, with disappointing consistency: everywhere; more than you think; and Halloween.

Now Halloween was already the biggest day of the year in the Castro—we didn't have so many tourists back then as later, but it was still Mardi Gras on acid, even when you weren't *on* acid. When you were, of course, it was Mardi Gras on acid, on acid. And when you were on blood—oh lordy!

I wasn't at first, mind you. Ripped to the tits on Thai Stick, sure, but Leon had cautioned me neither to hunt nor drink before he picked me up, and just to be sure he picked me up twenty minutes after sunset.

I got a wolf-whistle out of him, at any rate, when I appeared at the door in my finery. My high-necked red-lined opera cape was silk, my shirt a dazzling white-on-white, my dinner jacket black on black, and my fangs—my crowning glory—not the cheap plastic Hong Kong variety, but enamelled denture-grade ceramic.

As for Leon, he merited, not a whistle, but a quiet nod of admiration: his cape and tuxedo and silk opera-hat fit him so easily, and he wore them so naturally that they didn't seem to be part of a costume at all: he might well have been a Victorian gentleman out for a night on the seamy side of town: there should have been a London fog, carriage wheels squeaking, and the jingle of traces and the clopping of hooves.

Instead there wasn't even a San Francisco fog. On Castro Street the crowds milled under a benevolent sky: the men and boys were thick as hasty pudding, and still on came the queens: we had to jostle our way against a sea of taffeta all the way to the DuBoce Triangle, where we hopped a streetcar over the hill to Noe Valley. Two vampires on the J-Church. Never drew so much as a glance.

The house was a narrow Victorian, painted black, trimmed in walnut, built high and narrow like a Queen Anne row, but free-standing, with a steep front staircase behind an elaborate gate with the initials JMW worked in wrought iron. Carriage lamps on either side of the door lit the top landing, and a butler opened the door. Inside there were costumed vampires and witches everywhere: on the stairs, in the parlor, picking at hors d'oeuvres in the kitchen while a costumed, red-headed Bride of Dracula nagged at them to leave the food alone until it was time to serve it.

And the best part was this: Leon went up on tiptoes to whisper it in my ear: "Anyone you may meet tonight in this house who is attired in vam-pie regalia is a vam-pie in actuality."

"What about the witches?" I wanted to know, but before he could answer a tiny woman in a black dress and pointy hat had approached us.

"You must be Nicolas," she declared, handing me a glass of punch as Leon sidled off into the next room. "I'm Selene. Jamey's just *dying* to meet you—he's read all your books." She stood on tiptoes and craned her neck. "There he is. Jamey, dear, over here!" Waving a skinny arm over her head. "Jamey, this is Leon's friend Nick, that he was telling us about." We were joined by a slim, elegant man with a disarmingly languid manner, and cold gray eyes to die for. "Nicolas San Georgiou, this is Jamey Whistler."

"It's Nick Santos, actually—San Georgiou's my pen name." I toasted him with a sip of the peculiar-tasting punch—it occurred to me that perhaps it wasn't wise to accept beverages from witches, but I didn't want to seem an ungracious guest.

"Ah, Saint Nick—that's an even better name for the author of *The City of Blood*."

"How do you mean?"

"Well it *was* a bit naive, you'll have to admit, all that soul-searching, all that talk of good and evil." He smiled effortlessly. "Please, don't misunderstand me—I absolutely *adored* the book: all that sex and blood—

it reminded me of my own life." But he couldn't resist another dig. "On a slow night, of course."

"Of course." I returned his smile, and raised him a few watts for good measure.

"By the way, you'll have to forgive us our little Halloween *charade*." Rhymed with odd. "One night a year we indulge ourselves in that which must remain hidden the other three hundred and sixty-four."

Although we were standing in *his* hallway, I was required, in my position as King of the Castro, to remain rather less impressed with him than he was with himself. I turned to Selene somewhat stiffly—I had to rotate my torso along with my head, so as not to poke myself in the eye with that starched point of the cape collar—and offered to bet her that if you woke him up in the middle of the night he'd talk just like everybody else.

Whistler laughed heartily, though—or as heartily as he ever laughed, and for the first time I found myself starting to like him. "It's the god-damned tux," he said. "Everytime I put it on I end up sounding like Christopher Lee."

It *was* a magnificent tux. I complimented him on it, and he gave me the name and address of his tailor in Hong Kong. I jotted it down, feeling terribly urbane.

"Have you drunk tonight?" my host then inquired.

"You mean—?"

He nodded.

"Leon told me not to. He said—"

"Quite right: Selene and I had mentioned to him that we were hoping you would be free to drink with us this evening." He raised his eyebrows just high enough to convey inquiry, and not a hair higher.

"My pleasure," I said.

"You bet your ass," was the reply. Didn't sound a bit like Christopher Lee.

The party is in full noisy swing, but when Selene closes the door to the master bedroom behind us, all sound stops—*shoop!*—and I'm listening to the pulse in my ears. Half the room is taken up by a black-canopied king-size fourposter bed; the bedclothes are black as well. At the foot of the bed is a small round home-hooked black rug with a red pentacle. Selene positions us around the rug and says something about the greater evolution, then takes off her hat and tosses it into the corner of the room, and reaches behind her to unhook her dress. It falls to the floor with a rush. She's naked under it—slender, boyish—I barely have time to register any of this before Whistler wraps his cape around her one and a half times, like a burrito, and fastens it at her throat. Velcro. How clever.

Clad thus in a loose cape of black silk that covers her from neck to foot, Selene clambers up onto the high bed, and crawls into the center—long crawl: enormous bed—and sits waiting. "Do we prefer any vein in particular?" asks Whistler.

"Not really. Do you have any recommendations?"

"There's a very nice one just—" He climbs onto the bed without wrinkling his tux, unfastens her cape, and lays it open. "—here." Pointing out a cute little pulser that rests against the top front of the collarbone. "Shall I tap it for us?"

"Thank you, that'd be fine." Trying to maintain a professional demeanor, you understand.

"Have to get out of this monkey-suit, then. Recommend you do the same: so hard to get blood off these silk lapels, you know."

Selene hadn't said a word all this time—she appeared to be dropping into some sort of trance, but I'm pretty sure she watched us as we stripped with a good deal more interest than her expression betrayed.

It was an easy vein to tap with a scalpel—you could pin it against the clavicle, and get a nice clean cut: I made note of the location, and studied Whistler's technique assiduously. Selene appeared not to feel any pain, but she definitely started getting aroused when he began sucking at the hard bone below the throat, and by the time he ushered me to the wound she had begun to moan.

And while I can't swear that they had choreographed the whole dance, it sure worked out slick as spit: the tap was on the left collarbone, but I was on her right: the only way for me to reach the blood was to climb on top of her. It was awkward at first, but only until I had sucked a few times, and her blood had begun to flow again.

At this point the bottom begins to drop out of my consciousness. What the fuck was in that punch she'd handed me? I'd been mickeyed once in Saigon, and the drop-off felt a little like that—but instead of falling through to black, I find myself in some extraordinary psychedelic warp where hallucinations take the form of a hyper-reality: the warm naked flesh, the blood filling my mouth, the small breasts my clutching fingers have somehow found: all more real than real, while my thoughts run thick and slow and clumpish.

I open my eyes: I'm staring down into Selene's eyes. I don't know what color they are—black, all black. I have no peripheral vision, I can only stare down into her. I am inside her now—I don't know how long I have been inside her—inside her body, sure, but inside her trance as well. I can feel Whistler clambering about, but he is no longer hyper-real, not the way Selene is—I feel that if I turned my head I would not be able to see him.

Now here's the part that feels most like a dream: we have been making love, all blood-high and slick and sweaty, for time beyond time, when Selene slips from underneath me and rear-presents, anthropologically speaking, and it occurs to me that she has a tail—a small naked tail some three inches long, that moves easily aside, out of the way, as I enter her. And what is dreamlike is not the tail, which might as easily be an hallucination as an actual tail, or even the way I take it for granted (although that's what you do in dreams, you know: take odd things for granted), but rather the question I ask Whistler as he positions himself behind me.

"Do I have one, too?" I ask him. "Is it in the way?"

Now *that's* a dream state, Jack: I have found that no matter how high you may get in your everyday consciousness, you never actually lose track of whether you have a tail or not.

In the course of the next year or so I would have ample opportunity to ensure for myself that Selene did not, in fact, have a tail. She did, however, have the ability to cast spells. Wicca may well have been a religion, but at least the way Selene and her Coven (the other witches at the Halloween party: many of them had the same sort of arrangements with one or the other of the vampires as Selene had with Whistler) practiced it, it included the study of all the traditional witchly arts, both white and black. Still, as far as I could tell, her spells owed more to roots and herbs and telepathy and hypnotism than to supernatural factors—in any event, it was definitely the Goddess up there at the top of the Wicca organization chart, rather than Satan.

Selene had another talent besides spells: an amazing capacity for producing blood: I don't know how often Whistler drank from her, but I rarely let a week go by without paying them a visit.

At first, of course, it was largely for the blood, the sex and the new kink—there weren't many new kinks left by then—but after a year, which is about how long it took for my blood jones to reach the point where I dared not let a day go by without drinking, not crashing was as important as getting high. It wasn't the physical part of the crash I feared—that you could medicate—but the Elephant, which is what I called the depression that always showed up to take its perch on my soul if I woke up at night and did not drink within a few hours.

That meant I had to keep a stash: a one-day supply at first, then two, then five. And a padlocked refrigerator, and a virtual laboratory full of blood drawing and storing paraphernalia, and yet I still had to procure more blood nearly every night—how else do you keep the stash at the *m.c.l.*: minimum comfort level?—and sometimes the hunt turned . . . unpleasant. And after each unpleasant episode I would swear I'd cut back, and that vow would last a good, oh, thirty-seven hours, and there I'd be with my head in the refrigerator and my self-respect down the shitter.

But only until the blood got me high again: then I'd laugh at myself for being such a sentimental schmuck.

Of course if you were a vampire you were luckier than most junkies: you only had to score once a night. What's more, your particular drug wasn't even illegal. Some methods of procuring might have been, but a vampire attorney (no, that is not a redundancy) of my acquaintance announced one night that he had searched the criminal code, and that there was no statute currently on the books which prohibited one person buying blood from another in a personal and private capacity—or selling it, which rather amused several prostitutes I knew.

August Fetterman, the aforementioned vampire attorney, was a well-connected Deadhead. He had grown up in Menlo Park, and hung with a gang that lived out of cars and smoked marijuana and drank cheap wine. His parents had sent him east to college to get him away from the corrupting influence of "those beatniks." August turned into a lawyer; the beatniks turned into the Grateful Dead.

All of which is of interest only because Augie, who looked like a young Robert Morley (was there ever a young Robert Morley?) was always good for a backstage pass or two, or in this case four: Augie, Leon, Whistler and myself. The Dead were playing at the Greek Theater in Berkeley—it was June, the kick-off of the summer tour, and we each had our chores: Augie supplied the tickets, Whistler chauffeured us, and Leon and I took care of the drugs: he brought the blood and I supplied the acid, which had been lurking in my pharmacopoeia since my Awakening.

We drank first, at my place, but lightly, sipping refrigerated whole blood from aperitif glasses, then licked our Easter Seals (it had been the fashion that spring: one 250-mike drop on the back of each stamp: you could get high and contribute to your favorite charity at the same time) and hopped into Whistler's classic silver Jaguar sedan. And then, if I may paraphrase the Gonzo Master: *We were ten yards out of Frisco when the drugs took hold.*

Middle of the Bay Bridge, actually. We had left my apartment half an hour before sunset, but the sun was low enough, and the fog had poured through the Twin Peaks gap thick enough that we'd been able to avoid direct sunlight. It came strobing through the girders of the lower deck, though, and sent us all reaching for our wrap-arounds. The Dead were in the tape-deck, and I was riding shotgun, *going down the road feeling good*, at least until it occurred to me that the driver was easily as wrecked as I was, and *I* was watching white lines performing Native Hawaiian folk dances on the roadbed.

"Have we never tripped on blood before, then? Nicky?" With some difficulty I brought my attention backwards through the windshield, into the car again. Whistler was glancing over at me with as much concern as he could bring to those gunmetal eyes.

"Nope."

"Let the acid serve the blood, and not the blood the acid."

Leon piped in from the backseat. "Remember this, baby-heart: Vam-pies don't *have* bummers on acid. They *give* 'em."

I turned my attention back to the dancing lane-markers, narrowing my eyes like Clint Eastwood. That forced them back into line, but there was something different about them now: not just that they were alive—the blood alone would do that—but that now I understood that inside their straight little white-line hearts they were dying to get up and hula.

It was a playful combination, acid and blood, but not all its effects were as benign as the dancing lines. A few minutes into the Dead's first set I took off my glasses—the sun had dropped well behind the amphitheater wall—and wandered out front to merge with the tribal mass writhing before the stage. Now I'm no tie-dyed in the wool Deadhead, but I've found that if one is willing to take enough drugs to paralyze one's critical and ironic faculties, Dead shows can be awfully fun.

But not this time: this time I felt like Colonel Sanders dancing among the chickens: all I could think of was how much I wanted to drink blood—right then, right there. Not to get high—I could hardly get much higher—but just to be drinking, to have my mouth against warm flesh. For the first time, I could picture myself tearing open a vein with my teeth. Not a pretty picture. I tried to banish it, but it stayed with me as I pushed my way to the side of the stage and flashed my All-

Access badge to a large shaven-headed hoop-earringed black genie in the uniform of a Bill Graham security guard.

In my condition, though, even the open-air backstage seemed other-worldly, with its Grecian pillars and parapets and the gray-green eucalyptus and the new-fallen sun backlighting the clouds, and turning the western sky a glowing periwinkle. Nor did it help my attenuated sense of reality that the only person in sight was Wavy Gravy, everybody's clown but nobody's fool, in full red-nosed slap-shoed clown livery: the Hog Farm had the backstage child-care concession. He howdied me, and I thought about going downstairs to see the little Deads—I thought perhaps it would take my mind off blood. But then on my way down the stairs I thought again: what if it didn't? What if I looked at a child and couldn't stop myself from thinking about tearing its little throat open? Quel bummer, eh?

For good or ill, I never got the chance to find out: just as I reached the bottom of the stairs I glimpsed Leon ducking down a side corridor. I hurried after him, but he'd disappeared like the White Rabbit. "Leon? Augie? Guys? Whistler?" I called. The door nearest me opened a crack, and I slipped in sideways; Whistler locked the door behind me.

Augie was perched on the edge of a folding canvas cot, bent over the shirtless body of a pale young Deadhead. He looked up—his eyes were cartoon pinwheels, and a thin tracery of blood marked the corner of his mouth. "Jerry's good tonight, huh?" he said, then went back to his feeding.

Actually, from what I'd been able to tell out front, during my more lucid flashes, Jerry—Garcia, the Head Dead—seemed to be having trouble finding the neck of his guitar, but it was a moot point: down here all we could hear was the loopy beat of the bass booming through the cinderblock walls: I thought of Vonnegut's harmoniums in the caves of Mercury. In any case, I was hardly in a critical frame of mind. "Who's got nexts?"

"That'd be me." Leon raised a forefinger. "Why, you hurtin', baby-heart?"

"Jesus, Leon, I don't know what the fuck it is, but if I don't get some blood soon I'm gonna go werewolf." I'd heard others use the term for a vampire who'd gone over the edge—apparently it covered everything from ripping chests open with your bare hands to taking a nip out of your neighbor on the streetcar—but I'd never seen it myself. Or felt anywhere close to it until now.

"Calm down. Nobody's going werewolf around here," he replied soothingly. "Counsellor Fetterman, I believe it's time to introduce Nick to our new friend."

Augie sat up again, swaying, but he wasn't so far gone that he failed to pinch off the blue vein at the front of the boy's shoulder. "This is— well, I call him Tad: he couldn't quite recall his name when we first met," Augie explained as I approached the cot. I could hear voices in the corridor, and smell pot burning somewhere.

"What is he, out cold?" Leaning over, I positioned my thumb and forefinger outside of Augie's. We counted one, two, three, and at three he let go of the vein and I pinched it off without losing a drop.

"Hard to tell." He stood up unsteadily, and I took his place. "He was on his way to the freak-out tent with a major acid bummer, but luckily he ran into old Doc Fetterman, first, and we decided to medicate the problem."

"With?" I leaned down with my lips to the pinch of flesh between my fingers, rather like a man preparing to blow up a balloon.

" 'Lude and a Talwin. If he ain't asleep, he's close enough."

And the last thing I heard before I loosened my grip and tasted the hot salt blood spurting into my mouth was Whistler, across the room, humming the *shave and a haircut* tune.

'Lude and a Talwin, two bits.

Madness. By any definition, madness to be whirling through the crowd, to return again and again to the basement room to drink, to laugh when the shoulder vein collapses, to help Whistler find his favorite tap at the junction of the groin—I've drunk from Selene there, but Tad's groin is more to my taste: asleep or no, sometimes his cock flutters against my ear. The blood seems to pulse to the beat of the Dead through the walls, and the more I drink, the stronger the acid comes on. Then I have to dance, which makes me thirst again, and around we go.

It seems to be the same for the others: at one point I remember—I think I remember—Whistler opening the inside of an elbow, and the two of us sucking side by side like pigs at a sow, then heading back upstairs to a higher circle of hell, where we dance in the dark among the donors, the bleeders, the Tads of the world, until finally—it's late in the second set—I open that basement door to find the young Robert Morley sitting on the floor with his head pillowed on Tad's thigh, weeping.

"Augie? What is it, Augie? What's wrong?"

He looks up at me piteously. "It's Tad. He's got no more blood, Nicky. No more blood."

We got away with it, of course. Vampires almost always get away with it. It's not our fault that the side-effects of our drug include super-nally heightened senses and physical powers, not our fault that once Augie had gotten a grip on himself again, he and I were strong enough to suspend the now literally Deadhead between us and walk him through the crowd so casually that no one even noticed us (it looks easy in the movies, but we never could have done it if his blood had still been inside him, rather than us); that Leon was alert enough to spot us from the hill behind the last row of the amphitheater; or that Whistler was fast enough to dash down the hill to the parking lot, and return with the Jag in time for us to slide Tad into the back seat without any potentially embarrassing lag time on the sidewalk.

And given our powers, of course, it also made perfect sense that we take advantage of them when disposing of the body.

Perfect sense.

So why was it, then, that I opened my eyes the following evening at sunset with a sense of horror, not just of what I had done, but of what I had become, or that when I closed my eyes I found myself reliving it again, but with a vividness that went far beyond mortal recall: lying there in my bed I felt the dead weight of Tad's corpse as we carried it through the windswept grove of trees that crowned the bluff at Land's End, and out to the very edge of the dark cliffs, heard the soft thud when we rolled him over to strip the body of any clothes that might identify him, felt his dead ankle dislocate in my hand when I tugged off his boots, heard myself counting the cadence again at the precipice, a-one and a-two and a-three and a-*heave-ho*, and then was forced to watch, again and again and again, as the body, its nakedness somehow accentu-ated, made obscene by the snow-chains we'd wrapped around and around the pale torso to weight it, flew into the air, propelled by the su-perhuman strength of four vampires, and soared out over the ocean, thirty, forty, fifty yards before it began cart-wheeling end over end with all four limbs splayed out and flopping . . .

Nick broke off writing there—it was four in the morning, he was physically and emotionally exhausted, and he had what seemed to be a pretty powerful chapter ending. Even if it was not a chapter, and nobody was ever going to read it anyway. But it occurred to him, after he'd al-ready appended the new file to the protected floppy, and erased the backup shadow file from the hard disk, that it was a little self-serving, ending on that note.

Can't have that. He snatched up a pencil and a legal pad and jotted down one more paragraph:

"Twenty minutes later, however, after a short tussle with my conscience, which had it taken the form of Jiminy Cricket would now be a greasy green spot on the kitchen linoleum, I found myself standing at the refrigerator swigging blood out of a Clamato Juice jar."

Then, rereading it with some satisfaction, he thought: *Yeah, that'll do.* There's *the vampire life for you.* There's *a truth to shame the devil.*

Chapter 6

ONE

Nick parked the 'Vette by the side of the church and walked around behind it and up the short driveway. Betty Ruth was waiting for him out on the front porch of the parsonage. "What's up?" he called by way of greeting.

"Good morning, Nick," she replied formally. "Thanks for coming."

"The way you put it over the phone, it didn't seem like an optional activity." She'd awakened him from a using dream—Whistler had just handed him a bowl of brimming black blood—to tell him she had to see him right away, and no, she couldn't talk about it over the phone.

"Can I get you some coffee?" They both noticed that she had backed away as he mounted the porch, and he found himself growing more puzzled, if not panicked, by the minute.

"Thanks, I'm good. I stopped by Peets on the way over." He declined a wooden chair that had migrated from the kitchen—next stop would be the fireplace—and leaned back against one of the posts that held up the porch roof. "So what's up? Is this about the . . . the baby thing?"

Betty was startled. "How did you know about the baby?"

"What?"

"Nobody knew about the baby, Nick."

"Whew." He shook his head like a fighter who'd caught a haymaker at the opening bell. "I'm going to assume you haven't gone totally psychotic, Betty, and that we're now talking about two different babies. I don't know which one you were talking about, but I was referring to a prospective baby. Your prospective baby? Ours, maybe? Last week? Long talk? Sperm?"

"Oh my." Betty sat down heavily on an old fan-backed rattan loveseat that looked as if it had done time on the back of an elephant. "I'm sorry, Nick—I'm still a little shaky after what happened last night."

"Something about a baby?"

"No, that was last week. I'm—I'm sorry, I'm making such a muddle out of this. It's just that . . . I'm afraid this is going to be one of the weirdest, most uncomfortable conversations I've ever had, and having weird uncomfortable conversations is part of my job description."

"All I can say is, if the conversation has begun, I'm already lost. Maybe you should just cut to the chase."

"The chase? Okay, the chase. What does the *V* in V.A. stand for?"

To his surprise, Nick's heart did not stop. The earth did not cease turning on its axis, and neither did the birds fall screaming from the live oaks. His first instinct was to stall—he turned to face Jackson Street, and with his back to her, gripping the whitewashed railing with both hands, he said something Betty couldn't quite hear, something in either gibberish or Chinese.

"I beg your pardon?" she replied.

He said it again—definitely Chinese—then turned back to her, pale under his Mediterranean complexion. "That means 'This information is unworthy of another moment of your worthy consideration' in Mandarin. Useless in most Chinese restaurants, I might add."

"You're not going to shine me on this time, Nick. Not after last night."

"For crying out loud, Betty, I don't know what *happened* last night. And even if I wanted to tell you, our bylaws require a unanimous vote of the membership before any member can reveal that information."

"Then you might want to call an emergency session before ten o'clock this morning," she said, a little shaky, but determined to hold her ground. "Because unless you convince me otherwise before then, I'll be delivering an interesting sermon at the morning service."

"How interesting?"

"Very interesting." They both heard the echo of their first conversation in her words. "Would you like to hear it?"

By now, despite his lack of sleep, all of Nick's senses were alert, as if it were twenty-five years ago, back in the jungle with the Montagnards. "You bet."

She stood and gestured towards her vacated loveseat—again she gave him a wide berth as they changed places. He managed to force a pleasant, neutral expression as he settled back into the rattan loveseat—

it was the same expression he'd worn when the Montagnard chief had insisted on his presence at the Montagnard tribal banquet. Rat stew.

Betty took his spot at the porch railing, greeted the congregation of one, which greeted her back pleasantly, and began by sketching out the events of the previous weekend, the Very Anonymous stranger, the broken doors. He felt her studying his face as she talked—he could feel the pleasant smile locking into place when she got to the part about the curiously anemic baby Doe. *Mmm-mmm. Good eatin', that rat stew. And the guest of honor gets the bowl with the biggest chunks.*

"Now I've stood here before—well, not *here*, but you know what I mean—and preached that there are no accidents. But there are coincidences, so I didn't think anything more about it. Until last night, that is. Last night, after the last meeting left—it was a Very Anonymous meeting, coincidentally enough—I locked up the church behind them and went into my office to work on my sermon for this morning—not *this* sermon, but the sermon I was planning to deliver.

"I finished a little before one, but before going upstairs I made the rounds, like I've been doing every night since the break-in. Everything looked okay except that somehow the clock in the smaller meeting room had been smashed—but they'd left us a note, those thoughtful Very Anonymouses: they're going to replace it."

Nick allowed himself a sheepish look, and a shrug; Betty didn't appear to notice; he resumed his rat-eating expression.

"But then when I went back to make sure I'd locked the double doors, I thought I heard something outside—a moaning sound. My first thought, of course, was that it was another baby—that's the only thing that made me open the door. . . ."

It hadn't been another baby, though. It had been a young woman in a tight black long-sleeved mini-sheath, lying on her back under the live oak in the churchyard. Her eyes were open and staring, and upon reaching her, Betty was relieved to find her breathing. She waved her hand in front of the girl's face—it took those dazed eyes a pass or two before they focused on the movement in front of them.

"Jesus-*fuck*," were the young woman's first words. (Not exactly sermon-appropriate, but Betty repeated them for Nick anyway: by that point in her narration it had become increasingly obvious to her that she was only bluffing—there was no way that she'd be able to repeat this story to her congregation without losing a good half of them.) "Jesus goddamn fuck! For a minute there, right after I opened my eyes, I thought those branches were the ground, and I was hanging over them, like hanging upside down ten feet in the air. What a trip. Where's my purse?"

Betty felt around on the lawn, and handed her the black patent-leather bag. *My god, she's so young. Still got a smidge of baby fat. Sign of aging: hookers and cops look younger all the time.*

"Thanks." The girl struggled to a sitting position.

"Did you just pass out here, or did somebody dump you?"

"I dunno. Where's here?"

"El Cerrito."

"Then I been dumped, sweet cakes, 'cause that's too far to walk in these fucking heels." She snapped her purse open. "And if there ain't fifty bucks in here, I been robbed." She gave Betty a shaky wink. "If there's only fifty bucks, it's theft of services."

Betty offered to call the cops.

"Oh for chrissakes, lady—what planet you from? Yeah, the five-oh be a *big* help." Then she located the hundred-dollar bill folded carefully into her coin purse. "Scratch that, no problem, the mail has arrived."

She tried to stand up, but her legs wouldn't support her; Betty took one of her arms and helped her to her feet. The girl wobbled and went white under her makeup, except for her cheeks, which flushed tubercular red—the effect had been garish, ghastly in the moonlight. "Jesus-fuck." But softly this time, with a note of admiration, an appreciation at the edge of consciousness.

Rather than take her through the church, and up and down the parsonage stairs, Betty led the girl across the churchyard and around the Jackson Street side of the building. Then, feeling motherly, she helped her up the porch steps and into the parsonage kitchen.

"Would you like a cup of tea, darling?"

The girl looked up suspiciously. "I didn't say my name. How'd you know my name was Darlene?"

"Dar*ling*."

"Sorry. Naah, no tea. Just, could you call me a taxi?"

"Of course, if that's what you want. But wouldn't you rather I drive you to the emergency room instead, let them check you out—you're not looking at all well, you know."

"Just the cab. Please."

It wasn't a long wait for the cab—not as long as it seemed, anyway. It would have been charitable to describe their conversation as desultory, at least until Darlene asked if it was an old building, and Betty explained that while the church had been built in the 1920s, the parsonage had not been added on until the thirties.

"Wait a minute, did you say the church? This is a church?"

"Yes, of course."

"Then you must be the minister they were talking about! Well jesus-fuck. Oops, parn my french."

"It's all right," Betty replied automatically, as Darlene started to roll up her left sleeve. Then, a delayed reaction, "The minister *who* was talking about?"

"The vampires."

"The what?"

"You heard me." Darlene was plucking at her sleeve where it clung to the crook of her arm. "It's stuck."

Glad for something to do, Betty ripped a paper towel from the roll over the sink, moistened it, and handed it to Darlene. "Here, maybe you can soak it loose."

Darlene pressed the towel against the inside of her elbow; Betty watched in horror as the wet paper took on a faint pinkish tinge. "See, they took my blood." Darlene pushed the sleeve up the rest of the way: a crusty spot of dried black blood the size of a bread crumb crowned the bruise just beginning to spread out from the collapsed vein.

"Who? Who took your blood?"

Just then the cab honked its horn twice out on Jackson Street. "Duh! The *vampires*, of course." Darlene rolled down her sleeve again, grabbed her purse, and headed for the door. "The vampires took my blood. I can tell you on account of you're the minister."

Nick's first inclination, with those last chilling words still hanging in the cool Sunday air of the porch, was to simply tell her the truth. But even if his fellow addicts' anonymity hadn't been even more sacred to him than his own, outing V.A. was still an option denied to him by the V.A. bylaws, at least until after he had a chance to address a full meeting.

On the other hand, Betty obviously wasn't going to be put off much longer. Nick found himself thinking back to what Captain Harvey, his mentor at the Air Force Academy, had listed as the first three rules of Air Force Intelligence: "One, call in an air strike. Two, dazzle 'em with bull-shit. Three, call in an air strike."

Well, one and three are right out, he thought, reaching into his back pocket for his wallet, and extracting one of the business cards he and the other founders of V.A. had had printed for just this eventuality. He tried to decide what the appropriate tone of voice would be. Not amused—it was a serious story. But not aggrieved, either, because it was funny to be accused of being a vampire—at least if you weren't one.

He opted for caring: he could do caring. "Good lord, Betty, I can understand your being freaked. Either one of those things—the hooker *or* the baby—would have freaked me out too. But I sure am glad you called me first." He held the card out at arm's length; she crossed the porch and closed her fingers over it, but he held on for a second, and caught her eye. "Understand, I'm putting the anonymity, and possibly the lives, of twelve people in your hands, so first I need your promise: you can't tell anyone else—I mean *anyone.*"

"I promise," she said, still holding on to her end of the card. "If you want to tell me as a minister, you've even got some First Amendment protection—what's left of it."

"All right then. *In cathedra,* as it were." He let go.

She took the card, read it—"Victims Anonymous?"—and handed it back.

He smiled with more confidence than he felt as he replaced the card in his wallet. "Everyone in V.A. has been the victim of violence—domestic violence, stalking, that sort of thing. And for most of us it had reached the point where the stalker or the spouse had begun showing up at the more public twelve-step meetings. Remember a few years back, when a CODA meeting was attacked in the city?"

Betty had paled visibly. "This isn't all that reassuring, Nick. What if one of your stalkers is—"

Nick interrupted her with a dismissive laugh. "I've heard everybody's story two dozen times, and I give you my word—not a vampire among them." He hurried on. "I swear to you, Betty: your church is in absolutely no danger from V.A. That's why we put V.A. together, that's why we've maintained complete anonymity—no one but the members themselves even knows the group exists, much less where it meets."

He waited, trying to gauge her reaction. He'd never had to use the cover story before. It had always *sounded* plausible—but then, a cover story was like an antiaircraft missile: you never knew for sure if it was going to work until you used it. And by then, of course, if it didn't, it was generally too late to do anything about it.

TWO

Late autumn is such a lovely time of year to be a vampire. The sun is safely down before five, so there's always time for a crepuscular pick-me-up before embarking upon one's evening adventures. It hadn't taken Lourdes more than a few days with Whistler to discover the juice bar under the bed, and soon she settled into a happy routine: wake up a little before sunset in the blacked-out bedroom, sneak a quick jolt from the stash; if she timed it right, it would just be coming on when Whistler opened his eyes at sunset.

That was the fun part for Lourdes, lying there digging on the 'dor-phins, pretending to be asleep, watching Whistler while he woke up. He was like a little boy then—so rumpled and fussy and as close to vulnera-ble as he ever got.

He looked especially cute on Sunday evening, all sleepy-eyed, his yellow butch cut smashed flat on one side and poking out like Dag-wood on the other. She handed him the shotglass—he sat up in bed just high enough to drain it without spilling, then slid back down to a more bearable angle of repose. Lourdes leaned over him and delicately unbuttoned the top button of his pajamas so she could watch the blood flush rise.

"What are you thinking about?" were his first words of the evening.

"Last night," Lourdes whispered. "You and Darlene." She smiled, re-membering. Whistler liked to think of himself as so wicked, but it had ap-parently never crossed his mind to avail himself of the services that he had, after all, hired. It had been Lourdes who'd encouraged him to take advan-tage of the unconscious hooker, even going so far as to undress her for him.

(Of course, Lourdes had grown aroused too—there'd been a plump plangent prettiness to the young girl's body, despite the hard usage evident in the track marks along the forearms, in the crook of the elbow and the crook of the knee. Lourdes had stretched out at full length on the bed beside Darlene and watched from inches away as Whistler's face darkened with lust and effort, straining over the inert form. Eventually he'd turned his head to the side. "You like to watch?" he'd grunted.

"I sure do. You like to watch me watch?"

"Yes."

"But when you shoot it, baby, you look at me, not her."

"Honor bright.")

And Whistler had been as good as his word. He too smiled at the memory, and as the blood flush reached his eyes, the Creature bobbed to life under the silk comforter. "Is that mine, or Darlene's?" asked Lourdes coquettishly, nodding toward the bump in the middle of the bed.

"It was always yours, m'dear," was Whistler's reply. "Even when it was buried deep inside her."

When Lourdes came out of the shower in a white terry Sheraton Park bathrobe some twenty minutes later, Whistler was on the phone, sitting on the bed with his back to her. He turned and gave her a thumbs-up over his shoulder. "Not a problem. I'll call her in the morning. See you tomorrow night. Yes, you stay clean in between, too."

"Who was that?" She crossed the room to the dresser—he had turned over a few drawers to her, and she'd filled them in the course of the week.

"Nick." Whistler watched, enchanted, as she let her robe fall to the floor—there was such a confidence, a strength and balance in the smooth play of her calf and thigh muscles as she braced herself to open and close the drawers, and when she turned to the side to step into her white cotton panties, the brief glimpse of her breast in profile nearly broke his heart. "He asked me to call the minister in the morning and offer to upgrade the security system at the Church of the Higher Power. It seems some evildoer is trying to sabotage V.A."

She turned to face him, and in the instant of her turning, Whistler understood completely Elvis's reputed fetish for white cotton panties. "Now who would want to do a thing like that?"

"Fortunately, he hasn't the slightest idea. But he gave her the cover story."

"The one about the stalkers and shit? And she bought it?"

"Hooker, line, and sinker, as it were."

Lourdes laughed dutifully as she sat down beside him. "So what's our next move?"

"I can think of a few moves I'd like to make," he replied, waggling his eyebrows—his butch cut waggled too—and slipping an arm around her to cup the far breast.

"I mean about V.A. What's going to happen when I don't show up at work tomorrow morning? Nick's already gonna be suspicious of us, and when Beverly rats me out . . ."

Whistler stroked the side of her breast with tender concern. "Now now, m'dear. A little faith, a little faith."

She twisted out of his grasp and turned to face him. Her eyes were soft, but the lines of her mouth had hardened. "My whole life, the only person I could ever count on was myself. It's hard to all of a sudden have faith in somebody else."

"Then have faith in yourself. I do."

"You do?"

"I'll prove it. I'm going to take a shower now, and I'll bet you a penny to a pound—no, a hummer to a night of slavery—that by the time I'm out of the shower you'll have thought of a solution to both the Nick and the Beverly problems."

"How's that gonna work?"

"Simple. If you come up with something workable, I'm your sex slave for a night. If not, I'll tell you what I've worked out, while you hum 'God Save the Queen' to the Creature."

"While he's in my mouth?"

"Goes without saying."

He rose from the bed, but she tugged him back down by the waistband of his pajamas. "Wait. Before you leave, I just want to go over where we stand now."

"All right. Where *do* we stand?"

"Okay, well, we've got the minister right on the edge of either trusting us or calling the cops—we could push her either way. We've got Nick and the others suspicious. I don't know how suspicious—did he say how much she told him about what Darlene told *her?*"

"She seems to have followed instructions."

"Okay. But Nick's not stupid, so he probably suspects *us*—I know I would, after last night." She was thinking out loud now, as Whistler headed for the bathroom. "And we've only got each other for alibis. What we need is a skate-goat."

"A what?" He stopped at the bathroom door.

"You know, a skate-goat. Somebody to take the blame, take the heat off *us*. Especially if I don't show up at work tomorrow."

"Oh. Well, if I didn't know it was us, I'd suspect January."

"So would I. But what if she has a better alibi than we do?"

"Perhaps we should just skip town until things settle down." The bathroom door closed behind him.

"Yeah, right," she called. "That'd sure take the suspicion off of us. What are you, trying to throw me off the track just to get your blowjob?"

"No, really." He popped his head back out. "I'm never here for the holidays—why, they'd be suspicious if I were. Do you have a passport?"

"All Filipinos have passports."

"Then all you have to do is decide between Greece and—"

She interrupted him, her eyes narrowed in thought. "You know what, you might be onto something there. Go take your shower."

She was back a few minutes later, dressed in tight jeans and a loose denim shirt, tapping on the frosted glass door of the enormous shower stall. (The Depression-era theme of the farmhouse ended at the bathroom door: Whistler had never been one to sacrifice comfort for style, particularly if the style was a goof anyway.) "WANNA HEAR WHAT I'VE GOT?" she called over the roar. Whistler had a custom showerhead with the force of a firehose, and a water heater in the basement the size of a small silo.

"SURE." The shower had a rarely used pause button; he interrupted the stream. "Just let me rinse off, I'll be right out."

She closed the toilet lid and sat down to wait—she liked to see him when he stepped out of the shower, before he waxed his butch cut. He looked more his age then, and older men had always turned her on. In fact her first lover, not counting fumbles and squirts, had been her sophomore English teacher, whom Whistler resembled, in a classier sort of way.

"Okay, here goes—*slave*," she said when he'd emerged, dripping, and wrapped a towel around his still lean waist. "First thing, you offer to help Nick keep the minister cooled out. Go ahead and volunteer to beef up the church's security system. Let *him* tell her, though, get him in a little deeper.

"Now she's solid. Then we feed Nick our skate-goat, and he's solid too, and if he's solid, the rest of them are solid, and there's no problem with us going off on vacation."

He applied his deodorant—some kind of fancy stick with a solid black case and no label. "Close. Very close. Assuming we can come up with a suitable candidate. But have you considered that when we return, we're more or less back to square one?"

Lourdes stood next to him, pressing against his side. "But what would happen if while we were gone, somehow the minister found out Nick's been lying to her all along?"

"I don't know," he said to her reflection in the mirror. "What would happen?"

"I don't know either. But I bet whatever happens, they'll be so busy saving their own asses, they won't have much time to worry about ours."

Whistler had reached for his razor; he put it back down on the black marble counter. "Now you're cooking with gas. Next step: what have you thought of to throw Beverly off the scent?"

"I'll give you a hint," she replied. "It starts with you on your knees."

He raised his eyebrows in respectful surprise. "It's true, great minds do think alike." He dropped to his knees in his black silk pajamas, and proposed to her then and there, in the farmhouse bathroom. "Lourdes, will you marry me?"

She smiled down at him. "Yes, my darling Jamey. And will you give me a rock the size of Alcatraz to flash at Beverly tomorrow night?"

"I will."

"Do I win the bet?"

Whistler stood up. "Only if we can make it workable by coming up with a scapegoat to take the heat off us, and a trap to be sprung on Nick during our absence."

"Fair enough."

"It'll have to be something good, mind you. He's a clever fellow when cornered, that Nick. A regular dancer in midair."

Lourdes stood up on tiptoe. "So's Wile E. Coyote when he runs off the cliff after the Roadrunner," she whispered into her fiancé's ear. "But sooner or later, he always looks down."

THREE

Nick had put the top down on his Corvette and cruised back to Berkeley in style Sunday morning, after staying for Betty's sermon, which had nothing whatsoever to do with anemic babies or exsanguinated hookers. Not only had Betty bought the cover story, she'd been consumed with compassion for the poor Victims, offering her own services as a counselor. He'd managed to put her off when she asked about his own stalker—too painful to talk about, but some day he'd tell her the whole story.

She was still wracked with guilt when she called him back Sunday evening. "I've felt like such an idiot all day, Nick. I can't believe I actually accused you of being a vampire."

"I understand perfectly—don't give it another second's thought. Oh, by the way, one of our members—a man named James W.—is going to call you tomorrow morning about upgrading your security system. No, no cost to you. Just a little gift from V.A."

"All V.A. owes me is a new clock for the meeting-room wall."

"It's not entirely altruistic—we have our own reasons for wanting to meet in a secure environment."

"Well thanks." She sounded relieved. "I guess that means I haven't blown it, then?"

"Blown what?"

"I haven't scared you away."

"You mean V.A.? No, of course not."

"How about Nick Santos personally? Are you still thinking about . . . what I asked you to think about?"

"Entirely too much."

"What do you mean?"

"Just that it's such a momentous thing to try and come to a decision about. My general inclination is to say yes, but then I start thinking about all the details, and all the possibilities, and my head starts to swim. Do I want to be a father? Would you let me be, if I wanted to? Or could I handle just being a sperm donor, if that's what we both wanted? Or could I walk away even if *I* wanted to—do I have it in me to father a child and then act like it never happened? Not to mention the legal ramifications. I tell you, I almost wish we could just get it over with, and panic later, like everybody else." A pause. A long pause. "You still there, Betty?"

"Do you really mean that, Nick?" Dead serious now. "Because if you do, all you need to do is hop in that pretty little 'Vette and buzz over here."

"You mean . . . ?"

"If not, you'll have at least another twenty-eight days to think about it."

The first phrase that came to Nick's mind—*Piss or get off the pot*—did not seem to be quite *le mot juste*. Or, as they said in his native Detroit, the mo' juice. Neither did the next: *Fish or cut bait*. But the third, the one that actually escaped his lips, was, if neither eloquent nor romantic, at least a little more apropos: "Fuck it," he said. "I'll be right over."

But not directly. On his way to El Cerrito the marquee over the Adult Entertainment Center on the west side of San Pablo Avenue, across from the Safeway, caught Nick's eye (as well it might have: it was pink in color, a dozen feet long by a half dozen high). It occurred to him that he might need a little inspiration even to masturbate—his bitter joke to Betty the week before (about sex having given him up when he gave up drugs) had more truth to it than he liked to admit. Of course, it hadn't been just "drugs," it had been blood, without which regular sex—or even irregular sex—hardly seemed worth the bother.

He pulled into the lot at the side of the store. As he walked around to the front of the building, he caught himself angling his body away from the entrance even as he approached it: a misdirection ploy: same principle as backing out of a room in stages so it looked like you were walking in.

Once inside the Entertainment Center, though, Nick was surprised at how cheery the place was, with its pastel walls and counters, racks of glossy magazines, bubblegum pink dildos and glittering handcuffs. The only other thing that had changed much since his last visit to a porn shop was that now there were rows and rows of videos marked "Amateur." It occurred to Nick that they ought to be *giving* those away, but in fact they cost pretty much the same as the professional product.

His first thought was to buy a magazine. He sidled past the hetero racks—Big Boobs, Shaved Pussies, Interracial, Couples—to the smaller Men Men Men rack. Then he thought about the logistics of smuggling a magazine into the parsonage under his red James Dean windbreaker, and settled for a deck of playing cards featuring erect penises from around the world.

Betty came out onto the porch to greet Nick, wearing baggy jeans and a spacious GAIA sweatshirt. She gave him a hug and ushered him into the kitchen. "Are you as nervous as I am?" she wanted to know.

"I don't know. How nervous are you?" He took a seat on one of the three kitchen chairs—black lacquer ladderbacks with octagonal red Amish-looking designs painted on the front of the top rung, and rattan seats that seemed to be in the process of reverting to their natural state— set around a round water-stained drop-leaf garage-sale table Betty was going to get around to refinishing any day now.

"I frowed up." She winced as she heard herself. "And regressed, obviously."

"Oh. Well, I'm not quite that bad. Just a little performance anxiety, is all."

"But you'll be alone."

"I'll still have to perform. It's not something I've spent a lot of time at, lately."

"In that case . . ." She rose, and left the room; when she returned, she was obviously hiding something behind her back. "I wasn't sure whether you might want this or not." She tossed a derelict old porn magazine on the table. "Someone left this behind after the S.L.A. meeting last year—must have been Show and Tell night or something. I couldn't exactly leave it in the Lost and Found, but I didn't want to throw it away either—it's been at the bottom of my sweater drawer ever since."

Nick glanced down—the woman on the magazine cover had breasts that were quite literally the size of watermelons. He couldn't help but laugh, and once begun—he must have been more nervous than he was willing to admit—he found himself unable to stop. Every time he thought he had control of himself, he'd glance down at the magazine and lose it all over again.

Betty's already high color had flamed crimson—she was obviously taking this personally. Nick tried to shake his head—*no, not you, not laughing at you*. Finally, still guffawing, he reached into his windbreaker pocket, pulled out the still-sealed deck of cards, and tossed it down on the table beside *Humongous Hooters*.

"*Dicks of All Nations?*" Betty shrieked. "Oh my God and Goddess, Nick. *Dicks of All Nations?*" She collapsed, howling, into the chair beside him, fighting for control, not just of her laughter, but of her bladder. Finally she swung her chair all the way around until her back was to the table, and the offending publications. "I don't know, Nick," she said, when able to produce coherent sounds again. "Do you really think we're ready for parenthood?"

"I guess we'll find out over the course of the next thirty years or so," he replied, his abdominal muscles aching. "Just like the rest of humanity." He grabbed his deck of cards and followed her up the stairs to her bedroom.

FOUR

"I've been thinking it over," remarked Lourdes. "I think you're probably right, we probably could get away with blaming January, even if we have to plant something on her, or something." She and Whistler were lying in a Yucatan hammock strung between apple trees out in the orchard.

Two thick down comforters were spread under them, two rough Hudson's Bay blankets covered them. Their blood sex had been a little gentler this time, a little spacier. Of course, the hammock might have had something to do with that.

"If we have to. But a more suitable candidate has occurred to me."

"Who?" Lourdes turned on her side; the blankets slipped further, and the wind across her bare shoulders gave her a delicious chill.

"Someone who despises Nick every bit as much as she cares for both you and I."

Lourdes sat up suddenly, and threw the blankets off her shoulders. "Selene?" she said excitedly. "Would she do it?"

"Con gusto, I'm reasonably sure."

"Why does she hate Nick?"

"You know that ragged-edged scar on her throat?"

"The one that looks like somebody did it with their teeth?"

"That's because someone did." Whistler grabbed the ropes on either side of the hammock and pulled himself to a sitting position, setting the hammock swaying. "Guess who?"

"Not our St. Nick?" She threw her arms around him; if he hadn't still been holding on, the resultant heave of the hammock might have thrown him.

"Easy, easy. Yes, Nick. With his own little pearly-whites."

"Tell me," she insisted, hugging him tighter.

"Someday. It's not a story I enjoy particularly—he tore up another witch besides Selene, and caused the death of one of my oldest friends."

"Bummer," she said solemnly.

"Indeed."

She brightened. "At least we've got our skate-goat. Now all we need is the bombshell to leave behind us, and we're all set."

"Oh, I think you can leave that to me as well," he said mysteriously. "I believe I have the very thing we need, upstairs in my bookcase."

"Cool. As long as I still win my bet." She could tell she was supposed to ask him what it was, but didn't want to give him the satisfaction— even if she was dying of curiosity. She decided instead to check out the bookcase later, see if she could figure it out by herself.

"Absolutely. I'm yours to command for the night."

She felt something hard and cold bumping the side of her knee— it was the Clamato jar. She helped herself to a healthy swig, then handed him the jar. "Okay, slave. Take a hit off this—that's your first command."

"Bless you, Mistress." He took a draught. "And my next task?"

"Let's go climb a tree," she said, feeling the blood flush beginning to warm her chest. "I want you to tell me vampire stories until the moon goes down."

"I was born in Baltimore, but the family always wintered on the island of Santa Luz, in the West Indies," Whistler began, with only a hint of a British accent. He was perched on a low horizontal apple bough, with his legs dangling; next to him Lourdes, also naked from the waist up, squatted easily on her heels, comfortable as a monkey. In his mind's eye he saw them from the ground, from a distance, and as a connoisseur of color and line, of sex and absurdity, he was well aware of the delicious picture they made, in the tree, in the moonlight.

"Nanny Eames, my West Indian nurse, informed me years later that she'd known I was a vampire since I was three months old."

"But how did *she* know?"

He glanced up at her, surprised. "The same way any of us knows: she drank my blood and didn't get high."

"Your own nanny drank your blood?"

He appeared to be surprised again. "I keep forgetting—you haven't tasted baby-blood yet." Beyond her he saw a lone dark apple, shrivelled to the size of an apricot, still clinging to its branch. "In any event, when I was twelve my father moved my mother and I to London—he'd decided, during a delayed midlife crisis, that what he'd really wanted to do, all those years, was paint, and since he was a Whistler, it had to be London."

"I don't get it."

"Whistler? James McNeill Whistler the painter? He was my great-great-great-uncle. You *have* heard of him, haven't you?"

"Oh, you mean like, Whistler's M—"

He interrupted her. "If you say 'Whistler's Mother' I shall spank you and make you recite 'Arrangement in Gray and Black' a hundred times."

"Pretty fancy talk, for a slave." Lourdes dropped down to straddle the fat bough. "Is that where all your money comes from?"

Whistler swung his leg up and over, and turned to face her. "A portion of it. My branch of the family descends from the Whistler who built half a railroad for the czar of Russia, then sold the rest of the contract *back* to the czar for what history records only as a *screaming shitload* of rubles.

"The rest of the Whistler fortune does come from Great-great-great-uncle James, but indirectly: after he'd been cashiered from West Point for flunking chemistry ("If silicon had been a gas," he used to say, "I would have been a major general."), he went to work for his brother at the locomotive works. They had to sack him there, as well: the draftsmen always had fresh sheets of paper stretched and pinned to their desks, and he couldn't resist scribbling on them—anything, sketches, portraits, cartoons.

"Fortuitously, my great-grandfather Bartholomew, who was ten, was fascinated by his exotic Uncle Jem, and used to tag around after him at lunchtime and collect the drawings behind him. Seventy years later, when Bartholomew died, my grandfather Whelton Whistler found them in an enormous steamer trunk in the attic, and there you have the rest of the Whistler legacy, half of which devolved on yours truly upon the death of my grandfather. I'll inherit the other half when my father finally shuffles off this mortal coil, which the old bastard, who is now eighty-two years old, shows absolutely no intention of doing. Or so I hear—we haven't spoken since 1967."

"How rich are you, exactly?"

He frowned. "Only poor people know exactly how rich they are, m'dear."

"But you don't live like rich people—you don't have any, like, servants or anything."

"It didn't take me long, after coming into my inheritance, to learn that there are three primary uses for large sums of money. One can use it to make more money, or to buy responsibility, or to buy freedom from responsibility. I chose the third option. Servants are an enormous responsibility. A liability as well, if one has secrets one wishes kept. And besides, nowadays, there's no need for servants—one can simply lease the service itself."

Another question occurred to her. "How come you and your father haven't spoken in so long?"

Whistler laughed. "Servant trouble, oddly enough. Would you like to hear that story first?"

"Sure. If it has sex and blood in it."

"Oodles, m'dear. Oodles." He cleared his throat. "London. The mid-sixties. I don't know if you're old enough to know anything about London in the sixties—Swinging England, they called it. Ever heard anything about Swinging England? Carnaby Street, Mary Quant, the Beatles, and all that?"

"The Beatles, yeah. I was barely born, you know."

"Well, I was one-and-twenty and newly Awakened, and in that era London was *the* place to be, especially for a gentleman vampire who had just come into his inheritance."

"You said your nanny Awakened you?"

"Yes. Came as a complete surprise. On Santa Luz babies are checked for vampirism at three months—they actually have a ritual called the Tasting, held in the courtyard of a plantation Greathouse deep in the rainforest. They rub the foot with some sort of voodoo salve so the baby feels no pain, then take enough blood to fill a small gourd, and pass it around. If they get off, they have an orgy. If they don't, they still have an orgy—there's a standby baby.

"But the child itself is not told of the results of the Tasting until his or her twenty-first birthday. They came for me on the night of the full moon—"

He stopped. "That's the story I started to tell you in the first place. But you know what would be better?"

"What?"

"Instead of my simply telling you, we'll arrange to be on Santa Luz during a full moon. You can meet Nanny yourself, and be initiated, and see a traditional vampire culture—" He stopped. "Why, I actually feel quite enthused."

"Your nanny's still alive?"

"Oh yes. And kicking. But she never leaves the Greathouse anymore, and there's no electricity up there. I'll get in touch with her son Prescott, let him know we'll be coming."

"Let's do it now, let's not wait."

"Ah, but there's the tiger to be dismounted first."

"Fuck the tiger."

"We shall, m'dear. But all in good time. Now, back to my story. Where was I?"

"Vampires of London. Arooo!"

"Ah yes. Newly Awakened, and nowhere near as proficient at procuring blood regularly as I am now. The rush-and-crash cycle was beginning to wear on me. I was still living in my father's house at the time. Just the two of us—my mother had died two years before—and of course the servants, one of whom was a portly Bahamian cook and housekeeper named Mary Anne, who, it so happened, suffered from terrible megrims—migraine headaches, we call them here. 'Oh Mr. James, it feel lak gahn to split me head in two.'

"Now I already knew how to use a syringe—we used to inject heroin in one arm and have a friend inject cocaine into the other simultaneously. A Birmingham Train Wreck, we used to call it—why *Birmingham* I haven't the slightest idea, but the effect was rather like a train wreck.

"In any event, I took pity on her, and explained how in England doctors had been bleeding patients for centuries—nothing but the truth, of course—and although the custom had rather fallen out of favor lately, if she really wanted me to, I'd be happy to see what I could do."

"Cool."

"But too clever by half: it worked."

"No!"

"Yes. It was priceless. Picture for yourself—the poor woman comes to my room one day, face drawn, temples pounding, eyes shut tight against the pain. 'I'll try any-*ting*, Mr. James. Drah de blood, Mr. James. Jus' drah de blood.' Her skin the color of blanched mahogany, her heart so strong the blood virtually leaps into the syringe, dark as molasses, not too thick, not too thin. And lo and behold, her face begins to relax, her eyes flutter open, and it's 'Mr. James, Mr. James, you save me life, me son.'

"Alas, no happy ending. After several blissful, and may I add immodestly, headache-free months, one evening—"

"Wait a minute, what about the sex?"

Whistler laughed. "Here in the tree?"

"No, baby—you promised me blood and sex. Vampire stories have to have blood and sex."

"Well, one does hate to kiss and tell, but if I must. How shall I put this? . . . Mary Anne was five feet tall, a good fifteen stone, nearly twice my age, and could suck the wings off an angel when the mood was upon her. Does that help any?"

"Thanks."

"My pleasure. Now where was I? Ah yes—one evening she brought a friend to me—an older man, an Englishman who claimed to have megrims as well. But when I produced the syringe, he produced the manacles. Seems Mary Anne had told them all about her cure at home—"

"And the jig was up."

"So to speak. No charges were ever pressed—there was some talk about practicing medicine without a license, but nothing ever came of it. I was allowed—encouraged—to leave the country (fortunately I was still an American citizen) but I never *was* able to convince my father of my sudden interest in traditional British folk medicine, and he's refused to see me from that day to this."

"Did he know you were drinking the blood?"

"He must have, don't you think? Why else the never-darken-my-door-again treatment? My theory is that he's a frustrated vampire him-self—at least latently."

"So you think vampiring might be, like, congenitary?"

"Might very well be," he replied. "I honestly don't know." Then he swung his leg back over the bough, twisted around, and dropped lightly to the ground.

Lourdes jumped down after him. He stepped forward and covered her breasts with his hands. She unsnapped her jeans, lowered the zipper so the pale v of her lower belly was exposed, then placed her hands over his, and slid them downward from her breasts until his palms were pressing directly over her womb. "Shall we make a baby and find out?" she asked him.

He lowered his face to hers—when his tongue slipped into her mouth she nipped at it. He pulled his head away and caught her smiling her bared-teeth smile up at him. "Why not?" he said. "If it's not one of us, we can always feed off it."

The lips closed, the smile disappeared. "Only a little taste now and then," she said firmly.

FIVE

"Is there a problem, Nick?" Betty Ruth called through the closed bed-room door. She'd left him on the bed with his cards and her diaphragm half an hour before.

"Me and Rosie need a few more minutes," was the reply.

"Rosie?"

"You know, Rosie Palm and her five sisters. Don't panic, though—I'm only halfway through the deck. The hearts were a disappointment, but the spades look promising. Give us another twenty minutes."

Twenty minutes later: "I'm coming in, Nick."

"Hold on, hold on." She heard soft fumbling sounds, and pictured him pulling up his Levi's. "Okay."

He looked up sheepishly. He had indeed pulled on his pants and was sitting on the edge of the bed with the diaphragm lying beside him amidst the multi-national dicks spread across the Shaker quilt. She cleared a space and sat down beside him in her flannel nightgown. "How clever," she remarked. Each suit represented a different continent. The hearts were Europe. "I see what you mean about the hearts."

With a grin—hey, his worst fear had already come true; now maybe he could relax a little—he handed her the spades. Africa, of course. "Oh my," she said. Something about sitting there with a picture of a foot-long erection in her hand had put her beyond the reach of embarrassment as well. Actually, anything was better than some of the small talk she remembered from her courting days.

She turned to him. "Listen, Nick, we're not going to let a little thing like this stand in our way, are we?"

He couldn't help himself: "In the *first* place, it's not little; and in the *second* place, it's not standing." Totally cracked himself up—camping was something he'd pretty much given up along with sex and blood, and he was glad to know he hadn't lost his touch.

"I'm glad to see you've kept your sense of humor," said Betty. "They taught us in Hum Sex—" ("That's Human Sexuality, hon," was her aside in response to his raised eyebrows.) "—that the funny bone was one of the most powerful erogenous zones." Then, acting on impulse, she swept the cards from the bed. This was entirely unlike her—but then, entirely unlike her was what was going to be needed here, she realized, if she was going to get this thing off the ground. So to speak.

"Oh come on, Bet—"

"Don't move." She gathered up all her pillows from the head of the bed, heaped them behind Nick's back, then pushed him back gently until he was half reclining, with his legs over the edge of the bed and his feet on the floor. "Now lie back and close your eyes." Then she was on her knees in front of him, tugging down his jeans and his underwear in the same handful, so that she couldn't tell whether they were briefs or boxers until they were around his ankles. (Briefs. Red Calvins.)

"Please, Betty. What good do you think this is gonna do—you know I'm gay."

"That's why I'm down here on the floor instead of up there on the mattress with you, hon. And that's also what your imagination is for.

Now shut up and close your eyes like I told you. Oh, and hand me that diaphragm."

Twenty years ago I was the King of the Castro, thought Nick. *Now here I am getting a b.j. from a female minister.* Then, a minute later: *But you know what? It ain't bad.*

Nor did it last long—with an effort he remembered why they were there. "Soon," he called, without opening his eyes. "Real soon." Then he moaned: his testicles had been seized in a death grip and—of all things—a ministerial fingertip was inserting itself into his rectum. He came with a cry; Betty milked him expertly onto the diaphragm and rolled onto her back. "You're not going to want to see this next part," she warned him, as she rearranged the pillows under her thighs.

"You're right," he replied, closing his eyes again. A squishy sound, and then it was done.

And afterwards? A difficult feeling to assess, for either of them. Whether it had been a crossroads in both their lives or only a funny, futile little bump in the road was something they wouldn't know until after Christmas at the earliest. In the meantime Betty would be spending the next few hours flat on her back with her legs above her head, and the next few weeks praying to Higher Power for all she was worth.

So he threw a blanket over her, found the *Time* magazine she'd asked for in the bathroom rack, brought her a drink of water not from the bathroom tap but from the MultiPure filter in the kitchen, bent over her awkwardly so as not to dislodge anything, kissed her cheek in a brotherly fashion—she apologized for not being in a position to show him out—and left by the kitchen door, whistling an old Chicago blues song—the one where they spell out M-A-N and don't miss a letter.

He found himself whistling the same studly tune during the drive back to Berkeley, and then again in the shower, and afterwards as he put on a pair of crisp pajamas. *A Farewell to Arms* was on the midnight movie. Rock Hudson and Jennifer Jones. "You and me, Rock," he said, lifting a toast to the screen. "Breaking women's hearts from Paris to Frisco."

Then the phone rang. "Hellooo," he chirped—he was sure it was Betty.

"Is this Nick?"

It wasn't Betty, though. Not a minister of the Higher Power by any stretch of the imagination. Pretty much the opposite, as a matter of fact. Selene.

He hadn't heard her voice in over five years. It sounded about the same, though, which pleased him: after their last meeting, there'd been some question about whether she'd ever regain the use of it at all.

Chapter 7

ONE

Another mental snapshot for Whistler's scrapbook of color and line, sex and absurdity:

Eight o'clock Monday morning; the farmhouse kitchen; Lourdes puttering around, starting a pot of coffee, rinsing out last night's wineglasses, nuking frozen croissants in the microwave. What made the snapshot a keeper, though, was her costume for this display of domesticity: full dominatrix from the black seamed stockings attached by garters dangling from the beribboned black Merry Widow all the way down to the stiletto heels; a leather G-string completed the ensemble—her mask and whip lay on the counter next to the cow-shaped creamer filled with blood.

But try as he might to distance himself, Whistler couldn't deny the feelings that welled up in his chest just sitting at the kitchen table watching her—it was as if his heart was a Creature now. "Lourdes?"

"Jamey?"

"I adore you."

She put down the butter knife and brandished the whip at him. "You better."

"I do."

"No, Whistler, I mean it. 'Cause after I make this phone call, there's gonna be no going back."

"Phone away, my beloved. Phone away."

"Okay." She drew a deep breath, after which she had to tuck her bosom back into the bustier, then took the handset down from the wall and punched up Bev's number at the blood bank.

Answering machine, she mouthed to Whistler. "Hi Bev, this is

Lourdes. I'm sorry for the late notice, but I'm not coming in to work this morning. In fact, I'm not ever coming to work again. But it's not what you think—I haven't gone out or anything. I'll tell you all about it at the meeting tonight. Better yet, I'll show you. See you tonight."

Her face was flushed when she turned back from hanging up the phone, and her chest was heaving with emotion—an occurrence Whistler noted with appreciation. "I will have something to show her tonight, won't I?" she asked him.

"M'dear, we'll knock their eyes out. Just let me make a few calls, and then it's breakfast and beddy-bye for us."

Beside the phone they exchanged a lingering kiss, but when his fingers reached down and began to insinuate themselves under the G-string she stepped back gracefully—not an easy feat in stiletto heels, but easier for a ballerina: it was almost like being on point—and tapped him playfully with the whip. "Let's give pussy a rest, shall we?" she said, handing him the receiver. "Business first, then pleasure."

"Yes dear," he said meekly. He could afford to be meek: it would be his turn to hold the whip when they got upstairs.

"What can I say besides thank you? . . . Okay then: thank you. See you tonight." Betty replaced the receiver in a daze. She had taken the call in the parsonage kitchen, where she was brewing a pot of coffee in preparation for a nine o'clock counseling session with a couple suffering from lesbian bed-death syndrome, which was a sort of sexual Alphonse and Gaston deadlock that occurred when both partners in the relationship were women who had been brought up to be sexually passive.

It was a difficult problem, but after last night, she found herself feeling as if there weren't any obstacles of a sexual nature that couldn't be overcome. Then, as if to convince her that her luck was really turning, had come the phone call. She'd been expecting a few new locks or floodlights; instead this James W. seemed to be offering to provide both church and parsonage with a state-of-the-art security system wired up to a prepaid twenty-four-hour monitoring service. She reviewed the conversation in her mind: had it been some sort of shingle-salesman scheme after all? She didn't think so, but just to be sure she called Nick and left a message on his machine.

A few minutes later her phone rang again. "Hello? Oh, hi Nick. Thanks for getting back to me . . . Well thank *you*, hon. . . . I don't know. I can tell you I fell asleep in that position, so it was a downhill race for the little fellas. . . . Yes, well, let's hope the best man won. Listen, this

James W. just called me and offered to have something on the order of a ten-thousand-dollar security system installed in the church and parsonage. You did say this was a gift from your fellowship, didn't you? . . . Oh, well, if he's richer than God. . . . What? . . . Nick my friend, as my A.A. sponsor used to say, after you've been in recovery long enough, you don't just look a gift horse in the mouth, you take a flashlight around to the other end. . . . You take it easy, too, Nick. Talk to you later."

Nick had received Betty's message in his office that morning after staying up all night working on his Fourth Step, his *Life on Blood*. Somehow Selene's unexpected call had brought things round full circle for him—then, and only then, had he felt himself ready to go back to that last terrible night on baby-blood.

He'd written until dawn, then turned off the XT and signed on to one of his networked machines—a genetic engineering firm in Daly City had hired him a week ago to evaluate their system. He'd already proved to himself that the system was secure at night if properly shut down—now he wanted to see if he could hack his way in while it was up. He had just trap-doored through from their WAN to the LAN and was trying to create a fictitious security officer profile to get in a little further when Betty called.

He was unsettled at first—he'd forgotten all about having asked Whistler to call Betty, and now, after Selene's confession, there didn't seem to be the same need for beefed-up security at the church—it would only be a waste of Whistler's money.

Then it occurred to him that since he couldn't tell Betty about Selene anyway, it would be just as well to have her mind at ease. Besides, a waste of Whistler's money? Why, the very phrase was self-canceling, especially when Nick considered that someday that very same security system might well be protecting his own child.

Whip that wallet out, you Jamey Whistler, he thought to himself. *Whip it out. And don't spare the horses.*

TWO

By the close of the Monday night meeting, the remaining loose ends of Operation Dismount-the-Tiger had been tied up into a neat little package.

As always, Whistler's jewelry broker had done himself proud—maybe broken a few speed limits shuttling between El Sobrante and the direct diamond importers in Concord, but at his customary 60-percent markup, he could afford a ticket or two. And the exquisite engagement ring gracing Lourdes's left ring finger had silenced Beverly effectively enough. After all, what could she say? She'd taken her best shot at Whistler years before—if he'd ever popped the question, she'd have said goodbye to any job she'd ever held just as quickly as Lourdes had kissed off the blood bank.

Next Nick had explained to the others (as best he could without compromising Selene's anonymity) why it had become necessary to use the Victims Anonymous story. Then he had given them the good news— that the saboteur had come forward, was not one of them, and no longer presented a threat to the fellowship. After that, the meeting turned into such a love feast that Lourdes found herself wondering why it had taken a year or two for Whistler to get bored with fooling these people: the charm of it had already worn off for her.

The meeting itself ended early—or rather adjourned to the Dessert Inn, where the betrothed couple was feted with coffee and a hastily decorated, but still decadent, triple-chocolate cake by the entire membership of the so-called Victims Anonymous, with the exception of the youngest member, January, who had a pressing engagement elsewhere, as might be expected of an attractive girl her age, even at ten o'clock, even on a Monday night.

Besides, the happy twosome had a pressing appointment of their own, across the bay in Bolinas, where they presented Selene with a silver thank-you pendant in the shape of a crescent moon, for which she seemed grateful, and of course a slice of triple-chocolate cake, for which she seemed equally grateful.

"I truly am happy for both of you," remarked Selene, when she and Lourdes were alone out on the patio, undressing by the hot tub. "But especially for Jamey—I was getting awfully worried about him lately, but you seem to be doing him a world of good."

"Thank you," replied Lourdes, holding up the ring for Selene to examine more closely—between the two of them, that ring was all they were wearing. "Don't worry, I know I'll never replace you in Jamey's heart."

"You've got *that* right, dearie." Selene flashed her a signifying look from under the bushy eyebrows, and Lourdes understood her misstep: as she lowered herself into the hot water, she made a mental note never to come that close to patronizing the witch again.

"Ah, my harem awaits," called Whistler, opening the sliding glass door and stepping out onto the patio in another of his luxurious terry-cloth robes, this one from Caesars Tahoe.

"In your dreams, buster." Lourdes voiced their mutual reply.

But the position of the vein Selene chose for them to open, the one just behind her right ear, nearly cost her her celibacy. For the two vampires made a witch sandwich of her, and between Lourdes nibbling on her from the front, soft cushy press of round breasts against her chest, and Whistler bending down on her from behind, so that the Creature was nudging the small of her back, Selene came as close as she'd come in nearly five years to forgetting her vow.

Afterwards, as they drifted blissfully away on their blood high, she narrated the gist of her conversation with Nick. "I was good, dearies. Oh, but I was good, given how little I had to work with. My theme was, Hell hath no fury like a witch scorned. I wove my web from two coincidences: that this coming Yule would be the fifth anniversary of the night he gave me *this*." She lifted her chin and gestured toward the livid scar. "And that you two were now an item."

Lourdes had floated closer to Whistler; she reached down under the steaming black water to check on the Creature. Selene smiled across the tub at them: she knew all about the care and feeding of that beast and could only thank the Goddess that the burden was no longer hers to bear. "Shall I continue?"

Lourdes nodded. The Creature, while definitely a threat to navigation, had not yet reached critical mass.

"I explained that for a Wicca priestess of my standing to allow an injury to pass unrevenged for as long as five years would have cost me great loss of face, but that I had held off due to my obligations to you, Jamey."

" 'Oh, what a tangled web we weave. . . .' "

"Only amateurs weave tangled webs, dearie. It all tied together quite nicely. I told him that since you had abandoned me for a younger woman, destroying V.A. would serve quite nicely as my revenge upon all three of you."

She stilled Lourdes's nascent objection. "Yes, I'm aware the Doe was taken before you were in the picture, Lourdes. I told Nick I didn't know anything about that. It didn't seem to bother him any—we had quite a pleasant chat about the role of coincidence in human affairs. In fact, I think he'd have been more suspicious if I'd tied it all up with a neat little bow: the only loose ends in my webs, dearie, are the ones I leave dangling on purpose."

"And the hooker?" Whistler slipped an arm around Lourdes's back until his fingers rested against her far hip, so slick and soft and springy.

"That was the easy part: I simply told him she was one of the Coven, not a hooker at all but an accomplished actress. I then promised him that as far as I was concerned, he and I were even."

Lourdes giggled. "So when our little surprise comes off next week, poor Nick won't know what to think."

"That's the idea, dearie. Let him try to figure out whether I lied, and if so, whether I lied for Whistler or for myself. I'll be up in Tahoe by then—"

"And we'll be en route to Santa Luz—" offered Whistler.

Lourdes finished for them: "And St. Nick will be left holding the bag."

"Precisely." Selene raised herself up on her skinny arms. "And now, if you two lovebirds will excuse me, I'm going to get out of here before that thing—" She pointed towards the submerged Creature. "—goes off. I've made up your bed, Jamey. Call me if you need me, but call loud: I'll have my earplugs in. Oh, and before you leave for Santa Luz, you *will* have that list I asked you for?"

"Of the V.A. membership?"

"Yes, dearie. Names, addresses, your best guesses as to the weaknesses in their recovery—where they're going to be vulnerable to attack." She climbed out of the tub—the waves raised by her wake were still rippling as Lourdes swung her leg over Whistler and lowered herself upon the Creature.

THREE

The last meeting of Vampires Anonymous at the Church of the Higher Power—the meeting that Whistler and Lourdes expected would be their last at any location—began promptly at nine o'clock on Saturday, December 14. After the opening readings of the Steps and Traditions, Nick turned the floor over to Whistler, who announced that he and Lourdes would be leaving for the islands—he was careful not to say which islands—on Sunday morning, and would be away for much of the winter.

But during those few months, he assured them, they would be staying in touch with the fellowship, as well as holding their own dyadic satellite meeting regularly. "Furthermore," he promised, "every time we see that glorious sun in the sky, starting with our dawn flight out of SFO tomorrow morning, we will recall with love and respect the fellowship that's made it all possible."

He wondered as he looked around the circle if he hadn't laid it on a bit thick. January, at least, seemed moved—or perhaps only agitated: at this first pause her hand shot up and waved about violently, as if she were trying to catch his attention from the last row of an auditorium. "Yes, m'dear?"

"Here." She tossed her one-year chip in Whistler's general direction, but high and wide. He snatched it out of the air by the whirling chain far too deftly for a recovering vampire, but again no one seemed to notice. "I mean, Hi my name is January and I'm a vampire. It was burning a hole in my pocket—I don't deserve it anymore."

"Nonsense."

"I really don't—I don't have a year anymore."

"Doesn't matter, you've still earned it."

"I don't care, I don't want it."

"Why don't you just tell us about it?"

"I can't."

"I guarantee you, it's nothing everyone in this room hasn't gone through at one time or another."

An assenting murmur arose: *Right, all been through it, remember I went out once, still love you, here for you, yadda yadda. . .* until with a sniffle the fallen addict began the tale of the mosh pit:

There were resources available to Gen X vampires that their forebears could only have dreamed of. Body sculpting, for one: storefront shops dedicated to piercing and branding and scarification. Then there was the primal fount of serendipitous bleeding, the mosh pit: the area just below the stage at rock concerts, right at the feet of the band, where the moshers threw themselves about with such abandon that lacerations were commonplace, especially scalp wounds with their characteristically generous flow—not for nothing had the moshers originally been dubbed head-bangers, back in the heavy metal days.

But January swore to the meeting that she'd only gone to the Omni that Friday night because one of her favorite bands was playing—she never missed the Butthole Surfers. Hadn't even been moshing—just standing there on the outskirts of the pit—when, with the hollow sound of canteloupes colliding, a pair of moshers had banged their heads together like rutting moose. January had gone down in the resulting pileup, according to her story, found blood on her forearm, and had licked it off before she realized it was not her own.

That wasn't the worst part, though—she'd scarcely picked up a buzz. What she had picked up was the boy who'd received the more severe gash on his forehead. She'd ended up bringing him back to her room, where, during a bout of sex nearly as violent as the mosh pit itself, somehow the wound had been reopened. As her orgasm began she'd seized his head between her hands and sucked blood until he'd managed to pull her away.

"He didn't mind or anything—I think he thought it was so twisted it was cool. But then I woke up this morning alone in my bed with blood smeared all over my face and my pillow and sheets, and my chip was still hanging around my neck, and there was dried blood on that too...." Her hands were twisting violently in her lap as if she would wring the very blood out of them.

"Shhh," said Whistler, as sweetly as a father comforting his child. It was a peculiarly intimate tone, as if they were alone in the room, but it caught her attention. She looked up from her lap—he was polishing the silver chip with a snowy white handkerchief, but his eyes were fixed on hers, and with his voice he gentled her like a spooked horse. "None of that matters, January," he was saying. "That first year you got in before you slipped? That was hero's work, and no one can ever take that away from you."

"All that happens now is that you get to earn another one of these in a year." He rose and crossed the circle. "You're on the roller coaster of recovery now, m'dear—it's not like that safe old addiction merry-go-round: there are bound to be dips you never dreamed of." As he knelt before her with the chain spread between his long fingers, she tried to pull back and away from him, her chin carrying her head up and to the side, her body twisting after it, arching like a cerebral palsy victim in a wheel chair, so that when he leaned forward to drop the chain over her head his face came within inches of hers.

It was only for an instant, but that was all it took for her to smell the blood on his breath—to smell the blood and to *know*. Over his shoulder she caught a glimpse of Lourdes leaning forward, eyes trained adoringly on Whistler. Without thinking, January seized Whistler's head in both hands and pulled it toward her; her tongue darted into his mouth. Then she released him, grabbed her bag from the back of her chair, and ran from the room.

Slowly Whistler rose from his knees, the only sound the thump of January's footsteps overhead, followed by the banging of the double doors as she fled the church. He turned to the circle and shrugged like a borscht-belt comic. "Perhaps she doesn't care for roller coasters?"

Whistler and Lourdes offered to straighten up the room after the meeting. Their intention, of course, was to be the last couple to leave the church, so that on their way out they would have time to plant their little bomb on the lectern of the pulpit unobserved.

It went off without a hitch; they closed the double doors behind them and hurried out to the Jaguar, which was parked in the handicapped space with the chauffeur seemingly asleep behind the wheel, cap pulled down low. Whistler opened the back door for Lourdes, then followed her in. "You're supposed to come around and open the door," he remarked to the back of the driver's head. "I wish you'd pay a little more attention to duty."

The chauffeur removed her cap and handed it back to Whistler by way of reply. "Here," said Selene. "Wish in the front half of this, then shit in the back half and see which side fills up faster." The Jag pulled away from the curb. "Did you drop off the book?"

"Where it's bound to be found, no later than ten o'clock tomorrow morning," said Whistler, pulling the chauffeur's cap over his yellow hair for a goof, cocking it at a jaunty angle.

"And my list?"

"Got it right here. Names, addresses, and weak spots." Lourdes produced a small green spiral notebook from her purse and handed it up to Selene.

"You don't have to start working on this until after we get back, you know. Shouldn't be more than a few weeks," Whistler reminded her.

"I don't *have* to work on it at all," Selene reminded him in turn. "But I want to. I cast the runes last night, and got a new twist on the results I've been getting for a week." They turned right on Central Avenue, heading for the freeway. "The Oakland airport, you said?"

In the mirror, she saw Whistler nod.

"Oakland it is. Now, back to the runes. What I kept coming up with was beginnings and endings, birth and death. Pretty common for this time of the year, what with the Yule solstice and all. The numbers were a little weird, though. I ran them a few times, and they kept coming up two and one—two births, one death; two births, one death.

"But then when I threw the bones again last night, they came up reversed. Not clean beginnings and endings, but cycles. And the numbers were five and five."

Whistler nodded. "As I recall, it's been five years since Nick attacked you."

"Come the Yule, five years exactly. I think what the bones were telling me is that one five-year cycle has to end before the next can begin."

"Sounds reasonable to me," said Whistler. "Did the runes also happen to give you any hints as to how to go about it?"

"Not the runes. But I cast the Ching this morning—twice. Both times the yarrows came up Basic Principles." This time she caught Lourdes's eye in the rearview mirror. "Remember what I told you was one of the foundation stones of Wicca, dearie?"

Lourdes piped up again. "Do what thou wilt!"

Selene shook her head, amused. "Why is it that all you vampires only remember half of it? '*An it harm no one*, do what thou wilt.' But there's one more basic principle to Wicca, and that's from Heraclitus of Ephesus. 'The way Up and the way Down are One and the Same,' he said, about twenty-five hundred years ago."

"Which means?"

"A whole lot of things. In general, it means that when you're born into life, you're dying from death, and when you die from life, you're born into death. But you can apply it in an infinite number of ways. In this case, it's another way of saying that if you want to know how to tear down an edifice, you must look first to see how it was constructed, then reverse the process."

Selene waved the green notebook in the air. "Your little edifice was constructed one brick at a time, and that's exactly how we'll demolish it. One brick at a time."

FOUR

Betty finished working on her sermon a little after midnight, then made the rounds, mostly for the enjoyment of seeing the blinking red and green lights of the new security system, but also to make sure that the building was empty. She didn't want anyone listening when she stepped up to the pulpit to time her sermon. That was the only way she'd ever been able to do it accurately: aloud, at the pulpit.

But when she reached the lectern, she saw that someone had left a present there for her—a fat paperback with a glossy black cover, curling at the corners, embossed with stylized blood drops—vivid, red, raised.

The letters of the title, *The City of Blood*, were also raised, but in silver, as was the author's name, Nicolas San Georgiou.

The index cards for Betty's sermon fluttered to the floor. With fingers gone suddenly numb—so had the tip of her nose, for some reason—she opened the book to the dog-eared title page. It had been inscribed by the author in a careless hand:

> *To Jamey and Selene:*
> *Thanks for teaching me about the real thing!*
> *Every Inch Of Mah Love,*
> *Nick.*

The numbness passed; she turned the book over in her hand. "You son of a bitch," she said to the picture of the author smiling up at her from the back cover. "You lying son of a bitch." Then she remembered, and both the fear and the anger were supplanted by the same sad sudden understanding that must have washed over that bereaved mother in "The Monkey's Paw," hearing the thing that had once been her child dragging itself with agonizing slowness toward her door.

Only in Betty's case—it had to be true; it was too awful and too ironic and too perfect an answer to her prayer not to be true—the child had just taken root in her belly, and the father appeared to be a vampire.

Then Betty remembered a fragment of another story—a Sufi tale about a little girl who told her mother she was afraid to cross the graveyard on her way home from school, lest she encounter the bogeyman. "If you do see a bogeyman," had been the mother's advice, "run straight at him, because he's just as scared of you as you are of him."

But it was not until after she'd looked up Nick's address in the phone book, coaxed one more start out of her '77 Olds 88 (it took the Marin Street hill in second, with all eight cylinders growling and the tappets clacking like a troupe of demented flamenco dancers), located the house on Grizzly Peak with the red and black lacquer Feng Shui dragons on the mailbox, parked the exhausted Olds at the bottom of the steep driveway, and trudged up the lantern-lit flagstone walk that climbed steeply to the front door, that Betty remembered the punch line to the Sufi story.

"Mommy," the little girl had replied. "What if the bogeyman's mommy told him the same thing?"

Nick hadn't been sleeping—he'd been up in the office working on his Fourth Step—but he was in his pajamas when he answered the bell, with his *Dee*-troit security system (a little Saturday-night special guaranteed not to blow up in your hand three times out of four) behind his back. "Betty, what—?"

When she handed him the beat-up old paperback, it wasn't panic he felt—more like regret, along with the sort of awe that comes when you're white-water rafting, say, and you hear what might be the roar of a waterfall a little ways downstream.

What are the odds? was his first thought. The books were still fairly steady sellers—there'd been several editions—but only the earliest paperback had carried his picture. *What are the goddamn odds?* Then with one hand (the pistol was still behind his back) he turned to the title page. "Selene," he said aloud. "I should have known."

"Is she another *Victim*?" Betty asked bitterly.

He shook his head. "Witch."

"Of course. Silly me." She recognized where this new sardonic wisecracking persona was coming from: it was the way she used to act with a few beers in her. Funny, the whole ride over she'd been dying for a drink—once a drunk, always a drunk—and now here she was acting like she'd had a couple.

"Would you like to come in?" Nick tried to imagine what this must be like for her, and then in a flash of inspiration he produced the gun from behind his back, and holding it by the stubby barrel, handed it to her grip first.

"Does it have silver bullets?" She looked down at the cheesy weapon in her hand as if surprised to find it there—which she was, in a way: she'd never held a pistol before in her life.

"That's werewolves. Please, Betty, come in. I promise you, it's not as bad as you think."

"Well. If you *promise*. After all, it's not as if you've ever lied to me before." But she gestured with the barrel of the gun, feeling like Ida Lupino in a hundred black-and-white movies, and followed him through a small vestibule with straw mats on the floor and a pair of grimacing jade-green Fu dogs guarding the threshold, then down a few steps to a small parlor.

The sparse furniture was Pacific Rim contemporary. Two low woodframed futons formed an L, the long leg facing a wall of six-inch-square windowpanes looking out over a small, discreetly floodlit rock garden of bonsai and cacti. Beyond the terrace the ground fell away sharply to the wooded hillside, but trees planted below blocked the view.

Nick offered Betty the longer futon, then parked himself cross-legged on the floor with his back to the windows. "At moments like this," he informed her, "I always like to quote Jimmy Dean in *Rebel Without a Cause*: 'Well . . . now . . . then . . . there.' "

"Don't be charming, Nick," replied Betty. "I'm a lifelong pacifist, but if I knew how to take the safety off this thing, I'd shoot you for that alone."

"That doohickey with the ridges, right there on the side of the barrel? Just click it forward to release the safety. But before you shoot me, let me tell you a couple things to put your mind at ease."

"The only thing that's going to put my mind at ease is if you tell me this child you've knocked me up with—"

"You can't know that yet!"

"Let me give you a hint here, Nick: never tell a woman holding a gun what she can or can't know about her own body."

"You're really getting into that gun thing, aren't you?"

"Just answer my question—is this baby going to be . . . some kind of monster?"

"If you mean a vampire, I don't know. I can tell you it's no more or less likely to be a vampire than any other child—vampirism is congenital, but there's no clear evidence that it's hereditary. Neither of *my* parents, for instance, ever showed any indication of being a vampire—not that I ever asked."

"Damn it, Nick, I don't even know what that means. *Being a vampire.* Should I be holding garlic instead of a gun? Or waving a cross—oh—oh no!" For she had suddenly remembered that first meeting: *Do you mind if we take the cross down?*

He saw her feeling for the safety. "It's a drug for us, Betty," he said desperately. "Blood is only a drug, and we're only another sorry bunch of addicts, and we need your help." It seemed to be having an effect—her finger relaxed on the trigger. "It wasn't one of us that kidnapped that baby, or sent that hooker to you," he went on hurriedly. "It wasn't a vampire at all. Just the opposite—it was Selene trying to destroy us, to get to us through you. Please don't let her use you so easily."

Betty looked down again at the gun in her hand. It occurred to her that there were depths to this motherhood thing that she'd never dreamed of. She'd only been pregnant for a week, if at all, and yet there wasn't the slightest doubt in her mind that she would blow a hole straight through this man in front of her rather than let harm come to her baby.

Then she remembered that if she were pregnant, the man in front of her was that baby's father. "Convince me, Nick. I don't give a damn about your fellowship, but for the sake of our baby, you'd better convince me."

*   *   *

Betty followed Nick up to the second floor, holding the gun at her side, not at his back. The stairwell was done in that tranquilizing ecru so popular back in the early eighties, and the steps and banister were of a smooth yellow-blond wood. He ushered her into his darkened office and sat her down in front of the old XT. The screen was blank—he reached over her shoulder and tapped a few keys to activate the Quayle program. "Try the 'page down' key," he said.

She pressed it. Four words were now centered on the screen:

MY LIFE ON BLOOD

She looked up over her shoulder at Nick, who nodded. "Go ahead," he said. "It's all there. But don't try to print, copy, or save it—just page down, or if the screensaver blacks it out, press the space key. Any other keystrokes will wipe out the entire file, not to mention the hard drive."

She nodded that she understood, then tapped the key once more, and began reading about the man who thought he was the King of the Castro.

FIVE

It might have been an hour or two later—Betty couldn't tell, and she'd left her watch back at the church, on the lectern. She rocked her chair back twenty degrees and pressed the heels of her palms against her closed eyes. When she opened them again the screensaver had turned the screen black; she saw Nick's reflection in the depths of the blackness. "How long have you been there?" she asked him, swiveling the chair around to face him.

"Not long," said Nick. "What do you think?"

It took her a moment to identify his rapt, somewhat stricken expression; then she remembered that he was, after all, an author. "It's very well written," she said—anything rather than discuss the subject matter: she'd just finished reading about Tad, and was still somewhat shaken.

He seemed encouraged. "You really think so?"

"What I *really* think," she said, rubbing her aching neck, "is that I wish I was reading this at home, in bed, and that I'd got it off the Fiction shelf in the library, and that right under the title it had said 'A Novel' in great big huge letters." Betty looked away, weary again. "I knew Leon, you know."

"No!"

"I met him on an A.A. outreach program. You have him to the life. I tell you, the shock of . . . coming *upon* him like that in your story . . ." Betty used the arms of the chair to push herself up for a moment, put a little air between her jeans and the leather; she groaned as she lowered herself back down. "It's awfully hard, reading on screen like this. Couldn't you print out just one—no, I suppose not." Something occurred to her. "Writing it must have been like a Fourth Step for you."

He was impressed; he nodded solemnly. "And your reading it is a Fifth." *Admitted to God, to ourselves, and to another human being the exact nature of our wrongs.* "Could I make you some tea or coffee?"

"Coffee, please."

"How do you take it?"

"Half-and-half? Sugar?"

He nodded, turned away, then turned back from the doorway. "I didn't write this to be read—but if somebody had to read it, I'm glad it turned out to be you."

She bobbed her head—a gracious, seated curtsey—and spun her chair around to face the screen again. When she tapped the space key, the first word on the screen caught her eye. "Anomie," she said aloud: she hadn't heard that word since divinity school.

Anomie: n. [Fr., from *anomia*, lawlessness; *a-*, without, and *namos*, law.] Lack of ethical values in a person or in a society.

Is anomie a bad thing? Not if you have it—that'd be like caring about your own apathy. Besides, it got me through the seventies, and halfway through the eighties.

Got most of us through the seventies and halfway through the eighties, as I recall, vampires and bleeders alike. Didn't help Leon, though. One weekend shortly after the Dead debacle, while the rest of us were up at Whistler's Tahoe lodge (which he insisted on calling Whistler Manor), Leon backed a Ryder up to the rear door of the Pistachio Palace, and when we returned there was nothing left but a few deedly-balls on the back staircase, and some LaCoste-shirted twinky behind the bar who couldn't mix a decent Mary if his life depended on it.

And although at the time of his disappearance he had been perhaps my closest friend for a matter of years, I can't honestly say I missed him.

My own life had changed too much since the debacle: I so dreaded waking up sober every sunset that I installed a two-foot-high refrigerator, empty except for a Clamato jar, next to my bed so that my nightly caesura of sobriety might be as brief as possible. It was either that, or sleep in the kitchen.

Needless to say, I never got around to writing that fourth vampire book—or anything else, except quite a few checks. Fortunately, even after paying back the first third of the advance there was enough money coming in from royalties, and foreign sales, and movie options, and eventually the mini-series, for me to support myself in the style to which I'd grown accustomed. And it was only occasionally, perhaps on hearing a southern drawl in a bar late at night, or seeing some basement-theater Tennessee Williams production, that I'd find myself thinking about Leon, and wondering what had become of him.

As it turned out, he'd been thinking about me, too—about all of us. He'd been out in the desert, you see—the metaphorical desert, that is: The Last Temptation of Leon (he would never have subjected his constitutionally dry skin to the like of Joshua Tree)—and when he did finally return, it was with news that would shake our cozy little vampire world to its very foundations.

My god, that was a dreadful sentence. I've never understood *very* as a modifier—are very foundations stronger than plain old foundations? And *cozy little vampire world* doesn't begin to convey the sense we in the *Penang* (our coinage, so far as any of us knew, from the Malayan word for vampire) had of living, if not in a golden age, then in a soft golden pocket of time, at least.

Nowhere was the pocket cushier than over the Wiccan Yule at Whistler Manor on the eastern shore of Lake Tahoe. Credit for this belongs largely to the Coven. For the most part they were a harmless bunch of New Age space cadettes who worshipped various earth spirits and goddesses; but there were a few, like Selene and Carol, who had that *signifying* look about them, the look that said "Keep that up, buster, and tomorrow morning you'll be looking at a toad in your shaving mirror."

I asked Selene about Wicca and witchcraft once, on what turned out to be my last Yule up at Tahoe. It was the night before the solstice proper, actually. I had just drunk from her, up in her attic room in the Witch's Wing of the lodge, where men were allowed only on invitation. She and I never had sex after blood unless Whistler was around to spur us on, but she dearly loved to cuddle, and when I was high it was an intensely sensual, almost spiritual hit to feel her small body so warm and alive against me, and know its pulse and rhythm, softer than a man's, and higher-pitched. I could hear the sigh of her blood, and her low murmuring voice carried a calm so soothing it was practically a rush.

Wicca had been the dominant religion in pre-history, she explained, earth-worshipping and matriarchal, but it had for so many centuries been persecuted and linked to Satanism by patriarchal sky-worshipping religions attempting to discredit and thus supplant it, that some witches had indeed turned to the dark arts in self-defense.

"Was that an old spell you used on me, that first Halloween?" I asked her.

"A classic," she said, before realizing that she'd never actually admitted to me that she had indeed cast a spell over me. I felt her shrug—a little *oops* shrug—then she went on. "Remember Odysseus? How he and his men were bewitched by Circe, and turned into swine? Swine with little curly tails. The way the story was passed to me, by my teacher, the coven on Circe's island needed men desperately—for procreation only, of course—"

"Of course."

"—and when Odysseus' ship was blown onto their island they thought it had been sent by the Goddess. The only trouble was, all the sailors were gay—"

I nodded sagely. "Greeks."

"Sure. Why do you think Penelope had so much time to weave? Anyway, Circe went rooting around in her bag of tricks, and worked out a spell so that everytime a man would even look at another man's ass, he'd see this curly tail, and . . ."

"Oh, I see." I was somewhat offended. "An early attempt at deprogramming."

She smiled slyly. "I think I had more luck with it than Circe, though, even if it did misfire a little."

"Yeah, well, that tail *was* kind of cute on you."

"Want me to do it again?"

I turned on my side, intrigued. "Could you?"

She kissed the hollow of my shoulder coquettishly. "Sorry, handsome. You have to save your sperm for the kettle."

Sperm for the kettle. Pay-back time for the witches. Three hundred and sixty-three nights a year they sell us their blood (the economics are varied: Whistler supports Selene; Sherman will eventually marry

Catherine; Augie has the youngest witch on retainer; I have numbers I can call on nights when the pickings are slim), but when the solstices roll around, our precious bodily fluids are theirs for the taking.

And the taking is always an outrageous bit of fun. A few hours after midnight Selene sends me back to my own bedroom in the Penang Wing—we have all been sent to our rooms—they will come for us one at a time.

A rap at the door; three robed witches surround you, women's hands undress you; a hooded crimson robe with one hole for the mouth and another for the cock, but none for the eyes, is lowered over your head, and you are led through the Manor—you can hear the crackling of the great fire in the main room of the lodge, smell the books as they lead you through the library, and hear the creaking of the classic, not-very-secret revolving bookcase entrance to the Coven Wing.

Then a silvery bell rings, candlelight sends the hooded darkness dancing, you are seated on a velvet-cushioned chair, a goblet is brought to your lips, and you are given witch's blood to drink—fresh blood, hot blood.

Then black quiet, stillness, only breathing sounds, and the muffled movements of women in soft robes, circling you, closer and closer as the blood comes on; you feel the fabric brushing your skin, and the fingers—how small women's hands are—caressing you, and their soft scented lips nip at you; erect, you are led to the center of the room and milked by those tiny hands until you come so hard that your jism splashes against the far side of the black iron cauldron.

No man has ever seen the actual receptacle, by the way: that it is a black cauldron from a road-show Macbeth is only a joking supposition encouraged by the Coven. We used to speculate about it after the ritual. That was one of my favorite times during the Wiccan celebrations: after the night of the living sperm the Penang used to gather on the lawn that sloped down to the lake, and watch the pewter surface lighten as the dawn approached.

We would be alone, the Coven having retreated with our offerings to a nearby alder wood, to do whatever the hell they did. We liked to pass as much time as we could lolling on the redwood chaises, safe in the shadow of the mock-Tudor lodge, enjoying treasured glimpses of daylight—the dew on the grass, the ripples made by dawn-feeding fish on the lake, the breathtaking glory of the High Sierra—before the sun rose above the mountains.

Afterwards we would repair to our rooms to sleep the day away. And manufacture more sperm, of course: while our seminal fluid no longer had any ritual application, it was bound to come in handy at the Witch's Orgy scheduled to begin at sunset.

My room on the second floor of the Penang Wing faces west. I awaken at sunset, cop a little hair of the dog, and head for the shower. When I come out about ten minutes later, the floor to ceiling curtains and the casement windows have been opened, and Whistler is sitting in the Nantucket rocker, his yellow hair gilded in the western afterglow.

"Evening's calm and holy hour," he says without turning around, and raises a joint the size of a Tiparillo over his head.

With the towel wrapped around my waist I settle down in the windowseat; as I take the joint our eyes meet, and we smile, and I know we're remembering one of Leon's classic lines. We say it in unison: *Oh, but ah do love mah crepusculuh joint!*

I hand the joint back. "I wonder what the little guy's doing right about now?"

"Sleeping, drinking blood, or fucking, depending on the time zone." He takes a stiff toke, then exhales indolently. "Selene sent me to ask you if we could reserve the first slot on your dance-card."

"Hey, tell her if she'll do that Circe trick, she'll probably *be* the first slot."

"Now don't be crude . . . to a heart that's rude."

"That's *Don't be cruel to a heart that's true.*"

"Oh, you can be as cruel as you like—I think we'd rather enjoy that."

The Penang and the Coven gathered an hour past sunset in the keeping room—the main parlor of the Manor—and a black witch, or rather a "white witch" of African-American descent, Carol, conducted the opening rites of the orgy, which were also the closing rites of the Yule ceremony. We wore black formal wear—the vam-pie penguins, Leon had once dubbed us; the witches were in dark green robes, the folds of which took on the brassy glow of the hearth when they gathered before the great fireplace for the ritual.

I couldn't name the language Carol used, much less understand it, but I had learned over the years to recognize the closing syllables. All the vampires had—we couldn't drink until the ceremony was over, and a vampire who can't drink is an attentive vampire indeed: a sprinter in the starting blocks is less attentive.

The circle before the fireplace broke. Some of the women turned to each other for a first embrace, others fanned out to the waiting vampires; only Selene waited with her back to the fire, arms at her sides, hands down, palms out like pictures of St. Theresa.

Whistler and I approached her with our favorite blades drawn—mine was a slick silver Gerber Mini-Mag and Whistler's a choice turn-of-the-century folding scalpel, surgical steel with a mother-of-pearl handle. I knelt at the right hand, Whistler at the left; at her nod we each opened one of her wrist-veins—not the deep suicide vein, but a delicate blue surface vein—and drank.

Then, as the grandfather clock across the room struck eight, Whistler and I both turned to the assembled vampires and witches and opened our lips just wide enough to let the first flow of her blood spill over for the others to see.

Party trick: hell on the dry-cleaning bill if you don't do it right, but it always gets the orgy off to a swell start.

Once the blood hits, of course, there is no further need for party tricks. Orgies have their own momentum: one minute it's an absurd tangle of bodies; then a moan catches you up *just so*, and your answering moan is answered by a woman across the tangle being mounted from behind, and at the precise moment that your eyes meet, hers glaze over from a deep stroke, and your own abdominal muscles clench with hers, and your own partner moans, and his moan catches up the man thrusting into the woman whose eyes are locked to yours, and he comes, and she comes, and when you see that in her eyes you come, and the grandfather clock strikes ten, and you think, *how nice—Grampa came too.*

I enjoyed that last orgy as much as any I'd ever attended. There were even a few firsts: Sandy, a smooth-cheeked vampire with a wide freckled face, gave himself to me: it was his first time with a man, which always gave me a little shudder of enjoyment; the witch Catherine bit her tongue in a transport of joy and let me drink the watery blood; I even had Tacitus quoted to me while making love to a lord.

That last, that lord, was the Viscount, a pale (even for a vampire), enervated Englishman, an old University friend of Whistler's. The Viscount and I were lying together on one of the leather couches in the keeping room, and both happened to turn our heads at the same moment in time to catch Whistler buried somewhere in a daisy chain drinking blood from Carol's thigh, one hand resting on Selene's breast and the other holding a still-smoking joint aloft.

"I do admire the man," whispered the Viscount. "He reminds me of Tacitus' description of Petronius: *Unlike most who trod the road to ruin, he was never looked upon as either debauched or a wastrel, but rather as the finished artist in extravagance.*"

"A regular one-man band, as we say in Detroit," I allowed grudgingly. "Stick a broom up his ass and he could play the drums too."

I'd lost track of how many times Grampa came that night, and since it is as gauche to wear one's wristwatch to an orgy as it is to leave one's socks on, I have only my best guess, and the literary tradition that holds that St. John's true dark night of the soul arrives at three a.m., to suggest that it was probably around two that I wandered in my navy sweats down to the big industrial kitchen to find August Fetterman laying out lines for himself and the Viscount on a Teflon cookie sheet. I joined them, and within twenty minutes was reminded of the old junky adage *It ain't the coke that kills you, it's the cut.*

In this case the cut was Mannitol, a European baby laxative to which I happen to be particularly sensitive. Fortunately there was a small water-closet off the hallway behind the kitchen that housed an old-fashioned toilet with a walnut-wood seat and a tank up on the wall. I had plenty of time to take in all the charms of the place, seated on that walnut-wood seat whistling the Hershey Squirts with my sweatpants at my ankles and my knees nearly touching the door.

I wasn't suffering, mind you—not after all the blood I'd drunk that night—a little bored, maybe, but mostly just amused by the absurdity of the situation: after all, Bram Stoker never wrote about shit like this. But then, neither did Nicolas San Georgiou, not when he was writing fiction, anyway.

What happened next, though, was more Stevenson than Stoker or San Georgiou: like Jim Hawkins in the apple barrel, I overheard something I had not meant, and *was* not meant, to overhear—Whistler and the Viscount whispering in the kitchen.

WHISTLER: Is one alone?
VISCOUNT: *(A dry pause)* Obviously.
WHISTLER: Is one up for a little something special?
VISCOUNT: Such as?
WHISTLER: A special little something.
VISCOUNT: Delighted. Might one bring a guest?
WHISTLER: *(In tones quite as plummy as the Viscount's)* Whom did one have in mind?

VISCOUNT: That delightful Nick.

(Pause for a modest blush)

WHISTLER: No, not Nicky—anybody else but Nicky.

(Another pause—I was already planning my dramatic entrance—I freeze with my hand on the pull-chain)

VISCOUNT: *(As his chair scrapes back: he is rising)* Well, I'm sure you know best. But might I ask why not? You see, I seem to have fallen quite in love with the man. A demned foolish thing for an aging vampire to do, but there you are.

(Another modest blush)

WHISTLER: Why not? Conscience.

VISCOUNT: Surely not yours.

WHISTLER: His.

VISCOUNT: *(Dryly amazed)* No!

WHISTLER: Remnants, anyway. Dangerous remnants. Give him another few years.

VISCOUNT: And perhaps a copy of Disraeli's famous remark re Gladstone.

WHISTLER: Afraid I must have missed that one.

VISCOUNT: "He made his conscience not his guide, but his accomplice."

Well! I was not about to take an insult like that sitting down. I might not know diddly about Gladstone, but like most literate vampires I had read my Nietzsche—the philosopher of choice among those of us who become Übermenschen when we drink blood: "It is more convenient to follow one's conscience than one's intelligence. . . . That is why there are so many conscientious and so few intelligent people." I yanked the chain down and my pants up, and hurried after my faithless friends.

The path paralleled the lake, leading through the woods to the two-story bungalow where the overflow witches were housed. I could see my breath in the air; to my left the tame Tahoe waves slapped the pilings under Whistler's dock, and his boat bumped woodenly against it.

The door to the bungalow—a small gabled building as mockly Tudor as the lodge; serf's quarters once, no doubt—was already open a crack. I slipped in sideways. The entranceway was dark, as was the living room beyond, but at the top of the staircase to my left I could see a faint yellow glow. I crept upstairs as quietly as I could; a crooked trapezoid of yellow light leaked from under one of the two doors on either side of the panelled hallway; with my ear to this door I could hear a woman's voice. European accent. "Almost ready. Another few minutes. He always soon after falls asleep."

I opened the door quietly. A woman was sitting up in a narrow bed wearing a cotton nightgown that buttoned down the front. Or rather, unbuttoned: one plump white breast was exposed; attached to it was a baby of indeterminate age (all babies' ages are indeterminate to me: this one would have been a little over two feet long, if that helps any), eyes closed, tiny fingers clenching and unclenching as he sucked dreamily on a swollen brown nipple. The two vampires were standing with their backs to me, one at either side of the bed, Whistler in black slacks and turtleneck, and the Viscount shirtless, his tuxedo pants held up by narrow black suspenders that, when he turned to face me, made his bony ivory-white chest seem even paler—I thought of Lawrence of Arabia just before that wicked Jose Ferrer had him flogged.

"Hello, Mandy." I announced myself from the doorway.

"Hallo, Nick." Mandy was a bicontinental witch from the Netherlands—I tried to remember whether she'd been visibly pregnant at the previous Midsummer or not.

"Nick," said Whistler, affectless as ever. "You're just in time."

"For what, to hear Disraeli's collected speeches?"

"Oh dear." With the merest upward turn of his palm, the Viscount apologized. "It is good advice, though: if your conscience hasn't stopped you from doing something beforehand, it hasn't any right to nag at you afterwards."

"I'll keep that in mind." I shut the door behind me. "Motherhood seems to agree with you, Mandy."

"I feel goodt." She did look lovely: black hair in an early seventies shag, long cheekbones that gave her narrow black eyes a modest slant.

"How's the kid?"

"I just toldt the two men, soon he falls asleep."

Hmm. "Let me make a wild guess here," I said to Whistler.

"Does it upset you?" He was more curious than concerned.

I turned to Mandy, as if to pass the question on. She looked down at the baby, who had indeed fallen asleep at her breast, then back up at me. "It does him no harm."

"So it's true, what they say about baby-blood?"

"Ah, but you must see for yourself," the Viscount interjected. "Much more scientific, you see. I know how you Americans are about science."

"I prefer the liberal arts, myself," I said. "Very liberal." Trying to keep it light—but I couldn't take my eyes off that baby. "Is there—will there be enough for three of us?"

"For six. Three vampires and three consciences."

The actual taking of the blood was performed judiciously, almost tenderly: Whistler took his works from a drawer in the bedside table, tapped a vein in the baby's foot so smoothly he never even woke up, and drew three small vials of blood, each about the size of a fountain-pen cartridge. The Viscount took the filled ampules, capped them, slipped them into his trouser pocket, and after kissing Mandy good-night we tiptoed out. I turned at the door to see the mother and child snuggling up close in the iron-steaded bed, a rustic quilt pulled up to their chins.

We dragged three redwood lawn chaises down to the white crescent of Whistler's beach. Rumor was that he had sand shipped in from Maui. It was a moonless night, and even at three in the morning the casino lights brightened the sky to the south. The Viscount had borrowed a set of sweats from Whistler. If we hadn't already been blood-high we'd have been shivering, but as it was, the bite in the air added zest to the evening. The Viscount passed out the ampules; I was about to uncap mine when Whistler put his hand lightly on my arm. This was unusual: he was not a toucher, outside of sex. "You asked if what they said about baby-blood was true?"

"Is it?"

"Depends what they say."

"Different things. Augie says he freaked, his first time."

"Mmmmm. Yes, well … how to put this. …" Whistler looked about him, and, not surprisingly, found the lake; he gestured with a long, spectrally pale forefinger towards the sparkling blackness. "Let us posit that nighttime lake out there to be the world as it appears to a normal consciousness. The lake at night is all surface: one trusts there's depth down there, but basically it's impenetrable to the eye, and what one takes one takes on faith.

"But have you ever been out on that lake in the daytime? I never have, personally, but they say it's clear enough that one can see fish swimming fathoms below, even make out the lake-bed, until it drops off to the depths."

I nodded, and he continued; I couldn't see the Viscount in the next chair, but I was pretty sure he was smiling. "You've seen it then. Good. Let's say that's the world on blood. But a hundred years ago this lake was so clear that even in the deepest parts one could see as clearly looking down as looking up: it was transparent as the air: it was glass.

"That's what baby-blood does for one: that's the world on baby-blood: one sees clear to the bottom."

"And Augie didn't like what he saw?"

"It's what he didn't see, more likely."

"And what didn't he see?"

"An illusion. He didn't see a single, stinking illusion anywhere."

I uncapped my vial, and raised it to the dark lake. "Clear to the bottom, eh?" I said.

"Clear to the bottom." Whistler raised his vial, and then the Viscount joined our toast: "To the bottom," he said, and tossed back the contents of the little vial with a practiced gesture, like a man knocking back one of those tidy little bottles of airline booze.

Chapter 8

ONE

Betty pushed back Nick's chair and stretched tentatively, checking out her body a segment at a time: whatever position she'd been contorted into for the past hour or two, it had not been one for which the human body had been designed by its Maker. She groaned aloud, as much to hear a human sound as anything else, then pushed herself up from the chair and headed down the hall to the guest bathroom that Nick had pointed out, a small toilet-only water closet like the one in his story. The walls were covered with a textured Japanese willow–print wallpaper, white with delicate silver brush-stroke traceries.

When she returned to the office, Nick had freshened her coffee. But the screen was dark, and when she tapped the space key, she seemed to have jumped to a later place in the story. "Nick?"

"Yeah?" He was in the bedroom down the hall.

"Thanks for the refill. But it feels like I've missed some pages."

"What?" He hurried in, alarmed. "Where did you leave off?"

"You, Whistler, and the Viscount had just drunk the baby-blood."

Nick looked relieved as he glanced over her shoulder at the screen. "Sorry, my fault. I blocked real bad on the next part—I realized I could barely stand thinking about it. And as for writing it down, forget it. I tried it a dozen different ways—couldn't get over it, couldn't get around it. Finally I decided I'd sneak up on it—skip over the hairiest part, and flash back to it."

"I see," said Betty dubiously.

"Trust me, it'll all come clear if you just keep going."

Betty couldn't help herself: "Clear to the bottom?"
Nick flinched. "Something like that."

A white glare floods my dream. A heavenly white glare as though the sun had somehow slipped behind the sky. I try to bring my hand up to shield my eyes, but the hand will not move.

A face looms over me: a basset-eared, droop-nosed face, more lined now than when I'd seen it last, but still: "Leon?"

"Hush, baby-heart. It's all right now, it's going to be all right now."

"Are you real?"

"Real as I ever was. Now go back to sleep."

When I open my eyes again the white glare has resolved itself into a square luminous ceiling panel. Fleece-lined leather cuffs secure my wrists to the silver rails of a hospital bed. This seems like a terribly good idea. "Keep it tied up," I murmur.

"What?" Not Leon's voice: a woman.

"Where's Leon?"

"Here. I'm here, Nick." His goblin face at the foot of the bed.

"Am I in a hospital?"

"A clinic."

"Don't let them untie me?"

"Not till you' ready, baby-heart. Not till you' god-dayam good and ready."

"Mr. Shaw?"

I gather that's me: there's no one else in the room but me and the woman in the cardigan sweater leaning over me. "Yes?"

"Can you lift your hip up a little for me, and sort of twist to the side?"

"Why?"

She held up a syringe. "I thought you'd rather have it in the buttocks, now that you're awake."

"Story of my life, nurse. Story of my life."

"Leon?" Nighttime now.

"Talk to me."

"Did anybody . . . die?"

"Not that I know of."

I thought about that for a minute. I supposed I ought to be grateful, but I couldn't imagine to whom. "Got a joint?"

He shook his head. "Got a Camel."

"Have to do." A match flared in the darkened room, and a lit cigarette was placed between my lips. I took a drag, coughed, and the cigarette popped out of my mouth; Leon snatched it up and brushed the ashes off my chest before replacing it; when I was done he took the butt into the bathroom; I heard the hiss as it hit the water, and then the flush.

"Why is everything so quiet?" I asked him when he reappeared.

"It's Christmas Eve, baby-heart."

I thought about *that* for a while.

"Leon?"

"Still here."

"Know what I want for Christmas?"

"I sure don't."

"Nothing."

To his credit, he got it right away. "You don't want anything, or you want Nothing?"

"I want Nothing. I don't even want to die, I just want to already be dead."

"Why?"

"You know why."

"What, because you' an evil vam-pie?" He started to laugh, then made a spitting noise, worked his tongue around, and plucked a shred of tobacco from between his teeth. "Oooh, evil vam-pie!"

"It's not a joke, Leon. You of all people know it's not a joke."

"Au contraire, mon frere." He stood up then, drawing himself up to his full height, which put his chin an inch or two above the top rail of my bed. "I am quite possibly the *only* person on earth who knows precisely what a joke that is." He chuckled, and began unbuckling my restraints. "Evil vam-pie my ass! What you are, friend Nick, is a pitiful, powerless, chicken-shit ass-wipe of a dope addict, and the fact that your drug of choice is blood doesn't make you a snip more evil than some Sterno junky ralfing his liver out in some gutter someplace."

"You think so? Whyn't you ask Selene about that, see what she has to say." I began kneading my left hand with the numb fingers of my right—the pins and needles were making me testy.

"Selene won't be talking for a while."

"Or the Viscount?"

He gave me a blank look.

"The Viscount? Whistler's friend, from England?"

He shook his head, and I felt the first flutter of panic down deep in my intestines: if Leon didn't know anything about him, then his previous assurance—that no one had died—became a good deal less assuring. "Never mind. I'm not up for any metaphysical discussions anyway—you bring me any blood?"

He looked surprised? "Blood? Baby-heart, I thought you knew: I've been clean and sober for damn near two years now."

I was pretty sure he was bullshitting me—he had to be: as far as any of us knew, no vampire had ever given up drinking—but I was also pretty sure that I wasn't about to get any blood off him *this* night, for whatever reason: it's the sort of thing junkies just know. If begging would have done it, I'd have begged—as it was, I shifted my ground. "Okay. I'll settle for that shit the nurse has been shooting me up with."

"That I can do."

"What the hell is it, anyway?" I asked him, but he was already out the door. Fuck him, I didn't need him anyway. I worked my fingers around until the full feeling was back, and was just thinking about sitting up when Leon returned with the nurse.

"Experiencing a little discomfort, are we?" she remarked, unwrapping an alcohol wipe.

"I guess you could say that." Remember, this was the longest I'd been without blood in nearly a decade: I could almost *smell* hers: I may even have licked my lips before I turned away—on my side, without being asked—and felt the needle-prick. "But I sure feel better now."

I didn't, not yet, but I wanted an excuse for what I did next: rolled onto my back and took her hand in mine as I thanked her. Really all I wanted was her slender warm wrist in my grasp, so I could feel her pulse pounding through my fingertips. I could see it all now: next time, no Leon, grab the syringe, inject her, find a bigger gauge needle if I could, if not use the same needle to take her blood as she slept—that would give me the strength to blow this pop stand. And apparently they didn't even know my real name: that would be handy . . .

But I couldn't keep my eyes open long enough—the last thing I saw before falling back to sleep on Christmas Eve was the last thing I remembered from Yule: the Viscount. He seems to be underwater. His eyes are wide and staring, bloodshot red; his long hair floats dreamily upwards as if it were trying to tug him along with it. He opens his mouth to speak—or scream—only bubbles emerge, big ones at first, *ba-loop, ba-loop,* then smaller ones, tiny balls of mercury flashing up silver to the surface.

When I awoke the next morning it was with an oddly unfocused sense of excitement. I felt around in my mind, trying to figure out what it was attached to, this anticipation—for a moment I thought it was about Christmas, but I hadn't given a good goddamn about Christmas in twenty years: why would I start now? Then I remembered my plan to turn the syringe on the nurse, and take her blood—

Blood. How long had it been? Four days. I took inventory: nothing hurt—no wait, the back of my left hand was kind of sore. I turned it towards me like a man looking at his watch, and saw a little round band-aid centered in a yellowing bruise: I must have had an I.V. in at some point. Other than that, nothing physical, but I would gladly have traded a broken bone or two for the teeth-gritting ennui, the excruciating boredom that washed over me when I looked around the room. Nothing, nothing, nothing: it was all as flat and soul-crushing as a black-and-white Dana Andrews movie on the late show. I tried to remember whether reality had been like this before I was Awakened.

I couldn't remember, though, and I'd just about decided that it couldn't have been—I'd have killed myself years before—when the doorknob turned, and every cell of my body came to rigid attention . . .

. . . then collapsed—*as you were, men*—it was only Leon, looking even droopier than usual in a floppy red felt Santa cap with a dangling white deedly-ball. "Merry—"

I interrupted him. "Don't be chipper. Just don't fucking be chipper, I'll kill you with my bare hands."

"—Christmas." He lowered the left bed rail and held out his hand. "C'mon, up you go, baby-heart, come with me, I have something to show you."

I sat up—too fast—and found myself hanging on to his forearm as if it were a trapeze. The floor seemed awfully far away—even when my bare feet were on it, it still seemed like a long way down, and I had to sit back almost immediately. Made it on the second try, though, and shuffled the first few steps leaning on Leon like an old man after hernia surgery.

"Is this going to be worth it?" I asked him.

"I think so," he said. "It's something you haven't seen in a long time—just a few more steps now." We had crossed the room and were standing in front of the floor-to-ceiling black curtains. Suddenly he grabbed the curtain cord and tugged; the curtains parted with a diabolic creak; I whimpered out loud and threw my forearm across my eyes to shield them from the bright sunlight.

I shrieked, stumbled backwards. He leapt forward and caught me, but couldn't hold my weight; he settled for lowering me slowly to the carpet. "Quit whinin' and open your eyes," he said softly.

I did: no pain. Leon reached down and helped me to my feet again, then pulled open the sliding glass door. We were a good twenty stories in the air. I shook his hand off my arm and stepped out onto the balcony, tottered forward and grabbed the railing for balance. Leon was at my elbow in an instant—I waved him away weakly. "I just need to be alone for a minute, bud."

"You ain't gonna jump or anything, are you?"

"I don't know. I don't think so."

"I'll bring you a chair anyway."

I'd never seen Lake Tahoe in full sunlight before. They haven't got a name for that color yet. But the pale-washed turquoise of the sky, that's cerulean: I'd forgotten all about cerulean. Leon returned with a blanket for my lap, and one of those wooden-armed vinyl-seated side chairs you only find in hotels and hospitals. I sat down heavily. "Hey bud?"

"Hey what?"

"How long does it take? Before you stop wanting the blood?"

"I don't know—I haven't stopped yet. I long for it, sometimes. But I haven't *craved* it for over a year, if that's any help."

"I don't know if I can make it."

"That's good." He was standing behind me, his hands resting lightly on my shoulders. "See, the day you *know* you can make it, you call me. And until I get there, chain yourself down in the basement, 'cause that's the day you're gonna slip."

"That's not the problem." My eyes started tearing: I'd forgotten you can't stare at the sun, even if you're not a vampire.

"What is it?"

"I don't know if I want to make it."

He came around from behind me. "How 'bout jus' for today? You know, *one-day-at-a-time*, and all that."

I thought about it for a minute. "I can't give you an honest answer. And I don't care enough about anything to lie."

He turned his back to me, and leaned on the railing.

"Leon?"

"What?" Without turning.

"This isn't a clinic, is it?"

"Not exactly—it's the nineteenth floor of the Gold Dust Hotel and

Casino in lovely downtown Tahoe. And you, you're free to go, baby-heart. You can walk out that door anytime you want."

"Yeah?"

I started to push myself up from the chair, and he turned and looked down at me, grinning. "Absolutely. Well—you best get some clothes on first—they' picky about bare asses in casino, 'less they' in the revue." I sat back down—I'd forgotten for a moment that I was in a hospital gown—and Leon went on. "See, old bud, I can't do a minute of your recovery for you. I can take you this far, get you de-toxed, show you the sun, let you know you're not alone. The rest is up to you."

"Great. Where's my clothes?"

"In the closet there. But before you go—"

"A catch! I knew there was a catch."

He held his thumb and forefinger a half inch apart. "Little one. All I'm askin' is, before you make up your mind—"

"I've already made up my mind."

"Before you leave then. Before you leave I want you to sit down with me and tell me all about that last night of yours? The solstice?"

Ba-loop, ba-loop. "Didn't somebody give you a full report, all the juicy details?"

"Baby-heart, I was the ghost at the banquet—I showed up at five a.m.—oh, I had it all figured out—everybody'd be stroked out on the lawn per usual, waiting for dawn—I was just gonna tell all of you 'bout being clean and sober, I was gonna be so cool, no preachin', just bear witness, let everybody know it was possible, it could be done, we aren't doomed to live the rest of our lives hidin' from the sun. Instead what happens is I find you stretched out on the dock like a drowned rat, the witches are shriekin', the vampires are runnin' around like chickens with their heads cut off.

"So what I did, I took Whistler aside—he was the only one had his head about him, despite being wrecked on baby-blood, I gather, and worried sick about Selene—and offered to take you off his hands—at his expense, of course—and get you straightened out, de-toxed. I called AA to get a doctor referral, hired the nurse, had a few of the boys 'walk' you through the casino and up here to the suite. Mind you, I don't actually know if Whistler understood I was clean now, don't know if he took that in. He just wanted you gone before some of them witches got aholt of you."

I closed my eyes and saw a dozen yellow-white suns against the black field of my eyelids. "So you know by and large what happened, what do you need the details for?"

When I looked up, Leon was leaning back against the railing, propped on his elbows—man at leisure, except for that stupid Santa cap. "Oh, it's not for *me* to hear it: it's for you to hear it. See, when you make your choice, bud, I want you to know what it is you're choosin'. You owe yourself that much."

"Then I can go?"

He nodded, smiling slyly. "But I wouldn't go straight back to Whistler Manor if I were you—I gather some of those witches are fixing to tear you a new asshole, baby-heart, and it ain't gonna be near as pretty as the old one, either."

"All right, here goes: I guess about twenty minutes had passed since I dropped the baby-blood—"

"Try it in the present tense." Leon had dragged another chair out onto the balcony and placed it alongside mine; we were both looking out through the railings to the lake, and the surrounding bowl of mountains. The sky had darkened to the west—a high gray-bottomed anvil of clouds—perhaps a storm was on the way at last. The skiers would like that.

Leon had brought me a blanket; I tucked it in a little tighter around my lap, and started again. "About twenty minutes have gone by. Whistler and the Viscount are talking about going down to the casinos. Whistler explains to me that it's easy to make money when you're high on baby-blood. Says it's clear as glass from the minute you walk into the casino which players are lucky at that particular moment. Says they practically *glow.* So you find some shooter glowing at the craps tables, you bet with the shooter, you clean up.

"Anyway, I'm letting the talk wash over me. I know for a certainty they haven't the slightest intention of going down to the casinos—I don't know how I know—I just do—baby-blood, I suppose—and I'm paying more attention to the poor-will calling its name in the woods off to my right, and it seems as if the woods would be interesting in my condition. A line from old Uncle Frost is rolling around in my head— *Lovely, dark and deep. Lovely, dark and deep*—and off I go for a pleasant nocturnal stroll."

I could feel the words starting to come more smoothly now. My eyes were closed: I was back in the woods again: lovely, dark and deep they are, and sparkling like Sugar Frosted Flakes to my vampire eyes. The closer I got to the poor-will, the clearer its cry. "Poor Will my ass," I call, just to make trouble, and the startled hush that follows is as dark and deep as the woods themselves, but soon broken by a hollow

whistling   sound—*wheeeeee-wheeeee-wheeee-wheee-whee-wee-we.*   I
know that call: Peterson describes the rhythm as a rubber ball bouncing
down a flight of stairs: it's a screech owl.

I stop stock-still in the path. Silence again, then a smooth shudder-
ing in the air; a contained gray shadow drops like a stone; only when it
rises again is there a beating of wings, and over it a thin chittering
sound. For an instant the owl is silhouetted against the strip of starry
black sky directly overhead; in its talons a tiny mouse still struggles. But
not for long, I think. And although in a very cool way I feel some empathy for the mouse (I find myself wondering if, in its terror, it even sees
the woods receding below: what a strange vantage for a mouse!), it's
clear as the world on baby-blood that most of my fellow-feeling is reserved for the owl: what a warm bloody treat it has in store. And still
struggling: how much more savor that will add.

It occurs to me as I meander on up the path that I haven't felt anyone struggling in my talons for—oh, for absolute *ages!*—and with that
thought at the back of my mind I find myself at the door to the ginger-
bread house—the bungalow. The baby is upstairs, but I know before I
turn the knob that it's not the baby I want, but the mother. Sweet candy
Mandy. I can already feel her long-boned arms trapped in my own, the
warmth of her torso against mine, the feminine flutter of her throat. I
make my way up the stairs so stealthily that even *I* cannot hear my foot-
falls. The room is dark; I'm already standing over the bed when she
opens her eyes.

"Hallo Nick." Sleepily. "What is it? What do you want?"

Your blood, I think, but I don't really feel much like talking. I whistle,
instead: *Wheee-whee-whe-we.* A falling tone, a rubber ball bouncing
down the steps. There is a small sewing basket on the bedside table: the
scissors will do: all I need is a snip.

At first the struggle is all I'd hoped for. I even let her beat about with
her fists, and the screaming is relish for the blood—I have found a small
but satisfying vein behind her ear—picturesque really—now her fists
begin to annoy me, and I pin her arms behind her with one hand, and
tilt her head back with the other—dear mouse. I drink until the blood
smears my chin, and then hands—small hands—are tugging me away.
"Nick, enough. Nick, that's enough, you've got to stop now."

Selene. Doesn't understand: the mouse doesn't tell the owl when it's
time to stop. I turn, slowly, to show her my blood-smeared face, but
she's dived past me onto the bed, and taken Mandy's head between her
hands. Her clever fingers find the wound, pinch it off.

"Good," I say. "Good for you." I give her time to close the wound. Not so much an owl now as a cat. Fun with your food. And Selene not so much a mouse as a bird: small, hollow-boned, her heart beating with a shallower, quicker hop. I leap for her with a gleeful shout, and she begins to fight. But like a sparrow: those little fists a-hammering away: it's like being tickled when you want to be beaten, flutter-tongued when you want to be sucked dry. Tiring of the game now, I tear a hole in her throat with my teeth (not an easy thing to do, I assure you: nearly impossible unless you've already got your blood-strength), and lap a few drops from the welling wound before turning away. I'm not really thirsty anymore, you see.

"I don't imagine I could have gotten much higher anyway," I said to Leon. I was standing at the railing with the blanket thrown over my shoulders. A couple had appeared on the balcony next door: the florid gentleman probably owned a Pontiac dealership; the lady had that mummified Polly Bergen Turtle-Wax look.

"Try to stick with the present tense," he suggested as we tugged our chairs back inside and closed the sliding glass door. "Don't bail out now."

"Bail out? Baby, the plane has already gone down. In flames." I told him about the footsteps charging up the stairs, Mandy going off like an air-raid siren, Augie bellowing at the door. Me, I'm out the window: I slide inelegantly on my heels down the tiled roof—racketa-tacketa—jump the last ten feet and land lightly. A whole shitload of people are charging up the narrow path to the bungalow—to my eyes it's your basic Frankenstein mob, only without the torches. I cut through the woods, moving so fast it's like I don't even have to dodge the trees: they just seem to slide on out of the way like images in a negative, white against black.

I circle all the way around the bungalow, and behind the main lodge, enter through the back door, past the water-closet, through the kitchen, down the corridor, and up the staircase to my own room. I can hear them running around out there shouting to each other—part of me wants to go back out and show myself to them, just to taunt them: I can't believe they could actually catch me. I even roll a joint and smoke it on the window ledge, looking out over the lawn and the shallow beach to the lake beyond.

Leisurely, I stub the roach out on the sill, swing my legs back into the room, and see a vampire reflected in the full-length mirror on the back of the door. He looks like shit, frankly. Narrowing my eyes, I hop off the window seat and cross the room; the vampire narrows his eyes and crosses the mirror-room towards me; we meet at the cold glass pane of his world, and stare at each other: blood is smeared over his face—even his brow is splashed with red gouts of coagulating blood—and the neck of his navy sweatshirt sags from the weight of the blood which has soaked it black.

"Well, you've gone and done it now, old sport," I tell him—or he tells me. We hang our heads in mock abashment, and then, slowly, raise them again, looking each other over from feet to face until our eyes meet. *You talkin' a me?*, we ask each other. *You talkin' a me?*

Then we share a smirk, because of course we both know the answer to that question: *There's nobody else heee-eeere.*

"When they rushed the door of my room I went out the window again—a higher window, this time, a longer racketa-tacketa down the tiles, same ten-foot jump—vampire Olympics—I absolutely *stuck* the landing. Then a short run down the sloping lawn to the dock with the mob at my heels, and—"

"Present—"

But Leon, I wanted to say, *it didn't happen in the present tense.* See, time more or less stopped when I met my eyes in that mirror, and the full horror of the baby-blood high hit me. Of course, I say full horror: the fact is, the horror was that there was no horror: only me: only the blood-smeared monster in the mirror.

No value judgment there, y'understand. We attach words to things so that we can differentiate them from other things, and a monster wasn't a bad thing to be: no worse than a human, any more than an owl is worse than a mouse.

No, monster was as apt a word as any for this rather messy creature smirking at me in the mirror: that wasn't the trouble: the trouble was, he was no more Nicky from Greektown, or Captain Santos of Air Force Intelligence, or Nicolas San Georgiou the author than he was the man in the moon, and when they came through the door it was with a lift of his monstrous heart that he leapt through the open window; if he'd had a cape he would by god have gathered the corners in his outstretched hands as he rackety-tacked down the tiles so that he might have un-furled it like bat-wings when he jumped.

Monsters like that sort of thing: most villains tend toward the banal, but monsters are permitted drama. At any rate, I certainly could have used a cape when I was standing at the edge of the dock with my back to the water. Fangs would have come in handy, too: I could have hissed, and bared them with my cape raised on high. I must say, though, that for a mob that had me cornered, the assembly was not behaving in a terribly mob-like manner—mobs must never plead, anymore than monsters, but I was hearing things like *It's all right, Nick. Please, Nick, just calm down, just take it easy, nobody's going to hurt you.*

Pitiful, eh? I didn't stay around to hear anymore—monsters hate weakness: it makes them angry. Or thirsty, and we didn't want that, did we? Capeless, fangless, I could only shake my head in disgust, and turn . . .

". . . and dive. There's not the slightest doubt in my mind I could have swum the lake, but now I hear the splash behind me, labored strokes—the Viscount. I could easily outdistance him, but I slow down, tread water with my back to him, and at the touch of his hand on my shoulder I turn, grab both his hands in mine as if to twirl him at arm's length. 'Let's see who can hold his breath the longest,' I say, my fingers tightening on his forearms. Know what his last words were?"

Leon shook his head.

"Me either, 'cause he would have had to say them back on the dock. I remember the monster's, though."

"Tell me."

"*Ring around the rosie,*
Pocket full of posie,
Ashes, ashes, all fall down."

TWO

Whistler lay on his back on the bed that took up half the cabin of the Lear he'd chartered for their two-stage flight to Miami. Flying east wasn't easy for a vampire—you had to leave California right after sunset if you wanted to be sure of reaching the other coast before sunrise. Winter was easier, but Whistler still liked to break the journey into two stages just to be on the safe side.

They were somewhere over Oklahoma by now, and he was stark naked, the Creature pointing straight up. Lourdes, kimono-clad, stroked it thoughtfully with her hand curled into a relaxed fist. "You're different than most men your age, you know," she informed him.

He reached into his leather RAF kitbag for a small squeeze bottle of coconut oil. "Know a lot about men my age, do you?"

You'd be surprised, she thought, but "Girls talk" was what she said as she held her hand out, palm up; he squeezed a few drops of oil onto it.

"And what do the girls say?"

She began to stroke the Creature—it was almost purring. "They say that when most men get around fifty, instead of getting hard, they just get heavy. A girl can work with it, but it just ain't the same. They say."

Her fist tightened. "You, on the other hand . . ." She forced the Creature back against his oiled white belly, then released it: *boinng.*

Lourdes wiped her hands on the sheets and took a sip from a slim pewter thermos full of blood. "Here's to the fellowship!" The plane banked gently to the right; through the Plexiglas oval of the window the clouds below were mounded black seas, and the stars were fat and round, pulsing softly like stars do on blood.

She handed Whistler the thermos—rather than drink from the mouth of it, he sat up and poured himself a shot in a silver-rimmed glass. "To the fellowship. For however long they have left, poor bastards."

"I've still never been able to figure out how they ever got it off the ground," Lourdes mused as he lay back down and she resumed her gentle stroking. "What did Selene mean, one brick at a time? Did they just start out by kidnapping people one by one, Nick and that other guy, whatsisname?"

"Leon," said Whistler. It was quite a moment for him: she would be the first person other than Selene to learn the truth about Leon's death. "His name was Leon Stanton, and he was my best friend, up to the very moment I threw him over that guardrail."

Lourdes's hand never missed a beat. "No shit?"

He shook his head sadly, hiding his elation. "No shit. It was the old joke: one moment he's admiring the view, and the next he's part of it. I don't imagine he really believed I was going to do it until the last possible moment—never even screamed until he was halfway down."

"Talk to me, baby." Excited by the turn the conversation was taking, she grabbed the Creature tightly and climbed on; holding it inside her with one hand at first, she lay down on top of Whistler, then propped her weight up on her elbows. As long as he stayed hard, he'd stay in. And she meant for him to stay hard—it added something to the conversation.

"It was a few months after they'd so subtly persuaded me to join them by tying me to my bed. The others were growing impatient with attending A.A. and N.A. and M.A meetings, and using euphemisms for blood. I was rather comfortable with it, myself, but then, I was still using."

"So why didn't they just start their own meeting?"

Beneath her, Whistler spread his fingers modestly across his bare chest. "Yours truly kept pointing out to them, as often as necessary, that to start a new twelve-step program with integrity, one needs permission from Alcoholics Anonymous. They're rather generous with their permission, but one does have to tell them what addiction it is one is going to be Anonymous about. None of them were willing to do that, but neither were they willing to lie to A.A., or simply bootleg the program. They do tend to hamstring themselves with their integrity, these twelve-steppers.

"Then Leon called me one night to announce that he couldn't take it anymore—that he was going to save himself, and the rest of us, by getting it over with, by being the first to go public. 'How public?' I asked him.

"*Oprah,* was his reply."

"Ooo!" Lourdes was so horrified she nearly let the Creature slip out of her; she reached behind her and circled the base of it with thumb and forefinger, stroking it to full hardness inside her while he continued.

"I know. Would have been quite some show. The aftermath alone would have made the Salem witch trials look like an Easter egg hunt. 'Talked to any of the others?' I asked.

" 'No,' he said.

" 'If you do, I'll kill *myself*,' I said.

" 'Don't do that,' he said.

" 'I will, I'm on my way to the bridge right now,' I said.

" 'Wait,' he said.

" 'I'm gone,' I said.

" 'I'll meet you,' he said.

" 'Come alone,' I said."

Whistler reached inside Lourdes's kimono with his hands crossed, so that each palm cupped her opposite breast. She raised herself up to give him more room: it felt good, this trick of his, like suddenly being caressed by a whole different set of hands.

"Still can't bring myself to call it murder," he went on. "More a case of self-defense. Life without blood isn't worth living: who threatens my blood, threatens my life."

Now he put his arms around her and pulled her tightly against him;

they lay there, scarcely moving. "I told Nick and the others that Leon had killed himself in despair—that he felt he couldn't stay off blood—that he told me he'd rather be dead. I convinced them that all our lives were at stake, and that we had to start V.A. right away, permission or not. Told them A.A. would understand."

Through her breast she felt the rumble of his voice; in her ear she heard his whisper; and when the angle was just right, the head of the Creature brushed the sweet spot inside. "You went from talking them out of V.A. into talking them into it?" When she spoke her voice was husky, and she was surprised at how hot this was making her: there was something so sweetly twisted about having a conversation like this with a man's cock deep inside you.

"The idea of someone's going public had put a bit of a fright into me. I realized that if I could convince them to start a Vampires Anonymous, I could use the anonymity to my own purposes: we wrote into the bylaws that none of us could go public, or even tell another individual, without the unanimous consent of the fellowship."

She raised herself up on her elbows again. "But that doesn't explain why they all gave up blood in the first place."

"Step One: 'Our lives were unmanageable.' Personally, I've always thought of that as a sort of inside joke. After all, everyone's life is unmanageable. Frog race. Bump your ass every step." He gave a little upthrust with his hips for emphasis; she let her weight down so her breasts were pressed against his chest again. "Then factor in the particular problems that come with being a vampire—trying to earn a living 'twixt dusk and dawn, never seeing the sun. Not just the sun—*children*—how often do we see a child, for instance, you and I?"

"Mmmmhhmm."

"And as for someone like Sherman—back then his relationship with Catherine was shaky, his practice suffering. They took to calling on him around sunset—Nick and Leon would show up all bright-eyed and bushy-tailed, and having convinced themselves, by dint of constant repetition and reinforcement, that their own lives were now manageable, they were able to assure him that his would be, too, if only he would give up blood.

"The technique is the same for all cults—join us, and you'll be happy like we are. All you have to do is give up blood, or worship Jim Jones, or join the Party, or give Werner Erhard a thousand dollars."

"Whmmm?"

"Wern—never mind. Not important. One weekend when Catherine

was away at a meeting of the coven—Candlemas, I believe it was—they talked Sherman into agreeing to let them perform an intervention on him. And then when they had him hooked, there were *three* of them, three bright-eyed and bushy-tailed *my*-life-is-manageable examples of the value of giving up blood, to work on little Sandy. And then there were four, and so on and so forth—the thing snowballed, or rather dominoed, with the Penang falling one by one until only I was left.

"By then they had brought the twelve-step logic to its inescapable conclusion: Addiction is insane, therefore addicts are insane. Drinking blood is irrational, therefore the decision to drink blood can never be rational. Catch-twenty-two: If one doesn't agree one is insane and in need of treatment, then one is by definition insane, and in need of treatment."

"So they tied you to your bed."

"Yes. I was the first sailor they ever press-ganged."

"Ooo, sounds kinky." She grabbed his wrists, and they played their little wrestling game again; once more it ended with Whistler on top, and Lourdes stretched out on her back, hands crossed at the wrist over her head.

"It wasn't," said Whistler decisively. "And *that's* the real reason they talked themselves into it: despite all protestations to the contrary, twelve-steppers just can't stand to see anybody having fun."

"I don't know—my mother was a drunk. I think she'd of been better off in A.A."

She began grinding her hips against him; he let go of her wrists. "Drunks only *think* they're having fun, m'dear. Vampires really are."

They began making love in earnest again, and were still at it when the pilot informed them over the intercom that he was beginning his descent into Dallas/Fort Worth. "By the way, Mr. Whistler, ma'am, did I tell you Mick Jagger leased the plane just before you?"

"No you didn't," Whistler snapped, switching on the talk switch next to the speaker in the headboard. "And to tell you the truth, I'd just as soon not have known." Angrily, he switched off the intercom again, then turned back to Lourdes. "I've never forgiven the sons of bitches for throwing poor Brian out of the band."

"That was one of the original guys in the Stones, hunh?"

"Yes, Brian Jones."

"I heard they had him killed, Mick and Keith."

"Oh no."

"You said that like you know."

"Second hand—I'd already been deported by then. But I have it on good authority—" He switched to a cockney accent. "—that it was baby-blood wot done 'im in. Rather like Nick, I was told, except that it was Brian who drowned, and not my informant."

"Like Nick, huh?" She already knew the story about Nick and the Viscount, and of course had seen Selene's throat, had run her fingers wonderingly over the angry flesh of her scar. "Just couldn't handle it?"

"Not a problem you're ever likely to have, m'dear," he said, grinning down at her. "Now let's gird our loins and fasten our seatbelts. The vampires of Dallas await. There are only a few of them, so far as I know, but what they lack in numbers, they more than make up for in enthusiasm."

Lourdes had crawled over to the window to see if she could catch a glimpse of Dallas from the sky, but the sight of her on all fours proved irresistible to Whistler: as she looked out upon the lights of Dallas rising up from the dark plains to greet them, she felt the Creature nudging its questing head against the tender swollen lips of her sex from behind.

Then it was in her, and the front of Whistler's long-boned thighs were pressed against the back of hers, and his long arms had reached around and under her dangling breasts, but an agonizing millimeter or so too low, so that her swollen nipples were barely brushing against them. And every time she would lower her trunk, her breasts yearning to be held tightly, he would pull them away, until finally, in desperation, she grabbed his hands with her own to force them against her breasts.

Whistler sensed the orgasm beginning to build inside her—he arched his fingers so that only the fingertips were touching her, a circle of pressure all the way around the outside of each aureole, tightening, tightening from below until his fingertips were pressed against the hard place deep inside her breasts at the very root of the nipples, pulsing to the rhythm of her orgasm.

As Whistler groaned and the Creature throbbed and spurted deep inside her, she realized that they'd just touched down in Dallas. *Even the O's are bigger in Texas*, she thought wonderingly.

THREE

After Betty had paged down that last time, the screen had gone blank and the computer had beeped anxiously. Moments later Nick appeared in the doorway. Betty gestured to the screen, and he crossed the room to look over her shoulder. "Did you see a dotted line first?"

"Right after 'ashes, ashes, all fall down.' "

He winced, hearing the words. "Then you're done. That's as far as I've gotten." Betty scooted her chair away from the machine; Nick reached across her to switch the monitor off. It flashed white in the darkness—in the brief glare he appeared exhausted, the skin over his cheekbones opaque, like wax paper that had been crumpled and smoothed again.

She felt a surge of empathy. "What am I supposed to do, Nick? I know your letting me read this was a gamble. I appreciate the trust and the confidence, and I feel tremendous compassion for all of you, really I do. But I have a responsibility as a pastor to maintain my church as a sanctuary in every possible sense of the word, and it's not fair to ask me to let the problems of one fellowship jeopardize—"

"I'm not *asking* you to—"

"—all the other fellowships—"

"—jeopardize anything."

"—not to mention my home—"

"Oh bullshit."

She looked up at him angrily. "What do you mean, bullshit?"

"I mean *bullshit* bullshit. It doesn't take a degree in counseling to figure out what's got you more upset than any threat to your church, and that's something personal, something between you and me. *I* lied to you, not V.A., and I gave you my sperm under false pretenses, and it was wrong, and if you want to hate me, hate me, and if you want to take it out on me, take it out on me, and not on V.A."

"They lied, too."

"They lied because they had to. You know they had to. But what I did, I did out of pure selfishness. I was in the position you might have found yourself in after a few more years—I'd given up. I'd already accepted the fact that I was not ever going to enjoy the blessings of parenthood, which despite the legends is as close as even a vampire can get to immortality. Then you asked me to father your child—quick, you wanted it done quickly—and I gave in to the temptation."

Betty rose, heading for the door. He reached out and grabbed her by the elbow; she shook him off. "Get your hands off me, Nick. Don't you ever put your hands on me again. And don't try to turn this thing around so it's my fault somehow, either, and most of all, don't you ever try to tell me not to take a threat to my church personally."

Angrily, she plucked at the sleeve of her sweatshirt, as if his touch had disarranged it. "Everything about my church is personal. I've put every cent I ever saved into that church, I've lived like a miser for five years. You say you can't survive without V.A.? Well I can't survive without my church, and whether it's your fault or not, your fellowship has put it in jeopardy."

"But I've already told you, it wasn't one of us in the first place."

"No, it was a witch who's looking for revenge any way she can get it."

"We can protect you against Selene."

"I can protect myself against Selene. And here's how I'm going to do it." She folded her arms over her chest. "First of all, *Vampires* Anonymous—" She emphasized the word deliberately; she wanted Nick to know that she wasn't going to be shy about saying it aloud, now or ever. "—has had its last meeting at the Church of the Higher Power."

He nodded.

"Second, I don't want any of you coming to any other meetings at my church, either. I think I know what some of you look like by now, and I don't ever want to see any of you setting foot in my church for any reason."

"But the only other Friday M.A. meeting is out in Concord—some of us need M.A. too."

"Then drive to Concord," she said coldly. "Thirdly, if I am pregnant with your child, and *if* I decide to keep it—"

He started to say something; she silenced him with a look. "You don't have any say in the matter, not anymore, so just listen carefully: in the event I *choose* to bear this child, you are to keep as far away from us as possible. I don't want to see you, I don't want my child approached, I don't want our child to even know her father exists. In fact, if it ever reaches my ears that you've so much as *told* anyone that you're the father, I'll sue your ass from here to East Jabbip. Now what have you done with my coat?"

He retrieved her blue down jacket from the downstairs hall closet, and showed her out. Neither of them spoke. Nick found himself watching numbly from the doorway as she marched down the steep flagstone walk, then heard the roar of the Oldsmobile's engine from the bottom of the driveway and saw the red glow of the tail lights receding around the bend in the road.

He locked the door behind him and wandered back up to his bedroom. A peculiar numbness had overtaken him, as if he'd actually lost a child, albeit one he'd never known. He threw himself face down across the bed and tried to grieve, to let it out, to feel his feelings like a good twelve-stepper, but all he felt was self-conscious. He'd never ever been able to cry for Leon—how could he weep for a child he'd never see?

Then the phone rang. He glanced at the bedside clock—4:00 A.M.—and decided to let his machine take the call. He didn't even bother monitoring it, but a few minutes later curiosity got the better of him—it was practically the only emotion he hadn't worn out in the course of the harrowing night. He padded across the hall to his office and punched the playback button.

Hello? Hello, Nick. You there Nick? Please pick up the phone Nick. A woman's voice, not immediately recognizable. *Please, this is January, if you're there Nick pick up the phone.* Pitch rising desperately. *It's January. You gotta pick up the phone, Nick. I don't know if he's alive or dead. I think maybe I killed him . . .*

"Where are you? Are you home?" He found himself crouching down, fists clenched, nose to the speaker of the answering machine. "Goddammit, tell me where you are."

Nick? Are you there Nick? Nick, please pick up the phone . . .

BOOK TWO

At Feasts
Full Warm
of Blood

ONE

"Does it look anything like the Philippines?" asked Whistler.

Lourdes laughed. Her first glimpse of Santa Luz through the salt-rimmed oval window of the Blue Goose, a twelve-seater seaplane from St. Thomas, was of a wild black tangle of rainforest crowning the central hump of the island. "Yes and no, honey—there's seven thousand islands in the Philippines."

Then they were skimming low along a notched coast of small coves and inlets rimmed with pale curves of narrow crescent beaches, until finally the lights of the Old Town appeared directly ahead of them. The Goose touched down, bouncing like a skipping stone past the bare masts of moored sailboats towards the maze of wooden docks.

The seaplane terminal, a lighted shack at the edge of the Old Town docks, was deserted except for an agent in a white short-sleeved shirt with epaulets, and a cabdriver in a leather-billed cap, whose '50s vintage Checker was parked next to the shack.

"Mister Whistler, nice to see you again, sah." The Goose rocked gently on its pontoons while the cabdriver helped Lourdes up onto the dock, glancing appreciatively down the front of the scoop-neck silk blouse she'd bought in Miami. He still had hold of her hand when Whistler whispered something in his ear. Clearly flustered, the man dropped her hand and hurriedly turned back to help the agent with their luggage.

"What did you tell him?" whispered Lourdes as they climbed into the back of the taxi.

"That you were a Drinker, not a Drink—he'd mistaken you for a fellow slave."

"That's not very flattering. And how did he know to meet us in the first place?" They had been planning a full day's layover in St. Thomas, but when the flight from Miami had arrived in time for them to connect with the last Goose to Santa Luz, they'd decided on the spur of the moment to make the hop that same night.

"Francis! Miss Lourdes wants to know how you happen to be here to met us." Whistler relayed the question down to the cabbie, who had started up to the parking lot with a suitcase in each hand, and one under each arm.

"Been meetin' de last Goose every night since Mister Whistler called Mister Prescott last week, Miss."

"Oh," said Lourdes, surprised. "That was . . . thoughtful of you."

"Nanny Eames'd have my balls for breakfas' if I didn't," was the reply. It was Lourdes's first encounter with a Luzan accent—*balls* rhymed with pals, and for a minute there she thought she'd heard him say Nanny Eames would have his bowels for breakfast. For all she knew, it was a local delicacy—Whistler hadn't told her much about the island during their three-stage journey, and she hadn't asked, not because she wasn't curious, but because she despised the role of Orphan. *Tell me, oh learned Master, of the lore of vampires; teach me to suck wisely, oh great Whistler.* Plus Whistler had a didactic streak as wide as the continent they'd just crossed.

The road that climbed up through the rainforest was what the Luzans called dundo track—no sky. All Lourdes could make out through the windshield was a tunnel carved through the blackness by the narrow beam from the Checker's single headlight: a wall of jungle suddenly appearing in that spotlight would signal a turn in the road; the tree trunks at each of these curves were blazed with livid bumper-high scars.

Suddenly the cab stopped in what appeared to be the middle of nowhere—no driveway, no visible structures, just a row of ghostly-white limbless trees that turned out to be the thick-walled arches of a portico that surrounded the Greathouse compound. A little spooked now, Lourdes followed Whistler into a danker, closer, stony-smelling darkness. They emerged into a courtyard enclosed on three sides by the porticoed stone wall and on the fourth by the front wall of the Greathouse, which was so obscured by vines and branches that a yellow light in an upstairs window seemed to be glowing in the depths of the forest.

With the sky shut out overhead, it felt to Lourdes as if they were under a great black dome, courtyard, mansion and all. Her feeling of uneasiness grew when she noticed that she and Whistler were now alone in the courtyard: Francis had disappeared suddenly, the way people disappear in dreams. Their footsteps crunched on gravel as they approached the Greathouse; a parrot screamed somewhere in the surrounding forest. They climbed wide cracked stone steps; Whistler pushed open a great mahogany door, and Lourdes followed him inside.

There was a torch burning in a sconce in the wall next to the door, but the smoky light it cast barely reached the far wall of the entranceway. Lourdes had a sense of a staircase rising somewhere to the left, of an open balcony over their heads, of a wide corridor stretching into the darkness ahead of them, and of an open space, wide as a ballroom, to their right. The mansion was a vast and stony darkness surrounding her: if ever in her life Lourdes had felt as though she were in a fairy tale—perhaps in the castle of the Beast—it was now.

Withdrawing an extinguished taper from a cement urn full of sand that stood against the wall, Whistler lit it from the torch, then led the way up the wide curving stone staircase. Lourdes followed close behind, as the darkness hurried after her trailing shadow, reclaiming the staircase step by step.

The second-floor balcony had only a low stone balustrade on the right; the door at the far end was open. Voices spilled out, and smoky light, and quadrille music, and then the black figure of a crone appeared in the doorway, illuminated from behind, light streaming out around her as if she were appearing at the end of a tunnel in a barely-remembered dream. Her skin was a dusty, faded shade of black that never saw the sun, her dress a black bombazine so old it had a verdigris patina in the flickering light of Whistler's taper.

"Look a' you, you're gettin' old, me son," she said, in a voice like the dry whisper of stone crumbling to powder.

"I do seem to be catching up to you, Nanny Eames." Whistler dunked the taper into another cement urn. "This is Lourdes, that I told Prescott about."

"De Drinker dot ain' been initiated?" She closed the door behind her.

"That's the one."

"An' why not?" The ruffles and furbelows along the old woman's dress front rustled as she folded her arms across her bony chest. "De Drinkers ain' have no customs on dot island?"

"California is an island without customs, Nanny Eames."

The old woman turned to Lourdes and addressed her directly for the first time. "How often do you drink blood, gyirl?" She had great full bags under her eyes, and the whites were so bloodshot they seemed nearly black in the dim balcony light.

"Every night—since I met Whistler, anyway."

"Drink tonight yet?"

"On St. Thomas, before we left. But I sure could use a little boost right about— What? Did I say something wrong?" For Nanny had turned her glare upon Whistler.

"No, gyirl." Nanny's voice had softened with pity. "But your mon here should have told you—you cyan' drink on dis island until after you been initiated." She reached behind her and opened the door a crack, but without taking those baleful old eyes off Whistler. "Prescott!" she called.

"Yes, Mama?" A deep rumbling voice from behind the door.

"Get some clothes on, an' show Miss Lourdes to de tower." She turned to Lourdes. "Me an' Whistler must have a tack, gyirl. I'll send him up to you soon." Her smile was so ancient that the lips no longer moved, and the isolated narrowing of the wrinkled old eyes was more disconcerting than reassuring.

Nor was Lourdes exactly crazy about that "take her to the tower" stuff, but she decided to play along—she knew perfectly well that Whistler still had a flask of blood in one of the many pockets of his Banana Republic safari jacket.

Prescott proved to be a handsome ebony-skinned man with contrasting gray hair of so tight a curl that it reminded Lourdes of an old Persian-lamb coat her mother had once owned; his shoulders were broad under a blue and gold dashiki. She followed him up a narrow circular stone staircase, neither of them speaking, and he showed her into a stucco-walled chamber in what seemed to be some sort of turret with a curved outer wall, where he left her.

The room was furnished with a queen-size foam pad under a mosquito net suspended from a hook in the stucco ceiling, a dozen fat home-made candles, and not much more—but at least their luggage had been piled against the near wall. She made up a makeshift bed by unrolling Whistler's new sleeping bag across the foam pad and spreading her own matching bag over it, then crossed to the deep-silled window in the curving outer wall and pushed open the green-painted shutters. And now that she thought about it, yes, the smell of the forest out there did indeed remind her of the mahogany forests of the Philippines.

She was still at the window with her back to the door when Whistler arrived a few minutes later. She would not turn to him, or even greet him, but waited until he had crossed the room and was at her side before turning to face him—and then it was only to pat his pockets for the flask of blood. "C'mon, let's have it."

He drew away. "Sorry, m'dear. I had to turn it over to Nanny. Island custom—Eldest Drinker controls the stash." He started to put his arms around her; she twisted away to face the window again. "Like it or not, Lourdes, we are on an island with a traditional vampire culture—"

"Great. Here comes another lecture." She'd addressed the forest.

"There are advantages—no one calls us addicts, or forces us to attend meetings or talk about our feelings. And we don't have to waste any time agonizing over our vampire natures: we know precisely what we are, and where we fit, and where our next blood is coming from, and when." Whistler stopped—he could not tell from the back of her head or the quality of the silence whether Lourdes was listening or not. But then, it was never truly silent in the rainforest.

"But there *is* a price," he went on. "There are rules that we must live by. Because if we don't—" He stopped again. "How shall I put this? In that room behind Nanny Eames there were a dozen vampires, and at least two dozen slaves and donors and families—the categories tend to overlap—and if she ever took it into her head that you or I were a threat to the established order of things, there's not a one of them, not even that handsome Prescott or that helpful Francis, who wouldn't slit your throat and catch the blood in his hat if she ordered it."

"Why didn't you tell me all this before we came?"

"Quite frankly, m'dear, I'd forgotten that particular rule—that one doesn't Drink on Santa Luz until one has been initiated. My fault entirely. I should have remembered—when I was here in '73 a vampire from the mainland kidnapped a local girl. The Drinkers rescued her and explained the customs to him, but it was another two weeks until the full moon—apparently he wasn't willing to wait, or leave."

"What happened to him?"

"He was eaten by tourists."

"What?"

"Well, indirectly. First they chummed him, then they trolled him, then they sold the shark they caught with him to one of the resorts. Consequently: eaten by tourists. But you won't have to wait two weeks—the full moon happens to be tomorrow night."

"And how the hell do we make it until then?"

What do you mean we, Whistler started to say, then thought better of it. If she fell asleep, he might join the others downstairs; if not, he decided, he'd stay with her. Greater love hath no vampire, etc. With an apologetic grin, he extracted a bag of rock cocaine from a zippered front pocket, handed it to her, then reached under the mosquito net for the bottle of Jack Daniel's they'd purchased at the duty-free shop on St. Thomas.

"Crack 'n' Jack, m'dear," he replied. "A combination that has seen many a stranded vampire through many a bloodless night."

"You can stick that up your own crack, Jack." She turned on him furiously, jaw pushed forward, almond eyes flashing. "Me, I'm going downstairs to have a little talk with Nanny Eames myself. Woman to woman, and you *ain't* invited."

Her courage almost failed her at Nanny Eames's door. She extinguished her taper in the sand bucket, took a deep breath, let it out, and rapped on the door rather more loudly than she'd intended.

"Yes?"

Prescott's voice. She remembered Whistler's words: *He'll slit your throat and catch your blood in his hat.* "It's Miss Lourdes," she called boldly. "I have to speak with Nanny Eames."

Lourdes had just a moment to regret her rashness before the door opened and Nanny emerged. This time the high neck of her black bombazine dress was askew, and for some reason she was wearing a stiff black bonnet fastened to her head with a wicked-looking hatpin. "Yes, chyile?"

Lourdes plunged right in. "I'm sorry to bother you again, Nanny Eames, but I had to tell you I'm just not gonna be able to make it through a whole night without blood. If you want me to leave the island, I'll leave, and if you want to feed me to the tourists, then go ahead and feed me to the tourists, but I've got to have some blood."

That disconcerting narrowing of the ruined old eyes again—another smile?—and then Nanny Eames leaned forward and gave her a quick peck on the cheek. Along with the dry powdery smell of old age, Lourdes caught another scent too: the distinctive whiff of sex, of sweat and semen and pussy juice smeared across those aged cheeks. Then, in that powdery whisper of a voice: "Wait here."

A few seconds later Prescott emerged from the room, in boxer shorts and a build that wouldn't quit, and brushed by her on his way up the stairs; he returned with Whistler, who shrugged a *beats-me* in Lourdes's direction before following Prescott into Nanny's room.

The next time the door opened—ages had passed for Lourdes, waiting in the darkened hall—the cabdriver Francis emerged, followed by a fully dressed Prescott carrying a flashlight, and Whistler. They filed down the wide front stairs, across the courtyard, through the gate in the dank-smelling portico, and out to the old Checker.

Lourdes and Whistler got into the back seat, and Prescott climbed into the front beside Francis. "Where are we—" Lourdes began; Prescott silenced her with his finger to his lips. She took Whistler's hand as Francis started up the taxi. At a wide spot in the road a few hundred yards past the Greathouse compound Francis wrestled the Checker through a five-point turn and got them headed back in the direction they had come.

They drove back down the dundo road in silence; in silence they rolled through the cobblestone streets of the Old Town, deserted save for the feral-looking dogs that owned the town at night.

Then they were at the docks again—Lourdes wondered if she were being deported, but the seaplane terminal was dark and deserted now, and they passed it anyway, to stop instead at perhaps the most dilapidated of all the dilapidated piers of the Old Town docks. There was only a single ship tied up at this pier, a three-masted native sloop. Two-and-a-half-masted, rather, for the mainmast was snapped off ten feet above the debris-strewn deck.

Dubiously she followed Whistler and Prescott down a rusting iron gangway—Francis stayed behind in the cab, his leather visor pulled stolidly down over his eyes. Prescott pointed toward the stern line on his way into the deck-level cabin. "T'row dot off when I shout to you," he told Whistler. "An' Miss Lourdes, if you'd do de same wit' de bow line when you hear de engine cyatch."

It was not a sound she was confident of ever hearing, but the engine must have been in better shape than the rest of the tub: the motor started up with a chuffing roar. She seized the thick rope, the hemp wet and coarse against her fingers; a moment later the black water was sliding by on either side of the blunt bow.

Lourdes turned back to watch the island falling away behind them, wondering if she had just cast off her own life along with that line, fighting panic. Were they going to throw her over the side? How well did she know any of them, even Whistler? One thing she did know about him— he had killed before.

But no, he loved her, she told herself. Besides, her period was at least a week late—she could always tell him she might be carrying his child. All the same, she found herself measuring the distance back to shore until Santa Luz dropped out of sight below the horizon—then she started looking around for a weapon of some sort.

Prescott shut down the engines and emerged from the cabin; Lourdes heard the splash of the anchor, and the hiss of the anchor cable playing out.

"Lourdes," Whistler called from the stern. She made her way aft, past the cabin, hiding a length of sawed-off iron pipe behind her back. But when she reached the stern, Prescott was sitting on an upturned bucket with his sleeve rolled up past his elbow, holding a straight razor to his wrist.

"Oh thank God," she said, dropping her weapon surreptitiously over the side, and coughing to cover the splash.

"God ain' have a t'ing to do wit' it, miss," Prescott replied in that ringing baritone of his. "It was Nanny Eames dot took pity on you." Suddenly he sliced down with the corner of the blade; black blood welled as he held his wrist up to Lourdes's lips. She drank greedily, and relinquished his arm reluctantly. With his other hand he pinched off the wound and started to offer it to Whistler.

Lourdes stopped him. "Oh, that won't be necessary, thank you, Prescott. Mr. Whistler doesn't need any blood."

"I *beg* your pardon?" said Whistler archly.

Her lips parted, then her teeth. "Crack 'n' Jack, Prescott—Mr. Whistler says that'll get a vampire through a bloodless night just fine."

Underfoot the ship was coming alive, boards creaking and sighing like an old woman as it rocked in the gentle swell; overhead the stars above the Caribbean were flat and round, shimmering in a sky so plush and black and velvet that it looked to Lourdes, in the first flush of a blood high, as if it ought to have a portrait of Elvis splashed across it, to be sold at a flea market.

TWO

Her bosom heaved. One plump breast protruded from the torn bodice; he seized it with his hard, work-roughened hand . . .

Nick laughed. It was three in the morning, and he'd caught his hacker. He was dummied on to the only terminal in use at the gene-splicing firm; he watched as the cursor darted back to the word *protruded,* and changed it to *sprang.* Nick used his security-officer override to take over the screen.

Not much better, he typed. *In the future, please obtain permission from your supervisor before using your work station for personal business. Believe me, you're not ready to give up your day job!*

He decided to give the secretary in Daly City a few minutes of privacy to save her work, and went into the bedroom to check on January. She looked heartbreakingly young, curled up on her side with her mouth open, one arm flung out carelessly so that the light of the full moon creeping in past the bedroom curtains glinted off the silver bracelet of the manacles chaining her to the bedpost.

The screen was blank when he returned to his office. He checked the user queue—NO STATIONS LOGGED ON—and signed off, then windowed over to his accounting program to cut the final bill; it had just popped out of the LaserJet when he heard January calling his name. "Be right with you."

"Hurry up—I have to pee, and the chain got all tangled up."

"On my way ..." He had the key to the cuffs out by the time he reached the bed; he unlocked her.

"Thanks." She gave him a peck on the cheek. "You know what, I don't think I need the cuffs anymore—I didn't have a single bad dream."

"If you feel you're ready."

But Nick was dubious: he thought back to the scene that had awaited him in the motel room out by the Oakland airport, where the boy from the mosh pit had brought January on their second date. When Nick arrived, she'd been watching TV, naked as a jaybird and blitzed on Wild Turkey and arterial blood. The boy was also naked, lying on his side next to her on the bed, and obviously far from dead—he was, in fact, struggling quite vigorously against the sheets that bound him. He could not speak, though—he was gagged securely with what appeared to be his own underpants.

It had been an accident, January had explained—a small artery in his foot where an artery had no business being, in her limited experience. "It was his own fault. He thought it was so kinky the last time, me drinking his blood. He goes, like, it really turned him on, and everything. I told him I didn't want to, but he got me drunk, and he just kept insisting, so finally I just said what the hell."

Nick had turned to the boy, who appeared to be in his mid-twenties. "Is that true?" he asked. The boy had nodded weakly.

She'd recognized her mistake as soon as the wound began spurting, January explained, but had shielded the boy from the sight of the wound with her body, intending to take a few sips—no sense wasting *all* that blood. But she'd forgotten how seductive it could be, this drinking from a spurting wound—you didn't even have to suck, just time your swallows.

After a few minutes he'd begun struggling, but she hardly noticed.

She found herself twisting around until she was on top of him, drinking from his foot, breasts pressed against his thighs, pressing him back against the bed with the strength of her legs, growing stronger as he grew weaker. It wasn't until he'd stopped struggling entirely that she realized there was a problem.

With vampiric strength, she'd been able to pinch off the wound easily enough then, but she was already so stoned on his hot blood that she couldn't tell whether he was alive or dead. She'd pulled the V.A. phone list from her wallet and dialed Beverly's number, but couldn't get past her machine. Nick's was the second number she'd tried.

But then the boy had regained consciousness and tried to call the police—hence his bound and gagged condition. "I'm so sorry, Nick," she concluded. "I tried so hard to stay clean."

Nick had hugged her, told her everything was going to be fine, and sent her into the bathroom to clean up as best she could.

As soon as she'd closed the door behind her, he drew the only chair in the room up to the side of the bed and leaned down until his face was only inches from the boy's. "So you wanted to call the police, did you?" Nick said confidentially. "And what were you going to tell them? That you'd taken this underage girl with severe mental and emotional problems to a motel? Oh, I know, she looks older. That's what the last fellow said at his sentencing hearing for statutory rape. Know what they're giving out for statch now? Well trust me, you don't want to know."

The boy was still now, listening. He was pale—might have lost as much as a few pints of blood—but other than that he'd be all right. Nick sat back in his chair, laced his hands behind his head, and sighed. "Son, all I can say is, you should thank your lucky stars you never got to make that phone call. Can I take your gag off now?"

The boy nodded—Nick pulled the gag over his head. "I swear to God, I didn't—"

"Shut up," said Nick, leaning forward to untie the sheets that bound the boy. "I think you're despicable, and if it wasn't for the fact that having to testify against you would set her back years in her therapy, I'd see your ass in jail. Now grab your clothes and get out of here. You've lost some blood—you might feel a little dizzy for a day or two—eat some liver—but other than that, you're luckier than you deserve to be."

The boy was gone by the time January emerged from the bathroom. Nick helped her gather her things, and while she dressed he bundled up the bloodstained bedding and knotted sheets. These they deposited in a dumpster near the Oakland Coliseum on their way back to Berkeley.

January had slept all day Sunday, while Nick phoned around to try and find another place for V.A. to meet. Finally he worked out a schedule with one of the senior centers in Berkeley: it was a much larger room than they needed, but as long as they were willing to pay a building monitor after nine, they could keep their Monday, Wednesday, Saturday schedule. He had debated how much to tell the others—after weighing all the factors, and all the respective anonymities involved, including Betty's pregnancy and his own part in it, he finally decided to inform them only that the minister had changed her mind about allowing them to meet in the church, inferring that she was nervous about hosting Victims Anonymous.

January's Sunday-night handcuffs were Nick's idea—he had quite a collection of S&M gear he'd never been able to bring himself to throw away—and although January had protested that she wouldn't need them, when he'd come up to check on her the next morning—he'd bedded down on the futon in the parlor—he could see that she hadn't slept, and when he freed her from the cuffs he could tell from the scratches around the lock that she had indeed tried to pick it.

But the meeting Monday night seemed to have done her a world of good. She told them all about her second slip. When she got to the part about smelling blood on Whistler's breath, she could feel the electricity in the room. But they had to wait until she was finished—having a roomful of people who had to listen to her until she had finished was one of recovery's major compensatory factors for January.

After her share, predictably enough, the meeting had erupted. Augie the attorney had defended Whistler on the grounds that the evidence against him was a little thin—after all, January had drunk blood the night before for the first time in a year: she might have imagined it. Beverly, on the other hand, was all for performing an intervention on Whistler then and there—except of course he was no longer there then, but out of town.

Nick sat out the debate, but not because he had any personal doubts that Whistler had been drinking blood—he was convinced of it. Furthermore, he was convinced that Whistler was behind Selene's depredations. Of course it was true: Selene had always been Whistler's creature. She still was, and he'd been a fool to believe otherwise. But he'd wanted to trust Whistler—they'd been friends for too long, and lovers of a sort, at least during orgies, when they were both still on blood. . . .

So he did his best to talk himself out of what he knew to be true in his heart. Anybody can slip, he told himself. Whistler had been overconfident, his program had been getting a little sloppy lately. So maybe he did slip—

but only that once. Selene might have been telling the truth about all the rest. It was certainly easier to accept that than to believe his old friend was trying to tear down the fellowship after all they'd been through together . . .

Yeah, and maybe Uncle Sam would climb out of his ass strumming "O Susanna" on the banjo. Nick had worked too hard at his recovery to pay much attention to his addict self when it spouted nonsense. So he'd listened dispiritedly to the rest of the discussion at the meeting, which ended the only way it could: when Whistler returned from his winter vacation they would confront him, during daylight hours, and offer him a choice between being tied to his bed, or voluntarily marching out into the sunlight.

That was one of the convenient things about interventions on backsliding vampires, Nick had explained to January on the way back home: drug tests were quite unnecessary.

And January, at least, seemed to be feeling much better after the meeting: she not only managed to fall asleep Monday night, but went off to work Tuesday morning. They had left it to her whether she would sleep at Nick's again Tuesday night or return to her residence hotel on Telegraph Avenue; she had called him from work to tell him she didn't think she was ready to be on her own yet.

Which meant one more night on the futon for Nick. But he'd planned to be up half the night monitoring the gene-splicers anyway, so it wasn't all that much of a hardship. Besides, he liked having her around. And he did not cuff her again when she returned from the bathroom early Wednesday morning—enough of a bond had formed between them in the past few days that he felt he could trust her.

Of course, I also thought I could trust Whistler, he mused on his way downstairs. The only thing that would appease his anger was the thought of being there when they intervened on his old buddy. *Better have the lock on those cuffs checked out,* he told himself. *Make sure January didn't damage them any. And that chain—going to need a stronger chain than that to hold the likes of Jamey Whistler.*

THREE

With smoking torches twisted from the hemp of the baobab tree, in simple red ceremonial robes of purest cotton from the J. C. Penney in the Island Center mall, the vampires of Santa Luz came for Lourdes at the roughly appointed hour, a few minutes after sunset on the night of the full moon.

There was no particular order to their procession: they shuffled up the steps of the turret and surrounded her when she emerged, jostling each other like a fighter's entourage parading to the ring as they accompanied her down to the courtyard. Looking down so as not to stumble, Lourdes saw a riot of bare feet and legs casting a forest of stalky shadows. The shirts were ankle-length for most of the women, knee-length for most of the men, mid-thigh for the tallest, a scarified African-looking man with stilt-walker legs. One size fit all, none well.

The courtyard at dusk had the soft green glow of a cavern, but darkness in these latitudes falls swiftly, and by the time the procession reached the old stone well in the center of the court, the only illumination came from the flickering torches. The courtyard had emptied except for the dozen or so vampires, ranging in age from Nanny Eames, the crone of untold years, to last month's initiate, a chubby mocha-colored lad of one-and-twenty. A young Luzan woman stood apart with a blanket-clad bundle in her arms.

The old well was constructed in two tiers, with the low, outer tier serving as a round stone bench; the vampires shuffled around it as if in a stately game of musical chairs, fitting the shafts of their torches into sconces set into the well before seating themselves. When only Nanny Eames of the vampires remained standing, the young woman handed over her bundle and took a few steps back. Nanny unwrapped the blankets enough for a little arm to protrude, and Lourdes's heart leapt: it was a baby, after all.

The ritual that followed was remarkably compact, as rituals go—Nanny kissed the sleeping baby, then with the next-oldest vampire assisting, she rubbed a salve from a clay jar across the crook of the tiny elbow, and inserted a hollow quill of some sort—it looked a little like a porcupine's, but tapered at both ends.

This was all done silently. It was not until the baby had been returned to its mother, and Nanny Eames was holding aloft a small hollowed-out gourd the size of a mogul-base lightbulb, that the old woman spoke. "Wit' dis blood," she announced, crooking a forefinger at Lourdes, then handing the gourd to her as she rose, "we now Awake de new Drinker." Then, sotto voce: "Only a sip, now."

Lourdes tilted the gourd to her lips. The blood was hot in her mouth, warm going down. Nanny took the gourd back, motioned Lourdes back to the bench, and offered the gourd to the vampire who'd assisted her in the drawing of the blood. He was a wizened old fellow, so short his red shirt brushed the flagstones when he arose again.

The old man took a slash, then positioned himself so that he was standing opposite Lourdes, less than an arm's length away. He gestured for her to stand up, and when she had done so—his face across from her reminded her of a wise old monkey in a storybook—he reached out, placing his right hand along the left side of her throat, where it met her shoulder, and his left hand, palm forward, between her breasts, against her heart.

Nanny Eames nodded to her, and Lourdes understood that she was to place her hands on the little old vampire's throat and breast in the same manner. Then Nanny whispered for her to stare into the man's left eye, and when the baby-blood began to take effect, she felt an arc of energy building between her partner and herself as they stared into each other's left eyes.

By the time he spoke the ritual sentence—"Blood make us one"— Lourdes was higher than she'd ever been before, so high that high was scarcely a suitable word: it seemed as if she and her partner were on one level, while the rest of the world had been lowered beneath them like an old-fashioned orchestra pit.

She could feel the great artery pulsing under one palm, feel his heart against the other, and she knew what to do, then. "Blood make us one." She returned the phrase in a husky whisper, and he repeated it back to her.

"Blood make us one." The words were becoming reality: she and the old vampire were indeed as close to being one as if they were a single soul in two bodies. It was the eternal truth, the goal of meditation, an acidlike ego-melt that lasted until their eyes unlocked, leaving Lourdes with a soul-deep love for a wrinkled old vampire sporting a shirt stretching erection that must surely have placed a strain on his elderly heart, a yearning feeling in her own youthful heart, and a savage need calling from her womb.

Blood make us one. A dozen times the ritual was repeated. Whistler drank next to last, then held the gourd for Nanny Eames. One by one the torches had burned down, until the courtyard was as black as it had been the previous night—the full moon that had signaled the feast was no more than a rumor, somewhere high above the forest canopy.

Blood make us one. In the dark the circle of Drinkers shuffled around Lourdes. She kissed each of them—and they kissed back. Deep, open-mouthed kisses. And such was the spell of the ceremony, of the heart-touching and the left-eye-staring and the baby-blood, that no one kiss, no one kisser, no one body, was any more or less arousing than any other, and there was not one of them she would not have opened her legs to, from Nanny Eames right on down to the chubby lad who held her breast as he kissed her, cupping it, weighing it in his palm as reverently as if it were soft gold and he were Scrooge McDuck.

Blood make us one. The orgy that followed, back inside the Greathouse, though circumspect enough by Whistler's mainland standards, was generally agreed upon afterwards by the Luzan vampires to have been the finest in years, owing largely to the energy and visual contrast provided by the two whites. Whistler was particularly proud of Lourdes, who evinced neither jealousy nor reticence, actively seeking out new partners and combinations and variations, and adding an unaccustomed vocal note to the carryings-on.

Eventually even the shyest of the slaves, a young girl named Josephina, had taken to vocalizing—she developed a distinctive, aspirated high-pitched rhythmic squeal of her own under Whistler's insistent pounding, and as she began to come, the skin between her budding breasts darkening to an eggplant purple, Whistler found himself howling with her, and his first orgasm of the night was so strong it felt as if his balls were being turned inside out.

Lourdes heard him from the depths of her own impending orgasm; in response she placed her hands on the back of a woolly ancient head between her thighs—whether it was the old man or Nanny Eames she could not have said at the moment—and pulled it snugly against her; when she finally started coming it was in a series of short, sharp, nearly unbearable spasms. At first she feared she'd never stop coming; after a few minutes the fear turned to hope.

FOUR

Whistler had never taken Selene along with him to Santa Luz. "That island's no place for a Drink," he informed her, and from what he had told her of the local customs, she was inclined to believe him. But she thought of him when she saw the full moon rising over the snow-capped mountains to the east of Lake Tahoe that night, and then of Lourdes, wondering how the baby-blood was treating her. Personally, Selene had no doubts whatsoever that the woman who could snare Jamey Whistler would take to the stuff like mother's milk.

Not that she couldn't have had him herself, back in the sixties, Selene mused, standing at the window of her room at Whistler Manor, looking out over the grove of Jeffrey pines that shielded the manor from the highway. They'd even gone so far as to plan out one of those hippie-dippie Haight-Ashbury weddings in Golden Gate Park, with Steve Gaskin or Sufi Sam Lewis presiding.

But that would have meant giving up her witchly ambitions: her Coven followed the tradition of Dianic cults—no men allowed, and no married woman could serve as First Among Equals.

There was no rule against living with somebody, though, so when the High Priestess died and Selene succeeded to her place in the Cyrkle, she'd taken advantage of the technicality to remain Whistler's lover, and used her position to strengthen the bonds between the Coven and the Penang.

Which is why, after the disaster with Nick, there were others—not in her Coven, true, but priestesses in other covens—who blamed her for her own and Mandy's misfortune. Selene had gotten much too cozy with the vampires, they whispered, and allowed her coven to grow far too dependent upon them. Selene should have known better than to mix sex and recreational drugs with witchcraft, they also whispered—after all, that had been the downfall of Magister Cochrane for sure, and possibly Aleister Crowley as well.

And during the months of silence while her throat wounds healed, Selene began to think that perhaps they were right, at least about sex and drugs at her level of practice.

So she had refused Whistler's offer of plastic surgery for her disfigurement, and at Midsummer—the summer solstice—had taken a five-year vow of abstinence and celibacy. For the first year or so, every time she felt sexual stirrings all she had to do was run her fingers over the livid scars, and the feelings would pass. And then after a few years she found herself barely noticing the stirrings; her scars, though, had become old friends; she used them as allies, for strength.

A gust of wind shivered a high snow-laden bough and sent a curtain of shimmering powder cascading past her window in the moonlight. Selene started; instinctively her fingers went to her throat. In six months, she reminded herself, the five years of her vow would be up; she decided to use that as her timetable.

"By the summer solstice, then," she vowed to the full moon. "It will be done by Midsummer."

Nearly midnight: time to throw the runes again. She closed the window and retrieved her goat-bladder rune bag and the vampires' green notebook from her altar. Back in bed—an early American four-poster—she spread her feet wide under the covers, smoothed the quilt flat, then spilled the ivory tiles out across the blue-and-white-checked counterpane valley between her legs.

The bones had nothing to say to her on the first throw. Selene sighed and pulled her nightgown over her head, scooped the tiles up and warmed them between her palms before pouring them back into the sack; then she threw them again, naked as the bones themselves this time.

That did the trick. The tiles clacked and rolled and came to rest. She read them, gathered them, rolled them again. The message was clear enough: she thanked the runes, gathered up the bones, and poured them back into the goat bladder, tying up the neck of the bag with a thong made from the vocal cords of the same goat.

Selene's altar was set up in the northeast corner of the room—it was a wicker cabinet from Pier 1, draped with black damask, that held her paraphernalia, her hand-copied Book of Shadows, and her spells, which she'd copied onto index cards like recipes.

Squatting naked before it, Selene replaced the bag of rune stones, retrieved her athame (the ritual Wiccan dagger), lit the black candle on a saucer atop the altar, and with the athame carved four pentacles into the air around her, one for each of the four directions, to begin the process known as Drawing Down the Moon. This would invoke in her the qualities of the Goddess—only in Her aspect could the High Priestess convene a full meeting of the Coven.

ONE

Sherman ended the meeting of Vampires Anonymous the next Saturday by reminding them all that it was the night of the winter solstice, and warning them about what the psychologists were just beginning to refer to as S.A.D.—Seasonal Affective Disorder. "So if you find yourself feeling a little more down than usual, try turning on some bright lights, sunlamps, get some UV rays."

"Or P.V. Rays," suggested Henderson, the lanky musician.

"What's that?"

"Puerto Vallarta. That's where I'll be spending next week."

"That'll work too. Now is there any other business to take care of before the closing prayer? Nick?"

"Just a change for the phone tree. January's going to be staying with me for a while, so you can reach either of us at my number."

After the closing prayer, the others crowded around Nick and January at the coffee urn in the back of the room. "And will congratulations be in order?" asked Toshi.

"How about catering?" was Cheese Louise's question.

"Come on you guys," January protested, flattered at the attention. "I told you in my share I lost my job." Despite the fact that there was nothing romantic going on between them—or at least nothing sexual—January found herself blushing anyway. "And it's just, I mean, I can live on the streets, I done it before, but not without using. And nights are still real hard for me, you know?"

"No, no, congratulations are in order, I believe," Sherman interrupted her. "Unless you slipped again during the week, tonight's your one-week anniversary."

January seemed pleased. "I didn't think about it like that."

"Not only that, almost anybody who's ever slipped will tell you that in some ways, the *second* first week is even harder than the first first week, so you should be doubly congratulated." He then led the informal gathering in a round of applause, after which Nick invited everybody over to Fat Apple's for a celebration.

Sherman had to beg off, though, reminding Nick that Catherine was expecting him at home. This had come as something of a surprise, he'd explained during his share: she'd gone up to Tahoe on Friday night to spend Yule with the Coven, so he hadn't expected her back until late Sunday at the earliest. But then she'd called him a little after seven to say that she needed to talk to him, and that she was on her way home and would be arriving around eleven, traffic and weather permitting.

He had been obsessing about it ever since, he'd reported, and was dealing with it pretty well on a cognitive level: he'd performed a regression on himself during the drive over from Mill Valley, and traced the fear as far back as his mother telling a naughty three-year-old Sherman that she had called his father at the office to tell him about the crayoning of the walls of the dining room, and that said father would be having a "talk" with him that night.

He could have traced the fear back further—to the womb, no doubt, if the drive from Marin to the East Bay had taken a little longer—but it didn't matter, he'd explained to the meeting: the purpose of the regression had been to remind himself that fears of the future were almost always rooted in the past.

All of which self-knowledge was worth absolutely diddly—by the time he was halfway home he'd pretty much convinced himself that this was *it*: Catherine was going to tell him that it was all over, that she was leaving him now. Maybe that's what she'd been building up to all these months, maybe the other witches had finally talked her into it. . . .

Didn't matter. What got him through the rest of the drive was the understanding that if this was the kiss-off, he was going to have to talk about it in his men's group next week: he wanted to be able to tell them that he hadn't wussed out, that he'd marched up to the scaffold with his head high and at the very end had refused the blindfold.

But maybe a last cigarette if there's time, he told himself. Only there wasn't time:

Catherine's car was in the driveway. She'd beaten him home and was waiting for him in the living room, and the only difference he could see in her, apart from the stubborn set of her jaw, was the color of her hair.

For Catherine Roark Bailey, Registered Dietician for the City of Berkeley, chartered Witch, recovering Sex-and-Love addict, and black-belt Codependent, had been born the only brunette in a family of third-generation Mission Irish redheads. But when her hair had gone white in her early twenties, she'd turned to the bottle for the color that should have been hers by birthright, and over the years Sherman had seen her in every shade of red from Burgundy to Mahogany to Manic Panic.

When she'd left for the mountains yesterday she'd been Paprika, with a little Cinnamon thrown in for highlights. But all the spices of the Orient could not have produced the hue that adorned the curls of her new perm tonight. "Do you like it?" she asked him.

"I Love Lucy?" he said carefully.

"You've got an eye, Sherm, I'll give you that." It was genuine Egyptian henna, she explained. "I've been trying for this shade for years, but they stopped exporting it in the sixties, except for Lucy, because Nasser was a fan. Selene got me a bag through an herbalist she works with—we did it this morning."

"And then you rushed right back here to show me?" said Sherman hopefully.

"Fat chance, Bailey. Why don't you start a fire, and I'll go make us some tea, and then we'll have our little talk."

"I don't think I could stand—" he began.

She cut him off. "Fire, tea, talk."

A box of foot-long matches stood propped against the Amish hearth broom; from a wrought-iron rack hung a gleaming brass-tipped set of tongs and shovel and pokers—gleaming because they'd never been used. Sherman lit the Duraflame log and watched the paper cover flare up, gas blue at first, then a comfortable yellow. "There," he said, rubbing his hands together like Bob Cratchit, though in fact it was only a mild fifty degrees or so on the other side of the floor-to-ceiling picture window.

Sherman sat down on the white sectional, looking past their white-flocked dwarf Christmas tree to the heavily wooded hillside to the east. When Catherine returned with the tea tray he cleared a place on the glass-topped coffee table, and she sat down next to him. "Thank you for the fire," she said.

"Thank you for the tea," he replied.

"Thank You Falettin Me . . ."

"... Be Mice Elf Again. Sly and the Family Stone, 1970."

"Very good. Now can we get on with it, please?"

"Hey, you're the one who started the rock trivia."

"I'm sorry, Sherman. I guess I'm a little nervous too. But let's not fight. Tonight of all nights, let's not fight."

"But I don't even know what it's all about—and don't say *Alfie*."

"All right, I won't. It's about us, Sherman."

And there it was. He took a sip of tea—Earl Gray—she'd fixed it with cream and honey, just the way he liked it. "I thought it might be."

"Good. I was hoping you'd be thinking about it—that's why I called you first. I wanted you thinking about it good and hard, because I have a question for you, and I want you to give me the right answer the first time. Ready?"

" 'Ready when you are, C.B.' " he said bravely, thinking of his men's group again—boy, were they going to be proud of him.

She smiled in spite of herself. "Which do you love more, me or your sobriety?"

Sherman was pretty good at contacting his inner child—at moments like this it seemed to take over his face. His chubby cheeks plumped out like they'd just been slapped, and his walrus mustache quivered as if pasted on. "Jesus, baby, that's cold. How can you even—"

She stopped him with a gently upraised palm. "Is that your answer? Remember, I want the right answer the first time."

"Do you want the truth?"

"No," she replied, to his astonishment—and relief. "You don't even know the truth. What I want is the *right* answer."

"But—"

She interrupted him again. "I know what you're about to say, and I know all about situational ethics—I haven't been married to a shrink for twenty years for nothing. But just think hard: we're not in a meeting, so we don't need the right answer for a meeting. It's just you and your wife, and the right answer is the one that won't send me walking out that door. Now which is it, me or your sobriety?"

He stood up from the couch. "You don't have to leave, Catherine. Just let me pack up a few things. I guess I can stay with—"

He found himself yanked back down to the couch. "Shut up and sit down, you asshole. I was only bluffing."

"Fine," he replied. And it *was* fine: that one moment on his feet had made all the difference. Whatever was coming now, Sherman was ready for it.

"I can see I'm going to have to do this the hard way." She took both his hands in hers. "Do you know what tonight is?"

He made a puzzled face. "Sure. It's the winter solstice—Yule, you call it."

"Okay, rock trivia: what's the opening line of Sergeant Pepper?"

" 'It was twenty—' " His eyes widened behind the thick lenses of his wire-rimmed glasses. "Oh Cathy, it was twenty years ago today."

Catherine didn't bother to rub it in—her slow sad nod, her raised eyebrows and tolerant smile said it all: *Yes, darling, that's the sort of anniversary a man will seldom remember, and a woman will never forget.* "The night of my second initiation into Wicca—the Quest Perilous. Before then I'd been in the Outer Court, but I'd never been at a Yule with the vampires."

"It was down in Santa Cruz, right?"

"Close. Now hush, I'm going to tell you a story. But yes, this was before Whistler bought the Tahoe place—the house in Bolinas wasn't big enough for the Coven and the Penang both, so he rented two big old side-by-side houses. Only it wasn't Santa Cruz, it was Capitola. Or maybe Soquel. Anyway, the witches' house had about a dozen rooms and a trellised-in back porch, and to get to the beach you just walked out the back door and down the steps."

Catherine let herself slump down on the couch. When she was satisfactorily settled on the small of her back, she closed her eyes, and as she began to talk about the ceremony—a first, an astonishing first: never before had she so much as hinted at what took place in a Wicca ritual—Sherman noticed the hair on his forearms crackling to attention. An old bartender had told him about the phenomenon years before: *Sometimes people tell you the good stuff, and sometimes they tell you the true stuff, but rarely is the good stuff true, or the true stuff good: when it's both, the hair on your arms stands up.*

It was a particularly useful tip for a furry therapist such as Sherman—he found himself bristling all over like the hedgehog prince in the fairy tale as Catherine described the beach at sunset on Yule's eve, how the twelve other women formed a circle around her, stripping her, Selene administering the fivefold kiss; how they slid the forest green robe over her head.

She remembered it all: the satiny feel of the gown sliding down her body, the steely sky, the sun melting into a cold crimson puddle at the horizon, how she'd started trembling (not from the cold—it was a mild December evening even on the beach; more like the cell-deep shivers that sometimes accompany the second hour of an acid trip) as Selene raised her athame and cut the pentacle gate to the other world.

Catherine stopped there. No sense telling him the incantations, naming the Great Ones—she'd already told Sherman more than she should have. He knew it, too, and it frightened him a little. He couldn't take his eyes off her face—she had a sweet round Irish milkmaid's face, and her eyes were green as moss.

"After the initiation I was sent back to my room to meditate, and throw the runes. Eventually Selene came around with the athame and the bowl. I remember the bowl sitting on the calico comforter, the slow tipping sound of the blood dripping—she only nicked me ever so lightly—the most uncomfortable part was holding my wrist over the bowl for so long. Tip, tip, tip. The blood was darker than red. We talked about the vampires while it fell.

"I hadn't seen any of them yet—I'd only learned about them for sure the night before the initiation. I'd have been more shocked, but I'd pieced together some idea out of bits of overheard conversations, things like that. Anyway, I was sort of nervous—talk about your blind date!

"But Selene said she knew from my runes that I was going to fall in love with one of the vampires, and not only that, she knew exactly which one—but wouldn't tell me. Anybody else, you'd think that was bullshit, but with Selene you never knew.

"After that, naturally, I was dying of curiosity—I couldn't *wait* until midnight. And then, of course, all I ended up getting to see of them was their dicks.

"It didn't matter, though—the senior witches brought them in one at a time in dark red robes with holes cut out for their mouths and their dicks—" She closed her eyes, as if she could see them still. "—and they drank the blood and their dicks got hard, and along about the fourth or fifth dick—it wasn't the biggest one, but it was thick like a root, and ginger colored, and, I don't know, just . . . *cute* somehow, and zing went the strings of my heart.

"And at that exact moment I look up, and there's Selene watching me, her little face just grinning from ear to ear—she looked more like an elf than a witch—you could just *picture* the pointy ears under that green hood."

Sherman was blushing pink—not the fine red of a blood flush but a rubber-ball pink. She sat up, opened her eyes, and turned to face him. He found himself forgetting to breathe—it was the suspended feeling you get *during* the earthquake, now that she was talking to him directly again.

"After that it was like in a fairy tale: 'and so it came to pass.' We found each other at the Yule orgy the next night, and it was all my sexual fantasies come true: I loved teddy-bear men, and this was a teddy-bear man with a hard-on that wouldn't quit. There's one particular time from that night I still remember. It wasn't the biggest orgasm, it wasn't a screamer or anything—we'd been in the middle of a pretty intense cluster-fuck, when all of a sudden we looked at each other and without saying a word we knew we wanted to be alone together, and we went up to my room and locked the door and I lay down on my back and opened my legs and you dove into me, do you remember?"

"How could I forget?" He'd been on top of her and in her, but curled up like a pinchbug and slightly turned to the side so he could suckle at her breast while she moved dreamily beside him, underneath him, in a gentle wavelike lapping motion. They had gone on for hours: every so often he would reach for his razor-stropped pocketknife on the bedside table and nick at a vein, and together they would feel him swelling inside her, and then perhaps he'd piston into her for a few minutes—one of them might come, or both—and then they'd subside into their gently rocking, suckling trance.

"Okay. I gave you my blood, and you gave me what I needed, and in between we fell in love. And we went on like that for all those years, and sometimes it got weird, but the sex never let us down, did it? And if that's codependence, then so be it."

She turned away from him and stared at the Christmas tree for a minute; when she closed her eyes again she saw a cone of black dots behind her eyelids. "But then I went away for Candlemas five years ago, and when I came back you didn't want my blood anymore—you'd gone into recovery. So I went into recovery, and *that*—if you really think about it instead of letting the program think for you—is the biggest codependency of all: giving up your codependency for somebody else."

"How long have you felt this way?"

"In my heart of hearts? Always, I guess. Or at least—well, one of my first codependent exercises was to find myself a still quiet moment once a day—just after you wake up, just before you fall asleep is also cool—and ask myself, 'What do I really want?' Or better, 'What does Cathy really want?'

"But I had to give it up, because every time, what Cathy really wanted was blood-sex, and that simply wasn't an acceptable recovering codependent thing to want."

"So it's the sex? But you always said that our lovemaking had been so much more *real* since we went into recovery together."

"I'm a co, remember? What did you expect me to say?"

"But something must have triggered this off—you didn't just leave the Coven in the—" He stopped, alerted by something in the way she'd turned away, the way she'd chosen that moment to take a bite of Christmas cookie, then her first sip of tea. "Wait a minute, does this have something to do with the Coven?"

"I'm not supposed to talk about that."

He put his hand on the wrist of the hand that held her teacup, and guided it down to the table, then brought his face near enough to hers that he could smell her sweet vanilla Christmas cookie crumb breath. "It's too late for that now, and the stakes are too high. You've got to tell me what's going on, Cathy. After twenty years you owe me that."

She put her hand on his knee. "Wait here."

He followed her with his eyes as she left the living room; he heard her steps on the stairs; overhead he heard the shriek of the chronically untracked sliding closet door in the bedroom opening, closing. In the silence that followed, he found himself focusing on his reflection in the dark picture window; he imagined his eyes flushing blood red—then Catherine's reflection appeared behind him in the glass, in her diaphanous black Victoria's Secret nightgown with her right hand held behind her back.

She crossed the room and sat next to him, leaned into him with her breast pressed unsubtly against his arm, and produced from behind her back his trusty pocketknife. At the sight of it his eyes welled with tears. "I thought you'd thrown it away."

"You asked me to," she said. "I couldn't. Now listen to me, and if you love me don't ask me any questions. Will you do that for me?" Eyeball to eyeball. He nodded. "Okay then. Vampires Anonymous is going down." He started to protest—she placed her finger across his lips. "Now you promised, right? No questions?"

He nodded again, and she pulled her finger away. "I'm not saying your V.A. was a good thing or a bad thing—I do know you're lucky to have had it for a while. At least you got to talk about your issues sometimes without using euphemisms. But how about me? Can you imagine what it's like to try and talk about blood-sex at an S.L.A. meeting, trying to tell people what it was like and you know even before the words have left your mouth that they'll never have a *clue*."

She leaned closer as she spoke, until their foreheads were touching. "Or sharing at a CODA meeting—some poor woman is beating herself up cause she bought her husband a lousy six-pack, and I want to tell her, 'You think *that's* enabling? Practically every night for fifteen years, I opened a vein for *my* man. And if he'd only ask me, I'd do it again tonight.' "

She handed him the knife—to his surprise, he took it. "But that's all water under the bridge now. You're just going to have to believe me: the last recovering vampire will be drinking blood by the summer solstice. This *will* happen, Sherman—your only choice in the matter is whether you'll be that last recovering vampire or not. But let me warn you: if you are, I'll have left you long before that. You won't have me, and you won't have your precious sobriety either."

He looked down at the blade in his hand, but what he was seeing in his mind's eye was a glass snack bowl with about a quarter of an inch of blood in the bottom. Floating in the blood were a few left-over pretzel crumbs, rapidly staining red.

Sherman reached out for his wife's hand, and turned it palm up. "Do you think my knife's still sharp enough?" he asked her. Sherman was not, as he might have put it, entirely in touch with his feelings at this particular moment, elation and terror in equal parts forming an alloy difficult to assay.

Catherine, on the other hand, felt a sense of triumph and satisfaction so absolutely piercing that she could feel her sex growing moist. "If it ain't, lover," she purred, "you can hone it on my nipples, 'cause I guarantee you they're hard enough."

TWO

Whistler awoke at sunset to a faint popcorn sound: *Pop. Pop. Pop-pop. Pop-pop-pop. Popopopopopopopop* . . . On his back on the foam pallet, eyes closed, he sniffed the air. Ozone. He allowed himself a smile: he'd forgotten the sound of the rain on the forest canopy.

He listened as the storm passed overhead. When the popping slowed to two or three seconds between pops—the point at which, if it *were* popcorn, it would be time to take it out of the microwave—he sat up, taking care not to disturb Lourdes, who was snoring beside him. Whistler unzipped his sleeping bag, ducked out from under the mosquito net, stood up, pushed aside the wooden shutters, and reached out to catch in his palm the first clear drops of rain to filter through the canopy.

A rap at the door. "Just a moment." Whistler pulled a pair of jeans out of an open suitcase, slid them on without underwear, and crossed the room barefoot as a beachcomber. The door was massive and mahogany, as were all the doors in the Greathouse; when he turned the brass knob and yanked, it resisted him. Whistler, unaccustomed to doing anything physically strenuous before he'd had a little eye-opener, yanked harder; the door swung open—it was his old nanny.

"Merry Christmas, me son."

"Merry Christmas, Nanny Eames."

"Sleep well?"

He nodded. "The rain awakened me. I'd forgotten what a lovely sound it makes up there."

"You t'irsty now?"

"Do with a little pick-me-up."

"Wack wit' me, den."

He followed her down the winding staircase to the second floor, and along the balcony until they reached her room. She reminded him of a Gorey illustration—the funereal dress, the hovering, gliding walk that never left the floor but never quite seemed to touch it, either.

The room was empty, the couches pushed back against the walls, the cushions stacked in the corner, the massive black-canopied four-poster bed made up tidily—no orgy had raged Christmas Eve, only a circumspect threesome: Whistler, Lourdes, and Nanny Eames, and of course a carefully staggered succession of Drinks.

Nanny pushed aside the mosquito net around the bed, and waved Whistler on ahead of her. "Buoy or gyirl?" she asked, as he helped her up onto the bed.

"A girl, I think."

She reached through the mosquito net, and from the bedside table (which was something of a curiosity—a massive section of the trunk of an elephant-leg tree, hollowed out and overturned) she seized a hand-wrought iron bell and gave it two brisk clanks. A moment later a Luzan girl of about sixteen, dressed in a thin white cotton shift, with her nappy hair twisted into twin red-ribboned pigtails, was standing at the footboard.

It was Josephina; at a wordless signal from Nanny, she slid quietly around to Whistler's side of the bed and stepped through the netting. With a razor-edged utility knife that had been concealed in her left hand, she opened a lengthwise quarter-inch slit in a wormlike vein on the back of her right hand without wincing, presenting it to Whistler with her eyes turned down. He sucked for a minute or two, then relinquished the little brown hand—the skin was dry, the knuckles nearly black—with a lingering kiss that was both gentlemanly and lascivious at the same time. Josephina kept her head respectfully inclined, but the tip of her tongue darted in and out of sight, quick as a fat pink lizard.

Then she curtseyed and backed across the room, her left hand pressed against her right to stanch the wound. Whistler followed her with his eyes. When the door had shut behind her he lay back on the bed and closed his eyes. "Ah, that's much better."

Nanny Eames sat propped up against the headboard on several black-slipped pillows. "T'anks for de . . . how do you call dot t'ing?"

"It's a camera, Nanny."

"I know dot, rubbledehux." She rapped him on the side of the head with her knuckles. "What kyine?"

"Oh, it's a Polaroid."

She had taken one of the snaps from last night out from under her pillow—she examined it, shaking her head, then passed it to Whistler. "Dot's a ooool woman in dot picture, me son."

"Yes, but look how you've got the whole thing in your mouth, Nanny. And your position there? Why, I know women a quarter your age who aren't that supple."

She tilted her ancient head coquettishly. "You t'ink so?"

"Obsolutely," he said in dialect.

She laughed. "Now you be tackin' Luzan, Whistler. But Prescott say you gon' to leave de island nex' week."

Whistler nodded. "Spend Christmas here, New Year's in Tahoe, finish up some business over the winter, then spring in Greece."

"Will you let de chyile be bahn deh?"

Whistler's long jaw fell. "The what?"

"De chyile. She ain' tell you yet?"

Whistler could only shake his head.

Nanny shrugged, and her black dress made that whispering noise again. "Maybe she ain' know herself."

"Please, Nanny. It's too early in the evening for riddles."

"Your Lourdes, me son. She's wit' chyile."

Suddenly Whistler found himself wishing that Josephina had not left the room—lord lord lord, but he could have stood another Drink. "Are you telling me I'm going to be a father?"

Nanny Eames's laughter was as dry and whispery as the rustle of her black bombazine. "Only *she* can tell you if you be dot." She patted him on the thigh. "But probably so—she love you a bit."

"And I love her a bit as well," he said wonderingly. "But how did you know she was pregnant?"

Nanny smiled—she still had all her teeth. "Me *only* been tastin' her tun-tun juice since de second night she arrive, me son."

THREE

"Thank you *so* much for giving up your Christmas to help us out, Lou."

"My pleasure." Cheese Louise picked up the box of cooking utensils, garnishing tools, and sauces and spices she'd brought over with her for the Christmas dinner at the North Berkeley Senior Center, and followed Catherine out of the kitchen. They were both wearing jeans and soiled white chef's jackets. "To tell you the truth, I didn't exactly have a big evening planned."

"Could I get one more favor from you? I have to check that all the rooms are empty before I lock up—would you mind coming with me. It's always a little nervous-making, especially after one of these homeless feeds."

"Sure. Just a sec." She set down the box by the back door, and picked out a fearsome-looking cleaver. "Lead on."

Catherine took them up the back stairs, explaining that the elevator was a little too dangerous at night. "I hate this feeling of being helpless," she confided over her shoulder to Louise. "It's one of the only things I hate about being a woman." When there was no response she tried another cast. "It's also one of the things I used to envy you for, when you were still a vampire."

"I'm still a vampire," replied Louise. "I'm just in recovery."

"When you were using, then. How nobody could fuck with you."

They had reached the top of the stairs; Louise was breathing heavily. "Girl, do I ever remember!" She followed Catherine down the corridor, cleaver raised. "I was just talking about that at a meeting a few weeks ago—hey, has Sherman been blabbing about our shares in meetings?"

Catherine turned back. "Of course not. I was just remembering that time those guys tried to crash Augie's New Year's Eve party."

"That was fun, wasn't it?"

"The expression on the big one's face when you decked him? Priceless."

The second floor was clear; they checked out the front stairs, then the downstairs rooms, and returned to the back hallway, where Louise shouldered her box of tools again while Catherine punched in the code to arm the security system, then hurried them out the rear exit.

"This is the most dangerous part of the whole trip," Catherine remarked, surveying the unlighted parking lot.

"Cover me," said Louise dryly, handing Catherine the box while she searched her purse for her car keys. But they made it to the *Cheese Louise* van without incident; Catherine stowed the box in the back, remarking pointedly that the rear doors hadn't been locked.

"Nothing to steal anyway," Louise replied, turning on the engine and pulling onto Bonita. She'd gone about a block when she felt something cold and hard and metallic pressing against the little bump at the back of her shorn skull.

"Don't move, don't talk, don't turn around." It was a man's voice, a hoarse disguised whisper. She couldn't see his ski mask, but she could smell the wool. "And if your eyeballs so much as glance toward that mirror, I'll blow them all over the windshield."

"Who—?" Catherine's question was cut short by a blow—or at least by the sound of a blow, and the crack of her head against the passenger side window.

"You too, bitch. You so much as twitch, your girlfriend's one dead dyke." He jabbed the gun a little harder against Louise's head. "Just drive—I'll tell you where."

The gunman did not speak again, except to whisper monosyllabic directions—left, right, slow, here—that led them to a fire road deep in Wildcat Canyon east of El Cerrito, where Louise and Catherine were blindfolded and gagged, forced out of the van, hog-tied with a new-smelling rope while standing face to face, then pushed over into the damp grass.

He had left the motor running; it was all Louise could hear as she lay on her side on the cold ground. *Needs a tune-up,* she thought irrelevantly. At least she wouldn't be able to hear the sound when he cocked the pistol for the coup de grâce she just knew was coming. She wondered if it would hurt, a bullet through the brain, and decided probably not.

But then the car door slammed and the pitch of the engine changed from a rough idle to a deeper-throated low gear; she heard brush crackling and ground cover crunching—the van seemed to be turning around—and then the engine sounds receded. Louise held her breath—she could hear Catherine's breathing directly in front of her, felt Catherine's chin moving, then a spray of wetness as the other woman spat out her gag.

"Sorry," Catherine whispered. Then Louise felt the other woman's teeth closing around her own gag, pulling it away from her mouth, working it down her chin.

"Christ. Thanks. I thought we were dead."

"He still might come back," Catherine replied. "Why else would he have tied us up like this? Listen, we've got to hurry. Bend your face down, let me try to loosen your blindfold with my teeth."

A moment later Louise was blinking directly into Catherine's mouth; not long after that they were staring into each other's faces. "You're bleeding," said Louise. "Your forehead's bleeding."

"I know. He hit me with the barrel of the gun. Hurts like hell." Catherine waited a few seconds for Louise to come to the obvious conclusion. But it was cold out there, colder than she'd expected—she decided a hint was in order. "You know what you have to do, don't you?"

"Four years, three months, and two days," said Louise dully.

Catherine understood the reference. "Would you rather end your sobriety by drinking blood, or by dying?"

"Good point." Louise raised her head, and Catherine lowered hers—there was a surprisingly neat wound at her left temple, just at the hairline. Louise began sucking, but there wasn't enough blood at first—she opened the lips of the wound a little wider with her own lips, then nipped at it with her teeth.

"Hey, that hurts," Catherine protested.

"Shhh."

When Louise began sucking, it was all that Catherine could do not to squirm erotically—she could feel Louise's massive softness pressing against her; as her eyes grew accustomed to the dark, with her own chin at her chest she could see the blood flush creeping up above the neck of Louise's moon white chef's jacket.

A moment later they were free—Louise had snapped the rope as if it were dental floss—and running through the woods, Louise leading the way with her superior night vision, pulling Catherine along by the hand. Suddenly she stopped. "Wait a minute," she said, no longer whispering, not short of breath in the least. "What the fuck are we running away for? Let's wait and see if the son of a bitch does come back—I'll shove that gun so far up his ass we'll need tongs to pull the trigger."

Catherine drew close to her. "I'm cold, Louise," she whispered. "And I'm scared, and I'm not a vampire."

Louise put her arms around her. "Don't worry, kiddo, I'll take care of the both of us."

The big woman's body was pulsing warm—Catherine leaned closer to her. "I feel safer now," she said.

Louise swiped her forefinger against the other woman's bleeding wound, then licked the finger clean. "Maybe you shouldn't," she whispered. "I mean, you're alone in the woods with a vampire."

"I'm not afraid of vampires," Catherine whispered in return. Then she rubbed her own hand against her wound until the palm was smeared with blood, and brought it to Louise's mouth. "Hell, I married one."

FOUR

There wasn't a great deal of traffic at the Lake Tahoe airport on the last night of 1991, either air or vehicular. Whistler's charter was waved directly to the terminal, and his party met at the curb by a stretch limousine—there wouldn't have been room in the Jaguar for both him and Lourdes, along with Josephina and the twins (her younger siblings, brother and sister), as well as Nanny Parish, the midwife Nanny Eames had insisted on sending along with them, and Plum Rose, the midwife's three-month-old baby.

Selene met the limo at the front door of Whistler Manor. Barefoot, her long hair falling loosely around her shoulders to the shawl she'd pulled over her long white nightgown, carrying a jangling iron ring of keys, she reminded Whistler of Esther in *Bleak House.* "Happy New Year, Dame Durden!" he cried, holding out his arms for a hug. "Is the north wing open? As you can see, I've brought along a few friends."

"Who are currently freezing their tropical asses off," pointed out Lourdes.

Selene hurriedly ushered the little party inside and led them down the hall to warm up in the keeping room, where a fire blazed in a hearth large enough to roast a full-sized St. Bernard—standing up. Half an hour later, after the Drinks had been warmed sufficiently with hot cocoa, she showed them to their rooms in the north wing, and installed Nanny

Parish and Plum Rose in the maid's room that adjoined the master bedroom in the south wing.

When she returned to the keeping room, Whistler and Lourdes presented Selene with her Christmas present, a virtual pharmacopoeia of Virgin Island roots and herbs, grasses and mushrooms from the Weed Woman who served the vampires of Santa Luz. Piaba and ton-ton, powdered gully root and dried psilocybin, cowback, mandrake, and of course the famous Granny scratch-scratch, all in miniature colored glass apothecary jars and banana-leaf bindles, packed with excelsior in a compartmented wooden crate: it was a Hickory Farms Holiday Basket From Hell.

Selene was touched, but she only gave Whistler a peck on the cheek—Lourdes got a full-Selene, the enveloping hug that always left both women humming blissfully. "Thank you, dearie," said Selene. "This was too thoughtful a gift, and took too much time, to have been Jamey's idea."

He started to protest; Selene took his hand. "Now hush, you know it's true. Your idea of a Christmas present has always been a Rolex from the duty-free shop at the airport, Jamey. Don't get me wrong—a Rolex *is* a Rolex." She winked at Lourdes. "I have a safe-deposit box full of them back home."

Lourdes held up her left wrist in reply—a new Rolex with a diamond band; Whistler shrugged sheepishly.

Selene gave his hand a reassuring squeeze. "And now if you'll both accompany me to the bungalow, I'll give you your Christmas presents."

"Do you have any idea what this is all about?" Whistler muttered to Lourdes as they crossed the velvety lawn that sloped down towards the lake.

"Not a clue."

At the bottom of the lawn, just before the white crescent of beach, they turned right; as they followed the narrow path through the woods they could see light in the second-story windows of the bungalow; somebody was playing a Chieftains CD up there, and the Celtic music was appropriately druidic, groaning uilleann pipes and sawing fiddles, merry tin whistles and soaring flutes, and the heavy thump of the bodhran drifting out over the wintry woods.

Figures appeared in a window above as they reached the rustic wooden door; laughing voices called "Happy New Year" as someone leaned out the window and tossed a bucket of confetti into the air; it drifted down over them like psychedelic snow.

The music stopped, then started again; they trotted up the stairs, brushing confetti from their hair and shoulders, to the unmistakable, inescapable strains of the immortal Guy Lombardo and His Royal Canadians playing "Auld Lang Syne." Selene opened the door at the top of the stairs, then stepped back. "Well I'll be damned," she heard Whistler exclaim, and followed Lourdes into the room in time to catch the expression on her face when she caught sight of Selene's Christmas present to the couple.

Christmas presents, rather—three of them. Sherman Bailey in black tie—full vam-pie regalia, with the whites of his eyes glowing ruby red. Beside him, Catherine, in a loose witch's gown of deep forest green, her Lucy-red ringlets falling about her white shoulders, her bosom plumped up prettily. And behind them both, her cropped head rising from a crimson robe that could have covered a Volkswagen, her eyes quite as red as Sherman's, a broadly beaming Cheese Louise.

There was a pewter goblet on the mantelpiece over the small gas-fire hearth. Selene took it down and carried it carefully over to Whistler. "Will you take a cup of kindness yet?"

"For Auld Lang Syne?" he replied, grinning. The goblet in his hand was brimming with blood so fresh it was all but steaming. He took a sip and handed it to Lourdes.

"For Auld Lang—" she began, but stopped herself. "No. A better toast: Blood make us one."

"Blood make us one," each vampire proclaimed in turn. Then Selene took out her green notebook, and they set to work.

Chapter
3

ONE

August Fetterman, Esq., of the firm of Broadbent, Fetterman and Bennett, was two generations removed from the Fetterman of the letterhead, but as part of the firm's charter, any Broadbent or Fetterman or Bennett of direct lineage who could drag him- or herself through an accredited law school and then pass the bar was assured of a partnership. And since his recovery Augie had even come within a whisker of actually practicing law, if only to interview his wealthiest hereditary clients in his richly appointed corner office before passing them on to one of the associates.

Or, as was the case on this sixth day of January 1992, playing Sim City on the computer with a member of the technical support crew. It was an exercise in terror for the Simians—nuclear plants next to schools, that sort of thing—but a lucrative one for B.F.B., as Augie was billing his time to an oil company at two hundred dollars an hour.

Augie was a little surprised when his secretary buzzed him—he had inherited her when his father died, and she had never quite mastered the new phone system. "Yes, Evelyn?"

"You have a call, Mr. Fetterman," came the quavery voice over the speakerphone. "The gentleman who prefers not to give his name."

"All right, I'll take it." He dismissed the techie with a wave of his hand. "And, Evelyn, why don't you put the call through and then take off for lunch. . . . No, dear, it's perfectly safe for you to hang up. The blinking light means he's on hold—we won't lose him unless you push the button again *before* you hang up. Attagirl."

He picked up the receiver. "J.W.! I thought you were in the Virgins. . . . Oh yes, it hit the fan the very next meeting. . . . What do you mean, am I your attorney? I'm one of 'em—we're handling that offshore trust in the Caymans for you. . . . No, anything you tell me can be considered privileged communication. . . . I suppose so. Let me check my schedule. . . ."

Putting Whistler on hold, he pushed his considerable girth back from the massive teak-topped desk (Augie no longer resembled the young Robert Morley of Nick's description: since giving up blood the year before Whistler he had turned to sex and eating, bought his condoms by the case, ran a tab at Just Desserts, and by now could pass for the Morley of the *Beat the Devil* period), rose from the creaking leather chair he'd inherited from his father along with his creaking secretary, and left his office to check his calendar on Evelyn's desk, then picked up the receiver there.

"Yeah, I could do it, but it would help the confidentiality thing if I billed you. . . . Two hundred—but that would include the travel time. . . . Shall I bring one of my associates? . . ." He laughed dutifully. "I don't know if we have any with big tits—we're not allowed to look anymore. Besides, you know that's not my type. . . ." Another laugh. "Yes, you do know my type. Unfortunately, the 'I swear, your Honor, she *looked* eighteen' defense rarely works any more in statutory cases."

Humming a Grateful Dead tune to himself, Augie took his overcoat—a beautifully tailored black wool with long lapels that rolled with a satisfying swell across his respectable belly—down from the mahogany coat rack, wrapped his gray-on-gray muffler around his neck with a flourish, and strolled out to the twenty-second-floor elevator lobby, where one of the associates was just stepping into a down elevator and trying to pretend he hadn't seen Augie coming.

"Going down there, son?" Augie called heartily. Once in the elevator he let the kid push the Lobby button, waited a floor—21—then stuck out his hand, still heartily. He did not, however, remove his calfskin glove. "Don't believe we've met. I'm August Fetterman." *Of the letterhead Fettermans, asshole.* 20, 19, 18.

"An honor, sir. I'm Hershey. Neil Hershey." 17, 16, 15.

"First-year associate, Neil?" 14, 13, 12.

"Yes, sir." 11, 10, 9, 8.

"Want to try for a second year?" 7, 6, 5.

"Yes I do—sir." 4, 3, 2, 1.

"Then the next time you see a partner coming, hold the fucking door." Lobby.

Ka-whooosh: the bronze doors parted, and Augie marched out of the elevator without looking back. *I'm a simple man,* he thought, grinning to himself. *A simple man with simple pleasures.*

Augie's white Eldorado was fully loaded, from the climate-controlled cabin to the computerized seats that conformed to the shape of his ass at the push of a button. The sound system was about a year ahead of the curve, state-of-the-art-wise—before leaving home a few minutes after three, he stacked six Grateful Dead discs in the CD player next to the built-in refrigerator in the trunk, then pushed Random on the dashboard panel as he pulled out of his Hillsborough driveway. "Friend of the Devil" was the first song that came up—Augie laughed out loud.

It took him almost five hours to reach Tahoe—he could have done it in a little over three, but at two hundred bucks an hour, where was the incentive? He tried not to speculate on the nature of Whistler's business on the ride up—as an attorney it made absolutely no difference to him whether his client was drinking blood or not. As a recovering vampire, though, it was his obligation to look at it somewhat differently.

So why, he wondered, as he turned into the long gravel driveway winding down from the highway to Whistler Manor, was the very thought of it making his heart pound so?

He parked the Caddy under the fragrant grove of pines and followed the flagstone path around to the front of the manor. Whistler was waiting on the front steps.

"Glad you could make it, Counselor."

"When the client calls . . ." They clapped each other's shoulders vigorously like two old soldiers who hadn't set eyes on each other since the Crimean War; Whistler led him to the dark cavernous kitchen of the lodge.

"Sorry about the venue—the keeping room is being renovated. But we won't be disturbed here," said Whistler, indicating the bar stools arranged around the central butcher-block table. Overhead a collection of pots and pans and implements hung from the ceiling beams like so many shiny stalactites. "Do you need to freshen up first?"

"Took care of that at the gas station."

"Something to drink?"

"Rum 'n' cola, hold the rum." Augie draped his coat over the back of a bar stool, then sat down quickly before the weight of the coat over-tipped it. Whistler took a can of Coke from the refrigerator, filled two tumblers with cloudy crescent moons of ice from the ice maker, then divided the Coke as evenly as he could between them. It was a nostalgic gesture they both recognized: when they were vampiring together, they used to divide bags of blood that way: one guy pours, and the other takes his pick.

Augie took a sip. "Ah, that's better. Am I going to need to take notes?"

Whistler shook his head.

"So what can I do for you, my old friend?"

"You drew up the V.A. charter and bylaws, correct?"

"I did."

"Do you have any copies?"

"There's only one—it's on one of Nick's protected disks."

"But you remember it?"

"Word for word, I should think."

Whistler tinkled the ice in his glass by way of tribute. "Just a few questions, then. First: is there anything anywhere in those documents that says you can't have a slip—that is, that you can't drink blood and still be a member."

"Of course not," Augie replied. "That would go against everything the twelve-step programs stand for."

"But there is a clause that forbids any member from divulging the nature of the fellowship to someone outside it?"

"Without the unanimous consent of the membership. You know that."

"Just checking. Now are there any penalties spelled out for someone who would commit such a heinous act?"

"You mean drinking blood, or divulging the nature of the fellowship?"

"Divulging, divulging."

"Up to and including expulsion—it would be left to a vote of the membership."

"Great. Thanks, Counselor." Whistler reached across the corner of the butcher block and shook Augie's hand formally.

"Wait a minute, that's it? Just three questions, that's all you wanted to ask me?"

Whistler nodded.

Augie was still incredulous. "Jamey-o, at two hundred bucks an hour, this is going to cost you a grand a question."

"Oh, more than that," replied Whistler, turning back from the sink. "I've booked you a suite at the Gold Dust—can't have my attorney turning right around and trying to drive back tonight."

"If you insist," grinned Augie, relieved: apparently someone had warned Whistler of a possible confrontation with Nick, and he'd just wanted to be sure where he stood vis-à-vis the fellowship—or perhaps he might even have a counterattack planned. Still he couldn't deny a sense of uneasiness as Whistler showed him out the back way. And perhaps an element of disappointment as well, though he was not about to admit that, even to himself.

Augie left the Caddy with the parking valet at the Gold Dust. At the registration desk the clerk punched his name into the computer. Whatever she read there caused her to pick up the phone and mutter his name into the receiver; a moment later an impeccably coiffed and suited woman in her late middle years approached him carrying a clipboard. "Mr. Fetterman? I'm Holly Taylor, the concierge. No need for you to check in—we have Mr. Whistler's penthouse suite prepared for you. Do you have any luggage?"

He indicated his travel bag. A bellhop snatched it up as Augie followed Miss Taylor to a private elevator in an alcove around the corner from the bank of peasant elevators. There were only two buttons inside, an up and a down. The bellhop made the appropriate choice, and after a smooth ride of a few seconds' duration the elevator doors opened directly upon a glass-walled white-carpeted room with a sweeping vista of the lake and the surrounding mountains.

Augie whistled. "Nice jernt." The beribboned, cellophane-wrapped fruit basket on the coffee table by the window could have fed a Third World family for a week. As soon as he'd tipped the bellhop, accepted Miss Taylor's card, and pushed the lockout button on the elevator behind them, he tore the ribbon and red-tinted cellophane off the basket and was rummaging through it looking for something sweet when the door to the bedroom opened behind him.

"Mister Augie, sah?"

There in the doorway stood a pair of twins dressed in oversized red Gold Dust souvenir T-shirts that covered them to mid-thigh. Of course, Augie didn't know that they were twins, but they were obviously brother and sister—same narrow face and dark round possum nose, pretty much the same height (about five feet) and build (slender) and color (milk chocolate) and, if Augie was any judge, the same age as well—an extremely dangerous fourteen or so. So twins was a pretty fair bet.

Augie quickly raised both hands in the air—not as if he were being held up, but as if he had been caught at the cookie jar and were protesting his innocence. "Who the hell are you, and what are you doing in my hotel room?" he demanded.

"Mister Whistler send us, sah." The girl was obviously the spokesperson for the pair.

"And how old are you?"

"Four-*teen*, sah, nex' summer."

"Then you'll just have to hurry right back to Mr. Whistler, and tell him Mr. Augie said thanks, but no thanks. Tell him that inasmuch as Mr. Augie does not feel himself capable of doing the time, Mr. Augie prefers to avoid doing the crime. A bit of advice Mr. Whistler might do well to heed himself."

"Me ain' know about no crime, sah, but we cyan' go back to Mister Whistler until mornin'." The girl led her brother into the living room. "An' Mister Whistler say if you ain' drink our blood an' fuck us, he gon' to beat us stripe-ed."

They were standing between Augie and the light, so that he could see their slim-hipped outlines under the oversized T-shirts. The girl saw him staring, and nudged her brother—in unison they pulled their shirts over their heads, and stood there not six feet from Augie's clenched hands, both naked, neither with a trace of pubic hair, and the boy's little erection just starting to rise in the warm circulating air of the suite.

Then Augie saw that the boy was holding a Swiss Army knife in one hand, and watched, unable to speak, unable even to move except to tug his trousers away from his own desperate erection, as the lad took his sister's hand and raised her palm.

Wait, Augie tried to say as the knife sliced into the tender, lighter skin at the inside of the girl's wrist; his mouth opened and closed a few times, but no sound emerged.

TWO

The next time the white Eldorado made the trip to Tahoe, after the V.A. meeting the following Saturday night, it carried three passengers in addition to Augie. Louise occupied the shotgun seat, while Sherman and Catherine billed and cooed in the back.

Actually, they were considerably beyond billing by the time the Caddy reached the Sierra foothills, and Catherine's vocalizing had taken on an urgency more often associated with moaning than cooing. "*What is going on back there?*" Louise asked.

"Just don't turn around," Sherman replied jovially.

Louise's reaction was anything but jovial—Sherman felt a fierce yank at the fringe of hair that rimmed the back of his head, and found himself being tugged away from his husbandly duties by his puny new ponytail, while Catherine, squirming beneath him with her eyes closed, moaned, "No, don't stop," and tightened her grip on his buttocks.

" 'Now don't fight, girls, there's plenty of me to go around,' " he quoted from a thousand porno movies, but Louise only tugged harder. Reluctantly, Sherman made the sensible choice: he could always get laid later, but it would take him another six months to grow that pitiful fringe of hair long enough to twine into a ponytail again.

"What on earth, Lou?" he said, from his cramped position atop his wife, head tugged to the side like a pony on a lead. He pushed himself away from Catherine with one hand while attempting to loosen Louise's grip with the other.

"It was you, wasn't it?" Louise let go of his hair, unbuckled her seat belt, and knelt backwards on the front seat.

"I've always been me, as far back as I can remember," Sherman remarked, sitting up and rubbing the back of his head gingerly, his blood-induced erection pointing irrelevantly at the roof of the Caddy.

"You know what I mean. It was you that kidnapped us Christmas night, wasn't it? I kept telling myself it couldn't have been, until just now. The way you said 'Don't turn around'—I'll never forget the way he—you—said that."

"Actually, Lou, it was *us* that kidnapped *you*." Catherine had rolled on her side and drawn her knees up, the soles of her feet jammed against the side of Sherman's thigh. "Only it wasn't really kidnapping, was it?"

Louise's chins were quivering with rage. "How could you *do* that to somebody—to a friend? Do you know how terrifying that was?"

Sherman drew back into the corner of the back seat, out of reach. "Oh come on, you said the other night if you knew who the guy was, you'd thank him. I almost told you then. Besides, it worked, didn't it?"

"So you're saying what, that the end justifies the means?"

"If I may interrupt here?" Augie put his right hand on Louise's right shoulder, and gently urged her around. "First of all, Lou, please turn around and put your seatbelt on before we attract any unwanted attention." He slowed to sixty, pulling into the right-hand lane of the mountain highway.

"There, that's better. Now secondly, speaking as an attorney, let me say that this 'ends justifying the means' thing has always gotten a bad rap. Of course the ends justify the means—if I break into your home with the express intention of saving you from a fire, it's quite a different thing, legally, from breaking in to rob you, whether I actually steal anything or not.

"Conversely, the ends also unjustify the means: luring a lost child into your car with a lollipop in order to molest her is different, both legally and morally, from luring her into your car to return her to her parents. Same lollipop, though, same car." He glanced over at Louise. "That was a hypothetical example, of course."

"Of course."

"Take myself, for example: Whistler set me up like a bowling pin last week. For all I know, he even had my room bugged—"

"You should ask him to show you the videotape," interrupted Sherman from the back seat. "You done yourself proud, Aug."

"There, see?" He glanced to his right again; Louise's jaw was still set.

"Well he didn't have to call me a bitch," she muttered, but managed a reluctant laugh when Catherine pointed out that Sherman had actually called *her* a bitch.

"You he called my dyke girlfriend, which I thought was kind of a nice touch." Catherine slipped her toes under Sherman's thighs, and edged him forward so she could lie on her back again. "Now if you'll excuse us, my husband and I have some unfinished business to take care of. Love these roomy leather seats, Augie."

"General Motors would be so pleased."

They arrived at Whistler Manor a little after one-thirty on Sunday morning; Whistler met them at the back door, eager to show off the remodeling job he'd had done on the lodge. He led them along the wood-paneled passageway that led from the back door to the kitchen; where once a water closet had stood, there was now a pantry—Whistler demonstrated with pride how the rear wall swiveled to reveal the cellar steps.

He flicked on the light switch at the top of the stairs, and Augie and Lou and the Baileys followed him down to the newly dug cellar, which consisted of two rooms. The first was four feet wide and six feet long, both long walls lined with shelves and stocked with canned food. Hidden behind a swiveling section of one of the long walls was the second room, a refrigerated compartment with storage space for a few months' supply of blood for a dozen vampires.

It was not even half full as yet—Whistler said he figured that problem would take care of itself when they'd converted Beverly. He selected a Seal-a-Meal pouch so stuffed with blood it resembled a miniature crimson pillow, then ushered the others out of the cellar. When they had cleared the outer door, he slammed it behind him.

It was a hell of a door: four inches thick, with padding on the inside and a stout bolt on the outside. He'd had it built strong enough to resist even a vampire on blood, he explained, should it ever become necessary to contain one for a short time. Locking a vampire in need of a time-out into a vault full of blood rather appealed to Whistler's sense of the absurd.

Selene was waiting for them in the kitchen with five empty glasses and her green notebook at the ready. "Welcome, cabal," she greeted them. "Lourdes is taking a nap—she'll be down in about an hour." She took the bag from Whistler, snipped the corner with a pair of poultry shears, and poured them each a few fingers of blood. "Now don't get too loaded yet, we have some business to take care of first."

"How about a few minutes with the twins first?" requested Augie. "I've been looking forward to them all week."

"I sent them packing back to Santa Luz," said Selene firmly.

"But why?" he moaned.

"Vampires or no vampires," Selene replied, "you have to draw the line somewhere." She had left Augie's reclamation up to Whistler, but although she was far from ingenuous, when the nature of the twins' servitude had become clear to her, she'd hit the roof.

"What line? Since when?"

"Slavery and child molestation may be acceptable among the Caribbean vampires, Mr. Fetterman," she informed him, "but they are very much frowned upon by us California witches, who—" She raised her voice and her palm to cut off his objections: Selene and Whistler had already been over the morally squishy battleground of cultural relativity, and had trampled it to muck in the process. "Who, I might add, do not argue with lawyers. Or frogs!" Another warning gesture.

"I'm not Fre—" Augie began, then realized that the amphibian reference had been a threat and not a Francophobic slur. He decided not to pursue the point. "But their sister? The older girl?"

Whistler reached across the table and patted Augie's hand. "Currently in my employ, Counselor, and very possibly the highest-paid housemaid in the state of Nevada. Her duties, however, are wide-ranging—I'm sure you can work something out with her. But hold on to your wallet during the negotiations: she's taken to capitalism like a duck to water."

He took a sip of cold blood. "Now, on to business. Counselor, what's the report on the Henderson front?"

Augie pulled his hand out of the front pocket of his slacks—he'd been fingering his bankroll, trying to remember how much cash he'd brought with him. "Moving along just fine, Jamey-o."

"What are you going to do, hold a gun to his head, too?" asked Louise, still a little miffed about her own kidnapping.

"Not at all, Lou. We're working with one of the partners in my firm who specializes in entertainment law. He thinks he's helping me with a client that's looking for a tax write-off or possibly a cash laundry—you can move a lot of green around in the music business, as the mob has been proving for fifty years." He went on to explain how Henderson would be going into the studio next weekend with one of the most demanding producers in the record business. The idea was, when the Texan was good and stressed out, Augie would be waiting with blood and encouragement.

Selene performed a quick calculation in her notebook. "So by next Monday—what's that, the twentieth?" She looked over at Augie, who glanced at his watch for the current date, then counted on his fingers and nodded.

She turned to Whistler. "By the twentieth, then, we stand even: six vampires using, six in recovery. Do you want to risk a confrontation then, or wait until you have a majority?"

He nodded thoughtfully, took the notebook from her, and began flipping through it. "Better still," he mused, "let's try to actually *obtain* a majority by then."

"Whom did you have in mind?" asked Sherman, who was over by the cupboard looking for something to snack on with his cold blood. Which wasn't all that easy—the stuff was already salty enough, so pretzels and chips were out, but candy left a cloying aftertaste.

Whistler thumbed ahead a few pages in the notebook. "I'm not sure yet. Doesn't have to be anyone influential—let's just look for an easy nut to crack." Then—bang!—he slammed his fist down on the eleventh page. "Aha!" he cried. "Speaking of nuts . . ."

Sherman stepped up behind him to read over his shoulder. "January! I don't think so," he said. "She's still living at Nick's house—I'm not sure how we'd get to her."

"Leave that to me," said Whistler. "I'd like to handle this one personally."

THREE

"I think I'll call it a night," remarked Nick, yawning. You couldn't say something like that and not yawn.

"What else would you call it?" January asked, straight-faced. "I mean, it's practically midnight."

"When you're right, you're right." He stood up. "How about you?"

"I'll just surf awhile." She'd been crashing with Nick for over a month and still hadn't tired of his full cable setup. And if the futon in the parlor was a little narrower than her former bed in the residence hotel, it smelled a whole lot better, and the view of Nick's rock garden with its colored pools of light was a good deal more peaceful than the madness of Telegraph Avenue.

"Okay." Nick gave her an air kiss—"G'night"—then turned around in the doorway. "But don't forget, you've got that interview in the morning—you'll want to be fresh for that."

Yes Daddy. Another copy shop. Happy happy joy joy. She made up the futon, changed into her flannel nightgown in the downstairs bathroom, then set the sleep-timer on the TV to thirty minutes, turned off the light, and climbed into bed, planning to drift off watching Nirvana Unplugged on the thirty-two-inch screen built into the floor-to-ceiling bookshelves against the far wall.

Hog Heaven, she tried to tell herself, but then that little voice in her head—the one that she had learned to call her addict—couldn't help remarking on how much cooler that rock garden would have been if she were stoned on something, even just pot, the way the little floodlights splashed color across the gracefully distorted bonsai dwarves and jagged cacti set artfully among rolling hillocks of white pebbles.

She wasn't sure she saw it at first—a shadow at the edge of the garden. She held her breath, clicked off the TV, and lay still; after a minute, hearing nothing, she slipped out from under the covers and tiptoed two steps across the cold hardwood floor, then gasped and leapt back as Whistler appeared at the window with a finger to his lips.

Let me in, he mouthed. He was dressed in black slacks and a black turtleneck, one of the floodlights casting green highlights across his yellow hair.

She shook her head.

It's only a dream, he mouthed again—or perhaps he spoke the words—it was as if she were hearing them from inside her head. She wondered if perhaps she *was* dreaming. It sure felt like a dream—otherwise why wasn't she calling for Nick? So she did what they always did in movies: she pinched herself on the forearm. "Ow."

She saw Whistler laughing. Dream-weird again, his mouth open, but no sound through the cold glass panes. He pointed around the corner to the door that led in from the garden; she opened it a crack, but left the chain on. "What do you mean, it's only a dream?" she whispered.

"Everything's a dream, m'dear," he whispered back.

"I'm gonna call Nick." But the fact that she had whispered it told Whistler all he needed to know.

"Go ahead—you'll get him killed, but go ahead."

"What do you want?"

"I've brought you a birthday present."

"My birthday was in October."

"My mistake—your name, you know."

"Everybody gets that wrong. Count backwards nine months from October."

Whistler smiled. "Of course. That sounds more like Glory."

Suddenly January felt the chill for the first time; she gathered the neck of her nightgown tighter. "You knew my mom?"

He pointed to the latch on the door instead of answering. January was torn—she suspected he was only jerking her around, but what if he had known Glory? She shook her head again, resolutely. "I'm not letting you into Nick's house," she whispered. "You just said you were going to kill him."

"Only if you force the issue. Think about it, dear—if I wanted to harm Nick I could climb straight up the fucking wall to his bedroom, I am that stoned on blood. And if I wanted to harm you, I assure you I could snap that chain like a licorice whip."

"I knew it! I knew I smelled blood on your breath."

"Yes. Very clever of you. Now open this door."

"First tell me how you knew her?"

"Glory? I lived in Bobo. Do you want your birthday present or not?"

"Jan?" Nick's voice from up in the kitchen. "Somebody down there?"

Her eyes found Whistler's. Gray, amused, bloodshot. One of them winked. He pointed to himself, then up towards Nick, and made a throat-slitting motion.

"Nope," January called behind her.

"Sounded like you were talking to somebody."

"Just practicing for my interview." Her eyes had not left Whistler's.

"Okay, g'night."

"Night." January gestured for Whistler to step back from the door. She closed it in his face, then unhooked the chain and opened it again. Whistler slipped in sideways with one hand behind his back as she crossed the little room to close the door at the bottom of the stairs leading up to the first floor. When she turned back he had seated himself on the shorter futon that formed an L with January's bed.

"What about my mother?" she whispered, turning the TV on loud enough to cover their voices, but not so loud she wouldn't be able to hear Nick coming down the stairs.

"Just that I knew her. Most of us did." He patted her futon—she sat down cross-legged at the foot of the bed. "Not well, mind you. Wayne used to bring her to our parties sometimes. A beautiful woman—I used to call her Gilda, after a Rita Hayworth movie. He beat her, you know—that's why we kicked him out of our circle. We all felt so badly when we heard about . . . what happened."

"But why didn't anybody ever say anything at the meeting?" Suddenly she felt dislocated, cut off, disoriented—it was as though they'd had her mother hidden away this whole year. "Why hide something like that?"

"Oh, we discussed it out of your presence." Whistler was extemporizing—the mention of Glory had only been intended to get him through the door, but clearly he was onto something. "It was Nick and Beverly who argued the most forcefully against telling you. They think you're on the edge of madness anyway—they were afraid it might set you off."

"So you're all a bunch of fucking liars." She started to rise; he put his hand on her leg and seemingly without effort held her pinned to the spot.

"My poor little January." Whistler pressed his other long-fingered hand against his breast, and tilted his head to feign compassion. "The only people who come to twelve-step meetings to tell the truth, the whole truth, and nothing but the truth are either innocent newcomers like yourself, or broken spirits, cracked plates like St. Nick up there."

He removed his hand from his heart and pointed to the ceiling. Then the pressure of his other hand on her thigh eased slightly—he was gentling her like a spooked horse. "We've been watching you for a year, January. We wanted so to be able to tell you about us, so that we could then tell you about the others, their lies and their pretenses. But the time wasn't ripe yet."

He waited for her to ask him about *us* and *we*, watching her face with exaggerated concern, remembering something he'd read somewhere once, about how sincerity was all that mattered in this world—once you could fake that, you had it made. One more prompt: "But now the time *is* ripe: we want you to join us."

"Who's us?" More dazed than suspicious.

At last. "Let me see," he said thoughtfully, ticking off the names on the fingers of his left hand, beginning with the thumb. "There's Lourdes, of course. Sherman. Augie. Louise." He looked down at his hand, puzzled—the pinky was still bent against his palm. "I know there are two more. Myself of course." He unfolded the pinky. "Oh, and Henderson."

He removed his right hand from her leg to show her six fingers in the air—she was following his every gesture now, as if he were an astounding magician—then lowered it to her left thigh again, grasping her firmly, almost caressingly, just above the knee. "We know so much about you, January. We know who you are, and what you need, and we're going to help you get it, the way we wish we could have helped poor Glory."

He could feel the sinewy squirm of her quadriceps under his palm as she softened to him. "You see, what you need, first of all, is blood, and second of all, a family. Not to be alone. Believe me, I know—I lost my mother when I was around your age, and my father turned his back on me not long after. He gave me the same choice Nick is giving you— blood or family. I chose blood, but do you know what I discovered?"

Her eyes were still fixed on his—there was no need for her to shake her head.

"I discovered that I could have both, January." Suddenly his hand slipped all the way up her thigh so that his long fingers were pressing lightly against her hip and his thumb resting against the side of her sex. "And so can you." He reached behind his back with his left hand and presented her with a heavy cylindrical object, gift-wrapped in black foil. "Happy birthday."

She took it—it felt like a thermos, and when she held it to her ear and shook it, it sloshed like a thermos. And so it proved to be, when she tore the foil off: a silver and black *Star Trek: The Next Generation* beauty. She ran her fingers lovingly across Captain Picard's earnest shiny-domed visage, then rotated the bullet-shaped cylinder to see the *Enterprise* zooming across the quadrant at full warp speed. You could tell it was full warp by the streaming lights.

"Before you open it," said Whistler, though she had made no move to do so, "I want to tell you a few things. First, V.A. is already finished, done for, kaput—it's not your doing and it's not your fault and you couldn't save it if you wanted to. Second, Nick is in no danger—we don't want to harm him, or any of the others: we just want them to leave us alone to pursue our natures. Third, the choice is yours—you can join us or not, as you choose."

He removed his hand from its intimate position and noticed her thigh lifting slightly as if to follow it. "But you have to decide now." He took back the thermos, casually twisted off the cup from the top, then worked the plug loose and poured a splash of blood into the cup. "If you take this blood from me now, and drink it straight down, you become a member of our Penang. You'll never want for blood, and you'll never want for a home."

He held it out until she reached for it. "Your eyes are beautiful all sparkling with tears," he said gently as she took the plastic cup. "That's the girl."

But she paused with the cup to her lips, so he upped the ante. "By the way, did I mention that I'd like you to think of this thermos as a Big Gulp, and of myself as the Seven-Eleven?" Her eyes went wide over the rim of the cup. "That's right, free refills."

The cup tilted slightly, but froze again, and Whistler decided to play his last card. He knew it would tip her one way or the other—he just didn't know which. "The alternative is to stay on the *Titanic* until it's just you and Nick. But when that ship goes down—and it will, my dear child; believe me, it will—you'll end up just like your poor darling Glory: alone and drowning in a cold, black sea."

FOUR

"Hello, everybody. My name is Nick, and I'm a recovering vampire."

"Hi Nick, hi Nick, hi Nick, . . ." All the way around the table.

"This is our first full meeting—I mean, our first meeting with the full membership—in over a month, and our first full meeting ever in our new home." He gestured to the wide open conference room, which had a small stage, and could easily have accommodated a group ten times their size. It was separated from the lobby of the Senior Center only by an accordioned floor-to-ceiling plastic room divider; the dozen vampires were gathered around one of several conference tables on the opposite side of the room. "Before we read the Twelve Steps and Traditions, there's some business we need to get out of the way."

Nick—who was alone at the head of the long folding conference table, with Whistler seated directly to his left and January to his right—turned to Whistler. "James, after your last meeting—"

January was tugging at his sleeve. He turned all the way around to face her. "What?" he said, annoyed.

"I changed my mind."

"What do you mean, you—"

"I was thinking about it last night, trying to remember, and now I think I could of been wrong, it could of still been on my shirt or something, or I could of made it up."

"Wrong about *what*? Made *what* up?" Whistler addressed her directly, across the table.

"I'm sorry, James. Our last meeting, you remember how upset I was?"

"Because you'd slipped? Yes, of course."

"And I told everybody the reason I ran out was because I smelled blood on your breath. But I'm not sure anymore."

"Well *damn*, girl." It was Lourdes, next to Whistler—he put his hand on her arm.

"It's all right, Lourdes," he told her; then, to January: "I forgive you. I've done stupider things myself." Whistler didn't quite flash Nick a triumphant smile when he turned to him, but then, they knew each other well enough that he didn't have to. "You were about to say, Nick?"

Nick had to force himself not to turn around to question January—he couldn't imagine what had caused her to change her mind, but decided it didn't matter. He, for one, hadn't a doubt in the world that she had smelled blood on Whistler's breath back in December—he would salvage what he could. "I don't see where January's having second thoughts changes much, James. The membership voted for an intervention—we don't want to take your inventory for you, James, we're just asking to see you in the sunlight tomorrow morning, or afternoon, or whenever's—"

Sherman, seated to Lourdes's left, interrupted Nick. "Hi my name is Sherman and I'm a vampire." When the answering hi's had died away, he addressed Nick directly. "I think maybe January's retraction does change things, Nick. I know I'd change my vote."

"Me too," said Louise.

"Hold on, everybody." It was Augie, directly across from Nick at the foot of the table. "There's an easy way to settle this—let's just vote again."

"Good idea," said Whistler. "And for my part, I promise to go along with whatever you decide."

"Fine," said Nick, sensing defeat—but not yet disaster. "Let's vote. Aye means we confirm the first vote, for an intervention; nay means we drop the whole thing."

They went around the table, starting with Whistler, who gracefully recused himself. By the time the vote came around to Nick again, the tally was nine to one, with only Beverly of the still recovered vampires voting to intervene. "You win," Nick announced to Whistler. "My vote doesn't matter."

"I want to hear it, Nicky," replied Whistler evenly.

"I said it doesn't—"

"I said I want to hear it!"

"AYE THEN, GODDAMMIT!" Nick fought for control of himself, and of the meeting. "Let's just drop it now," he said quietly. "Who wants to read the Steps?"

Whistler put a hand on his arm. "Not so fast, Nick. We have one more piece of business."

"Save it for after the meeting." It took all the self-control he could muster not to shove Whistler's hand away; instead he withdrew his forearm from under it.

"It won't wait."

"Fine, go ahead." It sounded petulant even to Nick's ears. He tried to soften it. "Please."

"Why are we no longer meeting at the Church of the Higher Power?"

By dint of repetition and time, the half-lie came to Nick as easily as the truth would have. "Reverend Shoemaker changed her mind."

"Why?"

"I don't know—I think perhaps I oversold the dangers of being a Victim."

"You're a fucking liar, Nick." This was Lourdes—it was said completely without heat, but the effect on the meeting was electric. "Selene told us about how she left a copy of your vampire novel with your picture on it on the podium the night we left."

She turned to the others to explain: "Those of you who don't know her, Selene was an old girlfriend of James's—she was the one who left the hooker at the church—she's been trying to get even with James for getting engaged to me, and she's doing it through V.A."

Whistler took over again swiftly, before Nick could regain the floor. "So, Nick, now that you are possessed of this particular enlightening detail, would you like to explain how you managed to re-convince the good Reverend that you were only a Victim in the face of such persuasive evidence to the contrary? The truth, this time." He sat back, folding his arms with exaggerated patience.

Stunned as he was, Nick still had no idea what he was up against—after all, no one had ever been punished or even censured at a V.A. meeting before. He decided to tell the truth: "I let her read my V.A. Fourth Step."

Murmurs broke out around the table; at the far end Augie had risen angrily from his chair shaking his fist like an extra in *Spartacus*. Nick hurried on. "Please, you don't understand. I had to. She was going to go to the police—it was the only way."

Whistler had stilled the uproar with an upraised palm. "Let's hear him out."

"Thanks, James," Nick said, growing more confused by the moment. This time he told them everything, including his role in the possible impregnation of their former landlady. He thought he'd made a pretty good case for himself, too, but when he'd finished Whistler took the floor again. "Thanks, Nick. Augie, just for form's sake, does the charter say anything specifically about the penalty for breaking the fellowship's anonymity?"

"No penalty specified. Same as all the Will of the Membership issues in the bylaws. Majority vote."

"Fine. Well, I'm sure we all understand why Nick did what he felt he had to do."

There were nods, murmured assents around the table. Nick relaxed—at least until Sherman suggested they have a vote anyway: "Like James says, for form's sake."

And now—too late—Nick's professional instincts kicked in. "Wait a minute, what's going on here? A vote on what?"

Whistler turned to him ever so slowly. Twisting-in-the-wind slowly. "Why, not to take your *inventory*, Nick. Just to decide whether any punishment need be applied in the current situation. I'm sure you'll do just as well as I did in the vote you forced me to submit to."

He turned back to the others, almost as slowly. "I'm sure nobody wants to be unduly harsh. Myself, I think Nick actually saved the fellowship. On the other hand, we are a society of laws, and we don't want—oh, the hell with it." He'd almost forgotten that he'd already rigged the election. "Who votes that Nick be suspended for six months for breaking the anonymity of the fellowship? Hands?"

Stunned, Nick surveyed the table. He had turned his body to face Whistler, so his back was to January as he counted the upraised hands:

Whistler, Lourdes, Sherman, Louise, Henderson, Augie. "Six," he managed to say. "It's a tie." Then came a tap on the shoulder. He twisted around to face January.

"Sorry, Nick," she said, gazing implacably into his eyes as she slowly raised her hand.

"Seven, then," Whistler said briskly. "All opposed?"

Nick found himself counting again, as if somehow the principles of addition and subtraction had slipped out of whack along with the rest of his universe. There were only four hands raised this time: Beverly, Toshi, Sandy, Sally. *Seven and four makes eleven,* he thought dully. *But there are twelve of us.*

Then he remembered—but just as he started to raise his own hand, he heard Whistler's mocking voice again. "Now now, Nick—why don't you show a little class like I did, and abstain from voting for yourself? After all, it won't make any difference. . . . All right, have it your way: the vote is seven to five. See you in six months, pal."

But Lourdes was whispering something into his ear. Whistler inclined his head to her like a witness conferring with his lawyer at a congressional hearing, covered his mouth with his cupped hand as he replied, then addressed Nick directly again. "Lourdes suggests that your hiatus should run, not from today, but from the date of your transgression. That way you'll be reinstated in time to attend our wedding in June."

With a sweep of his hand he included the rest of the membership: "If that's all right with the rest of you, that is. We're planning a June wedding up at Tahoe. You're all invited, of course—we'll be sending out invitations soon, but in the meantime, just hold Midsummer—that's the solstice—open."

Whistler glanced behind him. "Oh Nick? You can put your hand down anytime. It's all over now."

Nick looked up at his own hand in the air. Somewhere in the distance Beverly was shouting, but it all seemed so far removed. He remembered feeling like this once before, back in 'Nam, during his only skirmish alongside the Montagnards—he'd heard the distant popping sound of a rifle, and it was not until he'd fired off an entire clip that he recognized from the subsequent silence that it had been his own weapon.

Slowly he lowered his hand. If he had any thought at all as he pushed himself back from the table and rose to his feet, it was some vague notion of leaving with a shred of dignity. But even that last hope was not moored firmly enough against the wave of rage that washed over him at the sight of Whistler's next gracefully understated gesture—a little bye-bye flick of the long fingers, and an infinitesimal lift of the yellow eyebrows.

The son of a bitch is dyeing his eyebrows too, was Nick's last thought before he launched himself across the table. After that, only red rage, a hunger for Whistler's throat between his hands, then the sensation of flying—an oddly peaceful feeling, even as the room turned upside down around him.

ONE

"Good evening, everyone," began Selene, looking around the keeping room, which had been remodeled into a low amphitheater with three horseshoe-shaped tiers lined with velveteen-covered cushions (red paisley: red to camouflage the bloodstains, paisley for the come) surrounding an orgy pit of foam pallets and leather bolsters. "I'd like to welcome you to the celebration of the vernal equinox. As I promised those of you who were with us at the Coven's last gathering back in February—I think that's most of you—on Candlemas, which was a celebration of the Goddess renewing herself and reembodying herself as a virgin, tonight's celebration centers around spring, and a ceremony of renewal to honor the coupling of the Goddess with the Lord of the Green, also known as the Goat-God, Pan . . . so it should be a lot more fun . . . than Candlemas."

Selene paused for a breath, relieved to have worked her way back to her original sentence. After twenty years as High Priestess, she was still not comfortable with public speaking. And this was a larger crowd than usual—arrayed before her across the top two tiers of cushions were the full Coven, including the first-level initiates, each in her green hooded robe slit up the crotch and sides, and the reestablished Penang (which by now encompassed the entire membership of V.A. with the exception of Nick and Beverly) in their crimson satin robes with crotch-high easy-access plackets fore and aft.

"Before we get started," Selene continued, "let me remind you of a few things. Firstly, the vernal equinox is all about the Horned Hunter roaming the greenwood hitting on everything that moves. He and the

Goddess don't settle down until Beltane, so—please, couples?—no sneaking away.

"Secondly, let's not be rigid about our roles—Jamey, don't snicker, it's unbecoming. You know what I mean. Women, feel free to embody Pan; there are all sorts of phalluses in the cabinets at the side of the room. And men, remember *you* don't need any extra equipment to embody the Goddess; lubricants and lotions are also available in the cabinets.

"Thirdly, the Coven has already completed the solemn part of the ritual, so—everybody?—just relax and have some fun."

She caught Whistler's eye and nodded. He and Lourdes rose from their seats in the middle of the top tier, and holding each other's hands for balance, with their feet sinking into the soft cushions, they descended tier by tier until they were standing next to Selene. "Our host and hostess have volunteered to kick things off," she announced unnecessarily, then closed her eyes and held both arms out from her sides, palms up—St. Theresa again.

Whistler knelt on one side of her, Lourdes at the other; they pushed up the sleeves of her gown, and then with his scalpel Whistler opened a small vein on one wrist while Lourdes wielded a miniature Luzan machete on the other. Together they performed the trick at which Nick had so excelled: they filled their mouths with blood, then turned to the serried ranks of witches and vampires, and let a few ceremonial drops trickle down their chins before swallowing the rest.

They drank for another few seconds, then closed the finely slitted wounds with a firm pressure of their thumbs as Selene slowed her breathing and heartbeat to assist the clotting. Then she opened her eyes and addressed the assembly: "By the way, dearies, I almost forgot—I'm still under my vow of celibacy, so I'll just be a spectator tonight."

Whistler, ever the gentleman, led the others in a disappointed *Awww*. Selene bowed, and swatted him across his crimson-swathed behind before hiking up her robe and ascending to the top row of the keeping room, just under the lozenge-shaped domed ceiling, which had been newly painted with a pastel frieze of nymphs and satyrs—the usual gambol—no vampires. The colors, turquoise sky and mango sunset clouds, were pure Maxfield Parrish, illuminated by glowing panels of light all the way around the base of the dome; ducts set between the light panels wafted in warm scented air.

By the time she'd turned around, Lourdes had already pulled her robe over her head, eliciting a gasp from the rapt audience. Her belly had a three-month curve that formed a shallow S with her as yet rounded ass; her breasts were swollen but still high, only beginning to hint at the ripe pear shape they would bear at fullness, and the aureolae distended, outlines blurred.

Another gasp as the Creature found the placket at the front of Whistler's robe and came poking through; then delighted laughter from the spectators as it grew, and grew. And grew. Lourdes dropped to her knees and took it in her mouth; the laughter of the spectators was now sprinkled with expressions of wonder, and doubt—could she eat the whole thing?—that turned to applause as she gracefully deep-throated the Creature. "*Put* that bad boy away," called one of the witches.

Then Whistler reached down and gently drew Lourdes to her feet again; they embraced; he bent his head to hers; she opened her mouth wide and soft and he entered it with his tongue. As the blood came on, they found themselves aware only of each other. Lips still locked onto hers, Whistler bent slightly and swept one arm behind her knees and the other behind her shoulders; he lifted her into his arms and laid her down carefully on the mats.

She raised her knees for him; he pulled his robe over his head and knelt between them, then lowered himself to enter her, belly muscles clenching as he fought for control with the Creature. The others had fallen silent—the room was quiet except for the hum of the air ducts and the lubricious sound of the Creature sliding slowly into harbor, inch by slippery inch.

Lourdes opened her eyes to see Whistler's face close above her, his iron gray eyes staring into hers as their lower bellies bumped; he shifted his hips down and forward so that the head of the Creature brushed her sweet spot. When he arched his back and bent his head to her left breast, she held it up for him in her palm, hefted it and fed him the dark distended aureole, so swollen with her pounding blood, the skin so thin and tender it felt ready to burst. He stretched his lips around the rim, sucked hard, pushed his tongue against a nipple swollen to the size of a thimble.

The sensation of the hard nipple pressing back into the soft tissue of her breast was excruciating; her hips lifted from the mat as she struggled to engulf the Creature and pull it deeper within her, somehow deeper though their groins were already pressed so tightly together that their pubic hairs were meshed like Velcro. She began to moan, and heard an

answering groan from deep in Whistler's chest that vibrated sympatheti-
cally at the center of the breast in his mouth as her orgasm began to
build.

Whistler and Lourdes beckoned to Cheese Louise to be the next embodiment of the Goddess; her great breasts and hams rolling and shifting
beneath her crimson robe like a sack of basketballs as she stepped carefully down to the floor of the amphitheater, Louise crooked her finger
for Josephina, the newest witch, to join her.

Selene watched from the cheap seats in the upper tier as the brown-
skinned Luzan girl in the shiny new forest green robe rose from her
seat and bowed gracefully; on her way down to the mats Josephina de-
toured over to the cabinet to select a toy, and retrieve her razor-edged
utility knife. Josephina may only have been a witch for a few weeks,
Selene had to remind herself, but she'd been a Drink since she was
three months old.

Louise had plunked herself down cross-legged on one of the mats,
with Whistler and Lourdes reclining on either side of her, resting their
cheeks against her enormous robed thighs. Josephina walked around behind Louise and positioned herself above her, then with her left hand
pinched her own left earlobe hard, and before the sensation of the pinch
died away made a quick slit in the earlobe with the blade of the utility
knife, stooping downward as Louise tilted her head back to catch the first
drops of blood in her mouth.

The more she drank, the farther back Louise leaned, her breasts shifting to the side beneath her robe; the farther she leaned, the lower
Josephina stooped, until finally Louise was lying on her back on the mat
with Josephina lying on her belly, drops of blood falling like grace notes
from her earlobe directly into the soft sucking mouth.

Selene had to sit on her hands to keep from touching herself as the
slim Luzan pinched off her wound, then rose and walked around past
Whistler to stand between Louise's feet, which were spread as wide as the
crimson robe permitted. Then Josephina lifted up the front of her own
green gown to reveal a small black phallus, much smaller than the Creature but beautifully molded into a pert upward curve, and detailed right
down to the swollen veins and ventral channel.

So engrossing was the spectacle of the young girl sliding the robe up
past Louise's thighs and spreading the great legs with her hands, kneeling between them, and inserting the hard rubbery tip of the phallus
gently between the lips of Louise's sex, that Selene hadn't noticed

Lourdes's departure from the sunken stage until she was beside her. "I'm not copping out on you," Lourdes whispered. "But Nanny Parish says I have to be more careful now—no more all-night all-comers until after the baby."

"I understand, dearie," replied Selene, patting her on the knee of her robe; they watched together as Whistler positioned himself behind Josephina. "Thanks for keeping me company."

Josephina may have been overacting a little as, sandwiched between Whistler and Louise, with the head of the Creature poking her pussy from behind and the base of the phallus rubbing her clitoris in front, she raised herself on her elbows to survey the ranks of witches and vampires. "Now who shall it be, who shall it be, who *shall* it be?" she asked out loud, then eeny-meeny-miny-moed Mr. Augie as if by random, though all the witches knew he had bribed her dearly for this place on her dance card.

Augie descended ponderously to the mats (without blood he exhibited none of the vaunted fat man's grace), drinking his first witch blood of the night from a silver flask: he'd always loved the bitter shiny aftertaste of silver and blood. As he reached her, Josephina slid out from between Whistler and Louise. Whistler stayed on top of Louise, greedily gathering her breasts up onto her chest under her robe and nuzzling his face between them while the Creature nuzzled against her soft belly. But they were both already looking up to the bleachers for the next Pan and Goddess.

Augie was oblivious to all of this—he only had eyes for Josephina, who had disrobed, and lasciviously masturbated the curved dildo a few times before unsnapping the leather harness around her waist. When it had fallen at her feet Augie gasped: she had shaved her pubic hair for him, and her little pussy was brown and bare as a walnut. He sank to his knees and buried his face between her legs. *I could die happy now,* he thought to himself, spreading first her pale brown outer lips, then her pink inner lips with his thumbs, and entering her with his tongue.

Soon there was no more room on the mats, and the orgy had begun lapping its way up the tiers of cushions in a tide of green and red robes, of pink and white and brown bodies, of hair and breasts and phalluses of all colors, both flesh and rubber, and bare feet sticking out here and there at odd angles. When the tide began bumping against their feet, in the persons of Sherman and Catherine, Selene and Lourdes left the orgy room by crawling around the top of the outer tier, then descending past the writhing bodies to the door, which was blocked by a striking couple.

Henderson, all six feet six inches of him, had spread-eagled himself in a standing position in the doorway, anchored against the door jamb with both hands while January clung to the front of him, both arms around him, both feet off the ground, impaled on a cock as improbably long and thin as its owner.

"Excuse us? Henderson? January? Coming through?" But there was no getting the attention of two vampires entwined on blood; Selene turned to Lourdes and shrugged, then dropped to her knees and crawled out of the keeping room through the portal of Henderson's bare legs.

Lourdes followed her; in the hallway outside the keeping room they rose from their hands and knees and fell laughing into each other's arms. "I would *kill* to watch Henderson fucking Cheese Louise," said Lourdes, when she could talk.

"Come down to the kitchen with me, dearie," replied Selene. "For some reason, I feel a craving for a popsicle."

TWO

Nick had been thinking about it all day that Monday, the twenty-third of March. Not exactly fighting it—just thinking about it. At work—a conference with the gene splicers south of San Francisco. At the A.A. nooner in Daly City. In the rush-hour traffic. Plenty of time to think about it there; he even reached for his car phone once or twice. At the N.A. meeting at Mandana House. Then, once he got home, he teased himself for another hour, forcing himself to sit through dinner—a Cornish pasty from Noble Pies—because he tended towards stringiness if he lost too much weight. Stringy pecs: heaven forfend.

He ate in his white pine breakfast nook, working with one hand on the acrostic puzzle he'd saved from Sunday's paper and shoveling in the meat-pie with the other. Most un-Nick-like behavior. Pasty crumbs all down the front of his salmon pink Polo. Brushing them would leave grease spots, so he grabbed the shirt by the neck and shook it, leaning forward.

Then he teased himself a little longer: he made himself sweep the crumbs off the beautiful blond hardwood kitchen floor. He would have started the dishes, but the still small voice inside told him he'd dicked around long enough. Without further delay he marched upstairs to his bedroom, took the cordless phone off the charger, lay down on his bed, unsnapped his tailored 501's and punched the fateful eleven-digit number.

It picked up on the second ring. *"Hi, big boy."*

"Hi," said Nick wryly.

"If you're into S&M, press 1; if your pleasure is—"

"I love it when you talk dirty," Nick said—but did not press 1: the trouble with the S&M calls, you could spent fifty bucks talking about the hardware alone. And Nick wasn't interested in leather or steel or rubber. Just a voice, a connection, the dirtier the better, then release, and at least a blessed spasm of forgetfulness.

The "call waiting" signal bleated in his ear before Nick had a chance to choose a subspecialty. Annoyed at the interruption, but grateful too, enjoying the faint flush of guilt he so rarely managed to indulge in nowadays, he broke off the first call. "Hello?"

"Hi Nick. Bev."

"Hey Bev. Zup?"

"Huh?"

"What's up. That's how the kids say 'What's happenin' ' nowadays. Zup."

"Oh. I called to tell you I decided to drop by the V.A. meeting tonight."

"That's fine—I've told you a dozen times, Bev: I appreciate what you did, walking out with me, but I don't want you screwing up your program on my account."

"That's not what I wanted to tell you. I only went to ask them to reconsider about you—"

"Thanks, but—"

"Will you *please* just hear me out? What I called for, *there wasn't any meeting.*"

"No!"

"Yes indeedy. I asked the woman at the desk, she said they hadn't been meeting Mondays for a couple of months, anyway, and when she checked the book for me, turned out they weren't meeting at the Senior Center at all."

"Maybe they found another room someplace?"

"Maybe. But I started calling around when I got home, and I couldn't reach a single member. Sherman finally returned my call about twenty minutes ago—he's going to meet me after the M.A. meeting tomorrow night—said he couldn't explain over the phone."

"Do you trust him?"

"If you asked me that question a couple months ago, I would have said yes without a hesitation. But now? I don't know."

"Do you want me to come along?" There was a pause. "Bev? I said—"

"I was thinking, I was thinking. I'm pretty sure I'll be safe—after all, it's Sherman, not Whistler. But I'll tell you what, I'll stay in touch with you by phone. And if I haven't called you by, say, midnight . . ."

"If you haven't called me by midnight, what?"

"I don't know. Come by my place in the morning and put a stake through my heart."

"Ain't funny, Bev."

"I'm from the Bronx, Nick: I can handle Sherman."

"To put it in the language of your people: Bronx schmonx. You tell Sherman that if I haven't heard from you by midnight, I'm going to call the cops and report you as a missing person. *And* give them his name and address. Tell him that before you even give him a hug. Because personally I don't trust any of them—there's not a one of them that's a match for Whistler."

"Hey, I'm still clean."

"Me too. Take it easy, Bev. Thanks for sticking with me."

"You take it easy too, Nick. Talk to you tomorrow."

When Nick leaned over to replace the handset of his phone in its cradle, he noticed his dick lolling pinkly out of the fly of his black jeans, still undone from the first call. He hadn't a trace of lust left in him, but decided to try and masturbate anyway, if only for the sake of his prostate. Feeling sorrier than dogshit in the rain, he reached into the drawer of his bedside table for the now well-worn *Dicks of All Nations*, and began thumbing through the deck.

But it was no use—the cards only served to remind him of Betty Ruth. They'd bumped into each other once since that night at his house—he was on his way in to the 7:30 meeting of M.A. at the Berkeley-Albany Recovery Center; she was just leaving the six o'clock A.A., wearing a puffy down jacket over baggy jeans, so he hadn't been able to tell whether she was pregnant or not—and when he'd started to speak to her, she'd turned away.

The memory of how she'd turned away—with revulsion, it had seemed to him—pretty much finished Nick off for the night. He didn't even have to stuff his penis back in his jeans: it had shrivelled up backwards like the empty socks of the Wicked Witch of the East, until it was about the size of a rock shrimp.

THREE

At the end of the prayer that closed the Tuesday night meeting of Marijuana Anonymous, Sherman rushed across the circle and threw his arms around Beverly. "Bev, I'm so sorry we never got in touch with you about moving the meeting. If I'd even *dreamed* you wanted to come back . . ." He hadn't shown up at the Recovery Center until after the opening prayers of the M.A. meeting, so this was their first chance to talk.

She stepped back from his embrace. "Tell me first, are you on blood?"

"Of course not."

"Where was everybody last night?"

"At the meeting. We're holding it at our houses, in rotation."

"Why'd you move it? And why couldn't you tell me that over the phone?"

"Same reason: Whistler." He drew her aside, away from the literature table where the ex-potheads were signing up on clipboards for Service assignments. "We should have figured out by the way he tossed Nick across the room that night that he was on blood, but it wasn't until he'd already seduced poor January that we figured out how he'd tricked us." He seemed sincere enough, if somewhat agitated. "Bev, he'll do anything to subvert the fellowship."

"I'm glad you've finally figured that out. Now how about letting Nick back in?"

"Absolutely." Then his high-colored face fell into its familiar puffy pout. "If you think he wants to have anything to do with us again, that is, after the way we treated him."

This time Beverly extended her arms and gave him a hug. "I'm sure he will. Let's call him together."

He glanced up at the clock on the wall at the Recovery Center—it was

Jonathan Nasaw

half past the Eighth Step. "I'm in kind of a hurry—I'm meeting Catherine over at Chez Panisse in half an hour. Tell you what, why don't you join us for dinner, and then we'll call him afterwards."

"God, I'd absolutely adore to. I haven't seen Cathy in ages. But Chez Penis?"

"Just the cafe upstairs. Cathy worked there for years. Oh, and Toshi's the chef tonight. Come on, it'll be fun. My treat—by way of apology."

"Okay, you twisted my arm. Just let me say goodbye to a few people, get a few numbers."

"Meet you in the parking lot—I could use a ride anyway."

They drove across town in Beverly's '61 Volvo—the model that resembled a cross between a Beetle and a '48 Plymouth—and met Catherine at the ivied entrance to the shrine of California Cuisine. Upstairs, Catherine and Sherman were greeted warmly by the host and shown to a table for three looking out past the sloping projection of the roof to the weirdly tiered branches of an araucaria tree.

Beverly whistled when she opened her menu. "Your practice must be going pretty good, Sherm, to be able to hack prices like these. Eighteen ninety-five for hand-cut noodles with yellow-fin? That's tuna noodle casserole, for crying out loud."

"Toshi said to order the duck. Said he'd fix it up special for us."

She checked the menu again. "I don't know—a sorrel-burgundy sauce with shiitake mushrooms, and a cherry glaze? Sounds a little rich to me."

Catherine shrugged. "It's up to you, honey," she said, as casually as she could manage. The truth was, it had sounded a little rich to her too. But she and Toshi had been experimenting for weeks, and there wasn't an ingredient in *Canard à la Whistler* that could be omitted: the burgundy was needed to disguise the salt-sweet taste of Catherine's own blood, and the funky sorrel was required to dispel the aftertaste, while the cherry glaze covered the telltale stickiness. It would have gone better with venison, Toshi had insisted, but Catherine had warned him that in her experience the only women who would eat Bambi would be wearing wool caps with earflaps.

The question now was, could she get Bev to order Donald? Catherine reached around the bread basket and patted the other woman's hand. "Take it from a food service professional," she advised. "A: it's going to be delicious. And B: when an Oriental chef recommends a dish, it's usually best to order it—they tend to pee in the soup when their feelings get hurt."

*   *   *

As the waiter cleared the entrée, Sherman, who'd also dined on doc-tored duck, excused himself and slipped away to the men's room for a blast of Visine—they wanted Bev to figure out she was high all by herself.

When he returned to the table by the window, dessert had arrived—a perfect orb of rose-geranium sorbet, drizzled with a tracery of raspberry sauce, afloat in a pond of mango syrup.

"The color scheme God was trying for when he designed the sunset," Beverly remarked, spooning up a sliver of sorbet. After letting it dissolve slowly in her mouth, she dipped her forefinger into the mango syrup, licked the finger clean with lascivious enjoyment, then closed her eyes and repeated the entire sequence several times.

By the time she opened them again, the whites had gone as red as the raspberry sauce; when she spoke, her tone was conversational. "It was in the duck, right?"

Sherman tensed. "How long have you known?"

She pointed at the shallow-rimmed dessert bowl in front of her. "Since that arrived."

"What tipped you off? The color? The taste?"

"I heard it melting."

Later, over coffee and biscotti, Beverly asked them why they'd gone to so much trouble to dose her. "Why didn't you just tie me down and pour it in my mouth—the end result would have been the same, once I was high. Even in V.A. meetings, we always used to say that nobody could resist blood, *on* blood."

Sherman answered. "Too crude, Whistler says. Says that just because V.A. used force, didn't mean we had to stoop to their level. And from a professional standpoint, I had to agree that force should always be a last resort. Besides, Whistler's picking up the tab anyway."

They lingered over their coffee until Toshi had finished work, then, with Sherman and Catherine following in their car, Beverly drove Toshi to the West County Blood Bank in order to pick up a nightcap for the orgy that was almost sure to follow.

Beverly opened the back door with her key and disabled the alarm; the others tiptoed in after her, waiting in the office while Beverly let herself into the refrigerated storage room. On her way out, carrying a fat plastic drip-bag full of blood that would pass its expiration date at midnight, she glanced at the clock on the wall, and nearly dropped the bag. "Oh shit."

"What's wrong, Beverly?" Toshi asked.

"It's almost midnight."

"Are you going to turn into a pumpkin? If so, let one of us hold the blood."

"No, but if I don't call Nick in the next five minutes, he's going to call the cops and tell them Sherman kidnapped me." She hurried into her office to pick up the phone, and Sherman hurried after her. When they returned a minute or so later, both were grinning.

"All done?" asked Toshi, sitting at the receptionist's desk with his feet up. Catherine was sitting on the desk itself.

"All done." Beverly sashayed across the office, her narrow hips swinging.

"How'd he take it?"

"He was devastated." She kissed Toshi on the top of his head, then leaned over him to kiss Catherine full on the lips. "Absolutely devastated."

"What did you tell him?" asked Catherine, after a respectful pause. She was still a little surprised by the vehemence with which Beverly had turned on her dear friend Nick, although Sherman had predicted it. "Basic psychology," he had informed his wife the night before. "The same elements of her psychological makeup that made her the most rabid of the reformers will now make her an equally rabid backslider."

And apparently he'd been right on the money. "I told Mr. Nick Santos exactly what Whistler told your husband to tell me to tell him," Beverly replied blithely, as she dropped the bag of blood into her oversized patent-leather purse. "I informed Mr. Santos that he was now the last recovering vampire on earth."

FOUR

Aluka. Asasabonsam. Lampir. Langsuyar . . .

By late March the Reverend Betty Ruth Shoemaker had researched vampire myths and legends from every culture on earth, from the flying Aswang of the Philippine Islands to the Zaloznye Pokojniki of the Russian steppes, from Elizabeth of Bathory in the early sixteenth century to the Highgate Vampire in the late twentieth, and had found an undeniable correspondence between vampire lore and vampire reality as she had recently come to understand it.

It all fit—the avoidance of daylight and the superhuman powers of the Nosferatu; the progressive madness of the historical Carpathians; the intense eroticism of the literary vampires; the baby-craving of the Malaysian Penangglan—all dovetailing nicely with Nick's story.

Betty Ruth had even taken it a step further: on a hunch she'd borrowed a new book about Jack the Ripper from the Richmond library. "Just the facts, ma'am," she mused aloud—ministerial perks again. It was a little past midnight; dressed in her bedtime sweatshirt and sweatpants, she was lying in her living room with her feet up on a garage-sale sofa that had once passed for Louis Quinze but was now more like Louis Wept. "One: All of the Ripper's victims were exsanguinated—drained of blood. Two: the experts always blame that on the disembowelments, but there was never as much blood on the scene as they would have expected to find. Three: The mystery of how he managed his escapes . . ."

Three was a corker: by the last few murders, there were cops all over Whitechapel, almost literally on every corner, but no one had ever caught so much as a glimpse of the killer. One of the bodies was even discovered within minutes, maybe seconds. "And the only way out of *that* particular alley was either right past a Bobby, or straight up and over a fourteen-foot wall."

Betty couldn't stop herself—she climbed off the couch slowly, feeling somewhat ponderous due to her recent weight gain, and walked over to the living room window, which was framed with silver tape from the security system. She glanced down to the ground a few feet below, then craned her head up towards the ceiling to measure the distance from the ground to the nursery windows directly overhead. Looked to be about fourteen feet, she estimated—maybe even a foot or two lower.

She was halfway up the stairs on her way to bed when the phone rang, but as she had the machine set to kick in after four rings, and was carrying a mug of chamomile tea, she decided to take her time. She could hear her ancient answering machine groaning through its tired repertory of clicks and whirrs; then, from the top of the stairs, a man's indecipherable voice through the crackling speaker.

When she reached the bedroom Betty set her tea on the dresser and picked up the phone by the bedside table. "Hello?"

"Thank for picking up. I know I'm the last person on earth you want to talk to, but I was getting pretty desp—"

"I didn't know it was you, Nick." She hung up, then rewound the message he'd been leaving without listening to it. A moment later the phone rang again. Betty turned off the machine before it could answer, then shut off the ringer on the phone and climbed into bed with an Annie Lamott novel and her tea, muttering to herself that she'd had quite enough of vampires for one night, " ' thank you very much, Mr. Santos. Or is it San Georgiou?' That's what I should have said."

She opened the book to her place and read the same page two or three times with an absolute lack of comprehension before curiosity got the better of her. She reached over and pushed playback on her answering machine. *Betty? It's Nick Santos. Sorry to call you so late, but I really have to speak with you. So please could you pick up the phone? Betty? Betty Ruth? Please? I'm begging you, Betty, it's a matter of life and death. Literally. In the name of God, Betty, you're a minister. Please pick up the ph—*

"And at this point," she remarked to herself, "Mother Teresa here picked up the phone and slammed it down in the desperate man's ear."

"SHIT!" She didn't even have to persuade herself to let out her anger.

"SHIT, SHIT, SHIT, SHIT, SHIT," at the top of her lungs all the way down to the kitchen, decreasing in volume but not vehemence. Only her Rolodex wasn't next to the kitchen phone, she realized when she got there: it was down in the office.

She took a chance and dialed 411—they had a listing, but only for his business line: she tried that, and reached his machine. "I'm sorry I hung up on you, Nick. I'm here—call me back."

On her way back up to bed, Betty Ruth tried to remember something called the Forgiveness Process that had been popular in the eighties. She remembered that it took a whole week to do, and that every day you forgave somebody—your parents one day, people who'd hurt you as a child the next, and so on until on the last day you forgave yourself.

And it occurred to her as she climbed back into bed that perhaps her anger at Nick was only a reflection of her anger at herself—she'd been the one who'd been in such a damn hurry here. "Wait forty-two years to decide to become a mother, and about forty-two minutes to decide on the father. Who had already told you he was recovering from practically every addiction known to mankind. Smooth move, Ex-lax."

She had turned the switch under the phone to the ring position and picked up her novel again when she heard someone banging on the kitchen door directly beneath the bedroom window and calling her name. She knelt up on her bed and threw open the sash. "Nick?" she called softly, leaning out.

"I'm sorry. I'm so sorry. But I have to—"

"I'll be right down."

The next time the phone rang, it was the man from ADT calling because Nick's banging had set off the silent alarm. "No, everything's fine. . . . My password? Let me th—I remember: Psalms 121:8. . . . No, thank *you.*" She hung up.

"What's Psalms 121:8?" Nick asked her from across the kitchen table.

" 'The Lord shall preserve thy going out and thy coming in from this time forth.' "

"How appropriate."

"A divinity degree ought to be good for something. Listen, Nick, I'm sorry I hung up on you before. All I can say in my defense is that I did call back and leave a message on your machine after I'd listened to your—"

He interrupted her. "I'm the one who should be apologizing to you. After all I've put you through, to call you in the middle of the night like this. But I was pretty desperate."

"So I gathered. Would you like some tea?"

"It won't take that long. I just have to know if . . . Well, you know—if it . . . if you . . ." He blew out a long breath. "Oh shit. Are you pregnant, and am I the father?"

"You said it's a matter of life and death?"

He looked into her eyes and nodded.

"Why?"

"I'll tell you, I promise. But it's important you answer me first."

She looked down at the table, then deliberately raised her eyes. "Yes I am. And yes you are. Now tell me why it's a matter of life and death."

But to her surprise he broke down before her eyes—she caught a glimpse of his handsome face distorting with anguish before he buried it in his hands. Betty walked around the table, leaned over him, and hugged him from behind while his shoulders heaved against her with unvoiced sobs. "You don't have to tell me," she whispered.

"I—I want to," he managed after a few false starts. It had occurred to him that there was no one else left to tell the story to.

". . . so for the past—" Nick glanced at his watch: 3 A.M. "—three hours or so, I have officially been the last recovering vampire on earth. I spent the first hour of that trying to think of just one good reason to go on living. If your answer had been no, I was on my way to the bridge."

She nodded: having lived in the Bay Area for nearly twenty years, she had no need to ask him which bridge, or why. "Has it occurred to you that that's exactly what Whistler's hoping you'll do?"

He shook his head. They were in the living room, Betty in the armchair and Nick on the yellow sofa; in the angle between them stood a three-legged wooden end table supporting a fringed lamp, a box of Kleenex, two mugs, a scattering of crumbs, and an empty box of Pim's Orange cookies. "He's already won—I don't think he cares what I do next."

"I do, Nick."

"Do what?"

"Care what you do next. Care what happens to you."

He waved off her concern. "It's all right, Betty, I'm not planning to kill myself anymore, if I ever really was."

"Good. Because I'm going to need all the help I can get with this baby." At what point she'd arrived at this decision, she could not have said. And how much of it was impelled by her sense of guilt at having turned her back on him professionally—either of her professions—and how much by the financial panic that had been a constant companion of hers since losing the prayed-for V.A. income, she could not have said either.

But Nick assumed a third—and fourth—possibility that had not occurred to her. "I didn't come here for that, Betty. If you let me into your life now, it would be out of pity or charity, and I don't want either of those."

The fatigue of the long night caught up to Betty all at once; she pushed herself up from the armchair—not an easy feat—and began clearing off the end table. "Pity, charity, self-interest, fear—those aren't things that bring people together, Nick. People just get together—life brings them together, or fate or Higher Power or something."

She brushed the crumbs into one of the empty cups; when she returned from the kitchen Nick was still sitting on the edge of the sofa, hunched forward with his hands between his knees. She sat down beside him on the sofa, nudging him with her hip to make him slide over. "Did you ever watch *The Honeymooners*, Nick?"

He nodded, surprised.

"Well, it's like Ralph Kramden always used to say: 'This thing is bigger than the both of us.' And it's certainly bigger than either of us alone. Me, I'm three and a half months pregnant with no medical coverage and no savings. You, you're trying to fight the most horrible addiction known to man—or woman. And we're both trying to do it alone. You tell me, Nick: what's wrong with this picture?"

After a minute or so he raised his head. Even at three in the morning, so wept out that his mustache was soggy, it occurred to her that he was still an awfully good looking man. "Actually, I think it was Arnold Stang who used to say that. But if you want Ralph Kramden, I'll give you Ralph Kramden." He brandished his fist weakly in the air. "One of these days, Alice, one of these days: pow, right in the kisser."

She laughed. "Oh yeah? Well, one of *these* days, Ralph, one of *these* days—" She grabbed his fist with both hands, and brought it to her lips. "Kiss! Right in the power."

ONE

Although Whistler's and Nick's paths did not cross for the next few months, their lives were running on curiously parallel tracks. Each was living a life of unaccustomed domesticity, and each, despite having learned a great deal more about the process of human gestation than he might have preferred to know, seemed to be thriving on it.

Of course, that said, it must be admitted that their respective circumstances could not have been more different. Nick and Betty maintained their separate residences and lives, getting together a few afternoons a week for therapy (for which Nick paid full retail price, thus conveniently solving the most pressing problems of both simultaneously) and once or twice a week for dinner and a movie—he'd donated one of his old VCRs to the Church of the Higher Power, and taken a nice deduction for it, as well.

All very comfy-cozy, of course—no sexual component that either of them would have acknowledged—but even without that, it was still more of a relationship than either Betty or Nick might have reasonably expected of each other back in December.

Whistler and Lourdes's domesticity was of a more conventional nature, insofar as anything having to do with those two might be described as conventional: they had spent the bulk of her second trimester at his villa in Greece while renovations were under way at Whistler Manor, and returned to Tahoe in time for high spring in the Sierras.

And there, almost every evening, Lourdes would awaken at sunset in vanilla satin pajamas, between vanilla satin sheets, and look around at the Impressionist paintings hanging on the textured cream-colored walls of her bedroom, and then out at the lake, an Impressionist masterpiece in its own right, framed by the thick brown beams of her bedroom window, hoarding the last few blurry ribbons of sunset gold in its turquoise blue depths.

Then she would ring a little enamel bell on the bedside table, Nanny Parish would bring her a thimbleful of blood (a thimbleful an hour—no more, no less—was the time-tested Luzan ration for pregnant vampires), and Lourdes would sip from a bejewelled silver thimble (a relic of sorts, reputed to have been the very thimble Nanny Eames had used while carrying Prescott) as the western sky turned a pink-edged charcoal gray above the darkening rim of mountains.

And as the blood came on, Lourdes would bare her teeth in a contented smile, and stretch, and wriggle languidly inside her pajamas, enjoying the kiss of satin against skin, as through the window the lake turned gravely purple.

You done good, girl, she'd think to herself at these moments. *For a poor little flip from West Mo, you done real good.* Then, when shc was good and ready, she'd unlock the door between her bedroom and Whistler's. No need to call him—he'd have been waiting for the snick of the bolt.

The reason for the locked door was her advanced pregnancy—after her fifth month, Nanny Parish had restricted Lourdes to shallow penetration only. To which the Creature had replied *Yeah, right.* Whistler himself had installed the bolt in late May.

But there was an old Filipino saying to the effect that a woman *managed* a man by withholding sex, but only *mastered* him by furnishing it. Fortunately, the farther her pregnancy advanced, the more her body seemed to fascinate Whistler; by mid-June they had settled into a routine that was not too taxing on Lourdes, but that so delighted both Whistler and the Creature that none of them saw any reason to abandon it even on the evening of the twentieth of June, which marked not only the Midsummer gathering of the Coven and Penang, but their wedding night as well.

So after drawing the bolt, Lourdes, wearing only her oversized pajama top, assumed her customary place at the window, pretending not to notice Whistler standing in the doorway in his lilac and black kimono, sipping his eye-opener from a brandy snifter held loosely in one long-fingered hand, with a joint of his usual exquisite weed burning in the other, not to gild the lily of his blood high, but to assure that both his hands were occupied.

She let him watch for a while, giving him the pleasure of peeping while she unbuttoned her top one slow button at a time; then, when the last satin button had slipped through the last satin buttonhole, she turned to him, eyes downcast, and opened the jacket; it stayed open, held in place by the great pear-shaped swell of her breasts and the breathtaking swoop of her belly. Then and only then did she allow him to make eye contact with her.

But that eye contact she held, firmly as a dominatrix's whip, as she shrugged off the jacket, which slid to the floor with a whispering sound that only vampires could hear. Nor would she set his eyes free to wander over her nude body until he was seated on the bed—she wanted him looking up at her, seeing the heavy blue-veined weight of her breasts and the taut mound of her belly from below.

For Whistler, the effect was always the same: he might have been looking up at a great stone fertility goddess come to life. And when she joined him on the bed, reclining leisurely on her side, and freed the Creature from Whistler's kimono, all it yearned for was to burrow its way up past her swollen belly to her distended breasts, bury its entire length between them, and be kneaded into a great gushing orgasm between their pillowing softness.

All of which was accomplished with Whistler still juggling his snifter of blood in one hand and his reefer, long since extinguished, in the other (a feat only a vampire would attempt—or need to). Then, spent, Whistler rolled onto his back and watched in amusement as his fertility goddess diligently rubbed his pearly offering into the soft skin of her breasts. "Nanny Parish says it'll prevent stretch marks," she explained.

"Delighted to be of help." He leaned across the bed to put down his glass and relight the joint. "Care for a taste?"

She refused the weed. "I can't get too stoned—there's too much to do."

"I'm sure Catherine and Cheese Louise have everything under control."

And a moment later, as if in response to Whistler's assurance, Catherine Bailey (who had quit her job with the City of Berkeley for a much better paying position as Whistler Manor's full-time housekeeper), rapped at the door with their continental breakfast—two lattes, croissants, English muffins, sweet butter, fruit compote and fresh-squeezed orange juice. "Enter," called Whistler grandly.

Neither of them had bothered to cover themselves—Catherine glanced towards them wryly as she set the tray down on the small drop-leaf secretaire against the bedroom wall. "Isn't there some superstition about the groom seeing the bride naked on the wedding day?"

"We're vampires," explained Whistler. "We don't believe in superstition."

"Toss me my top anyway," Lourdes asked her. "I don't want to get my boobs in the compote. Thanks. Hey, aren't you supposed to be at the Coven meeting?"

"The solstice occurred at seven o'clock—I just this minute changed out of my robe and made your breakfast."

"Are any of the vampires here yet?"

"Just Louise—she got in last night—beat the sun by about ten minutes, grabbed a couple hours' sleep, and has been down in the kitchen ever since. Yes, the cake is beautiful, and no, you can't see it."

Lourdes finished buttoning her pajama top, and carried her latte over to the south-facing window of her corner bedroom. It was her favorite spot, her *querencia*: she had taken to spending hours at a time there with her feet braced against one wall of the deep wide window ledge and her back against the other, contemplating the glow in the sky over the State-line casinos, and communing with her great curving belly.

Whistler, who was prone to nearly hourly fits of uxoriousness, had had the window sill padded royally when he saw she liked to nest there, and as he watched her climbing up carefully onto it, he made a mental note to have a low step installed, and perhaps even a plush-padded handrail. He sat up and closed his kimono over the nodding Creature. "Any word on our guest of honor?" he asked Catherine.

"All I know is that Selene says the runes say he'll be here in time for the wedding." Catherine left, closing the bedroom door behind her.

"I dunno, Jamey." Lourdes turned from the window. "Does it really matter all that much anymore what happens to him?"

"Apparently it does to Selene. And I must admit I tend to agree with her. You know how the twelve-steppers throw around the term 'disease'? Well, the more I've thought about it, the more it seems to me that they're the ones carrying the disease.

"Furthermore, the way it's spreading, chapters of Anonymous This and Anonymous That popping up in every village, town, and hamlet from one end of the country to the other—" He crossed over to the window and stood beside her. "—it seems obvious that *their* disease is far more threatening an epidemic than any of the so-called diseases they claim to be combating.

"All of which has led me to the following conclusion." He rested a hand on her thigh, looking out past her to the wooded curve of the lake shore. "I've decided that as long as there's a single recovering vampire left to infect the others with his pernicious beliefs, none of us should consider ourselves safe. Remember what I told you about Leon: 'He who threatens my blood, threatens my life.' "

Lourdes put her hand over his and squeezed. "But not like Leon, please Jamey? No bridges? It would really stomp my buzz to have somebody killed on our wedding night."

"Fear not, mother of my child—I have absolutely no intention of having him killed, and as far as I know, neither does Selene."

"No?"

"Of course not." He leaned over to kiss her on the cheek. "We're just going to vaccinate the son of a bitch."

TWO

Betty Ruth marked her place in her book with her finger, and looked up from the kitchen table as Nick let himself in with the key she'd given him. "Didn't you say Whistler's girlfriend was Filipino?" Six and a half months pregnant and twenty pounds heavier, she was wearing a pavilion-size orange and red flame-patterned maternity muumuu.

"Half." He set their suppers down on the counter—lemon thyme chicken, rice pilaf, small salads, chocolate cake, all boxed and bagged from one of the yuppie take-out places that had proliferated around Berkeley in the past five years—and hung his red nylon James Dean windbreaker over the back of one of the ladder-back chairs.

"Listen to this: 'Among the several varieties of vampirelike creatures known to Philippine mythology, perhaps the most terrifying is the Aswang. As she fills herself with her victim's blood, this demon gradually assumes the shape of a pregnant woman, then flies home and suckles her monstrous brood with a elixir of milk and blood from her swollen teats—' "

"Charming." Nick interrupted her. "Absolutely charming. And from which scholarly tome are we gleaning these latest tidbits?" She held the book up to show him the cover. "Ah, *Vampires: The True Story*. By Count Polozny, no less." He raised his eyebrows. "Have I ever mentioned that an obsessive interest in vampirology is one of the markers for the disease?"

Betty closed the book, and started to haul herself up from the table. Nick waved her back down. "Sit, sit." He found plates and bowls in the cupboard—none matching—and began transferring the meals. "How did it go today?"

Betty had facilitated a workshop on Self-Esteem for straight single women. "As usual, they spent the sessions talking about how great it was to be single, and the breaks talking about how to find men."

"Learn anything?"

"Houseplants. If a guy has houseplants—if he even knows the *names* of houseplants—it means he's gay."

Nick agreed, as he placed an artfully arranged dinner plate before her. "The only surer way to tell is if he puts take-out food on dishes."

Betty laughed. "I got us *Thelma and Louise* for tonight."

"Damn," said Nick.

"What, you saw it?"

"No, I forgot to tell you—I have to go out tonight."

"Abandoning me for some chippy, eh? I thought we had a date?" She meant it as a joke, but it hung in the air a little too heavily, a little too long.

"Hardly. It's program business." He might have told her which program—would have, if she'd asked—but didn't want to set a precedent by explaining. That was the sort of thing that could go far towards defining a relationship. After all, he'd never *said* anything about staying for a movie this evening—they'd just sort of fallen into the habit.

And after the way her joke had gone over, Betty wasn't *about* to ask. So they ate, and chatted companionably; he insisted on doing the dishes, and she let him—it's hard to wash dishes when your belly won't let you get within a foot of the sink.

After he'd left, promising to attend her morning service, she ascribed to hormones the dismal empty feeling that swept over her, then brushed back her tears and began calling the women who'd attended the workshop that afternoon, one after the other, until she found one who didn't have anything better to do on a Saturday night—most—and also hadn't seen *Thelma and Louise* yet—none. She settled for a recent divorcée who had seen it twice, but promised not to divulge the ending, or telegraph the good parts.

Nick drove to El Sobrante with the rag in the bag—top down on the 'Vette, that is—feeling a little conflicted about Betty. Even though it had been years since he'd been involved in a relationship responsible enough for guilt to come into play, he still recognized that he could have handled things better. On the other hand, he reasoned, would it have been less upsetting for her to have known that V.A. was the program he had business with, and that the business involved January, who'd apparently been house-sitting for Whistler in El Sobrante, had stumbled onto his stash, and hadn't been asleep for a week?

Even though he suspected that she was only calling *him* because all the other vampires were up at Tahoe for the wedding (Nick had received an engraved invitation in the mail, and torn it into pieces with a satisfaction as enjoyable as it was childish), it was still an opportunity—indeed a duty—he could not pass up. He had agreed to pick her up after dark, her habit having reached the point where she could no longer tolerate daylight, and bring her back to his place to help her detox.

Of course, for all he knew, January might already have changed her mind—she might not even be there. No sense in worrying Betty until after he saw how it went. But when he reached the end of Whistler's long driveway, January was indeed waiting for him in the farmhouse doorway, wearing funky black jeans and a purple tank top; leather armbands and wristbands highlighted the definition in her arm muscles as she hauled her heavy suitcase over to the 'Vette. In her other hand was a close-meshed net bag full of what appeared to be silver dollars.

"What's all this?" asked Nick, getting out of the car to open the trunk for her.

"Chips," said January, shaking the bag so that the coins jingled heavily. "Everybody turned in all their V.A. chips. Whistler said I could have them for watching the house. He gave me the suitcase, too, on account of we have the same initials." She pointed to the monogram. "See—J.M.W. James McNeill Whistler, January Moon Winters."

"Lucky for you," replied Nick. He lifted the suitcase into the trunk, but horizontally, facing up. "That's a six-hundred-dollar Vuitton. Mind if I open it?" He'd already reached for the catch. "I just have to make sure you aren't bringing any—"

But he never got to finish the sentence—she'd whacked him across the back of the skull with the sack of solid silver twelve-step anniversary chips, and he slumped face forward into the trunk with an unexpected sigh, then crumpled to the ground.

(The sack of chips, of course, had been Whistler's suggested weapon of choice. "He'll go out easy enough if you catch him right at the base of the skull," he had explained to her over the phone on Friday night. "The hard part's not cracking his head open."

"Do you really care?" she'd asked him.

"Of course I care," had been his immediate reply. "Why should you get to have all the fun?"

January grabbed Nick by the collar of his red windbreaker, tugged him around the car and hauled him up into the passenger seat, fastened the non-stock shoulder and lap belts around him, then went back to the trunk and opened the suitcase herself. There wasn't much in it—her clothes, a few things Lourdes had asked her to bring from the farmhouse, her Star Trek thermos, of course, and for Nick, a soft felt Rolled Crusher hat, an oversized pair of sunglasses, and a small bottle of ether in case he woke up during the drive.

She slapped the hat on his head and adjusted the glasses. "Hold this for me, will you?" she asked him, then tucked the thermos into his lap, strapped in place by the lap belt.

She ground the gears a few times, looking for reverse—she'd watched him carefully, but had never driven a three-speed before; she wondered for a moment if she were too stoned to drive, then decided no, the problem was she wasn't stoned enough. She was right, too: within moments of borrowing the thermos back from the unconscious Nick and taking another slash, she had become one with the car—a Vulcan mind-meld with a '56 Corvette.

"Thanks for letting me drive, Nick." January tucked the thermos back into his lap belt, and kissed him rather too hard on the cheek—he slid sideways and banged his head against the side window. "It's like that movie *Weekend At Bernie's*," she giggled, tugging Nick upright again, tightening the harness, and straightening his hat and glasses. "Only it's Weekend at Whistler's."

January revved the 'Vette's engine until the fiberglass doors vibrated, then threw it violently into first gear. She didn't quite manage to pop a wheelie, but the back end fishtailed satisfactorily like the drag racers out on the Great Highway at midnight; even more satisfying was the way Nick's body lurched backwards against the seat, then slumped forward against the shoulder harness.

THREE

Even before he opened his eyes, Nick knew that it was Selene's lap that cradled his aching head, knew it from the sense of well-being that had come over him, as familiar and recognizable as the smell outside his father's bakery on a sunny morning in Greektown.

But the pain when he did open them was blinding; he shut them quickly, having recorded a vague impression of being at the bottom of a bowl, with people in hooded robes looking down at him. But he doubted his senses, for he'd also seen a skyful of nymphs and satyrs floating directly over his head. "What . . . ?"

"Shhh," said Selene, raising his head, holding a silver chalice to his lips. "Drink this, it'll help the pain."

He knew it was blood he was drinking, of course—what he didn't know was where he was drinking it, or even more peculiarly, when: between the cotton-batting wooziness of the concussion, and Selene's sudden appearance, Nick had the indistinct impression of having, like Billy Pilgrim, become unstuck in time, of having been knocked back into the middle of his own life. And although it occurred to him as he drained the chalice that there was some reason not to, for the life of him he couldn't remember what it was.

Ironically enough, it was the blood that brought him back to himself—soon the throbbing in his head had disappeared entirely, leaving in its wake a blood-induced clarity that was nearly as blinding as the concussion had been.

"Open your eyes, Nick," said Selene softly.

He found himself staring up at her ravaged throat. "Is that mine?" he asked softly, referring to the livid scar.

She nodded—above him the scar creased and relaxed, creased and relaxed. "Yours, mine, and ours," she agreed.

"I never saw it before," he explained. He could see the tiered ranks of robed vampires and witches rising above him, but whatever play he and Selene were acting out, at this point in it, it was obviously perfectly appropriate for the two of them to be having a quiet little conversation. Even a banal one. "No wonder you're pissed off," he added.

"I never minded the scar, Nick." She wanted to be sure he understood. "At least, not after the first year or so."

"No, it's beautiful," he said, and meant it. "I'm still sorry, though."

"Sorry don't milk the toad, dearie." She put down the cup and picked up a folding mother-of-pearl-handled straight razor. "Tilt your chin back." She snapped the razor open with a flourish, like Al Capone's barber.

Even if he hadn't been high, he could easily have overpowered the slight, middle-aged witch; as it was, high on blood, and with the training the Air Force had given him, not to mention the Montagnards, he might even have stood a chance against the vampires. But something—perhaps that same blood high—was informing his instincts: there was no fight in him, no flight, just a softening of the muscles in his throat as he leaned back against Selene's welcoming lap and closed his eyes again.

The pain was exquisite—he'd forgotten how exquisite pain could be, on blood. He could feel his hard-on pressing against the front of his jeans as she drew the razor across his throat.

Nick opened his eyes. The hooded robed figures were at the edge of their seats, staring down at him. He remembered Ben Casey on television: the operating amphitheater. And now he was the patient. He noticed that he was breathing—no bubbling noise; glanced down—no spurting; touched curious fingers to his throat and then held his fingertips before his eyes—only a thin red tracery of blood.

He remembered a joke: guy slits another guy's throat with a straight razor; second guy says you missed; first guy says oh yeah, wait'll you try to turn your head.

Nick turned his head—when it didn't fall off he decided it was safe to sit up. "Does that milk the toad?"

Selene nodded. "Bygones are bygones."

"And I'm free to go?"

"Or to stay." She handed him the chalice.

The lake was lower than Nick had ever seen it. He placed the chalice down carefully on the brick step, pulled off his boots one at a time, then his socks, picked up the chalice again, and stepped down onto the lawn, which was cut low as a golf green. It felt glorious, like walking on cool green velvet. *The more skin, the more better,* he thought. *God help me but I love this drug.*

He was able to walk a long way out on the beach, in the moonshadow of the dock. He still hadn't taken that second sip from the chalice. On the other hand, he hadn't exactly poured it out, either, and what was going through his mind as he bent over to roll up the cuffs of his jeans was a prospect that he'd thought dead forever, buried under the derisive laughter of a hundred twelve-step meetings. It was the most dangerous of fantasies, covering the entire spectrum of addictions: *I can handle it. I'll just smoke pot on weekends / drink at parties / eat an ice-cream cone every Monday after work for a reward. The rest of the time I'll stay straight / sober/ thin.*

Nick waded into the lake until the cold black water was lapping at his ankles, and lifted the chalice towards the moon in a toast. "To the Dream of the Occasional User," he said aloud, then lowered the chalice, took a sip, smacked his lips. "And a delicious fucking Dream it is, too."

Nick opened the keeping-room door quietly and tiptoed in, wary of interrupting the wedding ceremony. But as the ceremony at that point seemed to involve the groom and the pregnant bride copulating naked on the floor of the amphitheater, there wasn't much danger of that. There was an empty space next to the door, on the first tier of cushions; he slid in.

"Hi Nick," whispered January. "You okay?"

"Okay?" He thought about it for a minute. "I suppose so. I'm stoned. I suppose I'm going to be fine so long as I'm stoned."

She laughed under her breath. "Tell me about it."

"Are these two married yet?" asked Nick.

"I dunno. They didn't say 'I do' or anything."

"Well what's going on at this point?"

"I didn't understand everything Selene said, but it's like on spring equinox the lord of the green fucks everything that moves, but in summer he has to settle down with the goddess."

"Oh, I remember Midsummer now. 'Forsaking all others, and cleaving only to each other,' right?"

"Right. You have to pick a partner and stick with 'em all night. You should have heard everybody bitching."

Lourdes was nearing a climax at their feet; Nick hoped she wouldn't hurt herself. Whistler and the Creature did seem to be taking extra care tonight, but still, he'd never seen so pregnant a woman naked before, much less *in flagrante.* He was getting off on it, too—but then he was high on blood for the first time in five years: he'd probably have gotten off watching Mr. and Mrs. Ed.

Nick glanced around the amphitheater—the pairing up had already begun. Sherman and Catherine were leading the procession out of the stands and towards the door. He felt January tugging at the sleeve of his nylon windbreaker. "Wanna cleave?" she asked.

"There's a problem," he replied carefully.

"I don't care," she said. "I'll keep my shirt on, strap on a dildo, and call you—" She lowered the register of her voice to a deep tenor: "Bud!"

He laughed. "Well, okay—but what are we going to do for blood?"

"At Whistler Manor?" It was January's turn to laugh. "Follow me."

"This used to be a bathroom," remarked Nick, in the pantry. Six months after Whistler's promise of all the blood she could drink, January still had a distinctly feral air, but with an edge of sleekness; her empurpled black hair, combed straight back and moussed to a shine, accentuated the length of her narrow skull, and she moved with a smooth confidence beneath the satin folds of her crimson robe.

"Well now it's a secret passage to a roomful of blood," she said enthusiastically, sounding about nine years old as she pushed open the door at the top of the cellar stairs.

When they reached the bottom, they found Louise and Sally in the blood cellar on a similar errand, so they waited in the four-by-six outer room, which had an ugly green indoor/outdoor carpet laid over an unpadded concrete floor, and a translucent light panel set into the high ceiling. Both long walls were lined with shelves, and the shelves lined with red windowpane-plaid contact paper and stocked with canned food—everything from creamed corn to caviar, peas to pâté. Apparently there was a fan up there too—they could hear it whirring.

"Hey Cheese, Sally," called Nick, feeling buoyant as a teenager himself. "You guys a couple too?"

"Yeah," said Louise, emerging from the inner room through a revolving section of the wall.

"But a couple of what, I couldn't tell you," added Sally, following her out with a bag of blood, her elegant head carried high and regal above her robe, waving like some exotic brown orchid on her long narrow stalk of a neck. "Come visit us later—we're in the bungalow."

"I'd *pay* to see those two naked together," remarked Nick when he and January were alone. "But I don't want to get in trouble with Selene again." That last he'd added only half jokingly.

"She just said we couldn't *cleave* with anybody else," replied January, leading Nick through the revolving door into the refrigerated room. "Didn't say nothing about watching. Besides, I'm not a witch—I only have to listen to Whistler, not Selene."

Nick gave her the mezzo-mezzo gesture, as if to say, *I'm not too sure of that.* "One thing you have to remember about Selene: she's Whistler's creature entirely. I forgot that once—just once—but I'm still paying for it."

On the other hand, there were worse forms of payment. Once inside the inner room of the blood cellar, there was nothing Nick could do but throw back his head and laugh. A room full of blood indeed: an entire wall lined with pigeonholes containing blood in sundry containers—thick plastic blood-bank bags; sparkling glass drip bottles used by hospitals half a century ago, refilled and resealed; test tubes and vials and labeled, dated Seal-a-Meal pouches.

"Estate bottled?" wondered Nick, selecting a pouch and holding it to the overhead light to read the label. *Selene. 5/5/92.* He handed it to January. "Ah yes, May 'ninety-two. An excellent vintage," he remarked, in a toothy British accent meant to mimic Whistler but sounding more like Terry-Thomas.

"Yeah, Selene's got killer blood," January agreed. "She takes herbs and shit. Come on, let's get this into my thermos while it's still cold. That way it'll keep all night."

All the rooms on the third floor of the north wing were slope-ceilinged and windowless—servants' quarters, originally, accessible only by a single back staircase. January's room was one of the smallest, containing only a king-size mattress, a tangled pile of bedding, and her open suitcase, but there were patterned tapestry-like cotton wall hangings billowing from three of the four walls—it felt as much like a womb as a cave.

Nick sat down cross-legged on the mattress to wait while January washed out her thermos in the dormitory-style bathroom down the hall. When she returned she tore open a corner of the pouch with her teeth, decanted the contents carefully, tossed the empty pouch into a corner, and handed the thermos to Nick.

He looked down into the wide mouth, hesitating.

"For fuck's sake, Nick, are you gonna like, soul-search all night every time you take a drink?" complained January.

He looked up. "I was just remembering something that used to happen at meetings, sometimes. M.A. meetings, especially. Some pothead with years of clean time would raise her hand and say—" He lifted his voice to a high-pitched singsong: " 'Hi, my name's Whatever, and I'm a pothead. I've been clean for . . .' "

Back to his own voice: "Only instead of saying two years, four months or whatever, it'd be two days, or ten hours, and everybody except her sponsor or phone buddies goes *Aaaah,* and then she talks about how she toked on some piddly roach or something, and she went out, and it was hell, and the paranoia hit almost right away, panic, remorse, despair, blah blah blah . . .

"And you know what I'd always think? I'd think, 'You silly bitch. Once your sobriety date's blown, it's blown—you might as well have had some fun.' "

"Want me to say it to you?" asked January.

"Sure. Why not?"

"Okay: You might as well have some fun, you silly bitch."

She stood up as he drank, and pulled the robe over her head. Nick handed back the thermos, looking her over frankly: long, small-breasted torso; muscled arms; legs that were long, white, slightly bowed, a triangle of hair emphasizing the empty space between her wiry thighs; a surprisingly shaggy pubic bush hanging down like a buffalo beard. A naked female body less like Lourdes's, the last he'd seen, could scarcely be imagined—the two women hardly seemed to belong to the same species, let alone the same sex.

January took one last belt from the thermos, replugged it, and screwed the cap back on. When she stooped to set it down at the foot of the mattress, her small breasts drooped forward like commas. She straightened up—the room was so small she only had to turn and reach for the light switch by the door, but a fetching turn and reach it was; the long line of her outstretched arm, smoothly knotted shoulder, long back, straining boyish buttocks and thighs was the vision he carried with him into the sudden, complete dark.

"I haven't done this in years," whispered Nick, pulling his jeans off. He was already rock-hard from the blood.

"It's easy," came the whispered reply. He felt the mattress give as she climbed on, felt also the heat of her palm even before she grabbed him. "You just stick that—" She lay back, pulling him forward over her. "—in here. No, wait . . . no, not . . . oh, okay, in there."

There was no clock in the room, and Nick had left his watch some-where—oh yes, in his boots, on the steps by the front door—but they seemed to have made love forever, well into the wee hours of Sunday morning. Nick, after all, had five years of blood lust stored up, and Janu-ary was young, wiry, and vampire-strong, and even with the lights on she didn't mind rolling over and playing at being a boy part of the time. That way, when he reached under her to play with her dangling little breasts and stroke the odd bony flatness between her legs, it seemed deliciously perverted and retro, the inverse of inverse.

And of course after he'd come it seemed only fair to tuck his penis back between his legs and pretend to be a girl for her. Not that she was a lesbian—just so that they were both playing at being something else. She pinched his pecs together so they looked like breasts, nipped at them with her teeth, howled like a wolf when she came.

"Hey," he protested mildly.

She rolled off him, breathing hard. "Dja ever kill a donor while you were fucking?"

He shook his head.

"It's fun. Right when you come you bite into their throat. It's like poppers, only a hundred times more intense."

"You must run through quite a few donors that way."

He must have looked dismayed, for she dug at his bare ribs with her knuckles, and laughed. "Gotcha. I never really did that—I just wanted to see your reaction."

"Whew."

"But you gotta admit it *sounds* cool."

"I do not," he said, but they both knew he was lying.

Nick lay propped on an elbow, watching January nap. In candlelit repose her wildness did not show—the lips were relaxed, not drawn back in a raptorial sneer. Upon closer inspection, though, the eyeballs were oscillating wildly under waxy, reptile-thin eyelids, and when he drew the sheet back he saw that she had clenched in upon herself, the way a fetus would, if fetuses had nightmares.

There was no window in the room, but he had the sense that it was nearly dawn. *Shortest night of the year,* he reminded himself. *No matter how long it seems.* He rolled over and felt around at the foot of the mattress for the thermos—he was long past the soul-searching phase. But he'd barely unscrewed the cap before January's arms came around him from behind, pinning his own arms lightly against his body. He sensed she was only teasing. "Mother, may I?" he asked.

She had pressed her front against his back; he felt her chin nodding into his shoulder, and took a swig. The blood was a touch stale—*my, haven't we gotten fussy fast.* Turning around on the bed, he spread his longer legs on either side of January's. She grabbed the thermos from him, sat back between his feet, upended it, and swallowed greedily; he could see her throat muscles working in her taut neck.

He watched the blush spreading between her little breasts, felt the heat in his own chest. "Thanks for taking me last night. I was afraid I'd be standing there like the nineteenth kid in a pick-up baseball game."

"I didn't take you." She held her hand out; he handed her the red plastic plug and she recapped the thermos. "Selene picked all the partners." Then she laughed delightedly. "Hey, if you didn't know, that means you said yeah on your own. Nick, that's so fucking romantic!"

"Fucking romantic: that's me." He wondered if he ought to feel worse, if only for having been beaten so soundly by Whistler and Selene. For he knew perfectly well that he'd been in some sort of cosmic contest with both of them over the past several months—or was it years? And sometimes, just to keep himself going when things were at their lowest, loneliest ebb, after losing Bev, he'd even pictured their struggle in terms of the Marvel comics he used to read as a teenager: the Silver Surfer and his archenemies hurtling thunderbolts at each other across trackless space.

And now he understood well enough that their victory could not have been more complete—that he'd just had the cosmic crap beat out of him. Fortunately, he was managing to stay high—he wondered how much it would hurt when he came down. "Want to go for a swim before the sun comes up?" he asked January.

"Are you kidding?" She'd tensed visibly. "I never even go near the water."

"How come?"

"My mother? Glory? Drowned herself?"

"Oh, right. Bummer."

"I haven't gone swimming since." January blew out the candle. "We have to rest up for tonight, anyway." But she'd curled up on the mattress with her head in his lap—face down.

"Why's that?"

She mumbled something around his rapidly inflating member.

"Beg pardon?" He couldn't understand—or rather, hoped he'd misunderstood.

She turned her head and looked up at him. "I said baby-blood tonight." She turned back to his penis. "Damn, now where did *you* disappear to?" She was referring to his erection, which had indeed gone the way of all flesh—only faster.

Nick crept out of the room in his black Levi's, with his red windbreaker open over his bare chest—those were all of his clothes he'd been able to locate. His polo shirt might have been under the mattress, but he didn't want to risk waking January, who'd finally dropped off to sleep with the aid of a few of the Quaaludes—Mexican, but pharmaceutical nonetheless—that Whistler handed out like after-dinner mints.

It took him a few minutes to find his way from the back stairs to the kitchen, but from there he knew his way to the front door. He opened it tentatively, but the morning light was not unbearable—he paused in the doorway to watch the silver mist rising from the lake.

Down by the water one of the Luzan servants, a boy of eighteen or so, wearing only a pair of tight cutoff jeans, was raking the beach. Nick crossed the lawn barefoot and sat down quietly on the end of one of the redwood chaises to watch him. He found himself growing aroused at the sight of the boy's lean muscular back and long calves, and it occurred to him as he stroked the growing bulge at the front of his own jeans that while the sex with January had been vigorous and twisted enough even for a vampire, there had been an emptiness at the core of it.

Suddenly the boy turned. "You need somet'ing, sah?"

Nick realized he must have moaned out loud. "No—don't let me interrupt."

"Finished anyway, sah." He set down the rake, tines down, and trotted up to the lawn. He was a handsome boy, and the bleached-out indigo of his cutoffs set off the chocolate brown of his lean midriff. He knelt at the foot of Nick's chaise. "You cyare to drink me blood, sah? Got plenty—I ain' give none all night."

"I suppose I could use a pick-me-up," Nick admitted, and in less time than he would have imagined, he was sucking from the heel of an up-turned palm, where several of the Luzan Drinks had developed scar tissue that made their bloodletting nearly painless.

As Nick sucked, the boy reached out with his other hand, and gingerly touched the bulge in Nick's jeans. "Cyare to fuck, too?"

Nick looked up from the boy's hand, took a last suck from it, then released it, pinching off the wound at the wrist. "What's your name, kid?"

"Hedley, sah." The boy put his hand over Nick's—at first Nick thought he wanted to hold hands, then realized the boy wanted to stanch his own wound, and let go.

"I'm Nick. You gay, Hedley?"

Hedley looked puzzled. "Gay? You mean am I happy, Mister Nick?"

Nick started to laugh, until he understood the boy was serious. "No, I mean gay. You know, homosexual?" A shake of the Hedley head—Nick reached out and touched the soft tight curls. "Queer? Fag?" Nothing. "Man who likes to fuck men?"

Still confused, Hedley checked his hand to be sure the bleeding had stopped, then stood up and pulled off his cutoffs. His penis was darker than the rest of him, almost black, and he did not have an erection. "At de Greathouse, sah, de Drinkers fuck everybody, and nobody cyare if de Drink is happy."

I care if you're happy, thought Nick, reaching around the boy, clasping a buttock in each hand, and pulling the boy's crotch against his face. *But I'll settle for hard.*

On the way back inside Nick noticed his boots on the front step, and Selene's empty chalice beside them. (Hedley, who'd been hard, and was now happy, was still resting on the chaise—Nick, having nothing else to give him, had told him to take the morning off.)

The boots he left inside the door; the chalice he took with him as he climbed the stairway that led up to the south wing. He had no idea which was Selene's room (last time he'd been in Whistler Manor, it had been divided into the Coven wing to the north, and the Penang to the south); he wandered down the hallway until he smelled incense coming from under the last door, and set the empty chalice down in front of it.

"Come in, Nick," called Selene, though he had neither knocked nor spoken.

He opened the door and saw her seated before her altar, dressed in her hooded green robe. "Sit down on the bed, I'll be right with you."

He climbed onto the four-poster while with a pentacular wave of her athame she sealed the gate to whichever region she'd been visiting, then blew out her black candle, replaced her *Book of Shadows* inside the altar, closed the wicker doors, and dropped the black damask altar cloth over the front as if she were putting a hamster to bed for the night.

"Thanks for not cutting my throat last night," he said when she turned around at last. "I brought your chalice back."

"Thank you. But it wasn't personal, Nick. And it wasn't about blood, either—it was about submission."

"In that case, I'm glad I didn't struggle."

"*Be* glad," she said, lowering her pointy little chin and regarded him from under dark bushy brows. "Be very, very glad."

"But it's behind us now. Bygones be bygones, you said?"

She raised his chin to examine her handiwork. "It's in the past, Nick. Insofar as there is a past, present, or future, it's in the past."

"And what's in the future? January says baby-blood is on the menu for tonight."

She looked surprised. "Planning to join us?"

He shook his head. "Not me, thanks much. I'm just hoping nobody gives any to January."

"Not my call, Nick. And she's no longer your responsibility, either."

"I'm not talking about that, Selene. I know when I'm beat: I'll be lucky not to be prowling People's Park myself in a few weeks—I'm not about to start preaching to anybody else. All I'm saying, as a friend, as somebody who knows her pretty well—from both sides now, if you'll pardon the expression—is that she's got a lot of heart, but I don't think she can handle baby-blood right now, any more than I could."

"The problem is, you've never seen what the problem is, have you, Nick?" She silenced him with a finger in the air. "Just listen to yourself—Nick Santos, St. Nick, out to save the world single-handed. Have you forgotten, dearie—Whistler never wanted to give *you* baby-blood in the first place. You're the one who insisted, and it cost him one of his dearest friends in the world." She touched her throat. "Nearly two."

To Nick's surprise—and it was as much of a surprise to him that he had any capacity for that emotion left—he felt the tears rolling down his cheeks.

"Don't worry, dearie," she went on smoothly, while he had his private epiphany. "Whistler hasn't the slightest intention of letting January drink baby-blood—we'll drop some Ecstasy in a bowl of my blood, and pull the old switcheroo. . . . There, there." For Nick had buried his face in his hands, and begun sobbing.

She patted his heaving shoulders and waited for him to sob it out.

It took a few minutes. When he looked up only her crinkled elfin eyes were visible above the covers. "I feel years younger," he remarked.

"You look years younger." She winked. "Quite a monkey to carry around on your back all these years, eh Nick? The responsibility for the addictions of humanity? Quite a monkey."

"I'm sure it'll come back when I'm straight," he replied. "At the moment, I don't care one way or the other."

"If it does come back, kindly take it on down the line, will you, dearie? Now take off those nasty clothes and climb in here. You're about to get the benefit of five years' enforced celibacy."

He put his hand to his bare chest. "I'm flattered, Selene, but—"

"Don't be." She sat up and stripped off her gown, then reached out a bare arm and zipped Nick's windbreaker the rest of the way down. "That ritual I just finished?" she said, caressing the fine brown hairs of his chest. "That was the completion of my vow—I have to fuck the first person I see afterwards." She lowered her hand to the crotch of his black jeans. "Guess who, dearie?"

"Selene, I've been fucking all night and half the morning, I was out of training to start with, and I've finally remembered, if I could ever have truly forgotten, that I am, to the heart and to the bone, queer as a three-dollar bill."

Selene's reply was to reach up and unsnap the waistband and crotch of Nick's 501's. "You can ask me if I give a shit after you drink my blood and fuck me," she said sweetly. "Otherwise, you're messing with the Great Horned God. Now say the words I long to hear."

Nick skinned his jeans down, grinning as his reddened, battered, but still game and semi-erect penis popped into view. "You mean, 'Roll over, baby, I think I love you'?"

Selene giggled. "Close enough."

FOUR

By 8:30 P.M. on Sunday the sun had sunk low enough behind the western mountains to allow the vampires to enjoy some unaccustomed, unfiltered daylight out on the lawn. Under his white panama hat, August Fetterman wore an ivory-colored linen suit and an open-necked shirt the color of a Palm Beach tan; little Sandy wore exquisitely faded jeans and a soft blue oxford-cloth shirt; and when a barefooted Whistler emerged from the lodge in a blousy black silk Armani sport jacket and slacks, Nick felt positively grungy in his Levi's and Jimmy Dean windbreaker.

He'd been awake a good thirty-six hours—Selene had had an awful lot of catching up to do, and fed him as much of her blood as was required to get it done, and then when she finally let him loose around one or two in the afternoon, he'd inadvertently awakened January crawling back into bed.

She'd been cross, to say the least, and had dispatched him to the cellar with her empty thermos, after which they'd played at their naughty retro sex for hours—it had occurred to Nick that if he didn't find himself a man again soon, the authorities might strip him of his homo card.

Then January had drifted off into what looked like a delicious Quaalude doze, while Nick had prowled the Manor looking for company; he'd stumbled across Sandy on a similar errand and renewed his card; the two of them had met Augie out on the lawn just after the sun dropped behind the mountains.

"Gentlemen!" called Whistler as he crossed the lawn.

"Squire." Augie tipped his panama, his billowing ivory suit invested with a faint lavender tinge in the fading sunset light; Sandy touched his forelock, which was that colorless shade of brown that redheads fade to after forty.

"Hello, Jamey," said Nick warily—it occurred to him that the two of them hadn't actually talked face to face since his expulsion from V.A. "Congratulations."

"On my marriage? Thank you," replied Whistler, thereby artfully reminding everyone that there was something else Nick might have been congratulating him on, without being so crass as to actually mention it.

Nick would have been happy enough to let it go at that, but Augie, standing facing the water with his legs spread wide and his arms behind his back, snickered under his hat. "Something funny, Fets?" An old, detested nickname.

"Get off your fucking high horse, Nick," said Augie without heat. "So we got you. So what? Before *you* got got, every one of us got got just as good, by everybody who'd gotten got before them. You want to hear the story of *my* fall from grace?"

The other three were all laughing by the time Augie had finished the tale of the teenage twins. "Yeah, laugh," he said, pretending to be offended as he took out his silver flask for a nip of Josephina-blood. "Me, I'm left with a broken heart."

They passed the flask once around, then Augie pocketed it again. "By the way, Nick, how did you and your partner hit it off last night?"

"I like January," he replied, somewhat defensively. "I've always liked her. She's got a lot of heart."

Augie snickered again. "Yeah, in jars in her refrigerator, probably—like that whatsisname, that Dahmer in Milwaukee."

"She'll be fine—as long as she stays away from baby-blood."

"Which reminds me . . ." Whistler glanced down at his Patek Philippe. "Gentlemen, we're due in the keeping room at ten o'clock. Nick, I understand you're going to pass?"

"I don't even trust myself in the same room with the stuff," Nick replied.

"Why don't you join us after midnight, then? And in the meantime—" Whistler patted the thin fabric of his Armani, then found his own silver flask in the hip pocket of his trousers, and held it out to Nick. "Here, take this—it's full."

"Thanks." Nick slipped the flask into the back pocket of his jeans.

"Don't mention it. Oh, and Nick? It's going to be good having you back."

The others seconded the motion, clapped him on the shoulders, and wandered back towards the manor, leaving Nick alone on the lawn still trying to think of an appropriate reply. He stooped to pluck a few errant blades of grass that were sticking up higher than the others, then tossed the offenders into the air like a golfer testing the wind.

But there was no wind: the air was violet and still, the lake as deep a purple as the cheapest properties on the Monopoly board. Nick could feel Whistler's flask rubbing against his hip as he rose; it occurred to him that he could leave now, and use the flask to detox. It was still his choice.

But then, it would still be his choice tomorrow, and the day after that, and the day after that. *One day at a time,* it seemed to Nick as he reached for the flask, was as good a motto for a user as it was for a twelve-stepper.

Besides, he realized later, strolling through the quiet woods where he'd met the owl five years before, if he ever wanted to come back, he knew that twelve-step rooms were the only places left in America that fit Frost's definition of home: the place where, when you have to go there, they have to take you in.

An hour or so later Nick found himself sitting cross-legged at the end of the dock, trying not to pay attention to the voice in his head that told him he'd be a fool ever to leave this place. He tried an old meditator's trick Leon had taught him—listening for the farthest sound. It was the only thing that worked, sometimes, when you felt you couldn't listen to that little voice a minute longer, and it was unusually rewarding on blood—at the moment, for instance, Nick was largely convinced that he could hear fish feeding below the surface of the lake.

But his tranquility ended suddenly when all the other sounds he'd been picking up, the music floating in from along the shore, the softest ripples of wavelets against the pilings, the snap-crackle-pop of his neck when he rolled his head, were overwhelmed by a muffled screaming coming from somewhere inside Whistler Manor.

He turned in time to see the front door of the lodge burst open, throwing a trapezoid of light over the threshold and onto the lawn, and was on his feet as January came backing through the door hauling a struggling body in a cross-chest carry. She turned sideways to stumble down the brick steps to the lawn. Nick saw Josephina, now gone limp in January's grasp, no longer screaming. There was a knife at her throat.

The vampires began crowding through the doorway. The light spilling through the open door was oddly angled—to Nick's stoned eyes it was like a painting, Hopper on blood: Whistler's hair a paintbrush dipped in yellow; Augie and Louise in their dark crimson robes crowding through the door at the same frozen moment, an unwieldy grace to their movements, as if they were going to take each other by the waist and waltz down the steps and across the sloping lawn. The lawn itself was billiard green where the light spilled across it, otherwise dusty black velvet, and the dancing angular shadows cast by the vampires on the porch were black as well, but with luminous, amethyst auras.

By the time Nick reached the beach, January was halfway down the lawn, her back to Nick, one arm across Josephina's chest, the other holding the knife to the girl's throat; the vampires had arrayed themselves in the doorway, on the porch, and along the two narrow steps, as if posing for a class photograph.

They saw him coming up behind her; she did not. Sherman was speaking in his most tranquilizing therapist's tones: "We're just having a little difference of opinion here, January . . . let's not give up, let's keep working with it . . . you want us to give you baby-blood, we want you to show us that you're ready for it . . . don't you think that putting down that knife might be a good way to start . . ." He was trying to keep her attention as Nick crept towards her in a crouch, placing one bare foot carefully before the other, so high he could feel the blades of grass bending under his soles with each step.

It was already evident to Nick that January hadn't drunk any baby-blood yet—if she had, he knew, recalling his own brief experience, there was no way he'd be able to get this close without her noticing.

He was only a few feet behind her when he felt, with a telepathic jolt, that she had sensed his presence. Her right arm—the knife arm—tensed; he leapt the gap between them and the three of them tumbled forward onto the lawn, Nick grabbing for January's right wrist with both hands as they fell, forcing it down and away as Josephina scrambled toward the manor on her hands and knees.

Nick could feel the pounding of footsteps across the lawn, then a picket fence of legs surrounded them. Someone reached down and took the knife; he smelled ether as he rolled off January and lay on his back on the soft damp grass.

"Don't hurt her," he said. The only other sounds were scuffling, and hard breathing, until Josephina began to wail. That was a good sound, Nick thought: it meant her throat hadn't been cut.

After the commotion died down (apparently Whistler's sleight of hand had not been quite as sleight as he'd hoped: January had seen him switch bowls when it was her turn to sip from the gourd), Nick volunteered to drive January back to Berkeley. Part of him wanted to stay, but he'd been getting the feeling, out there at the end of the dock, that if he didn't leave tonight he might never leave. Besides, he didn't think he'd be able to enjoy the orgy much anyway, if they'd had to lock January in the blood cellar.

As for January, for the first hour she was still drowsy from the ether, and by the time that had worn off, the Ecstasy with which they'd dosed her had begun coming on. They'd also spiked her refilled thermos with it—Nick took a hit at the top of the pass leading out of the Tahoe basin, and by the time they'd reached the flat street-light grid of the Sacramento valley they were both loopy and mellow. January didn't appear to know that it was Nick who'd jumped her—or if she did, she'd decided to ignore it, in the flush of Ecstasy empathy.

Nick encouraged her by pretending that they'd barred him from the ceremony, and refused him baby-blood as well; he really started getting into it under the influence of the Ecstasy-laced blood in the Star Trek thermos. "Who the fuck do they think they are?"

"Telling *us* what not to do. Nobody tells *us* what not to do." January's face had taken on a haggard beauty in the reflected glow of the dashboard lights. "Fuck 'em if they can't take a joke. Next time we'll bring our own goddamn baby."

"Although if I may make a suggestion?" offered Nick. "There are lots of ways to get blood other than by killing people."

"Yeah, but why?"

"For one thing, if you kill them, you never get to use them again. For another—I know this is hard to believe—but you'll feel better about yourself."

"Okay, well—and I'm not *even* saying you're right—but what's some ways? I mean, I never had anybody to teach me."

"Non-lethal ways to get blood. All right. Give me a minute here." Nick drummed his fingers on the steering wheel. "In general, for a woman of course, there's sex—men will do all sorts of goofy things if it gets them laid. Or you don't even have to screw them—you can always maneuver them in a position where you can accuse them of rape—you know, blackmail.

"Or, for a big strong girl like you, there are non-lethal blows—the Glasgow Kiss is a good one. Then there's the sob story—you tell them you're dying of a fatal disease and only blood keeps you alive. Hospitals are good—there must be a dozen ways to hunt blood in hospitals. Or did you ever hear about the Oops Ring? One of my personal favorites . . ."

Nick warmed to his subject as they drove through the warm Sacramento night. The sky was high and starry—a top-down convertible sky; in the distance they could make out the lights of a Denny's twinkling through the heat haze rising from the cooling highway.

It was not until they were nearing Vacaville that it occurred to Nick to ask himself just what the hell he was trying to accomplish here. Something about the situation had finally struck him as odd: he'd long since passed his original intention of saving the lives of January's potential donors—by now he was just junkie-rapping.

Having noticed that, he should have felt guilty—or at least uncomfortable. Instead there was another sensation, one that it took him to the county line to put a name to.

Ah, Anomie, my old friend. Hop in, make yourself at home. I can use a fellow like you—things are getting too godawful strange around here to have to deal with concepts like right and wrong.

Chapter 6

ONE

January was still sleeping soundly beside him when Nick heard the phone ringing in his office across the hall. He threw on the Percy Dove-tonsils dressing gown he found at the foot of the bed (from the back of what closet had that emerged, he wondered), and balancing his aching head carefully atop his neck, he went into the office to monitor the call.

Mr. Santos, this is Reverend Shoemaker's office calling. You had a three o'clock appoint—

He grabbed the receiver. "That you, Betty?"

"Of course it's me. Are you all right?"

"Except physically and emotionally—oh, and spiritually. Other than that, tip-top."

"Nick, what happened?"

"Long story. Can I come over?"

"If you'll pick up dinner on the way—otherwise I'm going to have to go out."

"What time is it?"

"After eight-thirty."

Sunset. He'd awakened at sunset. "K.F.C. okay?"

"The roasted—if they don't have that, extra crispy."

"Be over in half an hour."

Trying to ignore his aching head, Nick typed a note to January, then while it was printing stooped down and from a lock-box welded to the back of a two-drawer file cabinet bolted to the floor, he peeled two bills from a roll of hundreds, then two more, then—*the hell with it*—a fifth, and clipped them to the note without rereading it. He knew himself—

once he started editing it he'd be there for an hour. As it was, it was a masterpiece of compression:

> Thanks for everything, but I'm going to try to fight this thing anyway. If you want to fight it too, you're welcome to stay, but if you don't want to, here's money for a hotel. But please, give me your number when you have one—I care about you, but I can't help you unless I help myself first.

When Nick returned to the bedroom, January was still asleep, snoring in a high-decibel adenoidal Quaalude honk. He dressed quietly, having a bad moment when he started transferring his keys and change from his black Levi's into his Dockers, and found Whistler's flask in the back pocket of the jeans. He unscrewed the top—fortunately the smell alone was enough to tell him it had gone bad in the past twenty-four hours, otherwise, he understood, he'd probably have taken a snort.

Rather than leave the money on the dresser (where it might be misinterpreted by January—he knew that she'd tricked a few times in her young life), he placed it with the note in an envelope with her name on it, and left that on the kitchen table. Then he poured the contents of the flask down the sink, rinsed it out, and left it in the dish drainer with the cap off to dry.

January opened one eye when she heard Nick let himself out the front door. She didn't like to wake up with people—didn't even care to see anybody before her first drink, much less talk to them. She felt around at the side of the bed for her thermos, then remembered that she'd put it in the refrigerator that morning before going to sleep.

The elegant silk and satin quilted dressing gown she'd found in the back of the closet, and left at the foot of the bed, had somehow transported itself to the chair by the window. It wrapped one and a half times around her, and trailed on the floor; she secured it with the tasseled belt and trotted down to the kitchen.

She opened the envelope while sipping from her thermos—there was about an inch left in the bottom. "I fucking hate notes," she said aloud when she'd finished reading. Notes on the kitchen table were something Glory left when she wouldn't be home for dinner. Or sometimes breakfast. In fact, given the choice, she'd probably have preferred being treated like a hooker than a child—Glory used to leave her money for pizza too.

She was furious at Nick—still, five huns would buy a lot of pizza. She tucked the money into the pocket of the dressing gown, went back upstairs, and rummaged through Nick's clothes, donning a clean white T-shirt and a pair of jeans, both of which looked as if they'd been ironed, then rolling up the cuffs of the jeans a good four inches. A pair of wide red suspenders with clips completed the ensemble—and more importantly, kept the jeans up.

He had a full-length mirror on the back of the bedroom door. She frowned. "Too clowny." But there was a faded dungaree jacket in the closet—she slipped the T-shirt off, crossed the straps of the suspenders between her breasts (that effect by itself was pretty cool in the mirror), and put the T-shirt back on over that, untucked.

Now, with the hem of the oversized T-shirt hanging out from under the oversized jacket, she had a respectable outfit. January stuffed the dressing gown over the dirty clothes in her monogrammed Vuitton suitcase, along with a cashmere sweater of Nick's and a few bandannas. Feeling a little better about him now, she called a taxi from the bedroom phone and went downstairs to wait for it.

"Basically," Nick began, unloading the Colonel's red-striped bag onto the counter of the parsonage kitchen, "I was kidnapped, driven to Tahoe, forced to drink blood—you want cole slaw?—had my throat cut in some sort of satanic ritual—" He raised his chin to show her. "—and binged for thirty-six hours—mashed potatoes?—but as of—" He checked his watch. "—twenty minutes ago, I have twelve hours clean and sober, and every intention of remaining so. Gravy?"

"Let me see that. No, come closer." She tilted his chin, turning it left and right to examine the thready line that ran across his throat from one ear to the other. "Selene?" she asked.

He nodded. "But it's over now—she gave me her solemn word. We . . . shook hands on it—" The briefest hesitation before *shook hands*— of course, he and Selene had shaken a great deal more than hands. "—and agreed to let bygones be bygones. You want a leg or a breast?"

"Suddenly I'm not very hungry for some reason. Breast. And what's that piece there?"

"Either a thigh or a mutation."

"Never mind." She found herself eating anyway, one hand shoveling it in, and the other resting on her belly as if to protect the baby. "You sure you're all right?"

"Right as rain."

"So that's all there is to it? Just oops? Witches and vampires and throat cuttings and binges, so-sorry-no-problem?"

He shrugged. "It's the truth, what else can I say?"

"But you're clean and sober now?"

"As a judge. Listen, Betty, if I were still using, I wouldn't have told you any of that—I'd have given you a different story entirely." A story, he failed to mention, that he'd begun to prepare in the car on the way over, until he realized that he didn't need it—that the true circumstances of his weekend were all the exoneration he'd need.

"And we're not in any danger?" This time she patted her belly, to show him which we she was referring to.

"Your name never came up—they don't even know I've been seeing you. You're not involved in this—" He stilled her protest with an up-raised plastic spork of mashed potatoes. "Yes yes yes: except insofar as *I'm* involved in it. But that's what I'm trying to tell you—I'm not in-volved anymore."

They ate in silence for a few minutes, but she could sense him waiting for something—forgiveness? reassurance? She could have used some re-assurance herself. She knew she'd take him back, insofar as he'd ever been hers, insofar as he'd ever been away. What she was less sure of was her motivation: she needed him too much, if only financially. Suddenly, with an inner lurch, she thought of all the couples she'd counseled—wives with abusive husbands, lesbians with philandering lovers—and how she used to wonder, unprofessionally, even as she was doing her professional best to repair the relationship, why on earth the aggrieved client didn't just leave the asshole?

She wondered how much more she didn't know about relationships. *M.F.C.C., heal thyself.* "Hey Nick?"

"Mmm?" Around a mouthful of three-bean salad.

"Want to hear about my weekend? It wasn't quite as exciting as yours, but I think I found a crib."

January checked into the Bierce, a mid-range residence hotel on Tele-graph Avenue where she'd stayed before, tossed her suitcase on the bed, polished off the last of the thermos contents (apparently the Ecstasy had broken down overnight—nothing but Selene's own blood now, not that that was anything to sneeze at), and ten minutes later was back out on Telegraph.

January didn't particularly enjoy prowling Telegraph—before V.A., People's Park had been her prime hunting grounds, but that was also before the riots, and the volleyball courts, and the lights and the attention. In those days it had been relatively easy to isolate a stray wino or junkie or wacko. Tonight, as she passed by the boarded-up windows of a record store that had not survived the last round of riots, she sighed aloud, remembering just how easy it had been, and thinking that if she'd only confined herself to wino hunting, she'd never have been suckered into that twelve-step shit.

But no-o-o-o, not January. Winos weren't good enough for me anymore. I had to get greedy, had to break into the blood bank. . . .

She could feel herself flushing as she thought of what a sucker she'd been not to just have killed Beverly the moment she came upon her there in the back office, snapped her neck before she could even open her mouth. But she'd been a goner the second Bev started talking—Wayne, the Chinese vampire who'd initiated her, after a manner of speaking, had never exactly had a chance to explain much about vampirism to her. She'd always assumed that being a vampire was, well, a state of being—the notion that it was an addiction that could be kicked was a revelation. Beverly had talked January into accompanying her to a meeting that very night.

Still, it hadn't been a total loss: those last several months with Whistler had been as close to paradise as she'd known since the commune. Communes in Sebastapol are cool places when you're four—and come to think of it, being four is a lot like being on blood. But thinking about Whistler—his betrayal, her banishment—made her too angry. January needed a cool head to hunt, especially if she were going to try out some of the tricks Nick had taught her in the car.

She patted the pockets of his Levi jacket, found the note, and uncrumpled it as she strode up Channing Way—the lights of People's Park were bright enough to read by, now. *Fight this thing . . .* yeah, sure, blah blah . . . there it was: *I care about you.* She shook her head—people were so fucking weird. They got to be a vampire, and they wanted to give it up. They say they care about you, and write you off with a note.

Well it ain't that easy, Nick. You want blood as much as you want me—you just need a little encouragement. Besides, I'll make you proud, you'll see. The Glasgow Kiss, the Oops Ring—I'll get us both all the blood we need without hardly killing any—

"Hey, watch where you're going!"

"Sorry." She had walked smack into a high school kid. Good-looking kid, too. Backwards baseball cap. Baggy shorts, Berkeley High sweatshirt with the sleeves cut off. He was rubbing his nose, which gave her an idea. "You okay?"

"I guess."

"I'm such a space case—I'm always doing that." They'd each bounced back a step from the collision; she drew closer. He was all sweaty—probably on his way from the volleyball courts. How cool: those volleyball courts had cost her her favorite hunting grounds; only fair that they give something back. "You sure you're okay? I have a room right around the corner—I could put some ice on it."

But something had spooked him—he danced back nervously again, staring at her eyes. Oh fuck, she thought, they must be scary red under the security lights. What a stupid thing to forget about. It had been so long since she'd been stoned out in the world. At Whistler Manor, of course, red eyes had been the norm. She rubbed them. "Fucking chlorine." Her best excuse. "I'm on the swim team."

"At Cal? I'm starting in the fall."

"Great. What are you gonna major in?"

"Computer science."

"So you're smart too—I mean, besides good looking." He blushed as dark as if he'd been the one drinking blood—she closed the distance between them again. "I lied—I don't really have any ice up in my room." She touched the front of his shorts. "Just a bed." A single drop of perspiration emerged from under the band of his backwards cap and rolled down his forehead. "C'mon. Don't be such a kid. It'll beat volleyball all to shit."

January took him up the back stairs (no tricking at the Bierce, except with the assistant manager if you couldn't make the rent), closed the door behind them, threw the bolt, positioned him with his back to the door, hooked her thumbs into the waistband of his gym shorts and underpants, and as she knelt before him, tugged them down around his ankles and grabbed his penis in her hand. He came almost immediately—before her mouth was anywhere near him.

She stood up, wiping his limp penis clean on the hem of her T-shirt, then tilted her face up to his. "Lean down," she whispered, puckering her lips. As he did so, she drew her head back, then brought it forward violently, shattering the bridge of his nose with the top of her forehead: the Glasgow Kiss.

He moaned and crumpled; before he could topple over sideways, she propped him up into a sitting position with his back against the door and the lip of her Star Trek thermos under his gushing nose.

His bare legs were out in front of him, pants still around his ankles. He might or might not have been conscious; it was hard for her to tell, as his eyes had swelled shut almost immediately. He *was* groaning, but then, she'd known bleeders to groan when they were unconscious—even when they were almost dead.

Not that she had any intention of letting him die—in honor of Nick, sort of. When the thermos was full she grabbed his nose between her thumb and forefinger and squeezed. He screamed—*so you were conscious after all, you bad boy,* she thought—and fainted again from the pain. Pinching his nostrils closed, she took a swig from the thermos, then another, let the nose go, topped off the thermos with the resulting spurt of blood, then with one hand pinched off the flow again while with the other she deftly capped the thermos. This was a lot more complicated than slitting winos' throats, she had to admit, but a lot more fun, too.

She left the boy slumped against the door and darted into the kitchen. When she returned, he was groaning, and doing his best to see through his swollen eyes. What he saw—January approaching with a serrated knife—made him try to struggle to his feet, but he gave up when she sat across his legs and flicked his nose with her forefinger. He didn't pass out, this time, nor did she use the knife on him. Instead she lifted her sweatshirt and scraped the edge of the knife vertically against the top of her left chest a few times, from the collarbone down to the top of her breast. Then she ran the boy's fingertips under her shirt and along the path of the red shred marks.

It hurt him more than it did her. When he groaned again she looked him in the eye. "You conscious now?"

He nodded.

"Get out. If you tell anybody about this, I'll tell them you tried to rape me. Who do you think they'll believe, with your come on my clothes, and the scratch marks and the bruises and all, and my blood and skin under your fingernails?" She started to climb off him, then sat back. "But you could wash your hands, couldn't you? I better call nine-one-one now, instead."

"Nnn."

"What's that?"

"Nnn. Dnn."

"Don't?"

He nodded.

"You just gonna leave and never tell anybody?"

He nodded again.

"Cool." She climbed off his lap, then reached down and helped him to his feet. She had to help support his weight for a minute, and took advantage of the opportunity to slip his wallet out of his pocket. He was feeling well enough to protest—she jabbed a finger toward his nose, and he yelped—she didn't even have to touch him. "I just want to see where you live, cutie. In case you do decide to tell somebody."

True to her word, she replaced the wallet after checking his driver's license, then opened the door and shooed him out into the hall. "Stairs to the left."

She closed the door, then opened it immediately; he was already gone. She laughed, but the laughter died away as she realized she should have taken some money from him after all—she was going to need money. Then she hefted her thermos—it was so full it didn't even slosh. What was it the Furry Freak Brothers in her mother's old hippie comix used to say? Blood will get you through times of no money better than money will get you through times of no blood?

Or something like that. Never mind. She had enough of both to last a day or two. Then it would be time to call on Nick again—he'd probably be glad to see her by then. Because never mind about what that Furry Freak Brother said: blood *and* money, that was the ticket. Money and blood.

TWO

The week after Midsummer passed with measured grace up at Whistler Manor. It appeared to Lourdes that pregnancy was as safe a charm against vampiric malaise as was baby-blood. Every evening she awoke while the sky to the west was still that pink-tinged gray, and after peeing (her bladder by now had the capacity of a golf ball) she would ring for Nanny Parish, then waddle over to the window seat to wait for her.

It was not an ungraceful waddle: had there been troupes of pregnant ballerinas, Lourdes would have been prima among them. Nor did she need the plush padded railing and low cushioned step that Whistler had installed on Tuesday—but she'd thought of him and smiled fondly every time she'd used them since, so it was well worth it.

She'd drink her thimbleful of blood in the window seat, while in the Nantucket rocker Nanny would nurse little Plum Rose—nine months old now, with cheeks fat and purple-black as plums.

"Where'd the name come from?" Lourdes asked the shiny-faced Luzan midwife on Friday evening. She loved to watch Nanny Parish nursing her little girl, loved to watch the little mouth suck dreamily at the great brown breast. That was as close as she got to sexual desire lately: sometimes after drinking her hourly ration she'd fantasize about nursing from those swollen breasts herself. The aureolae were the size of the saucers in a doll's tea set; swallowing the warm spurting milk would be like drinking sweet blood from a fountain, she imagined. But whenever she thought about it too much, her own breasts would ache with fullness, and she'd have to look away.

"Plum Rose? Dot's de Jambu tree, Miss Lourdes. Bears de golden apple dot Odam and Eve ate of in de Gyarden."

"I think we've decided on a girl's name. Corazon, after my grandmother."

"Dot's a good name, too."

A boy was to be named Leon Stanton Whistler. A life for a life: advice on karmic maintenance from the High Priestess of the Coven. They would have considered the name Leona for a girl, had not that name been associated in recent years with a photo on the cover of *Time* magazine, under the legend: *Rhymes With Rich.*

After blood, breakfast—Catherine Bailey wheeled in a cart, and she and Nanny (Selene was in Bolinas) joined Lourdes for some calorie loading.

Whistler meanwhile had developed a sunset ritual of his own. This Friday, as he'd done every evening since Midsummer, he mixed up a pitcher of his special St. Thomas Extra Dry formulation (on Santa Luz this had involved pouring half a bottle of Tanqueray into a shaker, then waving the shaker in the general direction of the island of St. Thomas, where, presumably, it being the cocktail hour, someone would be opening a bottle of vermouth), and drank it with a blood chaser out on the lawn.

He was alone this evening. If any of his buddies had happened to be up at the lodge, they'd have been welcome to join him, but he was surprised to find how little he needed the company. Whistler, too, was finding impending parenthood an astoundingly effective antidote to the *weary, stale, flat, and unprofitable blues.*

Plans would be spinning in his head from the moment he opened his eyes in the evening: remodeling the lodge, putting in playrooms for the kid, childproofing the dock; or renovating the villa in Greece; or finding a grand old vampire house in the Garden District in New Orleans and living there a few months of the year, flying down to Santa Luz for the full moon celebrations.

It didn't matter whether any of it happened, he knew: what counted was that for the first time in years he had something to look forward to besides revenge, or his next drink of blood.

And while he missed making love to Lourdes (the Midsummer encounter had been their last: Nanny Parish's orders), the couple had worked out a rather civilized arrangement. Whistler was allowed to have a prostitute every night—a surrogate, Sherman had suggested she be called. Lourdes's only rule was, never the same woman twice, poor boy.

He lowered himself into one of the redwood chaises, poured himself a martini, set the pitcher down on the grass beside him, and drank to the retreating sun. Just for the hell of it, he decided, he'd ask for a big woman tonight. What was it the Viscount used to call them? He pictured Vy buried under an enormous barmaid he used to smuggle into his ground-floor room in the front quad. The Viscount had always preferred ground-floor rooms for his dates. "Otherwise they sweat so, climbing the stairs."

Ah yes, fifteen-stoners. Vy only fucked men (of any size), or fifteen-stone women. "It takes a great deal of jiggle to make up for the lack of a penis, doncha know."

Funny, it didn't hurt as much anymore, thinking about the Viscount. Time, Whistler supposed. And a sense of completion after Midsummer. Besides, the old reprobate would probably have been long dead by now anyway—stabbed in the back by one of his rough trade. Or smothered in his sleep by one of his fifteen-stoners.

Whistler reached into the pocket of his rust-colored silk sport jacket for the flask he'd bought in town to replace the one he'd given to Nick, tilted it to his lips, took a mouthful, held it, savoring the edge on it before swallowing. It was Catherine's blood—unlike Selene, she was a meat eater, and he could taste the difference. Not that he preferred one to the other.

"Some nights, you just crave meat," he said aloud, then laughed, delighted at the workings of his subconscious mind on blood. "Yes, definitely a fifteen-stone woman tonight!"

The Creature stirred—Whistler addressed it. "Oh, you approve of that, do you?" He took another swig. "And do you have any suggestions as to age or race?"

THREE

Nick was wide awake at midnight on Friday, monitoring the system of a software designer firm in Marin—they only made games, but then, games were big business, and somebody had been hacking at their system. Nick wasn't so much concerned with catching whoever it was (that just took up his time and the client's money, and rarely resulted in successful prosecution anyway: the laws were still being written, and full of holes as a junior programmer's first project), as letting *them* know that *he* knew that they were there—that was usually enough to send most crackers on to easier prey.

If not, then he'd have a battle on his hands. He found himself almost looking forward to the possibility—another archenemy for the Silver Surfer. Anything to get this Elephant off his back. He remembered writing about the Elephant in his Fourth Step back in December, but had forgotten what it actually felt like to have Jumbo sitting on your soul every morning when you awoke. He was back up to a two-meeting-a-day habit, and it was barely keeping his head above water.

When the doorbell rang, he thought at first it was one of his sponsorees. He signed off his computer and started downstairs barefoot, in jeans and a Reggae Explosion T-shirt from Hawaii; on his way down he noticed a cobweb in the far corner of the stairwell ceiling. Have to have somebody in, he thought. Nick liked his house spotless, and his twelve-step connections had always ensured him of an endless supply of inexpensive housecleaners. There were half a dozen in Marijuana Anonymous alone—potheads with attention-deficit disorders that left them unfit for McJobs involving deep fryers.

He peered through the peephole he had installed in the front door (not just a peephole, a Securit-Eye Vue-Hole—which was a lot like a peephole, only it cost forty bucks more), then hurriedly threw back the dead bolt and started to open the door.

January slipped through before he'd finished opening it. "You can stay on one condition," he warned her, by way of greeting. "Don't offer me any blood."

She laughed and held up her thermos—they were brushing against each other in the vestibule—he seized her by the waist to put her out the door. She laughed again and spun out of his grasp. "Yeah, sure. Good thinking, Nick. I'm high on blood, and you're not. Like *you're* really gonna throw *me* out."

He followed her to the kitchen. "Where's the little glasses?" She was opening the cabinets one after the other. "Ah, here we go." She took out a pair of octagonal juice glasses and placed them on the table built into the breakfast nook that overlooked the falling hillside, then sat down and filled both glasses. "Guaranteed one hundred percent non-lethal harvesting," she told him proudly. "The Glasgow Kiss!"

"Why are you doing this, January?"

"Jeez, I at least expected a congratulations." Pouting, she slid his glass across the table towards him. "I'm doing it because you want me to."

"I don't." He overturned the glass deliberately, the neat-freak in him protesting every bit as loudly as the vampire.

January jumped to her feet with a shout as the blood rolled towards her—it was thick, with a surface tension halfway between water and mercury. "Fuck you, Nick, I can *make* you drink it."

It took all the self-control he could muster not to grab for a paper towel. "Yes you can, January. And then you'll have a drinking buddy for a night. What you won't have is a friend."

January looked down at the spreading puddle of blood on the table, then up at Nick, then down at the blood again. "You asshole." More in resignation than anger. "Got a straw?"

Nick came to two conclusions after January was gone. First, that he could be around blood without drinking it; second, that he couldn't cut himself off from January completely. Not only would that be a battle that the Silver Surfer might not be able to win, but a lot of people might be endangered during the course of it. Not just January's victims (some or all of whom might die if he weren't around to encourage her pursuit of less mortal methods of procuring blood), but possibly Betty as well: it wasn't hard to picture January following him all the way to the door of the parsonage.

Which led him to a third conclusion: that there was no way, at this point, that he could tell Betty about January, not after having omitted her entirely from his previous, ostensibly complete, confession on Monday night.

No, the old *I wasn't telling you the whole truth the last time I told you that I hadn't told you the whole truth the time before but was telling you the whole truth now, but now I'm really telling you the whole truth* junkie rap just wasn't going to go over again, not a third (or was it a fourth?) time.

There was no way around it but to try and juggle the two women, never letting either one find out he was spending time with the other. He sighed—what a predicament for a gay man. Good thing he had no sex drive away from blood: he'd never be able to find the time.

And as for what he'd do once the baby was born, once he had a son (amniocentesis had assured them) to serve as a hostage to fortune, he had no idea. Whatever it took to protect him, he imagined, with another sigh. Whatever it took.

ONE

Even Selene was caught up in the excitement of Lourdes's pregnancy. It helped that the younger woman seemed to genuinely regard her as a mother figure—Selene had even started to give her lessons in Wicca practice.

And having such a dramatic embodiment of a fertility goddess around the house had made the celebration of Lammas, also known as Lughnasath, on the eve of August, particularly rewarding this year: the witches and female vampires had taken over the keeping room Friday night for a birth ritual, while the men, personifying the Corn King, had agreed to sacrifice themselves for the Harvest, to accept the ritual sentence of death, that they might begin their journey to the Underworld.

It was a sacrifice the Corn Gods accepted a good deal more enthusiastically than customary, as the Underworld had apparently been moved to the Gold Dust Hotel and Casino for the evening of July 31, and Whistler was handing out hundred-dollar chips like Quaaludes.

Technically, the Corn Gods weren't supposed to return until the autumn equinox, so since Lourdes would be having none of him anyway, Whistler had agreed to take part of the symbolic burden on his shoulders: he spent the night (his night, which is to say, the following day) in the penthouse suite with a three-thousand-dollar-a-night (-day) hooker named Lois (possibly) who had been flown in from Vegas for the occasion, and bore such a startling resemblance to the late Jayne Mansfield that he kept expecting her head to fall off at any moment.

His presence wasn't missed at the Manor. He returned after sunset Saturday night, entering the lodge via the back door; on his way up to see

Lourdes he passed Catherine and Selene in the kitchen, where they were engaged in a dangerous conspiracy to put some added poundage on the mother-to-be, per Nanny Parish's instructions.

A dangerous conspiracy to their own figures, that is: besides stocking the evening breakfast cart with high-calorie entrées like eggs Benedict and Belgian waffles, and pastries like cheese Danish, rugelach stuffed with almond paste, or flaky baklava dripping with honey, Catherine had taught Josephina to prepare *lumpia*, the little Filipino spring rolls that Lourdes's grandmother used to make.

Lucky thing Lourdes only has another month to go, Whistler thought on his way up the stairs to the south wing. *Else we'd have a whole houseful of fifteen-stone women by winter.*

"Hello, my darling!" he called through Lourdes's open door. The south wing was quiet, even though it was a Saturday night and the weekend of a Greater Sabbat, and the rest of the Manor was bustling with Coven and Penang guests in addition to the Luzan staff Whistler had imported for their discretion and smooth, full-bodied drinkability. (Also because they would have worked free, being in effect slaves, but Selene had put the kibosh on *that* little efficiency.)

"Hi Corn God. How was the Underworld?" Lourdes greeted him.

"Hades. Sheer Hades."

"I bet." She sat up a little higher in her enormous bed, and offered him her cheek to kiss. "Did the Creature miss me?"

"We thought of you the whole time." He gave her a peck, then pulled the rocker over to the side of the bed.

"Want to feel her kicking?" She took his hand and placed it on her belly.

"There . . . no, wait, *there.* Am I right?"

"Yeah, that was a good one."

"But what's this 'her' business?"

"Selene told me last night."

Just then they heard the clank of the elevator at the end of the hall; when Selene and Catherine arrived with the breakfast cart, Whistler asked the High Priestess how she knew that his son was going to be a daughter.

"Not difficult at all—for a witch," was the reply. "There's a woman in Petaluma who can sex chickens while they're still in the egg—compared to that, human babies are a snap."

"But you're sure?"

"Jamey, you can bet the farm on it."

"Never mind betting the farm—can I paint the nursery?"

"Pink as a virgin's nipples, dearie."

" 'So it shall be written, so it shall be done!' "

TWO

The sun had set at 8:18 PDT on that Lughnasath evening, the first of August. January was already awake, watching a *Get Smart* rerun on the Nickelodeon channel. With the money she had been wheedling from Nick every week on her promise (kept, so far) to use only non-lethal harvesting methods, as well as the occasional wallet or bankroll that came her way as a by-product of hunting, she had moved down the hall to a better room, one with a kitchenette (hot plate, sink, and a knee-high refrigerator) and cable TV.

What she really needed was a car—it was getting harder and harder to catch her customary quarry. Six weeks of preying on the weakest, drunkest, or craziest denizens of Telegraph Avenue and People's Park had winnowed down the local population with Darwinian rigor: the loners were cunning and watchful, the weak herded together.

Besides, while they'd been an ideal population for killing, most of the non-lethal methods of procuring blood were useless on them: they were impervious to blackmail, sob stories, or subtle trickery. But unless she could talk Nick into lending her the Corvette (fat chance) the best she could do was to expand her hunting grounds.

When her favorite *Get Smart*—the one with Hymie the Robot—had ended, she dressed in a new ribbed poorboy blouse over black jeans, threw her purse over her shoulder, and once out the door, instead of heading toward People's Park she set her course for the University of California.

It was a sweet summer night; even out on Telegraph Avenue, which was rapidly becoming the Skid Row of Berkeley, the air was still sunset-fresh and tinged with violet. January strode north with the traffic, past the boarded-up storefronts, stopping only when she reached Sather Gate. There she took the last swig from her thermos, and found herself a bench just off the path where she could eye the summer students until her hunting instincts took over.

The college kids—how young they seemed to her, how fresh and plump compared to her customary prey. It seemed as if their blood would be especially juicy. She recapped her thermos, closed her eyes, and settled back to wait for the blood to come on.

For her, the first symptom was always the same: a sweet feeling in her bones, spreading outwards from the marrow. When the tingle reached her skin, she would open her eyes without attempting to focus on any particular individual, and let her eyes select a victim. How they chose, she never knew, but they were rarely wrong. Eventually a figure would come into focus, one figure only out of the crowd, and that figure she would pursue the way a lioness stalked a single antelope through the distracting herd, faithfully, unswervingly, forsaking all others, however tempting or vulnerable.

This evening when she allowed her eyes to open, they settled on a blocky Chinese boy. January hopped off the bench and began tracking him at a distance. She followed him all the way to the BART station on Shattuck, where she lost him when the ticket machine rejected one of her crumpled dollar bills after another.

Fuck, she thought. *I bet he would of been good, too.* She trudged back to campus, mindful that she'd lost nearly half an hour of prime hunting time—if she didn't find someone in the next hour, she'd lose her edge entirely.

Back on the bench, she closed her eyes again, and opened them slowly. Another Chinese. (Not necessarily racism, despite her history with Wayne: the Chinese were simply the largest minority at Cal—and there *was* no majority.)

A girl this time. *Well helloooo Honey.* Reminded her of Duke's girlfriend in Doonesbury. Same little round glasses, same tragic haircut. Short steps. No hip action whatsoever, January noticed, following this one a little closer than she'd followed the first one, as she pitter-pattered towards the Student Union. Couldn't afford to lose her.

But she did—to a half dozen other Chinese students. *Probably a study group,* thought January bitterly, returning to her bench. *On Saturday night! No wonder they're gonna rule the world.* This time when she closed her eyes she felt the bench jar, and when she opened them found herself sitting next to a pale, spotty white girl in loopy carpenter pants and an oversized T-shirt, who turned to her and glowered. "Almost chickened out, eh?"

"What?" January was careful not to meet her eyes.

"We were supposed to meet at nine-thirty. I got here five minutes early, just in time to see you leave. You're not a Duggie, are you?"

"A what?" January had found her night shades in her purse. Blue-blockers—the amber lenses disguised the red. She put them on before turning to her bench mate, who turned away.

"Dyke Until Graduation. It's *so* P.C. now—where were they all when I was getting tortured in high school? The last woman that answered my ad was just *experimenting*."

"Your ad, right."

"You *are* Jill?"

"Sure."

The other young woman pursed her lips and nodded her head slowly, as if reaching a decision, then stuck out her hand. "What the hell, at least you came back. Hi Jill, I'm Patti. Want to go get a cup of coffee?"

"Cup of somep'n, anyway," said January, trying not to smile—for some reason, her smile often seemed to alarm her prey.

THREE

After a month and a half of juggling, Nick had a new respect for philandering heterosexual males. How they could manage to keep two women happy and also find the time for sex, he couldn't imagine. Take this Saturday—he and Betty had gone to their Lamaze class at the clinic in Richmond, then driven back to El Cerrito to open up for, and attend, the early A.A. meeting at the CHP, and then he'd taken her out to dinner at the Cape Cod in Albany to satisfy her sudden craving for sea bass.

It had occurred to Nick on the way back from the restaurant that Betty wouldn't be fitting into the front seat of the 'Vette for much longer—as it was, he had to help haul her out. *Don't worry, honey,* he reassured the car, *I'm never trading you in on a station wagon.*

"Want to come in?" she asked him, as he extracted her. "Bound to be something on HBO."

"Sure. Just let me check my messages first." He gave her his arm and she leaned on him as they mounted the porch steps. She was no lightweight, either: Betty was enormous approaching eight months—hadn't seen her feet since the Fourth of July.

Inside, she hauled herself upstairs to pee—again—while Nick checked his messages from the kitchen phone. Saturday was one of January's hunting nights, and Nick encouraged her to keep in touch, so he could give her some positive reinforcement in return for her adherence to non-lethal methods of blood harvesting. She also got two hundred bucks a week from him—between his two women, even Nick's generous resources were strained.

"So what's on the tube?" asked Betty upon her return. She had changed into a voluminous, wildly patterned maternity nightgown that was only a few ruffles short of a full Bozo, and settled its folds around her as she lowered herself to the Louis Wept sofa.

"*Green Card.*"

"Great—I just love that Gerard Depardieu—and *don't* try to tell me *he's* gay."

"A flamer," shrugged Nick. He had heard nothing of the sort about the rugged actor, but he couldn't resist tweaking Betty. Besides, the guy was French, and in the theater, so how bad could the odds have been?

But he found himself enjoying the movie anyway—in the old days, he told Betty, "I always had a secret thing for homely straight men. In fact, the only men I preferred to homely straights were handsome straights, handsome gays, and homely gays, in that order."

He expected a laugh, but when he looked over there was an expression of alarm on her face. His eye followed her gaze down to the lap of her clowny maternity nightgown. It was wrinkled from having been tucked between her thighs, but he could see the blood spot as she tugged it free: it was dark red, glistening, the size of a silver dollar, and spreading.

They'd called an ambulance, rather than risk stuffing Betty into the 'Vette again. And against all odds, the paramedics were at the parsonage in minutes, and were both compassionate *and* competent. Nick followed the ambulance to the county hospital in Martinez, where he was surprised at the small-town feeling of the place—no gunshot victims lying around bleeding, no junkies bouncing off the walls.

The doctor catching in the ER that evening was a Ghanaian intern with blue-black skin and a singsong accent; his initial diagnosis of placenta previa was both unusual and interesting enough to draw the attention of the OB resident, who confirmed it with an ultrasound.

"Here, see this blob down here?" The resident, a thirtyish woman with an air of frazzled resignation, pointed to the ultrasound screen. Betty squinted from the bed in the OB examining room; Nick leaned over her for a closer look. "That's the placenta, and it's slipped down here, covering the uterine—"

Betty interrupted. "It's blocking the way out, isn't it?"

"It surely is."

"So what do we do?"

"Well, the bleeding has stopped. You're how far along?" She thumbed through the chart. "About eight months?"

"Thirty-three weeks exactly—it was an artificial insemination."

"Then we wait. And at the first sign of a contraction, or if you start spotting again, or after you come to term, whichever comes first, we go in for a C-section."

"Will I be waiting at home?"

"Only if you live within thirty minutes of the hospital, have no major steps to climb, and can manage complete bed rest—potty breaks only."

"No problem," said Betty miserably, as the nurse began removing the fetal monitor. "The servants will be happy to work overtime."

"We can do it," Nick reminded her. "Set you up downstairs with a hospital bed—I'll have a line and a modem put in, and I can move in and work, and take shifts with the church ladies—be a lot cheaper than three weeks in here, and a lot more fun—"

"Doctor B.," the nurse interrupted, pointing to the bedding—she'd been changing the sterile towel under Betty, but the clean white towel she'd slipped underneath was soaked with dark red blood when she pulled it out.

"Lovely," said the doctor. She took a second to arrange her face, then smiled down at Betty. "What do you say, Mom? Ready for an eight-month Leo?"

"We were sort of counting on a Virgo," joked Betty bravely, reaching up to squeeze the hand Nick had placed on her shoulder.

"Yeah, but look on the bright side," suggested Nick.

"Which bright side would that be?" she managed.

"No more goddamn Lamaze classes."

At Betty's request, Nick donned mask and gown and sat beside her in the chilly operating room through it all: the administering of the anesthesia; the initial scalpel slit, with its thread of blood quickly sponged away; more cutting and stanching; Doctor B.'s hands wrist-deep in Betty; the baby lifted casually into the air.

Nick checked the clock on the wall—his own watch was under the long sleeve of the gown, and he didn't know if he was allowed to pull it back—and committed the time, 1:52 A.M., to memory. Betty had made it clear that it was his responsibility to note the precise time of birth for the baby's chart.

After the baby had been de-corded, he was whisked away to the side of the operating room, vacuumed and Apgar-ed and found to be pretty high on the scale, considering his truncated engagement in the womb. They'd held him up briefly for Nick to see while they were stitching Betty up: his head was round as Swee' Pea's, his features as blank and untroubled.

Later, in the neonatal intensive care unit, Nick had the baby all to himself until Betty came out of the anesthesia. What surprised him more than anything else, as he held his son, was the preemie's size.

Not that he was tiny—just the opposite: when Nick held him, the child who barely filled both his hands somehow managed to take up his entire field of vision. He was enormous, he was the most momentous thing his father had ever encountered. Nick then had only a brief moment to understand something that had always puzzled him—the peculiar shortsightedness, the tunnel vision that parenthood always seemed to inspire—before it sucked him under too.

After that it was too late, the understanding passed. He was a parent himself now: shortsighted, tunnel-visioned, obsessed.

Nick made a few phone calls while Betty and the as-yet-unnamed baby slept—most of them to the church ladies, and the aunt and uncle back in Williamsport who, along with their children, her two cousins, were Betty's only living relatives. Then he called his own number—one message. He played it back: *Hi Nick. It's like, around one. It worked, Nick! I did the Oops Ring and it worked like a charm.*

He checked his watch—4 A.M. Too late to call anybody but a using vampire. Still, congratulations were in order. The Oops Ring technique was tricky, involving a doctored ring with a sharp edge—you not only had to make it look like an accident when you severed your donor's vein, but you had to keep the blood flowing while appearing to try to stem the bleeding, and catch the blood while keeping your donor from panicking. If January could manage it, her social skills had advanced indeed.

She answered on the first ring, and accepted his acclamation with whispered thanks.

"I take it your donor is still there?"

"Sleeping like a baby," January whispered. "She's never been laid so good in her life."

"I can imagine," replied Nick, bursting to tell her his own good news. But then it dawned on him that there was now one more ball in the air, that his two-woman juggling act had now turned into one of those brain-teaser puzzles about how to get the wolf, the goat, and the cabbage across the river. So instead, he told her that he had been called out of town on a emergency job, gave her a line about a company in Portland whose system had contracted a virus. "I'll be back by Wednesday at the latest."

She sounded disappointed. "I haven't seen you all week, Nick."

"I promise, we'll get together as soon as I get back. And Jan? Congrats again on the Oops Ring—I'm so proud of you."

But his hand was shaking as he hung up the phone, and he cursed himself for a fool. Somehow, despite the absolute inevitability of this moment, until now he'd never quite put it all together. His charge, January, a vampire who craved baby-blood. And a baby, full of baby-blood. *Vampire, baby; vampire, baby; vampire, baby . . .*

What kind of an idiot would let a situation like that sneak up on him?

Wait a minute: *sneak?* The alarums had been blaring for months—he remembered his conversation with himself back in June. *Whatever it took,* he'd promised himself back then.

Vampire, baby; vampire, baby; vampire, baby.

Now he renewed the promise: somehow, whatever the threat, he would do whatever it took to protect his son. Whatever the hell his name was.

FOUR

For Selene, waking up a few hours before sunset at Whistler Manor gave her the same sense of spaciousness, of time and peace and opportunity, as waking up at four in the morning back home in Bolinas.

The light through the pine grove was a sere green-gold, somehow crisp and hazy at the same time. Summer in the High Sierra always carried a foreshadowing of autumn. Selene sat up in bed to throw her first runes of the day. But the bones' message—endings and beginnings, death and birth—was the same message they'd given her last Yule. It was a wintry message, easier to interpret in December than on the seventh of August.

She thought about consulting the tarot, then decided not to—the runes could be awfully jealous. And in any case, she'd never found foreknowledge to be of much practical use. It was like watching *Psycho*—you could yell to Janet Leigh all you wanted, but she'd never hear you with the shower running.

Selene decided to cast a protective spell anyway, just in case, asking the Norns—the Teutonic Fates—to extend their protection to all those under Selene's protection.

But only if such a thing could be done without altering Destiny—this was the most she was allowed to ask for. Sometimes being a witch wasn't all it was cracked up to be.

Spell cast, she showered, put on a *Year of Tibet* T-shirt and her baggy khaki shorts over her bathing suit, and went down to the kitchen to make herself a cup of tea. The kitchen was cool and dark, full of echoes; metal surfaces glinted in the dusky light.

After tea, Selene went for a dip in the lake, which involved a short hike across hard-packed sand and then a long wade to reach water deep enough to bathe in. When she returned to the Manor, Catherine was in the kitchen, wearing an apron over her corduroy bathrobe, with her red hair pinned up in a careless bun. Barefoot, pink-cheeked, and now that she'd had her coffee, pleased with the world.

"Sherman must have come up last night," Selene remarked. Catherine only glowed like that after a night with her furry vampire husband.

"Around four."

"No clients?"

"He's lightproofed his study and changed his schedule around. Now he sees clients straight through from nine in the morning to ten at night, Tuesday through Thursday. Stoned on blood the whole time, of course—he says it makes him a lot more empathetic."

"Which gives him four-day weekends up here," Selene noted with an impish grin. "So how are you holding up?"

"Chafed, but still game."

Later, as she helped Catherine prepare the breakfast cart, Selene mentioned the runes she'd thrown upon awakening. "I've never been as good at runes as I wanted to be," she complained. "Maybe it's because I'm half German."

"What's the other half?" Catherine inquired.

"Welsh."

"That's some help. But I'm all Irish, and I'm pretty sure that half the time I throw the bones, they're only mind-fucking with me, anyway." Catherine looked down at the tray. "Can you think of anything else that will tempt Lourdes?"

Selene looked over the cart. "Dearie, anybody who can't find a thousand-calorie nosh here, isn't trying."

After breakfast Catherine returned to the kitchen and brought her garnishing tools out from their hiding place behind the spice cupboard (she had to keep them away from the vampires—it wasn't the blood that dulled them, but the skin) to prepare an antipasto platter for the men's sunset ritual, while Selene stayed behind to give Lourdes another in a series of lessons on Wicca.

The lessons—which Whistler knew nothing about, since neither woman was exactly sure how a vampire witch would fit into the scheme of things—had been going on for over a month. This evening they were discussing snakes.

Wicca did not worship snakes, Selene explained, nor have them for familiars. "The only connection is medicinal—poisonous reptiles are quite useful—shamans have employed them for ages. There's even rumored to be a potion called mithradite, made of all the different snake venoms, that antidotes *any* poison."

"No shit?"

"It's probably mythical. But you can do a lot with reptile potions as backup spells. Amphibians, on the other hand, frogs and toads and such, are definitely overrated."

"What do you mean, backup spells?"

"You always have to back up spells. Suppose you put a curse of impotence on a man. In general, those are self-fulfilling: you tell a man he's going to be impotent, and he'll pretty much take care of the rest."

"Except vampires," Lourdes pointed out.

"God bless 'em," muttered Nanny Parish, who was nursing Plum Rose in the rocking chair.

Selene continued. "But if it doesn't work, there are quite a few substances that will induce impotence."

"How many?" Lourdes wanted to know.

"A lot more than there are to induce erections, I can tell you that," said Selene, and the other women laughed.

"So putting a spell on somebody, it's not just, like you chant the magic words or something?"

"We should *be* so lucky, dearie. Magic words and three bucks'll get you across the Golden Gate Bridge on a weeken—why, good evening, Jamey," she said lightly as Whistler popped his disheveled head into the room.

"Good evening, ladies." He was wearing black satin pajamas. "Actually, I was looking for Catherine—she's promised Sherman and myself an antipasto platter to go along with our martinis."

"Kitchen."

"Cheer-o." He closed the door, then opened it again. "Anyone care to join us for a little casino action later? I woke up feeling lucky this evening."

There was a muffled snicker from Nanny Parish in the rocker.

"What occasioned that, Nanny?" asked Whistler.

"Mister Whistler, y'already de luckiest mon in de world. You get any luckier, de rest of us gon' to flat give up." She chuckled, and turned back to her baby. "Yes mon, flat give up."

And suddenly he'd darted back into the room, and laid a wet sloppy kiss on Nanny's cheek. But even that wasn't enough to vent all the joy burbling up inside him—he dropped to his knees and threw his arms around her and the placid Plum Rose, and hugged as much of the two of them as his arms could encompass. "You're absolutely right, Nanny Parish," he declared simply, when he felt he could speak. "I am the luckiest man in the world. Thanks for reminding me."

FIVE

Nick might not have been the luckiest man in the world that first week in August, but he was certainly one of the busiest, what with tripping back and forth to the hospital to visit Betty and little Chicken Legs (which was what they were currently calling the still unnamed Baby Boy Santos-Shoemaker) and driving around the Bay Area meeting with potential clients: the hospital bills were inconceivable, and Nick, who had once been able to pick and choose his clients, had let the word go out that he was now available to all comers.

Of course, with all those balls in the air, one of them was bound to fall sooner or later: he'd just plain forgotten his promised meeting with January on the Wednesday after C.L.'s birth. But she'd seemed to be okay about it when he returned her call on Thursday evening, and they had rescheduled for Friday night, the seventh—he was going to pick her up at her hotel and take her out to dinner.

But he'd had a hidden agenda as well: he planned to sound her out about reducing her allowance. He wouldn't tell her anything about Betty or the baby, of course—just plead a temporary case of the shorts, see how it went.

Not well, as it turned out. Not well at all. She listened politely over the formica table at the International House of Burgers as he babbled on about extra expenses, and a downswing in business, and how he wasn't feeling exactly clean about bribing her, in effect, not to—

She didn't wait for him to finish. "Fuck you, Nick." She was wearing her amber blue-blockers, so he couldn't read her eyes, but her voice was shaking with emotion, and her hands—big hands, even for a rangy girl like January—had clenched so tightly around her Hula Burger that the pineapple slices were sliding out from under the bun. "I got expenses too—it isn't cheap, getting blood without killing people. You gotta stay clean, and dress nice, and buy coffee for 'em sometimes."

"But don't you feel better about yourself?" Nick's Greek burger—feta cheese, sliced olives, and crumbled bacon—lay untouched before him.

"Yeah, I guess."

"Come on, you know you do."

"Okay I do. But I also feel better about a refrigerator and a cable TV, so if you're kissing me off, Nick, you might as well tell me now, so I can start tricking or something before my money runs out."

"I'm not kissing you off as a friend, Jan—"

She interrupted him again. "A friend who's gonna let me go out tricking—I can get lots of friends like that."

"I don't want to see you tricking—it's just like I said, it's not feeling clean to me anymore. How about if I give you a hundred a week for a while, while you get back on your feet?"

January put down her burger, wiped her hands on the tablecloth just to fuck with the world, found her thermos in the roomy pocket of the coat draped over the back of her chair—a moss green man's overcoat she'd bought at a Telegraph thrift shop—and took a swig. It was either that, or kill him across the table.

The thermos blood was old—she'd have to hunt tonight—but it was working. She felt the world sharpening around her as the glow of the blood warmed her from the bones out. "I'm on my feet, Nick," she said. "And hunting twice a week. And right now you're giving me two hundred dollars a week. Even without a high school diploma, I can work out the math."

"What are you saying?"

Blpblpblpblpb. She blew a raspberry as she recapped the thermos. "And you a college graduate. I'm saying, if for two hundred bucks a week

I get blood your way twice, then for one hundred bucks a week I only get blood your way once."

"And the second time you hunt, it's your way?"

"Attaboy. But don't feel bad—it's not like you'll be killing somebody every week—just that you won't be paying me not to." She put her thermos away, and turned back to her burger. "Funny how, if you're eating, blood makes you hungrier, and if you aren't, it makes it so you're not even hungry in the first place."

Nick stood up. "Thanks for making it easier for me, Jan. I'd appreciate it if you'd stay as far away from me as possible from this point on."

She took off her blue-blockers, and fixed him with a blood red stare. "Sure Nick. I really give a shit what you'd *appreciate*. But at least you're not bullshitting me about being my friend any more, when we both know I was just the prize in your big fight with Whistler."

It's not true, Nick started to say. Then he realized that it might well have been—and that he didn't really care either way. He threw a twenty down on the table, and walked out.

Shaking with anger, but still hungry, January finished her Hula burger, and about half of Nick's Greek, then left, heading towards the U.C. campus. But when she reached Telegraph Avenue she turned left instead, striding through the night towards People's Park; in the doorway of yet another abandoned storefront near the corner of Channing and Telegraph, crumpled at an angle that left no doubt that the occupant was either asleep or unconscious, lay a footless sleeping bag with a pair of battered boots sticking out of one end and a ragged straw cowboy hat at the other.

January hopped over it without slowing her stride, but halfway up the block she ducked into the doorway of a bank to take her nearly empty Star Trek thermos out of her roomy overcoat pocket. She drained the last slash for a burst of strength before turning back, scooping the wino (or winette) out of the doorway, sleeping bag and all, swinging the bundle over her shoulder—it was astonishingly light to contain a human being—and racing up Channing towards the east end of People's Park, where there was still enough privacy to do what she had to do.

It was a man, as it turned out when January unwrapped him in the shadows of the bushes. She should have recognized him by the straw cowboy hat with the bedraggled feathers—it was old Hoopa Joe, who'd been panhandling around People's for years, and was so undernourished by now that he felt hollow. Fortunately, he wasn't—he was full of blood, and so drunk he didn't wake up until several seconds after January had pulled from her pocket a small longshoreman's hook with the inner edge of the tip honed sharp as a fishhook—stolen from the Copy Shoppe, where it had been used for opening cartons and bales of paper—and slit his throat from just below one ear to just below the other.

January didn't mind that puzzled stare—she'd seen the look before. There seemed to be only a few expressions available to humans as they watched, or felt, their lifeblood draining, or spurting, into a thermos held under their slit throats—anger, astonishment, curiosity—but this simple puzzled look was the most common, although January couldn't remember anyone who'd awakened so late in the process, and had consequently been so completely puzzled.

But only for a few more seconds—then the light, such as it was, went out of the dark eyes, and the heart stopped beating, and as the blood stopped spurting January had to elevate the corpse with one arm under the lower torso while trying with her other hand to position, then steady, the thermos under the failing trickle until it was filled to the top, and the dark blood spilling over.

Then, carefully, with the thermos held level, she drank from the brim like a woman sipping scorching coffee, screwed the top of the thermos down, and slid it back into her overcoat pocket as her strength surged again from the fresh blood. With a series of compact, violent downstrokes she hacked at the neck with the hook until first the hat and then the head came free. She grabbed the latter by the convenient ponytail and swung it around her head, spattering blood, until it was whirling so fast it was a blur even to her, and then let it go in the general direction of Emeryville.

It was a pretty cool trick that she'd conceived of in those first bloodless V.A. days, when all she could think about was blood, and all she could do about it was think. See, they'd find the body minus the head, and if they noticed it was missing a lot of blood, they'd figure it had been killed someplace else and brought to the park. The head minus the body they'd find God knows where, and think God knows what.

Or should I say, Higher Power knows what? She left the park at full speed, then slowed to a walk as she strolled back down towards Telegraph, laughing out loud at her own joke.

SIX

Lourdes's water broke around eleven-thirty in the evening on Friday, the twenty-eighth of August. The labor lasted less than two hours—short for a first child, long by vampire standards, but still relatively painless: Lourdes was allotted a thimbleful of blood at every contraction, and was so high when the time came to push that Nanny Parish had to warn her *not* to push with all her might, or little Corazon would have made her entrance into the world launched across the room like the human cannonball in the circus.

Occurring as it had on a weekend night at Whistler Manor, Cora's was one of the best-attended births this side of the royal family. Afterwards they all laughed and wept—the greatest laughter coming when Whistler called for something with which to cut the umbilical, and—snick, snick, snick—was instantly surrounded by proffered vampire blades of every description, knives, razors, scalpels.

He had managed to locate his own antique razor with the mother-of-pearl handle in his pocket, however, and waved the blade over the flame of a Bic to sterilize it. Nanny Parish showed him where to cut, and then tied the knot while Whistler handed round Cuban cigars of a brand so exclusive even Fidel couldn't get them.

"Anybody lights one of those in here has to deal with me," Selene announced, then slapped her forehead in dismay. "I forgot to check my watch. Did anyone get the exact time of birth?"

August Fetterman's moment followed: "One forty-three A.M., Pacific Daylight Time," he reported sonorously, trying not to sound *too* pleased with himself.

Selene nodded appreciatively. "A Virgo."

"And born in the summertime, appropriately enough," added Augie out of one side of his mouth; the other side now contained the cigar, still in its wrapper, pointing jauntily toward the ceiling.

"Oh?" Cheese Louise gave him the straight line.

"Her daddy couldn't be richer, and her ma is definitely good looking."

"Thank you, Augie," said Lourdes wanly.

Whistler hadn't heard any of this—he was holding his daughter in his arms for the first time. And vampire or no vampire, he was a parent now: shortsighted, tunnel-visioned, and obsessed.

Later, after the mess had been cleaned up, the bedding changed, the afterbirth placed in the refrigerator in a square casserole-size Tupperware container (unlabeled: woe betide the unwary seeker after leftovers) for subsequent ritual planting, and Lourdes and Cora sequestered for a nap, a strange urge came over Whistler, alone in his own bedroom, and without a second thought he gave in to it.

After all, it occurred to him as he reached for his bedside phone and dialed Berkeley information, what was the use of being the luckiest man in the world if you couldn't give in to even the strangest of urges without thinking twice?

The call came in on Nick's business line, jolting him awake in his ergonomic office chair. He had fallen asleep monitoring a hackers' bulletin board, and picked up the receiver without thinking about it. "Santos."

"Hullo, Nick."

Nick's first instinct was to hang up—the Silver Surfer was a little too busy at the moment to take on any more cosmic battles—but then for that very reason Nick decided to hear what his old archenemy had to say. "Whistler," he replied carefully.

"The very same. And the very different—I'm a father now. Lourdes just had the baby about an hour ago."

Caught off guard, Nick pictured a little brown Whistler baby, and almost smiled in spite of himself. "Congratulations. Boy or girl?"

"A little girl named Corazon. Cora, for short. And yours?"

Nick felt a stab of fear. "My what?"

"Your baby? With the Reverend Shoemaker? Surely you haven't forgotten."

"No, no—I just . . ."

But Whistler was on to him. "For heaven's sake, man, do you think I'm threatening your baby? A new father myself?"

"Then why did you call?"

Whistler sighed audibly, to let Nick know that his feelings had been hurt. "It just seemed like a good time to call old friends."

"We were that once, weren't we?" said Nick, almost sadly.

"Yes, we were."

Nick thought it over. "I don't know, Whistler. You understand I think what you did to V.A. was monstrously evil? I'm not even talking about what you had done to me—and don't tell me it was all Selene's idea, because I won't buy it."

Whistler's turn to think it over. "Before we end up back at square one, Nick, is it possible for you to understand that I feel just as strongly that what you and Leon did, both to myself and to the others, was also monstrously evil?"

"That you believe it? Yes, I suppose so."

"Good. Do you remember your Blake?"

"We didn't study at lot of Blake at the Academy, Jamey."

"Allow me to quote a relevant passage from a lesser-known poem entitled 'My Spectre Around Me Night and Day': *Throughout all Eternity/ I forgive you, you forgive me.*"

The pause that followed was surprisingly unstrained—it was if they had each decided to take a moment to think things over. Nick spoke first. "A boy. Leon."

"Well that's a lucky—" Whistler broke off the sentence. A lucky thing, he'd been about to say. A life for a life, and all that—but he'd remembered just in time that Nick didn't know anything about Leon Stanton's murder. "—boy, I'm sure. When was he born?"

"August first. He's supposed to be coming home from the hospital tomorrow."

"He's all right, though?" There was no mistaking Whistler's concern.

"He's fine. He was a month premature—they just wanted to make sure his lungs were fully developed."

"I'm so glad. And the new mother?"

"Doing fine."

"Excellent, excellent." Another pause. "Have you heard from January?" Whistler had—indirectly: Sherman had clipped a news article about a headless body in People's Park for him—but didn't want to bring it up if Nick hadn't seen it.

He hadn't. "We had a falling-out a few weeks ago—haven't seen her since. I gave up all the rest of my sponsorees, too—decided my own sobriety was about all I could handle."

"I take it you're on the wagon again, then?"

" 'One day at a time.' And I take it you're not?"

"Wrecked as the Hesperus, high as the Union Jack, stoned as—"

"I've got the picture." Nick phrased the next thought carefully. "I don't want you to get me wrong, what I said about my own sobriety. I mean, if you ever want to quit, if there's any way I could help, I'd want you to call me."

"I shouldn't think it likely. But yes, Nick, I will. I couldn't think of anyone else I'd call instead. And how about you? If you ever decide to start drinking blood again, will you call me?"

Another dead minute over the long-distance wires. "Same answer. I can't see it ever happening, but yeah. Yeah, Jamey, I suppose I would."

"Good. Well, I'm glad I gave in to my impulse to call you, Nick. Kiss little Leon hello to the world from his Uncle Whistler. They'll be twenty-tens, you know."

"Beg pardon?"

"Twenty-tens. I don't want to shock you, Nick, but our children will be graduating high school in the year 2010."

"Damn. We're gonna be in our sixties, with kids in high school?"

"Yes, Nick. So you'd better get your beauty sleep while you can—you're going to need it."

"You too—you've got a year or so on me, if I recall correctly."

Whistler decided not to remind him that thanks to blood, he himself would be aging at a much slower rate than Nick would. "And feeling every minute of it. Good night, old friend. Don't forget to kiss little Leon for me."

"Good night to you too, Jamey. And kiss Cora for me."

After hanging up, Nick signed off the hackers' bulletin board and began surfing the Internet for some sort of poetry or literary bulletin board. Eventually he found, not just a general board, but an actual listing for the Blake Society, in England. He hacked his way in and posted a query—when he woke up the next morning it had been answered. Some kindly Brit with the nom-de-net of Gryffon had typed in the entire text of "My Spectre Around Me Night and Day," which, although it may have been a minor poem, was certainly not a short one.

Nick found Whistler's quote on the second page down:

> *And throughout all Eternity*
> *I forgive you, you forgive me.*
> *As our dear Redeemer said:*
> *'This the Wine, and this the Bread.'*

He printed it out, along with one other verse, the first of the poem:

> *My Spectre around me night and day*
> *Like a wild beast guards my way;*
> *My Emanation far within*
> *Weeps incessantly for my sin.*

Not a bad description of a vampire, thought Nick. Even a recovering one.

ONE

While Whistler was gratified by the ease with which Lourdes had slipped into the role of Lady of the Manor as if to the Manor born, he found it no less admirable that she somehow seemed to be governing entirely without portfolio.

Catherine Bailey, for instance, had taken to bringing her notebook up along with the breakfast cart every evening, and while Lourdes nursed Cora in the window seat and Nanny Parish suckled Plum Rose in the Nantucket rocker, the three women would chat about the following night's menu. No one had ever told her to report to Lourdes, certainly not Whistler, yet by mid-September it would have been as unthinkable for Catherine to cook a meal that had not been approved by Lourdes as it would have been for Nanny Parish to take Cora out for a stroll without bringing her to her mother first to have her outfit checked out. (And oh, did Cora have outfits!)

So when it came time to plan the autumnal equinox celebration (it wouldn't be a simple holiday, either: some of the Coven and Penang would arrive as early as Friday evening, but since the equinox would not take place until 8:00 A.M. on the twenty-second, the ceremony itself couldn't begin until after midnight on Tuesday), it was to Lourde's window seat throne that Selene came with *her* notebook to plan room assignments, that Cheese Louise and Catherine came to discuss catering, and that Josephina reported to address housekeeping arrangements.

By Saturday night, the corridor outside her suite resembled the route to and from the royal bedchamber, with constant courtier traffic, and Whistler's admiration was growing a little strained. "I haven't spent ten uninterrupted minutes with my wife in two weeks," he announced, shooing Josephina from the room.

Lourdes finished nursing Cora, and handed her over to Nanny Parish to be burped. "You're exaggerating again, Jamey. That hummer this morning took at least twenty minutes." She had in fact been putting Whistler off since Cora's birth. Come the equinox ritual, when the Corn King returned to claim Persephone and carry her back to the Underworld with him, Lourdes was determined that the conquering hero, now Lord of the Underworld, would notice no diminution of pleasure upon coupling with his Queen, no slackness in Persephone's silky sheath.

To this end, she had been performing her vaginal exercises diligently for the intervening three weeks, and using a salve that Nanny Parish had brought with her from Santa Luz.

Whistler passed a palm over his yellow hair, rippling it like a field of overripe wheat—that was about as much frustration as he ever let himself show, but Lourdes recognized the signs. "Maybe you'd better give us a few minutes, Nanny."

The Luzan woman bustled off. "Come, Cora. We gon' to see Plum Rose, now. We know when we ain' wanted someplace." With a sniff she closed the nursery door behind her.

Lourdes edged closer to the window and patted the sill beside her. "Bring it right on over here, my Lord of the Underworld. You're looking awful handsome tonight."

He hopped up onto the window seat. "Thank you, m'dear." There was a part of Whistler that would have enjoyed wearing evening clothes to the casinos, the way they do in Monte Carlo, but in Tahoe it would have been *de trop* (in Tahoe, shirts that buttoned were *de trop*, and a necktie entirely out of the question), so he'd settled for a tropic-tan pongee shirt, casually pleated tailored slacks with his ourobouros belt, Topsiders with no socks, and Italian sunglasses that cost more than most Italian motorbikes. "But I'd prefer if you didn't manage *me* quite as diligently as the rest of the staff."

"No you wouldn't," she replied matter-of-factly. "You just don't want to know about it."

"Close—I want to be able to pretend I don't know about it—a willing suspension of disbelief, so to speak. And while we're on the subject, I'd like to ask of you the same courtesy Selene has always extended me: I don't mind you trying out your Wicca spells on me—I've always rather enjoyed them—but I do want to be know about it in advance. If you want controls and blind studies, kindly use the servants."

Lourdes had gone very still as he talked, and kept her eyes fixed on the view when she replied. "My Wicca lessons—you knew about my Wicca lessons? Did Selene—"

He interrupted. "She didn't have to. I've known Selene for nearly thirty years, and I'm as familiar with her tricks as she is with mine." Then he took Lourdes's chin in his long fingers, and turned her face towards him. "Listen to me, my darling," he said, staring deeply into her dark eyes. She remembered the look from her earliest nights with him—as if he were seeing straight through to his upside-down image across her retina.

"Lourdes, I've never cared for another woman as deeply as I care for you. In fact, if what I feel for you and Cora is love, then I've never truly loved anyone before. With one exception."

"Who?" It came out a little more sharply than Lourdes had intended.

"Myself. I have always had a deep and passionate regard and an abiding respect for myself. So let there be no more underestimating of your Whistler: the extent to which I am currently letting you manage my life is a measure of your competence at the task, and of my intelligence and good judgment; not a measure of your power over me, or of my weakness or lovesickness.

"You see, my darling, in a way you are proof of a pet theory of mine, that into *every* family, noble or pauper, there are born those fit only to rule, and those fit only to be ruled. And while being born into the right family for one's temperament is no guarantee of happiness, being born into the wrong one is a dead lock on unhappiness. Videlicet poor Prince Charles on one end of the spectrum, videlicet Lourdes Perez Whistler on the other."

"Viddie *what*'s it? And let go my head."

"Sorry. Videlicet. Usually abbreviated viz. By way of example. In your case, I was referring to the young woman who was once known as the worst receptionist in the history of the West County Blood Bank—"

"Hey—"

"Now now, just ask Beverly. And you *know* she adores you. As I was saying, the worst receptionist in history is the most effective administrator that Whistler Manor, or for that matter Whistler himself, if I may lapse into the third person, has ever known."

"Thank you, Jamey," Lourdes replied with a seated curtsey, and at least a measure of sincerity, if not abashment. "I give you my word of honor, I will never make that mistake again."

"Which mistake—underestimating me, or letting me know you're underestimating me?"

"You *are* good, aren't you?" With a forefinger she teased his butch cut back into place. "Both."

He pulled her hand away, and kissed her deeply there in the padded window seat, with the lights of Stateline, Nevada, lightening the sky to the south through the open casement window. "There," he said a few minutes later—for that was how long the kiss had lasted. "That was the worst fight of our married life, and it wasn't so bad after all." Then—fake afterthought: "By the way, m'dear, I also know all about your Kegels and your salve from Nanny Parish—or rather, all that I care to know—and I want *you* to understand that the Creature and I will be honored to wait until you're ready for us."

She kissed him back tenderly. "You lying fuck."

He laughed his careful laugh. "Only about the Creature."

TWO

The trouble with having a mother who had died like Glory was that when she came to you in your dreams, even if she looked okay and you were glad to see her, sooner or later you'd remember, and then in the middle of the dream, even if she was hugging you or something, her face would swell up all dead and drowned and you'd pray you could wake up quick.

January awoke bathed in sweat at sunset on Saturday night, though she was sleeping naked under a thin blanket. The TV was still on from last night—this morning rather. She threw back the covers and crossed the room to the kitchenette area, knelt sleepily, and checked the fluid level in her thermos in the tiny refrigerator. Still pretty full—she would be hunting tonight, not for blood, but for money.

The wind was blowing hard that summer night down on the Avenue, and the fog was thick and cold, driving the regulars into the doorways and the bars. This worked out for January—otherwise it would have been impossible to find an empty corner on a Saturday night. Besides, as long as a vampire kept nipping at her thermos, she'd be warm enough, even in her cutoff jeans and ribbed poorboy.

She didn't have to nip too long—within ten minutes a white Buick had pulled up to her corner with the window rolled down. "Hey, Long-legs." A skank-faced guy with a bad comb-over leaned across the front seat. He was wearing a gray sport jacket with a windowpane check.

"Hey yourself."

"You workin'?"

"No, I'm standing out in the cold just to get my nipples hard."

"Well bring 'em on in here." The door opened; she slid in.

"Haven't seen you on the Ave before," he said, looking down at her thighs, as if by her limbs alone he would have recognized her.

"I'm fresh."

"I don't suppose you'd consider coming back to my place with me?" he asked, as he pulled out into traffic.

"Sure." On the Ave, it was considered a dangerous thing to do. But then, most hookers weren't vampires with a good jolt of blood in them—if he did turn hinky, she figured she could handle him.

His place wasn't much better than the Bierce—a second-floor walk-up studio over a futon shop in Albany, with a kitchenette hardly bigger than hers. She wandered over to the refrigerator and grabbed a can of Sprite.

"Here, let me get a glass for you."

He reached for the can; she pulled it away. "No, I'm fine, I like it out of the—"

But he had taken it. "I insist. Please. Go on into the other room, I'll be right in."

Odd usage, because of course there was no other room—just a stained white sofa bed over by the window, and a glass-topped coffee table bare except for a telephone. She knelt on the sofa with her back to the room, and looked out over the broad, quiet, small-town-looking street below.

He brought her soda in a Golden Gate Fields highball glass. She turned around on the couch and tucked her legs under her—they seemed ever so long and bare to her: she'd have picked herself up if she was a john. He sat down cross-legged on the brown and orange shag carpet, on the other side of the coffee table, and watched her eagerly as she drank.

She in turn watched him watching her over the rim of her glass, and noticed that his eyeballs had a funny way of vibrating horizontally—*bzzt*—every few seconds. He was definitely giving her a creepy feeling. "Hey, are you *on* something?"

A goofy grin spread across his face—then he shivered involuntarily, and his eyeballs vibrated again. "A little a this, a little a that—you'll see." *Bzzt.*

"What do you mean I'll see?" But she'd just remembered where she'd seen that little eyeball zap before: when Glory was on acid. The creepy feeling threatened to give way to panic. "Did you dose me, you fucker?"

Zzzz. "That's why you had to drink out of the glaaass," he drawled, as if to a slow child. "I could have put it on the rim of the can, but it's so hard to mea—"

He was interrupted by the coffee table—January had reached forward with vampiric speed, grabbed him by the back of his head, and slammed his face into the thick glass with her full strength. "You stupid bastard, you know what you just did?" She reached into her purse for her thermos—might as well top 'er off—unscrewed the cap and popped the plug, picked up his head by the long strands of his comb-over, and positioned the mouth of the thermos under his smashed nose.

"I *said*, do you know what you just did?" She helped him nod his head, or possibly nodded it for him—*Weekend at Bernie's* again, but not so funny this time, not with his profile as flat as the glass of the coffee table. "You just dosed a vampire." When her thermos was full she let go of his hair and the head clunked back down onto the coffee table. "That was real stupid." She sipped hot blood from the mouth of the thermos, lifted his head again to top off, sipped until there was room for the cork, then let the head fall again.

It flopped sideways this time, and as the blood pulsed in waves from his nose and mouth, it formed a river flowing towards the table's edge. January snatched the telephone and her glass of soda out of the way; the river of blood pooled in an invisible depression of the glass, then resumed its course on the other side of the new pond while she watched, fascinated, to see whether it would eventually spill over and form a beautiful crimson waterfall in miniature.

THREE

The white building shaped like a Monopoly hotel on the corner of Jackson and Darling streets in El Cerrito had doubtless hosted christenings before, but the christening of a healthy-lung-ed (just ask his groggy parents) Leon Stanton Santos-Shoemaker on Sunday afternoon, the twentieth of September, had been its first in the guise of the Church of the Higher Power, and a great success by all accounts.

The attendance of virtually the entire congregation of the CHP, as well as a representative sampling from the various branches of the East Bay recovery community, had assured both a full house, and one hell of a potluck upon completion of a rather eclectic ceremony involving a few drops of water and a great flood of affirmations.

Afterwards (and say this for the twelve-steppers: they cleaned up after themselves without being told), Nick and Betty, still in their christening finery, a baggy white cotton suit for her, a blue Blass blazer, necktie, and tan slacks for him, drove the Oldsmobile up to Tilden Park with Leon's carseat in the back for his first ride on a merry-go-round (he spit up on Nick's blazer), a visit to the Little Farm, and a ride on the miniature railroad (he spit up again, this time on Betty's suit).

When they returned to a church cleaner than it had been before the party, they found the parsonage kitchen had been cleaned top to bottom as well. On the kitchen table rested a small package from Executive Couriers, with RUSH and SUNDAY DELIVERY and NIGHT DELIVERY and B.A.M.N. and similar sentiments stuck and stamped all over it.

But the space on the address form for the sender was blank. Betty opened the box to find an exquisite silver christening cup engraved with the letters *L.S.* "It's beautiful," she said.

"That ain't one of your mall gift-shop engraving jobs, either," agreed Nick, loosening his tie. "Is there a card?"

"Yes, but it's not signed." Betty read it aloud: " 'Tolstoy was wrong.' Now what could that mean?"

Nick took the card from her. "If I had to guess," he replied carefully, "I'd say it refers to the opening sentence of *Anna Karenina*: 'Happy families are all alike.' "

Betty looked the cup over again suspiciously. "And if you *had* to guess, who would you *guess* might have sent it?"

Nick shrugged—if there had ever been a window of opportunity for him to come clean about the string of evasions that had begun with him not telling her about bringing January back from Midsummer, and extended through Whistler's conciliatory phone call at the end of August, he had missed it—it was too late for the whole truth now.

But even if Nick hadn't recognized Whistler's careless handwriting immediately, he knew no one else who could afford a By Any Means

Necessary delivery from Executive Couriers—it would have cost him practically as much again as the cup itself, and that cup so heavy with silver it weighed more than Leon's head. Nor was the subtlety of Tolstoy's sentiment as a gesture of peace lost on Nick: it had JMW stamped all over it.

"Someone who doesn't believe all happy families have to be alike, obviously," was Nick's eventual answer. "And you know what? I think I agree."

Not only had the parsonage kitchen been cleaned, but the refrigerator was stuffed with leftovers—dinner for days. Nick served Betty while she nursed Leon, then left for his own house, promising to return for the 1:00 A.M. to dawn shift.

It was only fair—and as close as he and Betty ever got to resembling a married couple: there would be a bottle of expressed breast-milk on the bedside table; Nick would change into a pair of cotton pajamas he kept at the parsonage, then slip into bed beside Betty, who was often so exhausted she wouldn't even wake up (or at least acknowledge that she had awakened). When he heard Leon howling (usually around two or three, though it could be earlier—never later), he would feed him a bottle, change him, and put him back to sleep before either crawling back in beside Betty or, if he needed to work that night, returning home.

And he might indeed have some 'Net prowling to do tonight, he realized when he arrived back at his own house a little before seven-thirty: someone had posted a new, and rather sophisticated, entry to a dummy bulletin board Nick had set up to entrap unwary crackers.

He hit the PRINT SCREEN button, then went into the bedroom to change out of his christening clothes. He had just returned to the office in a softball-style Detroit Tigers jersey and his oldest, softest Levi's—no underwear—and removed the printout from his LaserJet when the office phone rang.

"Santos."

"Nick, please pick up the—"

"It's me."

"—phone, please—oh. I thought it was your machine."

"No, it's me. Is this January?"

"Please help me, Nick. Just this one time, and I'll never ask you for anything again."

"What happened?"

"This guy dosed me on acid last night—I been hiding behind the couch all night."

"Are you still tripping?"

"No. I don't know. Maybe."

"Where are you?"

"I don't know. His apartment."

"Is he there?"

"I don't know. I think he's gone." Not sounding very much like a vampire at all—more like a frightened little girl. "Nick, I'm scared and I'm having a bummer. Please come get me. I don't have anybody else to call."

"I don't want to start—"

"Please, Nick? I'll give up blood again, I'll do anything you want, please just help me this once."

"All right, all right. But you have to tell me where you are."

"I'm hiding behind the couch."

"No, I mean where the apartment is."

"Somewhere on Solano is all I remember. Second floor."

"Albany or Berkeley?"

"How should I know?"

"Can you see out a window?"

"Just a second." He heard the swoosh of curtains being drawn. "Yeah."

"Are there parking meters?"

"No."

"Okay, you're in Albany. What else do you see?"

"There's a bakery across the street, next to a frozen yogurt place."

"The bakery's on the corner?"

"Yup."

"Big clock in the window?"

"Yup."

"I know where you are. Hang on, I'll be there in ten minutes. Watch for the 'Vette."

He made it in five, including a minute to pull on his socks and Tony Lama boots and grab his fleece-lined Levi jacket from the closet. He cursed himself for a fool the entire way down to Solano, but when he saw January's pallid face peeking from between the drawn curtains of an upstairs window, he was glad he'd come.

For about another two minutes anyway, which was how long it took him to find the street door that led up to the second-story apartment.

Because when she opened the door for him, he saw over her shoulder a sight that would stay with him for a good long time: a dead man with his head resting on a low glass table-top coated with black and crusted blood.

"Fuck this," he said, starting to turn away.

She grabbed him by the shoulder and yanked him into the apartment. "I didn't know," she whispered. Her eyes were blood red, her grasp had been blood-strong, but her voice was tiny as a talking doll's. "I was scared to look. I swear, Nick, I been hiding behind the couch the whole time—I just pulled the phone over with the cord."

Nick moaned at the mention of her phone call—he'd realized suddenly that it was too late for him to back out now: the first thing the police would do would be to examine the telephone company printout. "What the fuck have you got me into?"

"Nick, I swear—"

"Shut up." He was trying to remember what he knew about Pac Bell's new computer system, whether it might be possible to delete the record without leaving footprints. No, it would be easier to camouflage it. "Here's what I—"

Once again, he never saw it coming—next thing he knew, he was lying on his back with the taste of blood in his mouth. His own blood, he hoped, but then he felt January prying his jaws open again, and opened his eyes to see her leaning over him with her uncapped thermos poised above his mouth.

"No!" He twisted his head away from her, and tried to strike at the thermos; she settled over him, pinning his shoulders with her knees as he clamped his lips tight; he felt the cool blood splashing over his face.

"I'll break your fucking jaw," she warned him, forcing the fingers of one hand between his lips, prying his teeth apart. He tried to bite her, but her fingers were stronger than his mandibles, and when she began pouring again, it was either swallow or choke.

When she finally let him up—she would have had to, sooner or later, when his strength came on—he rubbed the side of his head ruefully. She had only slapped him, but with vampiric strength. "I was going to help you anyway, you know."

"Yeah, but I like you better on blood," she pouted. "You never told me to shut up on blood."

He realized there was no sense trying to reason with her, especially if

ever so much better. As for Nick, he didn't seem all that upset as she drove him back to Albany to pick up the 'Vette—just a little quiet, and high on blood, looking out the window.

She had been assuming that he planned to follow her in the 'Vette while she ditched the Buick someplace deserted. Then, she hoped, if he was half as horny as she was (and how could he not be, high on blood), he'd drive her back to his place, and fuck her like a boy, like a girl, like a whore, like a virgin, fuck her all night and let her fuck him too. She'd have liked that.

But before he climbed out of the Buick back on Solano, he turned to her and said goodbye in a tone that seemed to mean goodbye.

"Aren't you going to follow me so we can ditch this car?" she'd asked, puzzled.

"Ditch it yourself." Coldly—so cold she couldn't believe her ears.

"Where?"

"I don't care. The farther away the better."

"But how will I get back?"

"That's not my problem, January." He seized her forearm tightly. "I've enabled you for the last time."

"Ouch. Hey." She tried to pull her arm away, but strong as she was, when they were both on blood he was stronger.

"Shut up and listen. It took every bit of self-control I could muster not to whack you with that tire iron and throw you into the bay after whoever that was I just helped you dispose of. And I'm still not sure it wouldn't have been the right move. So what I suggest, for both our sakes, is that you drive that sucker as far as you can without looking back— here, do you need money?"

He reached into his pocket, not waiting for an answer, turned her palm up, and shoved a few twenties into it. "Take this, drive as far as you can before dawn, leave the car in a twenty-four-hour supermarket park-ing lot someplace, and don't hitchhike away from it—just walk—not even to the nearest town, but the next town after that. Got all that?"

She nodded, rendered speechless by her sense of abandonment— again and again and again in her young life—and betrayal.

"Good. Now here's the part to really pay attention to: If I ever see you again—if you ever get within arm's reach of me—I will kill you. I will drive the bridge of your nose back into your brain with the flat of my hand—see, here?" He let go of her arm and flexed his wrist sharply to-wards her face to show her how the blow would be delivered. She was so stunned she never even flinched. "You've already sucker punched me twice—believe me, it will never happen again. In fact, if you ever even call me again, if you even so much as leave a message on my machine, I will drink enough blood to enable me to hunt you down, and then . . ."

Suddenly his wrist leapt forward again, the base of his palm stopping a millimeter short of her nose. She still hadn't moved. "Now have you got all that?"

Another nod.

"Good. I don't wish you harm, January—I just want you out of my life." Then he said it again: "Goodbye."

She saw the taillights of the 'Vette swinging right on San Pablo Avenue—right, towards El Cerrito, not left towards Berkeley—and suddenly she knew where he was heading: the Church of the Higher Power. "Fucking idiot," she said aloud—she was talking about herself, though. How could she have forgotten about that minister? What was it, back in January, the last meeting, that Nick had told the fellowship he'd donated sperm to her? She counted on her fingers: *February, March, April* . . . Then she realized that the impregnation had taken place at least a month before that.

She started again: *January, February, March.* This time she reached the ring finger of her right hand in September. She had to think again, squeeze today's date out of the whirlwind of thoughts. Saturday night— no, Sunday. The twentieth, something like that. Nick was either a father, or about to become one.

"Son of a bitch." This time she *was* referring to Nick, as she slid behind the wheel of the Buick. But it was not until she had passed the El Cerrito Plaza shopping center and turned onto Darling that the significance of the date struck her. Today, tomorrow, whatever, summer would be over. They'd be having the equinox orgy up at Whistler Manor this weekend. And serving baby-blood, no doubt. Suddenly she missed them all terribly, and the deserted feeling, the terrible loneliness she'd been fighting all her life, became unbearable, as if it had somehow slipped inside her, sharp and sweet and painful.

By the time she reached the church, she had it worked out in her mind—and just the working out of it, the focusing of her madly spinning thought processes, had made her feel considerably better.

If Nick had turned her away, then Whistler would take her in—after all, they'd been passing her back and forth all year. But they were having baby-blood at the Manor this weekend. That might be a problem.

Unless of course she brought her own baby.

What a welcome they'd give her then! She could see it all clearly in her mind as she parked the Buick out on Jackson, and tiptoed up the grassy border of the driveway so her feet wouldn't make any noise on the gravel.

Selene would hug her, and take the baby away to prepare it for the ceremony, and Whistler would kiss her on top of the head and whisper in her ear to save him a slot on her dahnce-card that night.

Then she could tell him the best news of all. *Anybody could of got you a baby,* she'd tell him. *But I got you Nick's baby.*

Whistler would never send her away again after that.

FOUR

If a good belch is truly a sign that one has enjoyed one's meal, then Leon's ten o'clock feeding must have been the greatest of his life, thought Betty, who had worked out a novel, if effective, program: she would nurse Leon downstairs, then carry him up the stairs over her shoulder—bump/burp, bump/burp, bump/burp.

She dressed him in a footed flannel sleeper—it was a cold night—put him into his crib, turned on the Yertle the Turtle Baby Minder (basically a plastic walkie-talkie with a turtle-shaped microphone unit in the nursery transmitting through an open circuit to a speaker turtle in the parents' bedroom), changed into a warm flannel nightgown herself, and climbed into bed with that rarest of treats, a new Armistead Maupin novel.

But not even Maupin's charms could keep the exhausted mother's eyes open for long. She turned out the light, rolled onto her side with her knees drawn up and both hands pressed warmly between her thighs, palms together—her comfort position—and quickly dropped into the waking doze so familiar to new parents, listening to the peaceful chuff of Leon's breathing through the Yertle on the bedside table.

From there, she must have passed into a deep sleep, for the next thing she knew Nick was in bed beside her, and she hadn't even felt the mattress settle. "Hi," she murmured, still half asleep; on her side with her back to him, she squirmed closer—some sort of thermal tropism, her body seeking the heat of his without her conscious volition.

And his body was warm—pulsing warm: to her surprise he had rolled on his side to spoon with her, snuggled down a little deeper in the bed, and was pressing gently against her from behind. Her eyes opened wide in the darkness at what she was feeling. She hadn't felt it for quite a while, but there was no mistaking the sensation: her nightgown had hiked up, and a hot hard erection poking at one's bare buttocks was not the sort of sense-memory a person ever completely forgets.

Oh yes, she thought, already growing moist. It had been so long. Then she thought she'd better say it out loud, to encourage him—though it didn't feel like he needed much encouragement. "Oh yes," she whispered; then, just in case there was any lingering doubt, she said it again, louder, as she reached behind her and seized his erection in her hand, guiding it towards her.

He had the angle all wrong—then she remembered with whom she was dealing. If he was pretending she was a boy, she realized, then, as much as she wanted him, she didn't want him. She let go, and rolled onto her back. "You have to want *me,* Nick," she said. "You have to make love to *me.*"

"I do." He passed his hand wonderingly over her heavy breasts, feeling the solid weight of them through the soft flannel. "I will."

"Good." She pulled her nightgown up to her waist, and spread her knees for him; he climbed on, and slipped inside her; as he entered her, she felt her nipples begin leaking, and laughed delightedly. "Here," she whispered, pulling the nightgown up to her neck and guiding his mouth to her breast. "Drink."

"It's so sweet." His voice in the darkness carried a tone of such horny wonder; his cock swelled inside her.

"*So* sweet," she agreed. "*So* sweet. You fuck me *so* sweet."

"Good."

Then he brought her a mouthful of her own milk, and she drank the warm sweetness from his lips as her orgasm began to build. She could feel him tensing. "Come inside me," she whispered. "Oh my sweet Nick, come deep inside me."

Then she wasn't whispering anymore, but moaning, louder and louder, building to an orgasmic series of yelps while he groaned like an old boiler about to blow as he came inside her, as deep as she'd begged him to come—Yertle the Turtle turned green with envy.

They were lying next to each other in afterglow when the phone rang, startling them both. Betty fumbled around the bedside table until she found the receiver. " 'Lo? What? Oh, Psalms 121:8. 'Kay. Bye."

"ADT?" said Nick.

"Yes, you must have set off the alarm."

"Fat lot of good it'd do now—I must have gotten here half an hour ago."

"Unless it wasn't you."

Not a fun thought. They both held their breath, listening. "I don't hear anything," whispered Nick. *And if I don't hear anything, believe me, there's nothing to hear,* he thought, although of course he couldn't say it aloud.

"I don't either."

A few minutes passed, and then a few more—Betty had almost fallen asleep again—before she realized what was so terribly wrong with silence: she should have been hearing the soft sound of Leon's breathing. She sat up then, and leaned closer to the Yertle the Turtle speaker next to the phone. She was perhaps already in denial: the only possibility she was as yet willing to consider was that Yertle's batteries had run down.

Noting with a sick sensation that the little red light was still on, she reminded herself as she climbed out of bed that it could be the other turtle, the transmitter, that had run down. When she reached the nursery, the first place she forced her eyes to look was not at the open nursery window, nor at the empty crib, but at that stupid green plastic turtle with its steady little red battery indicator glowing.

Yertle was working just fine: back in the bedroom, Nick heard Betty's anguished cry over the intercom as clearly as if she were still in bed beside him.

Chapter 9

ONE

The terrible scene burned in January's mind as she drove: high in the branches of the live oak she had watched through the window as Nick rolled onto that fat minister in the dark. She hadn't watched them for long, though. After all, she had a job to do . . .

She'd swung easily over to the nursery window, forced it open, squeezed through, taken the baby from his (sex wasn't hard to guess—blue all over) crib and placed him in a baby basket she found on the floor of the nursery, then scrawled a note on the wall with her black lipstick. Nick had to know who'd taken his baby, and what would be done to it, otherwise it wouldn't really count as *her* revenge this time.

Happy Equinox from January was the message she'd decided on. But she changed her mind and smeared out all the letters after the capital J; then, with the baby basket over her arm, she'd simply trotted down the stairs and exited via the kitchen door.

But now, driving east on 80, she wished she'd found the nursery first, and never seen Nick and the minister. It wasn't only the sight of them fucking missionary style that rankled her so, but what she'd heard through the window. "You have to want *me*, you have to make love to *me*."

And she understood suddenly that Nick had never wanted *her*, January, and never really fucked *her*, either: only what he saw when he closed his eyes and pretended.

But when she glanced down at the baby in his basket on the seat next to her, sleeping all peaceful and quiet with sweet little miniature lips and his eyelids fluttering, wrapped up snug in his sleeper and his blue blankie, she realized she couldn't carry her anger at Nick over to little Doofus here.

Wasn't his fault his father was such an asshole—even if he was the one who was going to have to pay blood for it.

Nick still had the dead man's Visine in the pocket of his fleece-lined Levi jacket. He gave himself a booster dose in the bathroom while Betty dressed. He had already decided to tell her as little as possible about his own, admittedly pivotal, role in this ongoing horror—he could feel guilty about it later, he reasoned: right now the truth would only get in the way.

Whistler's part in all this was something Nick had been chewing over since Betty's first scream. He didn't think his old friend and rival was involved directly—not after their warm phone call, and then the christening gift—but it wasn't farfetched to picture it as an extension of Whistler's original scheme, either. He might have seen Nick's sobriety as a threat.

Or perhaps the idea had just tickled his sense of humor. In any case, he'd fooled Nick before—repeatedly, and over a period of years. Where Whistler was concerned, Nick could be sure of nothing.

Scratch that: he could be sure of a few things. If January were indeed bringing Leon to the Manor (if not, then he was already dead, which was unthinkable), and if Nick and Betty got the cops involved, and if the cops somehow attempted to surround the Manor, or Tac squad their way in, the vampires would have had plenty of warning: no matter how good you were, you didn't sneak up on a vampire on blood unless you were a vampire on blood yourself.

And in that case, whether he was behind the kidnapping or not, there was no way on earth Whistler would ever let himself be caught with . . . with . . .

Faced with the choice of completing that thought with the word *Leon* or the words *the body,* Nick let it drop. When he emerged from the bathroom, Betty was just coming out of the bedroom wearing a T-shirt under a pair of the Can't Bust 'Em overalls favored by nursing mothers.

"I just got off the phone with ADT," she reported. "The alarm came in at 11:08, so she has about a half-hour head start on us."

"Make that up in the 'Vette easy. Grab a jacket, she handles better with the top down."

Betty didn't bother setting the church security system as they left—with Leon gone, there was nothing more that could be stolen from her.

TWO

"Shhh. Listen."

Two in the morning at Whistler Manor. Lourdes could hear it clearly from the window sill, but Selene and Nanny Parish, not being vampires, took another few seconds to pick up the sound coming through the open window: somewhere out there a baby was crying.

The three women were alone except for their own babies: Whistler had taken the vampires and witches who'd already arrived into town for a little casino action; the staff also had the night off—come the morning they'd be on duty for twenty-four to thirty-six hours straight, both as servants and Drinks.

All three started simultaneously for the door that led to the nursery. Lourdes got there first, and saw Cora and Plum Rose sleeping peacefully side by side in their cribs. "Both here," she said.

Selene put her finger to her lips for silence. She had closed her eyes, and was trying to pick up some sort of concrete image to go with the inchoate sense of danger she was feeling. No luck—just that it was about babies, which her ear had already told her. Then the front doorbell rang faintly.

"Lock the door behind me," Selene whispered to Nanny. Then, to Lourdes: "Go into the nursery. Whatever else happens, stay with the babies. If it's a vampire, only you can protect them." Selene hurried down to the front door and put her eye to the peephole.

It was indeed a vampire—January, looking all bowed and enormous through the fisheye lens, from the topmost spike of her purple hair to the incredibly long bare legs below the cutoffs. Selene stood on tiptoe, and saw the basket on the ground next to the incongruous Doc Martens boots. Quickly she unlocked the door.

"Why hello, January." Selene had to raise her voice to be heard over the outraged screaming of the baby in the basket. "Is that yours?"

"He is now. Little fucker's been howling like that since Placerville."

She stooped and picked up the basket, handing it over to Selene gingerly, as if she expected the baby to turn into an *Alice In Wonderland* pig at any second. "The scariest part was going through downtown Tahoe—I thought I was gonna get busted for sure." She followed Selene into the vestibule. "Nobody even noticed."

"He's probably just hungry." Selene locked the door behind them again. "How long since he's been fed?"

"How should I know?" said January crankily.

"In that case, how long since you've been fed?"

"Blood, you mean? Thermos went dry around Sacramento."

"Then which shall it be first?" Selene tried to sound as jolly as the good witch Glynda while shouting over the screaming infant, but every instinct she had, witchly or womanly, told her January was pretty close to the edge. What madness lay over that edge, Selene wasn't sure—nor could she chance finding out until there were more vampires around for safety. "Blood for you or milk for this beautiful little baby?"

"Both. I brought him for the equinox."

"And what wonderful timing!" Overdoing it now? Selene wasn't sure—her witchy talents were not always helpful in emergencies, as they tended to take a bit of preparation. "The ceremony's tomorrow night at midnight. But let me bring him up to Nanny Parish to get him fed—I can't think with all this noise."

Selene started up the stairs with the basket, but slowly, so January wouldn't get suspicious. "So where'd you get him, dearie?"

"The church," January announced triumphantly, having forgotten momentarily about surprising Whistler with the news.

"Which church?"

"The one where they used to have the V.A. meetings."

"So it's Nick's baby, is it? Whistler will be so pleased." The fine hairs at the nape of Selene's neck were singing like high-tension wires—she couldn't shake the feeling that she was about to be jumped from behind. "Have you had any of his blood yet?"

"No. I would of took some from him after my thermos went dry, but I wanted to bring him straight here. Plus I was a little scared to do baby-blood alone, on top of the acid last night."

"Acid, eh?" That explained the sense of danger Selene was picking up, beyond January's usual radio beams from just over the border of madness. "I'd say you showed excellent judgment."

She turned around again at the top of the stairs. The next part was going to be tricky—get the baby into the nursery with the others, but without either admitting January or making her suspicious. "Here's what let's do, dearie," she called over the howling Leon. "I'll take the baby in to Nanny Parish for his milk, while you go down to the cellar and pick out a nice bag of blood for yourself. In fact, why not fill your thermos—you deserve it."

"I left it in the car. Where is Whistler? Where's everybody?"

"Casino night—he's taken them all into town. If you'd like, I can have a car pick you up." Then, as suggestively as she could without tipping her hand: "As soon as you've had some blood. We'll fill your thermos for you later—such a generous gift deserves a reward."

It worked: January turned and started down the stairs. Selene waved after her, a little baby toodle-oo finger wave. "I'll be right down." As soon as January was out of sight around the curve of the staircase, Selene rapped at the door to Lourdes's suite.

Nanny Parish opened the door a crack. "Here," said Selene loudly, in case January was listening. "January brought him for the equinox, Nanny. Would you give him some milk, and start getting him ready for tomorrow night?"

Lock the door, Selene mouthed, pointing to the bolt as Nanny Parish took Leon from her. She didn't want to chance whispering anything— you couldn't tell how far a vampire could hear. Nanny nodded; Selene heard the snick of the bolt behind her as she started after January, praying to the Goddess under her breath. She had to time it just right, she knew: get down to the cellar after January had entered it, but before she had a chance to pick out her blood and leave.

As she neared the bottom of the narrow cellar stairs, Selene saw that she'd gotten her wish: January was still inside. She sent out one last prayer: *Help me now, Mother. Make me quick. If you can't make me quick, make me lucky.*

Then she jumped forward and shoved against the heavy door with all her might. January heard her in the inner room, and with unimaginable speed turned and lunged towards the pantry door. As it slammed between them Selene felt the reinforced door shudder from the force of the vampire's blow. It held, shuddered again just as Selene slammed the outer bolt into place, held again.

"It's just for a few minutes, dearie," Selene called, after mentally thanking the Mother. "Help yourself to some blood—as soon as some of the vampires get back I'll send them down to let you out."

She could hear the answering howl all the way back up the stairs, and clear through both pantry doors.

THREE

Rather than descend in a horde on any particular casino, the Coven and Penang had split up according to their individual tastes. One group of low-rolling witches converged on the Horizon to play the nickel slots; Louise and Beverly, who fancied themselves poker players, decided their fortune was to be made at the video poker machines at Harrah's. Sherman always preferred Caesar's, where employees of the female persuasion were forced to wear revealing tops; Whistler, on the other hand, despite owning a one-third interest in the Gold Dust, found himself drawn to Harvey's, at least partly because the change girls flounced around in buttock-length skirts cut high at the hip.

The table games—never the house specialty—weren't particularly hot at Harvey's that night, but the dollar slots were humming, and Whistler decided to slum. His technique was a variation on the hot-shooter theme that worked so well at the craps table: the theory was that luck came in waves.

If you were high enough on blood you could stake out a machine, feed it slowly while listening carefully, not just with your ears but with your body, to the sound of all the slots within hearing distance—the entire casino, on blood—and after a while you'd awaken to the rhythm of the ringing and the beeping and the peeping of payouts and the clattering of coins into bins and the rise and fall of the voices, and *then* was the time to throw the silver down the slot with one hand and mash the spin button with the other, fast as you could, never mind waiting for your payoff, until that particular wave had crashed. Then in the calm of the ebb tide you could rake in your coins.

Not big moneys, as Hemingway might have put it, not fast moneys, but a good honest 5-percent edge. There was a catch, of course—the more tense you were, the more you needed the money, say, then the more difficult it was to catch the subtle changes that heralded the wave.

Whistler was pumping a hot *Wild Cherry* machine in the dollar pit when he heard himself being paged. He scooped his winnings from the coin bin into a plastic cup, and spoke to Selene over a house phone while a caged teller cashed him out. It took him another few minutes to find Augie, over by the roulette wheel, and instruct him to round up at least one limo-ful of vampires and hurry back to the Manor with them; Whistler then commandeered a Harvey's car and driver and headed home ahead of the others.

* * *

Whistler had himself dropped off at the top of the drive; he noticed an unfamiliar white Buick as he raced through the parking lot towards the back door. Selene was waiting by the fenced-in trash can corral, and followed him inside. "Is anyone else coming?"

"Augie and some others are on the way." He threw open the door off the short white-washed passageway to the kitchen, strode through the pantry, shoved the revolving wall sideways, and trotted down the steps. "But I think I can handle January myself—why don't you go up and let Lourdes know that I'm back?"

"Okay, but be careful—she's probably pretty loaded by now."

That was the understatement of the year: the first thing January had done when she realized that Selene had been the latest in a long line of betrayers was to grab one of the Seal-a-Meal pouches at random from the cubbyholes in the inner room of the blood cellar, tear off a corner with her teeth, hold the bag above her head as if it were a wineskin, and squeeze.

It made quite a mess, the cold blood gushing over her face and down the front of her midriff-baring poorboy top, but she didn't mind—there was plenty. "Go ahead," she called to the ceiling, where a fan was whirring above the translucent light panel. "Lock me in a room full of blood—see if I care."

She comforted herself with the thought that when Whistler got back, Selene would catch hell. In the meantime, blood to drink, blood to spare. She thought of Ren and Stimpy, her favorite cartoon characters—*Happy happy joy joy*—as she tossed the not-quite-empty bag over her shoulder and grabbed another.

Growing more comfortable as the cold blood slowly warmed her, January idly browsed through the cubbyholes, reading labels, noticing and appreciating the slight variations in color—how rich, to a vampire, is the spectrum between pink and purple. At the sight of one particular shade she remembered suddenly a pair of shoes she'd craved in grade school. Oxblood, they'd called that color—she hadn't thought of oxblood in years.

She took a genteel sip from that one, another from a bag labeled CATHERINE 9/3/92, a third swig, less genteel, from a sparkling bottle; by the time she chanced upon the vial at the back of an otherwise empty pigeonhole on the top shelf, she was as high as she'd ever been in her life.

Too high to be afraid, even, when she noticed that the vial was clearly marked with the letters BB. "Well hello there!" she declared, her voice echoing in the cold chamber. "Let's see, now what could double B stand for?"

January pursed her lips like the Church Lady from *Saturday Night Live*. "Could it be . . . *Bitch's Blood?* Noooo, that's not it. Or maybe . . . *Boomin' Blood?* Nooo, that's not it either. Or could it be . . . I don't know . . ." She placed her hands on her hips and turned her head drastically to the left—she could feel the spirit of the Church Lady possessing her. "Could it perhaps be . . ." She whirled dramatically to her right, and shrieked the punchline: *"Baby Blood!!!"*

Quickly she popped the clever little plastic cork and tossed back the contents of the vial. It started coming on almost immediately; soon January's senses were heightened beyond anything in her previous experience. Apparently, baby-blood was to live blood as live blood was to fresh blood, as fresh blood was to cold blood, as cold blood was to no blood at all.

Not long after, from deep in the inner chamber, she heard Whistler coming down the steps, and it suddenly occurred to her that he might not be coming to free her at all. What if Selene had been acting under his orders? *That January's nuts,* he might have said. *If you see her coming, lock her in the cellar until I get there.*

He must have said that, January reasoned, for that's exactly what Selene had done. And then with a gasp she remembered something Nick had said to her in this very room, back at Midsummer. *Selene is Whistler's creature entirely.*

What else had he said back then? Oh yes: that he'd forgotten that once, and was still paying for it. *That's you, Nick,* she thought. *Not me.*

January smoothed back the sides of her blood-spattered purple hair with both palms, and attempted with limited success to wipe her face clean of clots with the hem of her ribbed poorboy, the front of which was black and heavy with spilled blood. Then she hurried back into the larder and swung the wall to the refrigerated room closed behind her, grabbed the first can that came to hand, crumpled herself into a squatting position in the far corner of the room, and tried, with no success at all, to rearrange her expression into one of woe and abandonment.

She settled for turning her torso away from the door just as it opened, and hiding her savage hunter's grin by burying her face in the fanned fingers of her left hand.

"January," she heard Whistler say, in a fondly exasperated, almost parental tone. "Jan, Jan, Jan. Now *what* are we going to do with you?" She had to bite down on her palm to hold back the giggles. He took the sound that emerged for a stifled sob; she could feel him approaching, hear his Topsiders whispering across the scratchy carpeting. It seemed to take him forever to cross the floor.

The can was in January's right hand, bootlegged behind her right hip—as he approached, she twisted farther to her right, as if to avoid his eyes. At the last second he saw the can, but by then January had worked up enough torque: she came whirling out of her crouch like a discus thrower.

If he'd been higher on blood, Whistler might have avoided the blow; if he'd been less high, he would surely have been killed. As it was, he barely saw it coming—a yellow blur in her hand—and was just high enough to do two things. The first was to throw up his left arm, partially deflecting the blow so that instead of crushing his temple like a sugar-shelled Easter egg, the can only glanced off the upper curve of his skull. The second was to record one indelibly irrelevant detail as he crumpled to the floor. *Creamed corn,* was his last conscious thought.

It was a can of Lady Lee creamed corn wot done 'im in.

FOUR

"All right, Mr. Santos, I'm going to let you off with a warning this time. But if I ever catch you running a light in this town again, I don't care *what* time it is, I'm going to write you up."

"Thank you, officer," replied Nick numbly. Something else to castigate himself about later. Not enough that he'd lied to the mother of his child almost from the moment they'd met, and impregnated her under false pretenses; not enough that on top of those lies he'd taken advantage of her sexually tonight; not even enough that his careless treatment of January might result in Leon's death.

But now, after driving the 'Vette all the way from El Cerrito to the Nevada border at speeds of up to a hundred and ten miles per hour without drawing any attention from the highway patrol, he'd pulled the lamest move of all: getting popped for running a red light on the Tahoe strip at 2:30 in the morning, and undoubtedly blowing whatever chance they'd had of catching January before she reached the fastness of Whistler Manor.

He'd had plenty of time on the drive up to second-guess himself about all his earlier mistakes. He should have either stayed with January and helped her ditch the Buick, or else killed her on the spot. But tossing that body into the bay at Point Isabel had thrown him into a state not unlike shock: it had been his recurring Tad nightmare, only for real this time, and he'd simply freaked.

Or was freaked too kind a word? Wimped might be better, or wussed or bailed. Whatever he called it, it amounted to cowardice: he'd gone running to Betty for comfort like a three-year-old climbing into Mommy's bed after a bad dream.

And now this—a moment of carelessness, and their best hope dashed. Nick threw the 'Vette into gear and pulled away from the curb carefully, conscious of the cop's eyes on him. Betty's eyes, too. He glanced at her—the look on her face was the sort of look you see on people in hospital waiting rooms, hopeful and despairing at the same time.

"A minor setback," he grinned. Amazing that he could still pull a grin out of his ass when he really needed one. But he couldn't let her freak too—he was going to need her very soon. "We'll be there in about another ten minutes."

Betty pulled herself together with a shudder. "What's the plan?"

"Depends on whether you trust me or not," replied Nick.

"Of course I trust you," said Betty. "But what's that got to do with anything?"

"I *might* be able to get *into* the lodge sober, but there's no way I could get *out*—not with the baby—not snatch it from a bunch of blood-high vampires, unless I can see and hear as well as they can see and hear, move as fast as they can move, and if necessary, strike as hard. For that, *I'm* going to need to be as high as they are."

"Meaning?"

"Meaning I'm going to need to drink some blood."

Betty sighed. "Somehow I knew you were going to say that."

Nick pulled over into a turnaround by a copse of trees across the highway and about two hundred yards up from the driveway that led to the lodge. He climbed out stiffly after nearly three cramped hours behind the wheel, and closed the car door as quietly as he could. It was already a cool night here in the mountains—soon it would be cold, not that that would bother him once he'd topped up on blood. A surprisingly quiet night, too, considering they were only a few yards from a four-lane highway: there was no traffic, just the birds, and the good old

Detroit sound of the manifold cooling, and the smell of the high thin piney air.

"Oh shit."

"What?" Betty climbed out the passenger side. She was as stiff and sore as Nick, but even more uncomfortable—her breasts were beginning to ache dully, as they filled with milk for Leon's next feeding.

"I don't have a knife."

She reached back into the car and hauled out her purse, rummaged through it unsuccessfully for a minute or so, then dumped the purse out across the 'Vette's hood (Nick winced), picked through the detritus for a two-blade-one-scissors Swiss Army knife, and handed it to Nick along with a packet of Wash 'n Dri's. "The small blade? At least?" she asked Nick, who nodded, wiped the blade, and tossed the used Wash 'n Dri back into the car.

Betty held out her left arm, palm up, and closed her eyes. Nick turned it palm down, wiped off the back of her hand with another towelette, gathered up a pinch of flesh along with the vein he had his eye on, and then actually pinched the pinch to distract her attention from the knife.

"Ouch." She winced, waited for more pain, but it was already over—when Betty opened her eyes, Nick was sucking from a wound at the back of her hand. She watched his downturned eyes, wondering if they would turn red like in his manuscript.

But even after Nick had ceased his sucking, expertly stanched the bleeding, and wrapped his red plaid pocket handkerchief around the wound, the whites of his eyes looked pretty much the same, as far as she could tell in the dark. He was grinning again, though, and shaking his head.

"What?" she asked. "What is it?" She had to ask a few more times, until it was more of a demand than a question; even then it took another minute before Nick replied.

"Good news and bad news."

"I'm not in the mood for jokes, Nick."

"That's too bad," came the answer. "Because Higher Power apparently is."

"Is what?"

"In the mood for jokes."

"What the hell does that mean?" she asked him, half afraid she already knew the answer.

"It means I'm not high."

He steadied her as she swayed. He thought he'd have to help her lie down there on the soft fall of maple leaves in the clearing, but she was made of sterner stuff than that. "So what's . . ." she began. Her voice failed her; she tried again. "So what's the good news?"

"The good news is, there's two vampires on our side now. I want you to wait here—I'm going to go in by the back door, and down to the cellar to get us some blood—I'll bring it back, we'll both get high, then we'll go get Leon."

"Why don't I just go with you?"

"I think I can sneak in—I don't know about two of us." He didn't think it was a good time to tell her that the reason he thought he could sneak in was that he was still a little high from the blood January had forced upon him earlier. "I'll be back in five minutes."

He left before she could protest again. In the parking lot he saw the empty Buick—the driver's side window was open. He reached through, opened the door, and popped the trunk and hood releases. The trunk was empty except for blood stains; under the hood the manifold was still warm—she couldn't have gotten here more than an hour ago, at the earliest.

Nick walked back around to the driver's door, reached in to take the keys out of the ignition, and saw the Star Trek thermos on the floor of the passenger compartment. A moment of hope—but it was empty. Leaving the Buick door ajar rather than risk the noise of closing it, he tiptoed past the cars scattered under the pines. There was only one open stretch; he covered it at a combat crouch, taking cover behind the board fence that enclosed the trash cans.

He peeked out. He was only a few yards from the back door—and, incredibly enough, only a few feet from what appeared to be a full Seal-a-Meal pouch of blood lying on the path leading from the doorstep. He darted over, snatched it up. There was another bag a few yards farther from the house—he grabbed that too, noticing a spattered, smeared, trodden trail of blood leading away from the back door.

Or towards it. But there was no time for forensics—Nick raced back up the slight incline towards the highway, tearing open one of the pouches with his teeth as he ran.

Betty had already followed Nick across the road and into the trees on the other side when the blood hit her. The first thing she noticed was how light her step had become—it was as if her body understood everything now.

And the woods had come alive as her senses sharpened. She could pick up the faint distinctive smell of the bark of the Jeffrey pines—some naturalists have likened it to pineapple, others to vanilla, but to Betty it was a piña colada forest—and she had absolutely no sense of danger as she ran, even when Nick was briefly out of her sight, for she could hear not only the twigs but the needles themselves being crushed under the soles of his boots as he preceded her.

Where have you *been* all my *life?* she asked, to the pounding rhythm of her steps. *Where* have you *been* all my *life?* She asked it of the world on blood; and in the voice of the wind, and the crackle of the pine needles underfoot, and the feel of the night air on her skin, the world responded: *Right here all the time, Rev. It just took a little blood for you to notice.*

Betty followed Nick through a small parking lot where a dozen or more cars were scattered at angles in the grove of sweet pines. "That it?" She pointed to the white car with the hood, trunk, and driver's door open.

"That's the one." He had lied to her earlier, in order to account for the fact that he knew which car to look for during their chase. He'd told her January owned the white Buick, figuring correctly that she didn't know enough about January to catch the fib. "She left her thermos inside—no sign of Leon."

"It just occurred to me, if I can hear pine needles crunching at fifty yards, can't they hear us from inside? Shouldn't we get going?"

"You're right." He took off in his running crouch for the back of the lodge again, zigzagging as if he were under fire, taking cover again behind the trash can corral.

Betty caught up to him, not even breathing hard. "How are we going to get in?"

"That door there leads through to the kitchen. Might as well try it—if they're watching for us we haven't got a chance in hell anyway."

"I suppose." Betty raised her head and looked around—her vision was as clear as if she were wearing infrared goggles. "Look, up in that pine! Do you see it?"

Nick followed her eyes—it took him a second to pick out the hunched gray figure of the screech owl perched high in the branches of one of the Jeffrey pines over the parking lot. "I see it," he whispered back.

"Do you think it's the same one from your . . . ?" She had started to say, *from your book.* Only it wasn't just Nick's book she was referring to, she understood now—*truly* understood, perhaps for the first time. It was Nick's life. His life on blood.

Hers, too.

*   *   *

The back door was unlocked. Nick turned the knob silently; Betty followed him down a whitewashed passageway that led towards a large darkened kitchen. Suddenly a door in the wall on their right burst open, and their way was blocked by a stout man in a wheat-colored linen suit and tan panama; the front of the coat was smeared with blood, as were the knees of the linen pants. "Nick!" he shouted; then, inexplicably: "Am I glad to see you! He's down in the cellar."

Nick answered carefully. "Who's down in the cellar?"

"Whistler. He's hurt—badly, I think. We don't know where January is."

"How's Leon?"

Augie looked baffled. "He's dead, Nick."

Betty moaned, and sank to her knees. Augie seemed to notice her for the first time. "You okay?"

Beyond words, she shook her head.

"You're the minister, right? Your baby's fine—Selene took him up to the nursery." Then Augie took in her bloodshot eyes. "I didn't know you were one of us."

Nick, equally stricken but still on his feet, found his voice. "I thought you said Leon was dead."

Augie's turn to be confused again. "He's been dead for years, Nick," he said cautiously, as if Nick had gone around the bend. "The bridge—he jumped—remember?"

And Betty dropped face forward onto the wooden floor of the corridor, like a Muslim at prayer, her shoulders heaving. At that particular moment, not even she could have said whether she was laughing or crying—not until Nick had dropped to his knees beside her: then they were both roaring with laughter.

Betty rolled over onto her back, pulling Nick down over her, showering his face with kisses. He collapsed onto her; they hugged and laughed and wept and kissed until Augie separated them like a pair of rutting dogs, grabbing Nick by the fleece-lined collar of his jacket and hauling him easily to his feet.

"Whistler's half dead, January's running around outside totally werewolf, and you're cracking up because Leon killed himself? Somehow I'm missing the humor here."

"The baby," Nick explained. "Our baby—his name is Leon, too."

"Oh." Then, as the larger picture dawned on him, "Oh! I'm so sorry—I didn't realize—you must have thought . . ." The stout man pulled himself together, touched the brim of his straw hat. "My apologies, Reverend. Come on, I'll take you up to your baby. Nick, why don't—"

But Nick was already halfway down the cellar steps. As the sound of his footsteps receded, Augie reached down to help Betty to her feet. She sprang up lightly—more lightly than she had in a good twenty-five years—noticing as she brushed off her overalls the heavenly smell of the pantry through the open door: bread and grain, chocolate and smooth-worn wood.

"Where is he?" she demanded of Augie—at the news that Leon was alive, that he was near, her milk had begun to leak, dampening the absorbent pads in the cups of her nursing bra.

The cellar floor was awash with blood—fortunately, most of it had been spilled, not shed. Whistler was barely conscious, his head in Selene's lap as she fed him blood from a bottle one sip at a time, a vampire's Florence Nightingale. He tried to sit up when Nick entered, but Selene pressed him back down with a hand at his chest.

"Shh. Rest until your strength comes back." She tipped the bottle of blood to his lips, then turned to Nick. "Leon's fine. He's up with—"

"I know. We saw Augie upstairs. Betty's with him." He squatted down beside her. "What happened here?"

"She hit him with that." Selene indicated the dented can of corn. "Then she grabbed as much blood as she could carry, and ran out the back—I just caught a glimpse of her on my way down."

"Girl packs a wallop," said Nick, leaning over Whistler, staring into his eyes. "Believe me, I'm the one who should know." He lifted Whistler's eyelids one at a time. "Both pupils equal and responsive. If I had a penlight . . . ?"

"Never mind that," said Selene. "Do you have a knife?" She indicated the bottle of blood in her hand. "This stuff's too slow."

Nick found Betty's Swiss Army knife in the pocket of his jacket; quickly, Selene opened a vein in her wrist and held it to Whistler's lips. He sucked greedily; Nick could see his color beginning to rise, even as Selene's drained. But she let him drink on, until Nick was afraid for her. "That's enough, Selene."

So earnestly had Whistler been sucking that his lips made a popping sound—*thwup*—as she tugged her wrist away. His eyes fluttered open again. "Nick. I thought that was you."

"In the flesh. How're you doing?"

"Little woozy. Give me a minute."

"Take your time."

"We don't have time." He struggled to sit up, failed, made it on the second try. "She has to be stopped."

No need to ask who. "I know," said Nick. "I'm going after her."

FIVE

In the alder wood where January stopped running, the leaves closed out the stars above her. She could smell the lake to her left, and moved towards it. A rail fence blocked her way; a tin sign the size of a license plate was nailed to a tree behind the fence. PRIVATE PROPERTY. TRESPASSERS WILL BE PROSECUTED.

Something in the moment took hold of her. A warm marshmallowy feeling spreading outward. *"Set the Wayback Machine, Sherman!"* *"Right, Professor Peabody!"* TRESPASSERS WILL BE PROSECUTED. TRESPASSERS WILL . . . TRESPASSERS W . . . Of course. Piglet's grandfather. Trespassers W. Three years old, in her nightgown, in the trailer, on her mother's lap, being read to from *Winnie the Pooh*. January closed her eyes and arched her head back, smelled pot and Herbal Essence shampoo, felt Glory's long wild hair against her cheek.

She dropped the blood she was carrying and climbed up onto the fence, balancing herself lightly on the top rail as she reached up for the sign; the whole while she was experiencing the odd sensation of being Dorothy climbing into the cornfield to free the Scarecrow from his pole.

What was even odder, it was every bit as vivid a sensation as the memory she'd just had of being three years old on her mother's lap, and only a little less real than the feel of the jagged edge of the grateful old sign against her fingers as she tore it free.

She hopped off on the far side of the fence. Looking down at her hand, she saw she'd sliced open the inside of three fingers, and the ring-finger side of her pinky; the black blood was beginning to well. "Don't . . . even . . . *start* with me," she commanded her fingers, severally; her delighted bark rang out in the alder wood as the wounds closed themselves like night-blooming flowers.

The wood gave out abruptly on a small rocky beach. Her moan, at the sight of the vast shiny lake, was not unlike the breathy vocalized shudder that men sometimes produce at orgasm. She bent down to untie the laces of her boots, and tugged them off, then walked into the lake purposefully, feeling the cold gentle swell lapping at her ankles, knees, thighs.

Her shirt, sticky with blood, was clinging to her chest; she had to tug it away from her skin before she could pull it over her head. Then she took off her shorts and her panties. Satisfactorily naked now, she dove forward and swam a few strokes—it was easy, on blood, anyway—then rolled over. Floating on her back in the light of the stars, she watched her panties drifting away, filmy white like a huge jellyfish.

Her mother's face floated in front of her—the baby-blood told her it was only an acid-flash hallucination, but it comforted her nonetheless. "I love you, Glory," January shouted.

I love you too, honey, mouthed the phantom.

No longer afraid of drowning—no longer afraid of anything, now that she knew what was going to happen—January raised her chin. She could see Nick standing on the shore, holding one of her boots in his hands, peering out towards her. She rolled over onto her stomach, and struck out for deeper water.

It was a terrible thing, thought Nick, standing on the rocky beach a few properties north of Whistler's on the eastern shore of Lake Tahoe, to know what you have to do, and to be unable to do it.

Tracking January hadn't been all that difficult—her boots had been drenched in blood: he'd had only to follow the bloody prints as far as the trail through the alder wood. The no-trespassing sign on the ground caught his eye, the discarded pouches of blood by the fence told him where she'd abandoned the trail, and her boots showed him where she'd entered the lake.

He knew he had to go in after her—whether to bring her out or to make sure she never left it, he could not yet have said—but he couldn't take the first step, not even after she had turned her shiny white ass to the sky and begun swimming away from him.

Nick tore open another pouch of blood, poured the cool sticky liquid down his throat until he started to gag, then tossed it aside. He was already higher than he'd been at Midsummer—but not high enough yet, not high enough to go back into that black water. Calling to her to wait for him, he stooped to pull his boots off, but all the while that stupid nursery rhyme was going around and around in his brain.

Ring around the rosie . . .

He could barely see January anymore, but when he closed his eyes he could hear her splashing about fifty yards from the shore.

Pocket full of posie . . .

Off came the Levi jacket, then the jersey; when he tugged his jeans down, a semierection popped up into the cool night air. It was only from the blood, he knew. But what the fuck—he'd always said he wanted to die with a hard-on.

He stepped out of his jeans and waded into the cold black water.

Ashes, ashes, all fall down.

January floated, spread-eagled on her back. She was dead tired, hadn't the strength for another stroke. She'd closed her eyes; still she sensed the lake round about her, the bowl of mountains round about the lake, and knew herself to be at the center of the whole round world. Just to check, she opened her eyes: the sky was a starry black disk overhead, and sure enough, she was right smack in the middle of that, too.

When she heard Nick splashing towards her, she let her feet sink under her, and began treading water. "Stay back, Nick."

He was treading water about five feet away. "Don't worry, I'm not all that crazy about getting within swinging distance of you, either. But I never had any intention of killing you, January. That was all bullshit back there—I was just angry."

"So I took your baby, and now you're not mad anymore? Yeah, right, Nick."

"But you didn't hurt him, did you? Don't you think I can take that into account?"

Her purple hair was blacker than black, slicked back over her narrow skull, and her eyes round in their narrow sockets as water lapped at her chin. "Yeah, but how about Whistler? Did I kill him?"

"He was sitting up when I left—he said no hard feelings."

"I bet." With a cupped hand, she sent a playful splash of water his way. "Don't try to bullshit me anymore, Nick. I've had my baby-blood now—I found some in the cellar—and you know what? I don't think anybody can ever bullshit me again. If I go back with you, Whistler's gonna lock me in that cellar."

"I won't let anyone lock you in the cellar. But I won't let you just swim away, either. You know I can't let you do that."

She lowered her voice. It was quiet this far out on the lake; he could hear the liquid sound her hands made, paddling just under the surface.

"I saw my mom, Nick. I saw Glory. And she wasn't all drowned and ugly, either—she's just as beautiful as she ever was."

"That's good, Jan. That's real good." *Hypothermia and baby-blood— it's a wonder she didn't see the whole goddamn cast of* Hair. "What can I do to get you to come back with me? I've got to turn back soon—this water's too cold, even on blood."

"You could fuck me. Face to face with your eyes open, the way you fucked *her.*" She paddled a little closer.

"Honey, this water's so cold, I couldn't find my dick with tweezers."

"Just hug me, then." She was within arm's reach.

"And you'll come back with me?" Face to face.

"Not exactly." She slipped her arms around him and drew him close; there was no appreciable difference in temperature between her pebbled skin and the water of the lake. "I want you to come with me," she whispered into his ear, wrapping her legs around his waist.

"Where?"

"To see Glory." She kissed him—then her arms tightened convulsively, driving the air out of him with a rush.

A moment of blackness—suddenly they were underwater. Nick's hands were free; he wrenched her arms from around him and drove for the surface, breached it, gasping, while a fathom down, January flailed her arms wildly until she bumped against one of his legs, then wrapped both hands around an ankle, and tugged. He kicked her in the head with the heel of his free foot as hard as he could against the resistance of the water, kicked again and again until her grip weakened.

One last blow and he was free. Free, but disoriented—rather than risk swimming further from shore, he spun around wildly, trying to spot the little beach where he'd entered the lake. He saw a figure swimming towards him—it was still pretty far away—all he could make out was a little white ball of a head bobbing halfway between him and the shore.

Then came a roar behind him as January broke the surface—she was all over him, hands and arms slapping, grabbing frantically, legs kicking. She clamped onto his back; he tried to reach around and throw her over his head, but jiujitsu was useless in the water.

Twisting around to face her, Nick forced the heel of his hand under her jaw, and began levering her head back. But her hands were clawing for his eyes; as he drew his head back, she managed to get both hands around his throat.

He had to let go of her face then, to grab at her wrists, but she had air now, and he had none—his eyes were open, but everything was going black except for the starry pinpoints of light streaking across his vision. As he struggled to bring his feet up and force her away with his legs, suddenly there was a hideous rolling, popping sound, like somebody cracking ten knuckles at once, or twisting a sheet of inch-thick bubble wrap between both hands.

The hands around Nick's throat had gone limp. He gasped for air, and sucked in a lungful of icy water. Choking, sinking, he was grabbed from the front again—but this time the hands were under his armpits, buoying him up. He opened his eyes: it was Whistler, his head wrapped in a bloodstained makeshift turban that had come half undone, and was trailing behind him in the water like a gauzy winding sheet.

You're a better man than I am, Gunga Din, was Nick's last thought before he lost consciousness, and slipped back under the shining black surface of the lake.

S I X

Selene hadn't even bothered trying to talk Whistler out of going after Nick and January. After using three rolls of gauze and two of hypoallergenic (also, unfortunately, hypoadhesive) tape to provide his skull with at least a little cushioning against a second concussion, she gave him a peck on the cheek, and started him off on the trail of blood that led up the cellar stairs, through the back door, and towards the neighboring alder wood.

That one of the three of them would not be returning to Whistler Manor, Selene had little doubt: after all, the two births promised by the runes had already taken place. But she was too busy for more than a perfunctory prayer to the Norns as she hurried out to meet the guests and staff returning in limos and cabs from the casinos to the south.

Fortunately, Catherine had been among the first carload from the Horizon; she took over the job of organizing the cleanup while Selene hurried back to the nursery suite, where Augie Fetterman was still standing watch outside Lourdes's door; down the hall Cheese Louise in all her vastness guarded the back entrance to the nursery.

"They kicked me out," said Augie mournfully, opening the door for Selene. "One little comment about Titzapoppin', and they kicked me out."

Titzapoppin', indeed, thought Selene, locking the door behind her. For Lourdes was nursing Cora in the window seat with her vanilla satin bed jacket around her waist; in the Nantucket rocker Plum Rose sucked greedily at Nanny Parish; and there on Lourde's enormous bed Leon was hard at work at an engorged breast.

That the owner of that blue-veined breast was a vampire would have been obvious to Selene from the vampire blush of the chest and throat alone; when the new mother opened her eyes to see who had intruded upon her nursing bliss, they were crimson as well, and Selene had to force back a gasp—she'd had no forewarning from Nick.

Lourdes did the honors from the window seat, with a full sense of occasion. "Reverend Betty Ruth Shoemaker, meet the High Priestess Selene of the Coven of Wicca. High Priestess Selene, this is the Reverend Betty Ruth Shoemaker, minister of the Church of the Higher Power."

"And a vampire, apparently," said Selene, recovering quickly. "I had no idea."

"Neither did she," replied Lourdes. "How's Whistler?"

"Fine when he left. Not so much as a headache."

"When he left?"

"He and Nick have gone after January." Selene turned back to Betty. Over the years, she had seen a few vampires lose their virginity—it was normally the sweetest thing to watch the way their eyes opened like a three-year-old toddling down the stairs on Christmas morning. "How are you doing, dearie?"

But Betty was still dazed from the sensation of nursing—she had nearly cried out with orgasmic surprise a few minutes before, when her milk had first let down, and though she was trying to grapple with the larger issues looming over the horizon, she couldn't quite get past the physicality of it all. *If nursing feels this good,* had been the thought going through her mind when Selene entered, *sex must be absolutely unbearable.*

Oddly enough, Selene's seemingly innocuous question took her completely by surprise, as if she'd been asked to name the fourteenth president. Betty shrugged as demonstratively as she could without setting her occupied breast jiggling out of Leon's greedy grasp. "Remember the Firesign Theater?"

"Oh-oh, boomer alert," remarked Lourdes.

Betty ignored her. "Well, I feel like . . ." She deepened her voice, trying to sound like Walter Cronkite on acid: " 'Everything *you* know, is *wrong!*' "

How very Zen, Selene was about to reply, when Lourdes waved wildly from the window seat, put a warning forefinger to her lips when she'd got their attention, and then cupped a hand to her ear. A moment later Selene heard the shouting from the lawn, crossed to the western window, unlatched it, and threw it open.

"Little help down here," Whistler was shouting. But even shouting, he kept his voice at a civilized *tennis, anyone?* pitch: he might have been calling for his ball from an adjacent court, rather than standing naked and dripping on the lawn, with Nick's limp body in his arms.

As Selene watched, Lourdes and Betty crowding the window behind her, others came running to Whistler's aid—vampires first, with their superior speed, Henderson and Toshi from around the side of the house, Beverly and Sandy from the parking lot; then the front door opened, casting an angular patch of yellow light on the deep green grass, and Catherine hurried out with the cordless phone at her ear, followed by several witches, Josephina, and two of the houseboys.

"Nick!" called Betty, despairingly. Leon had begun to howl, and as Selene hurried out the door and down the stairs she could hear Cora and Plum Rose joining the choir.

ONE

Whistler Manor was quiet on the evening of the autumn equinox—as quiet as it ever got on a sabbat. Whistler had been all for going on with the ceremony as if nothing had happened, but Selene had put her pointy little foot down.

"We've had a death here, Jamey," she informed him in his bedroom Monday evening shortly after sunset. "It may have been a convenient death for you, but it was a death nonetheless, and by the Great Horned God, we're going to treat it with the respect it deserves."

Whistler, having learned decades before never to mess with the Great Horned God, could only spread his hands in surrender. "It's not as if we're going to ignore it—there's the plan for the foun—"

She cut him off. "That's for your conscience."

"And this is for yours."

"Fine. I'll take it."

Which left Whistler back at the point of his original surrender. He changed the subject. "Do you think our newest Drinker will be staying over for the equinox celebration?"

"I don't know—she didn't say anything last night. How do you think she's taking it?"

"If I know Nick, right up the—"

But Selene cut him off again, this time with the aid of a raised, bushy eyebrow—even though she suspected the Great Horned God might have approved the sentiment. "I meant about being a vampire."

"She seemed chipper enough when she went off to bed."

Selene had another question: "How much does Nick know?"

Whistler thought it over. He was still in bed, not yet high—but of course, being Whistler, he was not yet sober, either. "Hard to say. He knows January's dead, and he knows she tried to take him with her. He also knows we got the body out—it was all he kept saying when he came to—that we couldn't leave her down there. Whether he knows the rest is anybody's guess."

By 'the rest' Whistler meant of course the unutterable fact that January had not died from drowning—that when he had finally located the body, in about fifty feet of water (and it had been a grueling two hours' work, diving again and again into that cold blackness with a feeble scuba diver's torch—only a vampire could have managed it), the head had been turned the wrong way around.

Not that he regretted what he'd done, having had little enough choice in the matter if he'd wanted to save Nick. And the manner of her death, while hideous-sounding, had been remarkably quick, and presumably painless.

Still, that noise when he'd broken her neck, and that quick glimpse of her face, made all the more horrible by the fact that he was still positioned behind her in the water (had she still been sentient? . . . had those eyes been staring into his own? . . . lord, he hoped not) were not anything he'd ever want to think about straight.

Ah well, little danger of that, thought Whistler, reaching a long arm under the bed, and feeling around for the handle to the little refrigerator containing his Clamato jar.

"Have you told Lourdes?" Selene asked him after he'd drunk, when the color had returned to his face.

"Of course not. And I don't want her ever knowing. Cora, either. You're the only one I've told, and lord knows I wouldn't have told you if I thought I had a chance in hell of keeping it from you."

She acknowledged the compliment. "You're a wise man, dearie. But a guilty secret in Nick's hands is about as safe as a pint of blood in yours. You'd better find out for sure what he knows—and the Reverend Shoemaker, as well."

"I have great hopes for the Reverend," Whistler replied, climbing out of bed, but for Selene's sake adjusting the folds of his nightshirt to conceal the burgeoning Creature. "Not only do I have the feeling that she would make a valued addition to the Penang, should she so choose, but she might even manage to knock Nick off his high horse occasionally."

Selene laughed. "Nick and *his* high horse? You know what I think, Jamey?"

"No, but I suppose you're—"

"I think if you'd reached January first, you'd have done exactly what he did—tried to save her." Whistler started to protest; she cut him off again. "Not only that, I think if Nick had been in your position, he'd have done exactly what you did."

"Save me, you mean? Or kill her?" Whistler's turn to laugh, on his way into the bathroom. "Either way, now you've gone and insulted both of us."

TWO

Betty and Nick had not made love that morning, despite Whistler's crude assumption. Nick had accepted blood from the others the night before, but only until his body had recovered from the hypothermia. After that, he and Betty had retreated to the bungalow, changed into borrowed sleepwear—a Cheese Louise flannel nightgown for Betty and a pair of Whistler's paisley pajamas for Nick—and had spent the rest of the night, and half the morning, simply talking.

And *this* time there had been no need for him to promise that *this* time he was telling the whole truth, etc., etc. He had talked until his strength was gone, refusing more blood but accepting a few Quaaludes around eight o'clock, and had fallen asleep by nine.

No sedatives for Betty, though: she had an infant to nurse. Afterwards, she had remembered to make some calls back to El Cerrito, to be sure that church affairs would be taken care of in her absence. A few white lies—Leon fallen ill, but in no danger—and it was done: the church ladies, bless their hearts, would go ahead with the healing circle in Betty's absence later that morning, and see that the building was open for meetings, and locked at night, until her return.

At first she felt a little guilty about lying, but then she realized that the truth would have been equally unkind.

Could you cover the church for a few days, Ellen? I'm stuck up in Tahoe . . . Oh, nothing serious—vampire kidnapped my baby, and then I found out I'm a vampire too. Bye-bye, hon, talk to you later. And there was a silver lining: she understood suddenly why Nick had been forced to lie to her so often during the past year—if she'd been hanging on to any lingering resentment over his having misled her, it was surely gone by now.

Pastoral responsibilities handled, Betty found that sleep came to her more easily than she'd imagined, the six hours between 10 A.M. and 4 P.M. representing the longest period of uninterrupted slumber the new mother had known since giving birth back in August.

In fact she'd found herself wondering, as Leon did his level best to suck both breasts dry upon awakening that afternoon, whether her milk was somehow fortified, now that she was a vampire—after all, he'd always been such a fussy eater before, and had never slept as long as four hours in a single session.

And after he'd uttered an ecstatic burp and fallen cheerfully back to sleep chortling at the ceiling, she'd decided in the affirmative—to her confusion, if not outright dismay. It wasn't fair, this blood. Drugs were supposed to ruin your health and wreck your life—that was the Second Step, the lynchpin of twelve-step thinking: *Realized our lives were unmanageable.* But all this drug had done so far was give her nursing orgasms while curing her baby of colic. That seemed manageable enough for the Reverend Betty Ruth.

Then the Elephant arrived. She didn't recognize it at first, Nick having given the pachyderm relatively short shrift in *My Life on Blood.* It started as a vague dissatisfaction with the ceiling—she was lying on her back, and it occurred to her that she'd never seen a drearier ceiling in her life—and soon extended to the entire room, which had seemed so charming to her only a few hours before.

So distasteful had the room become, that after checking on Leon one more time and finding no pleasure even in his gnomic sleeping visage, she fled downstairs in her nightgown. But the little parlor of the bungalow was not much of an improvement—nothing but walls and furniture and a Monet (or was it Manet? didn't seem worth the effort required to cross the room to check out the vowel in the signature).

She opened the door and stepped outside, but found that the little wood that had seemed so magical last night had lost its luster in the daylight. Trees, dirt—surely Mother Nature was vastly overrated. "It's only the drug," Betty tried to tell herself; that was a classic treatment technique for acid bummers. "Only the drug, only the drug . . ." But of course it wasn't the drug at all: Betty's problem was, the drug had worn off.

Since that truth was no easier to live with, she hurriedly changed her mantra: "It's only the crash, it's only the crash." With a heavy heart, she turned back from the dreary wood. Then it occurred to her as she trudged back up the stairs—and this was perhaps the worst shock of all—that maybe the problem wasn't the crash, either. Maybe the problem was the world.

"What if it's the world that's sad and—oh Goddess, it's true: '*All the world is sad and dreary*'—and I never knew it until I'd seen it on blood."

And then her heart was worse than heavy, it was practically broken as she found herself kneeling by the trundle bed, looking down at Leon, and feeling . . . *nothing*.

Nothing, not a goddamn thing. Just another dreary little creature of flesh and bone. Then she looked past Leon's trundle bed, noticed the cabinet built into the side of the king-size bed, and knew somehow as she reached for the chrome handle that behind that little door lay the answer to her immediate problem.

It was a refrigerator, of course, and inside it was a 32-oz Clamato Juice jar. And while it wouldn't be quite accurate to say that Betty had reached for the jar, twisted open the top, and taken a hearty swig almost before she knew it, it would be equally inaccurate to attribute her actions to a conscious decision, and downright misleading to call them the end result of a carefully reasoned moral choice.

Nor, at the time, had her bending of the elbow represented a considered rejection of twelve-step principles, or of her life to date, or even a preference for a life on blood over a life of sobriety. And although sober she'd have rejected whatever mentation had gone on 'twixt Clamato jar and lip as specious, once the blood hit her stomach Betty recalled clearly that even in recovery she'd always thought that NarcAnons who refused pain medication after surgery were downright silly. There'd never been a doubt in *her* mind that if she'd been rescued from an Alpine blizzard by a St. Bernard, she'd have sucked the life-giving brandy out of that cask in a New York minute, and the hell with a sobriety date.

So between pain and no pain, it was no contest. Blame it on the Elephant, was her last sober thought; then she was high on blood, and the concept of assigning blame for her bliss was, well, inconceivable. Especially after Leon awoke pink-cheeked and chortling again, and fed upon her with such a hearty appetite that he would have drained her dry, had not her mammaries been producing vampire milk at such a rapid rate that she could practically hear it gurgling into her breasts.

She closed her eyes in a nursing ecstasy. Sooner or later, she knew, she'd have to face the Elephant again. But not yet. Not tonight.

*   *   *

Nick was awakened a little after sunset by the bleat of a telephone, and wondered for a moment if he weren't still asleep. He was in a room furnished like a Swiss chalet, lit by a cozy yellow lamp; beside him in bed Betty Ruth nursed a cherubic Leon in the cradle of her arms; and when she turned her placid gaze upon Nick, the whites of her eyes were red as blood. It sure had all the elements of a dream.

It took him a minute to shake off the Quaalude haze. "I don't know," Betty was saying into the phone. "Nick just woke up. Let me ask him, and I'll call you right back." She hung up. "That was Selene," she explained to Nick, as if continuing a conversation. Then her face fell, the features forming a comic mask of dismay. "She wants to know if we're going to attend the ceremony tonight, and I just realized, I don't know *how* to call her back."

Leon's head lolled away from her nipple; one-handed, she tucked her breast back into her borrowed nightgown, flapped a hand towel over her shoulder to protect the flannel, then with both hands lifted Leon up into the air, lowered him for a kiss, and settled him over her shoulder.

A hearty burp was immediately forthcoming. Betty glanced over at Nick as triumphantly as if she had produced the belch herself, but to her surprise, tears were flooding his eyes, and there was nothing even faintly comic about the mask of dismay his features had assumed. "What is it, Nick? What's the matter?" she asked, genuinely puzzled.

"You're stoned," he replied.

"It seemed like a reasonable alternative to suicide," she said lightly. "Want some? There's the cutest little fridge built into—"

Nick shook his head miserably. "I'm so sorry, Betty. I'm so sorry I got you involved in this."

"I'm not sorry at all," she said. "In fact, I'm having the time of my life."

"Of course you are—you're high on blood. A drug that I turned you on to in the first place." He rolled onto his side, away from her. "I shouldn't be surprised," he went on, more to himself than to her. "It's like the perfect ending to the whole V.A. experiment—now *everybody* it's touched is either dead or drinking blood."

Betty sighed as she settled Leon into his trundle bed. "I think I'd better tell Selene we'll be staying for the ceremony tonight."

"How come?" Nick asked the opposite wall.

"Speaking as your therapist, I'd say you need the completion only a funeral can bring."

Perhaps it was the finality of the word funeral that finally released his anguished sobs—in any event, Betty knew better than to try and jolly him. Instead she pressed tight up against his back, threw her arms around him, and hugged him tightly until he was done, then released him and sat up, giving him time to compose himself.

He wasn't looking quite as dapper as usual when he finally rolled over to face her with his cheeks drained of color and his Magnum P.I. mustache matted with snot and tears. Betty swiped a Kleenex from the pop-up decorator box on the bedside table, and began dabbing him clean.

Her next move probably would have been to hold the tissue to his nose and say "Blow," but Nick recovered in time to spare himself that embarrassment. Sitting up in bed in his borrowed paisley pajamas, he took the Kleenex from her, turned his back, and blew and blew and blew, feeling a little foolish, but better for having cried. Somebody needed to cry for January.

When he was done, and had turned back to Betty, she reached for the sodden tissue. He almost handed it to her, then caught himself at the last second, wadded it up, and tossed it in the general direction of the wastebasket in the far corner of the room, next to the secretaire. A man might cry, and still be a man; a man might even let a woman blot his tears. But he had to blow his own nose, and he had to discard his own used tissues.

He also had to go after his own rebounds: Nick climbed out of bed, retrieved the Kleenex from under the secretaire, and slam-dunked it directly into the wastebasket. When he turned back to the bed, Betty was on her stomach, leaning over the side and dangling her fingers into the trundle bed, evidently to Leon's great amusement.

Nick lay down on his stomach next to her. Leon appeared to recognize him, and laughed so hard you could barely see his eyes. Baby Leon's eyes had turned brown over the past few weeks, brown as Nick's own, and it occurred to him that he didn't know what color Betty's eyes were. He glanced sideways to check them out just as she turned her head to look at him. Brown as well, but a lighter shade than his or Leon's.

They looked down at their son again—Leon had seized Betty's forefinger in his fist, and howled with joy when she tugged at it gently. This was high slapstick for the kid, this was commedia dell'arte, Punch and Judy, and Moe, Larry and Curly all rolled into one. "You know what I was thinking before?" Betty mused. "When he was nursing, and you asleep so sweet beside me?"

"What?"

"That the one thing you and Whistler have managed to agree on, so far, you were both dead right about."

"And that was?" He was trying to remember if he and Whistler had agreed on anything lately.

"The cup. Leon's christening cup. Tolstoy *was* wrong—happy families *aren't* all alike."

Nick thought it over again. He dearly loved his Tolstoy: he'd read *Anna Karenina* (the Garnett translation, of course) on blood, in one thirty-six-hour sitting. "Maybe Tolstoy was just being ironic. He liked to do that, you know, fuck with his readers. He said one time that a story leaves a deeper impression when it's impossible to tell which side the author is on."

"Sometimes . . ." But Betty couldn't go on—she was laughing too hard—the bed shook with her laughter. Finally, with an effort, she managed to complete the thought: "Sometimes I feel the same way about Higher Power."

THREE

The ceremony began in the keeping room at midnight. Informal. Street clothes. The Coven and the Penang arrayed around the lower two tiers of cushions. Only Selene, sitting cross-legged at the bottom of the orgy pit, was in her robe, with her athame in her lap.

"The ceremony of the autumn equinox," she began, "is normally one of my favorites in the round. I mean, we're not supposed to have favorites, but without getting too specific, basically what happens in autumn is that the Corn King returns from the Underworld, only now he's the God of the Underworld, and he wants to carry his Goddess back with him."

Betty Ruth tightened her grip on Nick's hand. Neither of them was high on blood, Betty having abstained since her hair of the Elephant six or seven hours before, and Nick not having drunk at all since the previous night. On the other hand, nothing about the keeping room promoted a sense of reality: Betty, at least, was as stoned on adrenaline, disorientation, and anticipation as she used to get on a shot of Stoli, while Nick was adrift on a sea of anomie.

Lourdes, on the other side of Betty on the first tier of cushions, was riveted to the High Priestess's every word: she had decided recently to go on with her Wiccan studies, and perhaps someday become the first vampire High Priestess in the Coven's history.

Even with the strictures against married High Priestesses, it still seemed like a more attainable goal than becoming a prima ballerina at this late stage (though Whistler had offered to buy her a troupe). And now that she had attained all her other goals—a rich sexy husband whom she adored, and who adored her; financial security beyond even *her* dreams of avarice; a beautiful daughter; and, last but probably not least, all the blood she could drink—she knew she'd better have something else to shoot for: unlike pregnancy, motherhood alone definitely wasn't going to cut it as a cure for the weary, stale, flat, and unprofitable blues.

Whistler, on the other side of Lourdes, was also paying more attention to Selene than was customary for him. January's death had affected him more than he was letting on—more than Leon Stanton's death, certainly, though by any common reckoning that had been a cold-blooded murder, while the more recent death was unarguably justifiable homicide, if not outright self-defense. He supposed his current unease represented at least a measure of maturity, by some twisted standard—deeper than that he did not wish to delve.

"But here's the part I like best," Selene continued. She'd been disturbed by January's death as well, particularly by the knowledge that she had, in effect, prayed for it—not directly, but by praying only for Whistler's and Nick's protection, knowing all the while that one of the three of them almost certainly owed the runes a death.

"The God pursues the Goddess, and pursues, and pursues, but however hard he pursues her, he can't catch her. The only way he catches her is to stop chasing—stop dead in his tracks and ask her to wait. And she always stops, and laughs, and says he could have saved a lot of trouble by just asking her that at the beginning."

Something else was bothering Selene: she was not unaware that the entire tragedy might perhaps have been averted if she'd forsworn her vengeance on Nick in the first place. It wasn't your garden-variety guilt: Selene knew too much about fate for that—or rather, knew better than most how *little* she knew about fate. Still, she'd been thinking about resigning as High Priestess. She'd polled the runes about it that morning—the results were inconclusive.

Even so, she knew this might be her last sabbat, which gave it more resonance and poignance for her than it already carried, even doubling as a funeral: Wiccans weren't real big on mourning. After all, the way down was the only way up. Old Heraclitus again. Clever fellow.

"Now the Coven will be enacting the Legend around four A.M., witches only, and I can't tell you others much about that. But those of you not in the Coven have some idea of what's involved from the ceremony we used to do with the Penang, which involved a striptease with the seven veils of existence, and a Goddess willing to let herself be chained up and scourged by the God, and the Hierophant, and then lastly by Death. It's the only time everybody wants to be Death, because of course he gets to make love to her."

She looked up at the witches and vampires—several of them were smiling, and Catherine Bailey had blushed to the roots of her orange hair. The last time they'd performed the ritual with the Penang, before the V.A. days, she had played the Goddess, and turned the Dance of the Seven Veils into a voluptuous belly dance, to the recorded music of Evelyn "Champagne" King. And Death that year had been an absolute teddy bear of a man, who ravished her tenderly all night long.

"But tonight, I think," Selene went on, "nobody really wants to mock Death—or to be ravished by him, either. Because we've just been paid a visit by the genuine article, and we're still a little shaken. So all I want to do at this point is just remind everybody how the rest of the round goes."

Selene caught Sherman's eye—he was on the far left of the upper tier—and beginning with him, she made eye contact with every person in the keeping room, left to right across the second tier, then right to left across the lowest, until she reached Cheese Louise, whose own eyes were brimming with tears.

"How it goes is, the Goddess descends to the Underworld, but does not die. Nor does she fear Death. Instead she loves him with all her heart, and they rule as equals until Candlemas. Then he gives her back the necklace of rebirth, and the earth is reborn in the springtime."

She turned back to the middle of the first tier for the next part— Whistler and Lourdes, Betty and Nick. "What we here on earth have to bear in mind is that there would have been no spring had it not been for the sacrifice of the Goddess in the autumn. We don't know exactly how it works—that's why we have our rituals—but what we do know for certain is that there is no birth without death, and what we hope is that there is no death without birth, and that's all I have to say for now. Jamey?"

She had turned away suddenly, her thin shoulders shaking under the forest green robe. Whistler raised an arm languidly. "Vampires, drink 'em if you got 'em. If you don't got 'em, see me. We meet on the front lawn in thirty minutes."

There were tiki torches flaring on the lawn, next to a chest-high stack of sod that to Betty Ruth resembled a mossy green cairn. The good Reverend was stoned again, on her first taste of live blood: Catherine had presented herself to Betty immediately after Whistler's recess, and the two women had fallen into each other's arms laughing—turned out they'd been in Codependents Anonymous together for years, until the Baileys had moved to Marin.

And as one good codependent, Catherine had been obliged to offer her blood (as a postrecovery pothead, she was already stoned herself), and as another good co, Betty had been obliged to accept.

Falling into line beside Nick, Betty joined the procession, took three squares of sod from the pile, and—carrying them out in front of her so as not to soil the overalls that had magically reappeared at the door of the bungalow that evening, washed and pressed—followed the procession down the lawn, turning right just before the beach and entering the path that meandered through the woods towards the bungalow.

The path had been strung with Japanese lanterns. On blood, they cast the most beautiful light Betty had ever seen—they were like little colored moons come to earth. Halfway to the bungalow, the aisle of lanterns turned left, into the woods, toward the lake. And in the densest part of the woods, there was a clearing of newly-turned earth six feet wide and six feet long—and presumably six feet deep, though no one mentioned that.

In fact, no one mentioned anything until each of the twelve vampires had laid his or her three squares of sod neatly in place, forming a bright green patch in the lantern light in the depth of the wood. Then Whistler cleared his throat—too loudly for the little clearing: it sounded like a bark.

He noticed that he was standing like a preacher before the grave, with his feet apart and his hands clasped in front of him—quickly he thrust one hand into the pocket of his Italian sports jacket. "My attorney has advised me not to be too specific. So in general, all I want to say is—and I include myself; first and foremost I include myself—vampires, let's try to take better care of one another, all year round. Because if we don't, who will?"

He looked around at the circle of vampires surrounding the new grave, which bore no headstone, nor ever would. "To that end, let me add that I've met briefly with the eminent psychologist Dr. Bailey, along with the eminent therapist and clergywoman Dr. Shoemaker." The latter title had been bestowed by Whistler without Betty's approval—she had never finished her doctoral studies—but she let it pass. Perhaps now she would. Anything seemed possible to her, at the moment. Might even be fun, cramming on blood. "And together with the eminent barrister, Dr. Fetterman, and the eminent everything else, Dr. Santos, we will be meeting over the course of the next month or so, to discuss the formation of a foundation dedicated to that end.

"We don't know much about it yet—whether it will be centered here at the Manor, or at the Church of the Higher Power, or on an island somewhere where we have a chance to legitimize the drinking of blood entirely, and thus remove some of the other societal pressures which complicate our lives. At any rate, we'll be discussing the details over the course of the next few months.

"What we do know is that we want it to be available on equal terms to those of us who wish to pursue the Dream of the Occasional User—" with a nod to Nick "—or who, for reasons still quite mystifying to me personally, might want to avoid blood entirely, as well as to those of us— the vast majority, I suspect—who want to drink our fill as often as practicable and still lead 'manageable' lives.

"The only other thing we've agreed upon so far is the name—we're going to call it the Winters' Night Foundation, after January." He looked down at the brilliant patch of green sod. "It ain't a headstone, m'dear, but it'll have to do."

Nick and Betty turned back to look at the grave when they reached the path again—the lanterns were so pretty, and the square patch of new sod so sweetly green, but the servants were already taking the former down, and trampling the latter so it wouldn't buckle overnight.

The other vampires were turning to the right, heading back to their rooms in the Manor, where they and the witches would pair up into Gods and Goddesses (though not strictly by sex, of course) and rule the Underworld jointly for a night.

Nick and Betty waved goodbye and started in the other direction, towards the bungalow, but suddenly Betty stopped Nick with a hand on his arm. "I just want to run up to the nursery and check on Leon."

"I'm sure he's fine, Betty."

"I'd feel better."

"Whatever. But as long as you're there, why don't you drop by the cellar and pick us out a bag of blood for the night?"

"Sure. Anything I should know in advance? I've never picked out blood before."

"Doesn't matter," said Whistler, startling them—they hadn't heard him approaching through the woods. " 'The pedigree of honey/ Does not concern the bee;/ A clover, any time, to him/ Is aristocracy.' " He bowed to Betty. "Emily Dickinson. But if you'll allow me, I'd be happy to help you select a vintage."

"Thank you, Emily," Betty said flirtatiously, and took his arm. A few yards up the trail, she turned back, the lantern directly over her head casting raspberry-colored streaks across her graying dark hair. "If I'm not back in fifteen minutes," she informed Nick, "start without me."

But she was back in ten. Leon had been fast asleep in the girls' playpen, Cora and Plum Rose snoring above him in their cribs, and Whistler—under the rather severe urging of the Creature, which had been banned from its own perfect Underworld for the past five months—was obviously chafing to return to his Goddess.

Nevertheless, he did escort Betty to the cellar, which was newly scrubbed and painted, though the smell of blood still lingered. Then the impeccably mannered, impeccably dressed vampire had accompanied her to the front door of Whistler Manor and pressed upon her a few Quaaludes, as well as a small canvas tote-bag he had retrieved from a cabinet in the keeping room. "You might want this later," he told her, as with a hug he bade her a warm good night.

Nick was waiting for her on the bed, wearing only a plush Caesar's Tahoe bathrobe. Seeing him, Betty turned shy. She handed the blood to him and hurried into the bathroom, undressed, ran the water to cover the sound of her peeing, and then slipped on her overalls again, over her bare skin.

Not quite your Victoria's Secret negligee, she knew—but then, that was another, unexpected benefit of this strange new high: confidence. She didn't recall Nick having written about that much. Of course, he was a devastatingly handsome man and might have taken his sexual attractiveness for granted.

But on Betty, a woman who'd never been sure of hers, this new drug had wrought a wonder: she could feel her sexiness from the inside out.

And when she opened the door and caught sight of Nick catching sight of her; when she sashayed over to the bed, watching his erection pushing out the front of his bathrobe as his eyes followed the heavy shifting of her breasts under the bib of the Can't Bust Em's; when she sat down cross-legged on the bed before him and he passed her the bag of blood with one hand while with the other unsnapping the brass button of one of the bib straps and freeing a breast for his widening, crimson eyes; when, in short, she understood that gay as this gorgeous man might be, down to the very core of his being, he was nonetheless hers for the night, bound to her with a bond of blood strong enough to overcome all prejudices, even those of sexual preference, then she knew she would never think of herself, of her body and her sexuality, the same way again.

As for Nick, who was soon lying on his back with his face buried between a pair of blue-veined breasts just beginning to leak sweet mother's milk, he had given up trying to make sense of the fact that every time he drank blood lately, he seemed to end up in bed with a woman. There were so many other much more important things to give up trying to make sense of, that he was just as glad to get this one out of the way.

Later, when Betty was back in the bathroom changing—into what, he hadn't a hint—he realized that he still didn't know what he was going to do tomorrow. Other than take it one day—or night—at a time, of course. He might drink blood often, or occasionally, or not at all. He might move in with Betty, or Betty and Leon might move in with him. Or neither: maybe he'd start dating again.

In fact, all he did know about the future, he realized, was that he was going to do either the right thing or the wrong thing, for either the right or the wrong reasons.

And even that uncomplicated epiphany deserted him at the sight of the Reverend Shoemaker emerging from the upstairs bathroom of the bungalow naked as the dawn except for a leather harness that fitted over her waist and thighs and supported a small, elegantly carved black dildo.

"Well, helloooo Sailor," Nick announced, abandoning further philosophical reflection for the remainder of the evening.

Three is not always a crowd—not when two of them are vampires and the third a donor. Selene lay face down on Whistler's bed, feeling the familiar light-headed rush as Whistler drank from the hollow behind her left knee, and Lourdes from the right.

But when they had pinched off the wounds and begun kissing their way up the back of her thighs, she rolled over and sat up, tugging down the hem of her flannel nightgown. "Tonight is for the God and Goddess," she reminded them. "Perhaps some other time, dearies."

"Promise?" asked Lourdes, only partially insincere: curious as she was about what it would be like to make love to the High Priestess, she was of decidedly mixed emotions about having a threesome with the other great love of her husband's life.

"The last promise I made was to myself," replied Selene. "It was not to make any more promises, and I'm going to keep it. You two have a wonderful evening."

Whistler walked her to the door. "I spoke to Nick," he whispered into her ear as they hugged goodnight. "He doesn't remember anything about . . . you know."

She gave him a peck on the cheek. "I didn't think so. I'd have seen it in his eyes."

"What are you two whispering about?" Lourdes called from Whistler's walk-in closet—she was browsing through his costumes.

Selene slipped out the door. Whistler locked it behind her. "Nothing, m'dear."

"C'mere, Jamey."

He poked his head into the closet.

"If I wear this—" She held up a long flannel mommy nightgown. "—will you wear these?" Daddy pajamas, light blue cotton with dark blue piping.

"And make love in them?" he said hesitantly, not quite sure if he'd caught her drift.

But he had. "Yes," she replied breathily.

"Under the covers?"

"Yes."

"With the lights out? Missionary position, no wiggling?"

"Oh yes, Jamey. Oh god, yes."

"Betty, I'm gay."

A voice in the dark: Nick and Betty lay side by side on the bed, naked in afterglow. Either would have killed for a postcoital cigarette; neither would have admitted it under torture.

"I know, Nick."

"No, really. I really, really am."

"I'm your therapist. I really, really know."

"As in, I will never be truly happy unless I'm in a sexual relationship with a man."

Betty laughed: "Yeah, right, tell me about it." Then, after a moment. "But what about blood? Can you ever be truly happy again without blood?"

But just asking the question had frightened her a little—he must have sensed it, for he took her hand in the dark. "I don't know. I used to think I did, but I don't anymore. What I do know, even now, even high, is that staying high all the time won't do it for me either—tried that: didn't work."

"Do you think there's a middle path?"

"What I think is, you have to learn to ride the Elephant. If you can beat the Elephant, then the First Step doesn't apply."

Realized we were powerless over blood. Betty thought it over—thought, and thought, and thought, then climbed out of bed, crossed to the casement window, opened it, sniffed the sweet piney air, and thought about it some more.

Finally she turned back from the window, leaving it open behind her despite the chill. Her body loved the night air—there was life to it.

"Want to face the Elephant together, this next time?" she asked Nick, climbing back under the covers. "I think maybe I could do it, if there was somebody there to remind me that it wasn't the world that was sad and dreary, but only the crash."

The bed shifted as he turned towards her—he had scooted farther under the covers, having had enough of a chill the night before to last him a lifetime. "Be crazy not to try it. The sooner the better, though, I'd imagine."

"Not too soon," she moaned.

He laughed. "Tomorrow night, then. Otherwise the Elephant'll be too big to ride."

"Bigger than the both of us?"

He thought back to that night in March—the night he had learned that he was the last recovering vampire on earth—and crawled up a little higher in the bed so that he could whisper directly into the ear of the woman who had saved his life that night, the woman who had kissed him right in the power.

"How I'll feel about it tomorrow night at this time, I haven't the slightest idea," was what he whispered. "But as of this moment, Reverend, I don't think there's an Elephant in the world too big for the both of *us.*"

AFTERWARD

With smoking torches twisted from the hemp of the baobab tree, in their simple red cotton J. C. Penney souvenir sleeping-shirt robes, the vampires of Santa Luz came for Betty Ruth and Leon at the roughly appointed hour: a few minutes after sunset on the night of the first full moon after the three-month anniversary of Leon's birth.

Darkness, as always, fell swiftly in the courtyard in the clearing; an unearthly green glow flared and faded, then there was only the torchlight flickering across the mortared stones of the old well. Betty handed Leon to Nanny Eames, and took her seat on the lower tier of stones.

She and Leon had arrived on the Blue Goose the night before, been met by Francis, and proceeded directly to the Greathouse. There they'd been welcomed by Nanny Eames herself, who inquired solicitously after her welfare. Nanny worried about the Drinkers out in California—she knew it was hard to be a vampire on an island without customs.

But Betty assured the old crone that it was not necessary for her to drink blood every night. In fact, she and Nick had been getting along well enough drinking blood every Friday night (Beverly had turned into the Penang's pusher-woman, but at least her prices were still reasonable, and she sold only outdated blood) and riding the Elephant together on Sunday. It was no damn fun, that Elephant—but then, neither was life entirely without blood.

And except for the weekends, their lives had gone on pretty much the same as before Leon's kidnapping. Betty had continued to attend her twelve-step meetings, and had thus far preserved all her other sobriety dates intact. This was good business as well as good mental health: the Church of the Higher Power was booked solid by the end of October, as the Great Recovery Scare of the early '90s continued to build up steam. It appeared that Reverend Shoemaker had finally landed herself in a growth industry, and she didn't want to screw it up, even if she had begun wondering, in her heart of hearts, whether perhaps some of her other drugs didn't have Elephants that might be ridden just as successfully. Not that the idea of getting shit-faced drunk was all that attractive to her, compared to the world on blood.

Nick meanwhile was working double shifts trying to service all the new clients he'd managed to land over the summer, so when Whistler invited all three of them down to Santa Luz for the full-moon ceremony in November, he'd had to beg off.

Betty, though, having decided that a free Caribbean vacation (the Winters' Night Foundation was picking up the tab) would be eminently manageable, had accepted with alacrity. She and Nick had enjoyed a blood-filled bon voyage party two nights before her departure and ridden the Elephant on the eve. And if, as Betty noted, there was still half a bag of blood left in the refrigerator when Nick drove his happy family to the airport the following afternoon; and if he decided to have a nip and go cruising across the bay—perhaps revisit the Kingdom of the Castro in search of true happiness—why, she knew, it was nobody's business but his own. And his Elephant, of course.

Betty looked up at Nanny Eames, who was smiling tenderly at the infant Leon in her arms—his Tasting would precede his mother's initiation—and watched tensely as Nanny rubbed the magic rain-forest salve into Leon's tiny instep. Beside her on the lower tier around the well, Lourdes watched just as tensely: Cora was not yet three months old—her Tasting would come in twenty-eight days—but Lourdes could imagine only too well how Betty was feeling. She took Betty's hand, and squeezed it for support.

Betty forced herself not to close her eyes as Nanny bent to her task, the baby in the crook of her left arm and a needle-thin quill tapered at both ends in her right hand. But there must not have been any pain, for the sleeping Leon barely stirred when the crone inserted the quill. Quickly Nanny brought the tiny foot to her mouth and sucked a few drops of baby-blood through the quill, then a few more.

Betty gripped Lourdes's hand tighter. "Well?" she started to ask. Whistler, flanking her on the other side, held up a forefinger. It was not a question permitted by the ritual. She had to wait—they all had to wait.

A minute passed, then another. Finally Nanny turned and smiled. "I have good news," she declared, and all the vampires of Santa Luz cheered.

So did Betty, until it occurred to her that she hadn't the slightest idea what that good news might be.